Books by Stephen Harrigan

Aransas

Jacob's Well

Jacob's Well

a novel by

Stephen Harrigan

SIMON AND SCHUSTER
NEW YORK

I want to acknowledge the generous assistance given to me during the writing of this novel by the National Endowment for the Arts. For various kinds of help along the way I am indebted to Tom Byrd, Alan Tennant, Dwight Deal, Suzanne Winckler, Rachel Zirkel, Norman Chenven, and Lawrence Wright. To Gregory Curtis and to William D. Wittliff I am especially grateful.

Copyright © 1984 by Stephen Harrigan
All rights reserved
including the right of reproduction
in whole or in part in any form
Published by Simon and Schuster
A Division of Simon & Schuster, Inc.
Simon & Schuster Building
Rockefeller Center
1230 Avenue of the Americas
New York, New York 10020
SIMON AND SCHUSTER and colophon are registered trademarks
of Simon & Schuster, Inc.
Designed by Elizabeth Woll
Manufactured in the United States of America

1 2 3 4 5 6 7 8 9 10

Library of Congress Cataloging in Publication Data

Harrigan, Stephen, date.
Jacob's well.

I. Title.
PS3558.A626J3   1984   813'.54   83-27148

ISBN 0-671-44945-1

FOR SUE ELLEN

AUTHOR'S NOTE

The Jacob's Well of this novel is mostly a literary invention. There is a real Jacob's Well in Central Texas, however, and people familiar with it will see that I have borrowed more than its name. The cavern in this book shares some of that place's physical characteristics and some of its sad history. But past a certain point it is solely the product of my imagination.

Libby takes up scuba diving under the instruction of Rick, who is fascinated by a dangerous underwater cave near Austin, Texas. A tense emotional triangle forms when Libby's estranged husband is drawn into the underwater exploration. _____

HE was awake at the first dim waver of light, watching the gray night shapes become slowly infused with color. On most mornings out here the sun rose abruptly into a clear sky and, topping the range to the east, sent a pure advancing arc of light across the desert floor. Today, with the overcast, there was only the idea of daylight, the faintest possible pulse in the comatose blackness. But he felt its insistent, steady rousing, the call to wakefulness.

He was Sam Marsh, a geologist, one of a herd of specialists doing contract work that summer for the Texas Wilderness Survey. He had been in the field for two weeks, and after the first few shakedown days he had settled into a comfortable routine. Every morning he would wake before dawn, take a quick bath in the stock tank, and then sit on the rotting veranda of the old hunting lodge, sipping tea and studying the rumpled, homely desert peaks as the new daylight pooled and eddied in their drainages.

The two peaks were called Los Abuelos—The Grandparents. That was also the name of the minor, isolated range they dominated. Before he came out here Sam had spent hours in Austin gazing intensely at 3–D quad maps of the area, and what he had seen through the stereoscope seemed so real that it had entered his mind as firsthand observation. He knew the vast Abuelo country better than he knew his own front yard.

A little of the overcast had burned away by now, and he could see the gleaming blue outline of the peaks standing out against a milder shade of sky. The Grandfather, El Abuelo, was larger and older. It had been here long ago, even before the caldera from which La Abuela had risen to meet it had formed. The Grandfather rose abruptly from the bastion of the caldera rim, but its summit was as smooth and broad as an elephant's brow, with a swale in the middle through which the raw tooth shape of the Grandmother was visible.

The ranch that contained them was immense, like all the ranches in this part of Texas. It took a fence rider the entire summer to inspect its perimeters, and though the ranching operations were said to be considerable, Sam had not yet, in his two weeks of wandering here, even caught sight of the headquarters. Every so often, though, atop some hogback or volcanic knob, he would see distant milling shapes that he took to be cattle.

He had seen a remnant herd of pronghorn once, and some exotic game that were maintained for the sporting pleasure of the overlords. The ranch was owned by a consortium of Houston orthodontists who came down once or twice a year to take drunken joyrides in their all-terrain vehicles and blast away at aoudads or axis deer. The orthodontists apparently did not mind the Wilderness Survey arriving to assess the value of the property as potential parkland—no doubt the whole arrangement was part of an intricate tax scheme. So for much of the summer the survey had been coming here in waves, taking inventory, scouring the harsh acreage for certifiable natural phenomena.

Sam looked at the country and saw a classic volcanic landscape, the traces of distant, unimaginable violence. He could see the eroded ash skirts on the slopes of the mountains and the threadbare greenery and assorted debris covering the pure lava material underneath. Up on the Cap Rock there were long vertical seams, cracks that occurred thirty-odd million years ago when the rock began to cool. From a distance the joints looked deliberate and precise, like friezes cut into the summits of the mountains.

Closer at hand he saw a heavy gray lizard climbing one of the cedar posts that held up the porch roof. The lizard's flanks were broken out in a nuptial flush, and it would stop climbing every

6

few inches to bob its head up and down with a fierce mechanical motion. When he heard a travel alarm go off inside the lodge, Sam stood up and shooed the lizard away, fearful that one of the zoologists would notice the creature, dispatch it with a sling, stuff it and tag it and send it back to Austin to be put in a specimen drawer with a hundred others just like it.

But the alarm had no effect. It had evidently been turned off and ignored, and Sam suspected he had a few more minutes of peace. Everyone else in the survey slept inside the lodge, bundled in their sleeping bags on rusted bed frames while woodrats clawed above them in the decaying rafters. Sam preferred his own cramped little tent, since he was habitually solitary, and a little grumpy, when he was in the field. And the tent, its ripe mildew smell, reminded him of Libby, of the years when they were close and well married, and likely as not to sleep out on the weekends at a second-rate state park or on the bluffs overlooking the lake. They had bought the tent just before they were married and had taken it along when they climbed to the top of the great dome of Enchanted Rock, located just enough soil to anchor their stakes, and then each took a small sacramental dose of mescaline and sat at the summit in the subsiding wind, watching the hill country below them pulse and thrum in the sunset.

That had been five years ago, and in a way it was a debilitating memory. But he held it squarely in his mind each night as he lay in the tent with his eyes open, gazing upward at the thin nylon fabric that was softly irradiated with moonlight. He was older now, and he believed that he was in almost every way calmer and more able.

A pale graduate student wearing only a pair of cutoff fatigue pants stumbled out onto the porch. He held a toothbrush idle in his mouth, and he looked blearily and distastefully at the peaks for a long moment before muttering a good morning to Sam and going back inside to rinse out his mouth.

The rest of them were coming awake as well now, walking out of the lodge with the untied laces of their hiking boots trailing behind them, carrying their unlaundered towels over one shoulder as they meandered down to the stock tank. Sam said hello to a few of them and then went down to his tent to arrange the things he would need for the next few days. He had an old backpack—another legacy—and he inspected it with affectionate concern, wondering if it would make the trip. The fabric was under severe stress where it was mounted onto the frame and the side pockets were almost worn through, but he supposed it would hold up if he did not load it with too many rock samples.

Janet Sullivan was walking toward him. She was barefoot, picking her way painfully along the pebbly ground.

"There's one of your golden eagles," he said.

She turned around and looked with her binoculars, but the eagle was close, circling about the little peak that rose behind the camp. Even without binoculars Sam could see the flush of gold feathers at the back of the bird's neck that Janet had taught him to look for.

"I hear you have the jeep today," she said, still looking through the binoculars. "You going far afield?"

"Over to the peaks. I thought I'd climb the Grandmother and then walk down some of the drainages in the basin."

"What are you looking for?"

"Moonstones, ideally. Maybe if I get real lucky I'll find a vent plug."

"Were you looking forward to being alone?"

"You're welcome to come, Janet."

"You're sure?"

"Sure. What are you after?"

"I don't know. I know there are bound to be some Lucifer hummingbirds hanging around those agaves. Maybe a peregrine'll pop up. Hell, maybe a penguin. I just want to get away from base camp for a while."

"I'm going to be gone at least overnight. The idea was to park the jeep near the peaks and then pack in."

"That's fine. Let me have a cup of coffee and then I'll get my equipment together and meet you at the jeep in half an hour. You sure you don't mind?"

"Of course not."

He took his time getting ready. He had known Janet for years, and one of the unspoken conditions of their friendship had been his indulgence toward her lackadaisical drift through life. She

8

was more or less a spoiled ranch kid. Her father had a place down near Falfurrias about the size of Costa Rica where he entertained especially heavy contributors to the prevailing status quo of state government. Janet had spent much of her childhood sitting in paneled deer blinds with governors and railroad commissioners, listening to inebriated boardroom talk. As long as Sam had known her she had been in a state of rebellion, first as a full-bore hippie, who would bring home scraggly, barely conscious boyfriends to sip Scotch with her father in the trophy room. Sam remembered only one of them with any clarity, an emaciated character with an alarmed look in his eyes named Astral Dominicus Marvin, who slept in his van and claimed to be a correspondent for *National Geographic*.

But she had thrown all of that over for natural history, for anthropology at first, and then marine science, and then finally for birds. After all those years of dissolution, she retained a keen, shrewd, ironic mind. Sam knew she had gotten her job on the survey not through her father, who could probably have made her its director, but through her own skill.

But he knew her well enough not to expect her to be punctual. He put his equipment in the jeep and strolled about the camp. Things were perking up. The archeologists were leaving in the old white utility van to look for middens, the botanists fanning out into the washes, and the zoologists beginning to clean and catalogue their prey.

Sam watched a girl in a pair of rock-climbing shorts and a T-shirt commemorating a women's marathon set up her things in the warm sunlight outside the lodge and commence the day's work. She took a live bat from a shoe box, held it in one hand in such a manner that she was able to pin back its wings with her fingers, and then stuck a syringe deep into its thorax, injecting a few cc's of sodium pentathol. It was such a massive dose for the bat that Sam could see the creature's chest swell with the volume of the fluid. The bat snarled and twisted its neck, snapping at the air with its brilliant white canines. It had the face of a tiny, tormented bear.

When the bat stopped flapping its wings, the girl began to skin it. He watched the whole process, the way she tore the

9

bloody carcass away from the skin and discarded it, then rubbed the empty skin pouch in cornmeal to stop the bleeding. She stuck a wad of cotton into the cavity and then kneaded and molded it till it bore a poor resemblance to the living bat it had been twenty minutes earlier.

She arranged its wings just so, and then looked up and smiled at Sam. She had blood and cornmeal on her fingers. She wore her thick blond hair in a braid behind her back, and she had the same serene look in her eyes that might have come from another happy industry, such as baking bread.

"We had good luck with the nets last night," she explained.

He nodded and tried to look pleasant. There was something so dim and happy about the girl, and the bat was so small it seemed that even its death was a diminutive thing. But death, Sam knew, was an enormous thing to the tiniest creatures. He knew that from watching his newborn boy die in the incubator and feeling the silent force of that little pinpoint of suffering that had sucked the whole universe into itself.

Janet arrived, carrying her backpack on one shoulder and her well-worn, off-brand field guide in her hand. She was wearing a baseball cap that said United Mud on the crown, and she had on a pair of Polaroid sunglasses and a smear of white sunscreen on her nose.

"You look like a lifeguard," he told her as they drove out of camp.

"Maybe I should donate my services over at the stock tank. You ever notice how ripped some of these kids get at night? When they get over there and start splashing around it's a wonder they have the sense to come up for breath."

"I've seen you ripped," he said.

"Not in a stock tank. Out on the desert at twilight."

"I've seen you wandering around in the Minit Mart, gawking at the Rice-A-Roni."

"That was a long time ago, Sam. That was ten years ago. I'm a full-fledged adult now."

They were on a good dirt road that Sam knew would soon degenerate into a jeep trail. He drove with only one hand on the wheel, scanning the road ahead for nothing in particular. A roadrunner skittered out in front of the jeep and then turned back into the brush.

"I'm homesick," she announced.

"We're leaving next week," he said. "You can hold out."

"You know what I'd like to do when we get back to Austin? I'd like to go to Barton Springs real early in the morning, like about seven o'clock, before anybody else is there to muddy up the water. I'd swim an entire mile, and then I'd drive over to Cisco's and have *migas* for breakfast. In the afternoon I'd go to a movie, and then when it got cool in the evening, I'd ride my bike somewhere to hear some music. I think that would be a perfect Austin day. Want to do that with me when we get back?"

"Yes," he said, remembering an occasional day like that with Libby, "I'd like to."

They drove through an ocotillo thicket, then up a long shallow wash bordered by free-standing volcanic hills. At the top of one of them he noticed a big anomalous chunk of limestone, a piece of sedimentary rock that had rafted up out of the earth long ago with the lava that had formed the hill.

Everything looked worn to him, no longer new. He was tired of the ranch too, but it was so easy for him here, with his few trustworthy possessions and his intimate working knowledge of the landscape.

"How's Libby?" Janet asked him.

"I called her last week from Presidio. She's all right."

"Things looking up?"

He shook his head. "I don't know if either of us knows what's going on."

He was aware of a thoughtful silence on her part. From the corner of his eye he saw her tracing with her finger a little scab on the back of her hand—a thorn wound, perhaps.

"Is this little outing," Janet asked, "just going to be rocks and birds?"

He tried to think of what to answer.

"You're pretending not to understand me," she said.

"We've been friends a long time, Janet. You think we can just switch modes like that?"

"I like your use of the word mode."

11

Janet raised her binoculars to her eyes, but the jeep bounced so violently that she gave up and returned them to her lap.

"Do you see anything?" Sam asked her. "Do you want me to stop?"

"Nope. I'm just scoping things out."

So they were back, for a time at least, to rocks and birds.

Sam's official function for the survey was very basic: to review the literature on the Abuelos, field-check it, and then write it up in layman's language for the final survey report. So far the only literature he had turned up was a twenty-year-old master's thesis by somebody named Ferguson, who had done his degree work at some remote state system college. No one else, apparently, had ever studied the Abuelos.

Sam had spent the better part of his time so far locating Ferguson's measured sections and double-checking them. They had turned out to be surprisingly accurate, except for the occasional formation whose name had been changed by academic decree in the intervening years.

All very well for Ferguson, but it was vaguely boring work, and Sam had something else on his mind. He was looking for the source of the Sleeping Beauty Welded Tuff, a species of hardened volcanic ash that outcropped all over the place in this part of the state. The raw material of the Sleeping Beauty had been laterally ejected from the side of a volcano one afternoon about 32 million years ago. It had been a collection of ash and molten rock that had traveled across the landscape at two hundred miles an hour, slopping way over to the Chisos in the east and as far south as Mexico, cooling so rapidly that the tracery of sanidine crystals within it had compressed into the iridescent blue flecks known as moonstones.

Sam suspected the Abuelos as the source of that explosion. There was good circumstantial evidence: the potassium argon dates for the Sleeping Beauty showed it to be about the same age as the caldera, there were outcroppings near the Abuelos, and the tuff bed itself thickened the closer to the mountains you came. If he were industrious enough and took enough samples, he might find the lost moonstone graveyard, or at any rate feldspars with the same chemical composition.

They were on the jeep trail now, and he had to look close and make educated guesses about the terrain ahead even to get some idea where the trail existed. Janet held onto the grip in front of her seat, lurching gracelessly, unable to find the rhythm.

"Four more hours of this," he warned her.

"I'm getting seasick." She looked over to her right, where three or four turkey vultures were circling. Sam noted the professionalism with which she took out her notebook and listed them. She must have listed ten thousand vultures by this time.

The sun was high now, and the greenery and the cool mountain shadows had washed out in the force of the light. Sometimes in the morning, when the sun hit them just right and flared in the sparse vegetation on their slopes, the mountains could almost be mistaken for some lush alpine glade. But by noon it was always clear that the bright colors had been some sort of atmospheric effect. It was a worn, gray, minor landscape, such a backwater that it was no wonder he was the first geologist to visit it in twenty years.

They were not far now from one of Ferguson's measured sections. Sam stopped the jeep and checked the map. It coincided with the map of his imagination, the one he had formed by staring through the stereoscope at the 3–D pictures until his eyes were crossed. That black-and-white vision was more real to him now than the landscape they were driving across, and in evoking it Sam imagined himself as one of those golden eagles, peering down with magical vision at the clean detailing below, teetering in the thermal from one wingtip to the other to keep his point of view stationary.

Ferguson's section was in a drainage of a low ridge that overlooked a vast desert basin. It was as precise as a road cut, and the thick bed of basaltic lava at its base dipped southwest at 12 degrees, just as Ferguson said it did. It didn't take long for Sam to double-check—there was Morrow Tuff above the basalt, veined with a thin lava belt, and then above that the usual tiers of lava and gravels. All in order.

"Do you want to look at this?" Janet called to him from the top of the ridge. She was looking through her binoculars out into the basin.

"What?" he asked.

"Come see."

13

He made a few notations in his field book and then climbed up the ridge after her, breaking immediately into a fierce sweat from the exertion of moving uphill. She had her binoculars trained at the center of the basin, where he could make out unaided a group of about ten human figures.

"Who are they?" he asked. "Wetbacks?"

"No. Take a look."

Through the binoculars he could see twelve naked people walking along in hiking boots and staring at the ground. One of them, a woman, stood off to the side studying a map.

"It's the archeologists," he told Janet. "Miranda has this thing about working her crews in the nude."

"No kidding."

"She's got some theory about it. She thinks it enhances your perception when you're looking for artifacts if you don't wear clothes."

"I'm constantly amazed," Janet said. She lifted the binoculars to her eyes again. Sam looked at her, feeling some vague excitement, absurdly fueled by the sexless, unclothed grazing of the forms far below in the basin. But he felt as well the habits of five years of marriage, that easy, unquestioned fidelity to Libby. Over the years he had developed a reductive scheme for living his life: discover those things that you care about most, close around them, and do not allow yourself to be distracted. He had once made a list, and on it he had written, in order, Libby, Family, Friends, Work.

He looked at Janet and saw the end of that plain, wholesome order. Their friendship, with its good-natured sexual tension, was doomed. He would lose Janet too.

They watched the forms wander off into the canyon, where Sam knew there was a *tinaja*, a beveled depression in the bedrock filled with rainwater where the archeologists would undoubtedly pass the heat of the day.

He and Janet walked down the ridge, picking their way among the *lechugilla* and ocotillo thorns, and ate their lunch sitting in the jeep. Janet had some of her homemade bread left, and they spread the stale slices with chicken salad and set a bag of dried apricots between them by the gearshift.

"Are you doing all right?" she asked. "In general?"

14

"I'm a little glum from time to time."

"Breaking up is hard to do."

"I'm just watching it all slide away from me, and I don't seem to have the emotional energy to step in and stop it."

"And Libby doesn't either?"

"Apparently not."

"Well, then, maybe it's for the best."

"That's what I wish I could believe."

Janet took a drink from her canteen, leaving a ring of moisture to evaporate on her chapped lips.

"I like you better when you're not so lethargic," she said.

"You're the one who brought it up. I was being very industrious."

She carefully removed the bag of fruit and leaned over and kissed him. It startled him a little, to have her so close. She seemed so unfamiliar.

"There you have it," she said, moving away from him, but taking his hand.

"Back in the old days," she went on, "I used to pine for you, for somebody stable like you."

"I just appeared stable to you. Your perceptions were warped."

"That may be," she laughed. "Let's drive on."

They bumped about in the jeep for another two hours, and then they were at the foot of the Grandfather, where the trail vanished utterly. Close up the peak looked stubby, its slope gradual. Through the saddle on top he could see the purer, intrusive shape of the Grandmother, bare and notched like some primitive implement.

He filled his pack with two gallon bottles of water and clipped a two-quart canteen to his belt. On top of the water in the pack he put another stiff, sweat-stained T-shirt that he had washed in the stock tank and an extra pair of socks. When he had put his Brunton around his neck and his hammer through his belt, he hoisted on his pack and then helped Janet with hers. They set off wordlessly up the gradual slope of the Grandfather, still not sure where they stood with one another.

The heavy pack, held scientifically out and away from his body by the frame, bore down on him with an almost ghostly weight, a burden that seemed to exist only in his imagination. He made

15

a point of walking steadily and in a sprightly manner, to take the weight evenly on the climb.

Janet walked up the mountain with great efficiency, locking her knee automatically after each step to brace the advancing leg. But between them they made little forward progress, with Janet stopping every few yards to watch for birds and Sam bending down under the weight of his pack to knock away a rock sample.

He took a childish pleasure in bashing rocks, but he did his best to restrain himself from hammering away simply out of idleness. All of the rock was badly weathered, and he had to look closely with his hand lens to see the minute crystals within the gray matrix of the rock face.

The face of the slope was occasionally stippled by vertical, upstanding rills like miniature dikes. This was the bedrock poking through, and it was hard and heat-fused. But elsewhere the rock was as brittle as clay, a cold ash-white except where the chemical seepage of the intrusive rock had sullied its color.

This was all recent stuff, compared to the Sleeping Beauty, which, if he was correct, had burst out of the earth very close to where they were now, an almost instantaneous event, a shock wave of smothering volcanic ash.

Ahead of him, Janet was nearing the saddle. He looked up for a moment, catching his breath, admiring the economy and grace of her stride. When he reached the top she was waiting for him there, sucking on a lemon drop and holding out the bag for him.

They sat there a while in the unshaded sun while Janet looked for birds.

"Oh boy," she said. "If this is what I think it is, it makes my day."

"What have you got?"

"A possible zone-tailed hawk. Yep, that's what I've got. See him?"

"He looks like a vulture."

"That's the point. He mimics a vulture. See the white under his wings? And he soars like one too, and then he swoops down on all these unsuspecting little fuzzy-wuzzies who think vultures are only interested in them when they're dead."

She made notes, quietly and almost illegibly, while she held the bird in her sight. When it finally disappeared she was reluctant to give it up.

"That was a good bird," she said, standing now and brushing the dust off the seat of her pants. "I may enter the literature with that one."

The high hard force of the sun bore down on the unprotected summit but neither of them made a move to leave. Like Janet, Sam was buoyed by the sighting, though he would still not have been able to identify the zone-tailed hawk if it flew up to him and perched at his feet. But he was glad for her; he liked to see her win like that.

The patternless volcanic hills stretched out before them. Twelve miles in that direction was the Rio Grande in one of its last accessible stretches before it began to carve the steep canyons farther downstream. To the north was a grove of cottonwoods and a scattered clump of adobe buildings. Sam could see the flat gleam of water there too and a herd of spindly quadrupeds— goats.

"A *curandero* lives there," Janet said.

"How do you know?"

"Powell told me. It's a hot spring. Used to be a spa or something. Mexicans would come over here from Ojinaga to take the waters. Now it's just this guy and his herbs. You'd think a healer would want to be near a population center."

When they were walking again, Janet suggested that the *curandero's* spread might be a good place to camp that night, but Sam did not commit himself. Janet loved old codgers and recluses, anyone whose conscious mind was in the slightest way addled. She would love to lie in one of those hot springs tonight, sipping peyote tea, and listen to the *curandero's* mystic tall tales. Why did he have such a peevish desire to thwart her?

In the steep, gravel-filled drainage they had to walk downhill with the weight on their heels. Before them was the caldera itself, very much the giant bowl he had memorized from the maps, with the awesome rock face of La Abuela looming in its center. Sam thought that the world could be so simply grasped if it were possible to imagine the impermanence of such things,

17

the molten, forming rim of the caldera as momentary in the final scheme as the perfect crown that surrounds a raindrop during that millisecond when it hits the sidewalk. Every day the world changed form, and from the human time-track this riotous activity seemed labored, incremental, eternal. From that vantage you did not see the molten rock in bloom, or see it weathered or cooled or crushed. You did not see it ground and worried into sand, you did not see it disappear.

That was a question he would have liked answered. Did rock, finally, pass out of being? At what point did the microscopic grains cease to exist, become the materials of spirit and mingle with the souls of the organic dead? Geology, Sam suspected, was as much as anything else the study of mortality, the true analogue for our own flickering lives and deaths.

His Brunton, swinging on its lanyard, thumped him rhythmically in the center of the chest, but he did not bother to correct it. They kept moving down through the scree, avoiding the hostile plants. They crossed the eroded ash skirt of the mountain and then down into a wide, dry creekbed with a strip of foliage in its center. There were curious worn places in the grass that Sam recognized as a javelina habitat. Their droppings were scattered about, little clusters of recycled desert scrap.

In the strata that rose on either side of them, the contact between the beds was as definable as the layers of a cake. Now and then it was possible to see the cutaway arch shape of an old stream channel choked with gravel.

They had not gone far along the creekbed when Sam saw a glimmer in one of these channels, a glimmer so faint that it disappeared if he shifted his axis of perception just slightly. It could have been glass, or the reflection from a pop-top, but it felt right to him. It seemed to emanate from the rock itself.

"I need to climb up there," he told Janet. "I think I see something."

"Careful."

He took off his pack and began to look for handholds along the rock face. The wall was vertical, and he was no climber, but there were enough knobs and depressions that he was able to make his way up with a cautious, steady rhythm, enjoying the way his body's center of gravity shifted and shimmied with every

18

forward commitment. Soon he was poised at the gravel deposit, fifteen or twenty feet off the ground, angling his head to catch the gleam. It was still faint, but he saw now he was looking at the real thing: a big cobble flecked with blue light—a moonstone.

He grabbed the rock, holding himself to the wall with one hand and by the flexion of his knees. Where had it come from? It could have washed in from the rim of the caldera, or from some distant Sleeping Beauty outcropping. As an isolated rock it proved nothing about his little theory, but he felt so warm toward it, that strange affection that it is possible to feel toward the inanimate.

"Eureka?" Janet called from below.

"Eureka," he answered.

He took his fieldbook out of his hip pocket and made a note of the location, as Janet warned him sternly that he was about to fall. Then he put the book and the moonstone back into the same pocket and began climbing down, feeling through the thick sole of his boot for purchase on the cliff. He was becoming exhilarated over the find of the moonstone and the feel of the sheer body knowledge that seemed to aid him in his descent.

Halfway down he felt his toe sliding through a little clump of vegetation that he thought would have provided solid footing, and he realized he had lost it. The drop was only seven or eight feet by then, and he knew he was in no real danger from falling, but on the way down he was overcome by an extreme sense of recklessness, of total commitment to an unconsidered course. Falling, he kept grabbing for handholds, skinning his palms, and watching the microscopic striations in the lava unreel before his eyes. He landed painfully on the moonstone in his hip pocket, and as his body swiveled on that point he reached out blindly for support with his left hand.

What he felt then was a slight flicker just above his wrist—a precise, delicate touch, like a consoling hand laid on the shoulder. But his own hand automatically shot away from the source of this feeling, and it was only then that he heard the rattle and saw the snake there beneath the crevice, coiled and cowering. Sam had the strangest urge to console the snake, to somehow draw it into his confidence. He saw with brilliant, shock-induced clarity the flat tabletop of its head, the black band like a raccoon's

19

mask stretching from eye to eye, and the palsied twitching of the rattle at the end of its black tail.

He moved away and the snake, as if by some unspoken agreement between them, did not strike again. Sam sat there watching it and thought, well, I have a few seconds before things start to get really bad. He tried hard to think calmly.

But then here was Janet, screaming, throwing large rocks at the rattler.

"Janet," he said, "leave the snake alone."

"He bit you!" She was in tears. "Sam, he bit you!"

She looked at him, silent now, stunned, ready to obey. He could feel the pain now, as if the snake itself were inside his forearm, a fine burning coil. Abruptly, he vomited, and then before he could catch his breath he did so again, his chest and stomach heaving, working against him. He desperately wanted a moment of peace to decide what to do.

Janet was wiping the tears off her cheeks with her fists, like a child. Her sudden, copious crying seemed like an odd reaction to him, but it had helped to calm her.

"What are we supposed to do?" she said. "Cut it? Freeze it? What?"

"Let me think," he gasped. He had done some research into this several months ago. He had a snakebite kit in his pack, but he remembered reading that the prevailing accepted attitudes held that cut-and-suction did more harm than good. He seemed to remember that cryotherapy was in disfavor as well, but in any event he had no ice.

"I think I'm going to have to ride it out," he told her.

"No, we have to get you to a hospital."

He shook his head. "We're eight hours away from camp. We're at least that far away from Presidio. I can't walk back to the jeep, much less bounce around in it. I've got to stay here and take my chances."

Janet turned frantically around in circles while he sat there, growing detached.

"Sam, you'll *die!*"

But he knew his system could take it. He felt he knew the venom intimately. He could feel it in there, he could feel its

20

strength. The thing to do was let it seep through him and become absorbed in his own good blood.

He retched again and felt the terrible burning in his arm. He began to shake uncontrollably, but without fear. The venom was like a charge of energy, a slow, quiet, brooding charge.

"What about the *curandero?*" Janet said. "We could make it there. It's only about a mile and a half. Maybe he'll have a phone or a shortwave or something."

Sam wondered about this plan. Walking would increase his circulation and joggle the pace of the poison. On the other hand, he told himself, be reasonable. He knew he was not quite himself, that he was in thrall to some deadly fantasy. The thing to do was to reconnect with the real world, to find a way back. He stood up, leaving his pack where it was and holding his hideously blackened and swollen forearm close to his body. The arm seemed to seethe, as if something was trying to emerge from it. His awareness was only a thin slit of light against the field of nothingness where the rocks lay, harboring their patient, mysterious knowledge.

He was glad he had not cut the arm, though it was so swollen it looked as if it were about to explode of its own accord. Some functioning part of his conventional mind told him he had used sound judgment. Vaguely, he was aware of Janet's frantic instructions about where to place his feet and of their passage through the dry creekbed, which seemed to him an event of great time magnitude, like the creation of the caldera.

He thought they had walked very far but they had only begun, and turning around he could still see the rattlesnake coiled a few yards away, wrathful, expended. It was yawning now, waggling its fangs. He felt close to the snake, allied with it.

But Janet was crying again and he realized his responsibility now toward her. He owed her the courtesy of trying to stay in his right mind. He put his good arm around her to somehow demonstrate that he would live.

"We'll make it," he said.

Behind them the sun glinted on the dry scales of the snake, and on its dark, banded face.

21

Chapter 2

LIBBY'S desk was away from the sales floor, in the dark and musty perimeter where stacks of overstocked textbooks were kept on wooden skids, waiting to be returned to the publisher. It was her job to type up the invoices and to make sure the Co-op received credit on the books it was sending back. It had been shocking to her, when she first came to work here, how thoroughly her job was grounded on mismanagement and waste. She relied for her livelihood on the certainty that supply and demand would never fall into balance.

Shortly after she arrived she had put a throw rug under her desk, covering a little the bare concrete floor, which was so cracked and buckled that it seemed to her—here was Sam's influence again—a little model of geological stress. And a while back she had made one other adjustment: six months pregnant, she had climbed up on top of the desk and then stood on a stack of organic chemistry books so that she could reach the Muzak speaker that was nested on the ceiling among the air-conditioning ducts and raw wiring. She had twisted the volume screw with a letter opener until that malevolent, feverish sound was below human range.

She was proud of that little bit of sabotage, and it was enough to make her content. She was no anarchist. She sat behind her desk now, dreamily, cynically perhaps, but doing her job. It was a dull job, but it was what she had wanted: something that would be easy to quit when the baby came. Now that the baby had come—and gone—and the hole he had made in passing had not quite closed, the job was all she had anymore.

"What are you thinking?" she asked Bancock, to keep herself from thinking.

He was sitting on the floor, surrounded by stacks of Psychology 301 books whose price tags had to be removed before they could be boxed and returned. It was Bancock's favorite job—he derived some peculiar satisfaction from the act of peeling. Libby remembered how, when Sam used to visit her here, he would take a few books from Bancock's stack and idly peel off the tags while he talked.

"I'm trying to decide," Bancock said, after some moments of reflection, "what sort of system I'll want to go with if I ever get a real job and make some money. I was excited about these video discs for a while, but when you get right down to it they're really limited. I hate to say it, Libby, but I think I'm going to have to stay with tapes."

"New technologies are being created all the time," Libby said. "There's still hope."

"What do you know? All you've got is that little black and white fuzzball, and all you watch on it is assassination attempts. I'm a video kid, Libby. I've got to have it. I want it all now."

He laughed to himself and smoothed back his greasy forelock. "I read somewhere that that's the motto of my generation: 'We want it all and we want it now.' But I thought that was *your* motto."

"No," Libby said, cranking the tabulation arm of her ancient adding machine, "ours was 'Get it while you can' or something like that."

"A person should have a motto," Bancock mused. "You know what Sam Houston's motto was?"

"'Be sure you're right, then go away.'"

"No, that was Davy Crockett. Sam Houston's motto was 'Honor.' You know what Sam Houston's last words were?"

"'Come here, Watson, I need you.'"

"His last words were 'Texas... Texas... Margaret!'"

Libby stopped adding for a moment; she was actually touched. Bancock sat back among his books, growing silent and still

23

more reflective as he heated the adhesive of the tags with a miniature iron. He was wearing a T-shirt, which was torn and faded and at least a size too large, that read "Junior Newt Clubs of America."

God knows what that was. Bancock had a certain pathetic mystique. When he left work he went next door and played Pac-Man and Galaxians for two hours, then wandered up and down the drag looking in the store windows and reading the flyers advertising punk groups and poetry readings that were taped three or four deep on the walls. Finally, he would settle in for dinner at the Whataburger.

Maybe, she thought, she should invite Bancock to dinner at her house tonight. She would enjoy that, really, cooking for such a lonely and disheveled video kid. Toward him she felt the minor, day-in-and-day-out affection that it is possible to feel toward colleagues with whom one has nothing in common except the concerns and confines of the workplace. But she knew he would misinterpret such an invitation. Surely he knew the condition of her marriage, and it was evident to her that in his hopeless way he cared for her. An isolated act of kindness would only confuse him; it would have to be tied to a larger promise, one she could not give.

From her desk she had a circumscribed view, through an open door, of the vast sales floor of the textbook department, with its bright fluorescent lights and legions of clerks and ceiling-high bins filled with the thirty-dollar nuts-and-bolts texts and with the trendy paperbacks that had been adopted as supplementary reading.

All of the clerks were younger than she was, but most of them had that willful grubbiness that she still associated with the hippies and agitators and dealers she had known at their age. Whenever one of these kids walked by her pushing a dolly filled with books, she caught the sour and—after all these years—still-illicit scent of marijuana.

She could see the truly enfranchised students out there as well, the girls strolling through the aisles with little shopping baskets held loosely on their forearms like purses, giddy with the license to buy. Two summers ago all of these girls had worn gym shorts, and last year it was those Spandex cargo shorts they sold over at Whole Earth, and now there was hardly an item of clothing that did not have an alligator on it.

She did not know what to make of the boys, those poor, lumbering, slow-witted dears who wandered the aisles as if they were sleepwalking, with the uneven tails of their polo shirts hanging out over their creased blue jeans. They seemed to her even more helpless and ill-prepared for life than the girls.

She felt so savvy now, watching them from this distance. But she remembered how unremarkable she herself had been at their age, how pliant and witless, except for one small irritating grain of common sense.

It was the common sense, as much as anything, that had finally delivered her to Sam. There was a picture of him that she especially liked, taken twelve or thirteen years ago, before she had known him. It showed him simply smiling at the camera, squinting a little against the sun, wearing a work shirt on whose pocket flaps some early girlfriend had embroidered twin seagulls. His hair was just beginning to grow over his ears, and he was wearing a string of flat wooden beads around his neck. It was a picture of a boy, really, a boy who was about to be blown this way and that by the prevailing winds. But she responded to the person in this photograph as if he were already a man: there was such warmth and steadiness in his eyes, so much about him that still seemed exceptional and fresh.

Once or twice during those years she had met him—not *met* him, since it had been a part of the code of that time not to introduce people to one another—but she had seen him at parties or at movies or peace marches, and known that he was the friend of some people at the outer edge of her own circle. He was vaguely notorious for the fact that he did not smoke dope, and there was occasional hushed speculation that he might be a narc. The speculation never held up, and his abstinence was regarded simply as eccentric behavior. In any case he seemed to be held in real respect by her own friends, whose personalities had been thoroughly laundered by drugs. In their hazy, simplified manner they had pegged him as a brooder.

Those were such dim memories. When she and Sam were

finally introduced, in no less a forum than a blind date, they had not seen each other for years and had to sit down and sort it all out and remind each other who they were.

And then the one year of living together and the five of marriage, and that intimacy that had seemed no more astonishing after the first few weeks than the feel of clothing against the skin and that now was gone.

She felt so solitary now. It was as if the slow, incremental deterioration of her marriage—the unstoppable tedium that seemed at first to have nothing to do with the quality of their affection for one another—had been in reality a whirlwind that had simply deposited her here, behind this desk in a dead-end job, with no one to love anymore.

Bancock looked very serene, surrounded by his stack of books. She watched the regular, autonomic way he removed the tags— it was like a form of Zen for him. Perhaps at this moment he was reaching toward a higher level of consciousness.

For the rest of the afternoon she did not disturb him, simply sat behind her desk in silence toting up credits and freight charges. When she left work, at 5:30, the heat outside was still intense. Walking out of the air-conditioned Co-op, she felt wobbly.

Maybe at the age of thirty she no longer had the necessary resistance to an Austin summer. The students were out basking in it. She saw the shirtless boys with their hair tied back or covered pirate-fashion with a bandana, their arms and legs thin and taut from some gloomy and exotic diet, straining righteously uphill on ten-speed bikes.

A street mime stepped out in front of her, batted his eyes, and placed both hands over his heart. She could see the beads of sweat on his greasepaint, and she was repelled by and sorry for him. Why would anyone give up so easily, retreat like that into such fawning silliness?

But she smiled politely and sidestepped around him as he tipped his hat to her.

When she got to her car she realized she had forgotten to leave the windows down that morning. The plastic upholstery was close to the melting point and the steering wheel so hot she could touch it only tentatively with the heels of her palms. Just for fun she turned on the air conditioner, but it had not come back to life. There was merely an exhausted wheeze, as if the machine had suddenly been overcome by the heat itself.

With the windows down and the car still steaming inside, she drove through the congested campus streets, where droves of student pedestrians, thinking no doubt they would live forever, crossed blithely against the lights. Watching them, she felt mortal and much older even than thirty. She felt like a cranky, exasperated elder who could not remember or had never experienced her own youth.

Dumptruck was out in her front yard. That was a bad sign. He should have been in the house, lazing about in the air conditioning and shedding on her furniture. The air conditioner was a ridiculous expense, but her backyard was unfenced and Dumptruck had a history of hostile encounters with mailmen. So he had to stay inside during the day until Sam came back to claim him, and she could not let the poor beast roast in a sealed house.

He was lounging by the curb when she saw him, but the sound of her car alerted him and he sat up, startled, the way he sometimes came suddenly awake from a deep sleep. The dog pranced around the car as she pulled into the driveway, and then followed her up onto the porch. But when she noticed the window he began to skulk away.

The window was entirely absent, and there was a deep drift of shatterproof glass covering the porch below the frame.

She looked at Dumptruck, who regarded her frankly now, and decided it was all more than she could stand. The mailman had been kind enough to leave a note:

> Dog jumped through window to get at me but did not bite just looked confused. He does not seem to be hurt. No hard feelings but I'll have to curtail your mail deliveries if you can't contain him.
>
> Your mailman

Standing on the porch, near tears, she felt the cool air from inside the house wafting through the empty window frame. Sam could pay for the window, she decided, and he could also pay for every single one of those escaping Btu's.

She got a broom and dustpan and swept up the glass, and then went inside and made herself a gin and tonic and brought it back out onto the porch. Dumptruck watched her warily, but finally she called him over and scratched the top of his head a little and allowed him to look deep into her eyes.

He was a large black dog of some vague and tangled Labrador heritage, a water dog. As a puppy he had spent many happy hours retrieving rocks thrown into the lake by zonked hippies whose appreciation of this game could not have been much more sophisticated than his own.

Dumptruck was old now, ten or eleven, but it did not appear that he would ever run down. He had started out as Libby's dog, not Sam's, the offspring of Bart, Hudson's famous mongrel. Bart was still remembered among the elite dealers of Austin for a certain shambling cool that mirrored the behavior of his owner. Hudson had given Dumptruck to Libby on her birthday, assuring her that the puppy was the pick of the litter. She remembered accepting Hudson's gift with a trusting and absurdly full heart.

When she made her break from Hudson—so long ago—Dumptruck came with her. Hudson had grown cold and self-absorbed by then, and even now she remembered his wrathful silence with numbing fear.

"You don't know what I'm capable of," he told her once during the worst of it. "I'm capable—and I really believe this—of reaching into my drawer here, pulling out my .22 and putting a bullet through Dumptruck's head. Simply out of spite."

She had hated that paranoid swagger of his. He had developed the dealer's occupational hazard—feeding on his own outlaw image until he could no longer tolerate anything that was not harsh and lean and proven in fire. He had, finally, the coldest, most brutal, and most absent look in his eyes. He was in the deep zones where she did not care to follow.

He lived out at the lake now, in a house patrolled by killer dogs. But that part was for show, since most of Hudson's business was now legitimate. He had a company that refurbished period buildings on Sixth Street and turned them into fern bars.

Looking at Dumptruck, Libby remembered the good, shabby days as well, and it hurt her to realize how much she and the dog were estranged. She had not known her affection for him had been a burden until Sam had come into her life and lifted it from her.

Dumptruck had recognized him at once, like some redemptive figure who had been presaged in one of his fervent canine dreams. Sam took the dog very seriously. It was one of the things she liked about him at first, that expansive concern.

Dumptruck was his now. There had been no question of that when Sam moved out. Almost from the moment she realized she was pregnant, Libby had given up all claims to the dog. The thought of that shedding, hulking beast—that carnivore—had sent her into some primal, protective wrath from which she had never quite recovered.

So she cared for the dog in Sam's absence grudgingly, knowing it was the wrong attitude. Libby was a West Texas girl, and sometimes she thought that that accident of birth was the origin of something harsh and impatient within her—something arid. She had to fight against that harshness now, she knew, or it could overcome her so easily.

The late afternoon light was beginning to dim a little, and she sat back in her porch chair trying to calm herself, to sink away from her aggravations. She breathed slowly and deliberately, remembering a scrap of mantra that some meditation zealot— against all the rules, he emphasized—had imparted to her.

In the pyracantha bush she saw the husk of a cicada, and nearby was the green, wide-bodied creature that had just emerged from it. This new thing was as motionless as the form it had left behind. Its wings were still furled, and it looked craven and exhausted.

She recalled hearing somewhere that newborn cicada larvae, deposited in the ground, remain there for as long as twenty years, developing witlessly in the dark, moist earth until they are impelled to emerge and burst out of their old skins. They are transformed, and mate, and die within a week.

How old was this one? It could have been placed in the earth when Libby was ten years old. It would have been here when she made her valedictorian speech in high school, when she came to college in Austin, during that miserable winter with Hudson

29

in Maine when she worked at a café to support him while he sat at home purifying his system, bombed out of his wits on the effects of an all-mucus diet that consisted solely of grapes.

When she married Sam five years ago, the cicada would have been in the ground for fifteen years. Her little baby's life had been like that: seven months of burrowing in the warm, moist cavity of her body, and then one shocking, painful day bursting forth into a terrible fulfillment—tubes and catheters and artificial air. And then folded into the blanket of nothingness, where this bug was going, where she was going.

At the thought of the baby she felt a quick, rude spasm at the center of her body. That had been such a wound, such a breathtaking piece of natural cruelty. She had a little store of acceptance now, built up laboriously bit by bit, but every so often she would feel a wave of hard memory come and wipe it all out.

The phone rang at the same moment she realized how desperately she wanted it to.

"*The Swarm?*"

"I don't think so, Bobby."

"Michael Caine, Katherine Ross, Richard Widmark. And Fred MacMurray as Horace."

"Thanks anyway."

"Kathleen says she'll only go if you go. Come on, Libby, this is Irwin Allen at the nadir of his career. It's something you want to see with your friends. Wait a minute, I'll put Kathleen on."

"What he says is true," Kathleen said. "I won't go with him unless you come along. It's on your conscience."

They came by for her in the pickup truck that Bobby used for his yard work, and he made a show of climbing out of the cab and opening the passenger door for her. Kathleen was sitting in the middle holding Daphne, feeding her from an engorged breast.

"Still batching it?" Bobby asked her.

"That's indelicate," Kathleen said.

"I know," said Bobby, "but I'm her friend and I want to know what the story is."

"There's no story," Libby said. "He should be back in a few days, if you want to call him."

They were, after all, Sam's friends originally. She reminded herself of that, but it was touching, their concern for her.

She looked over at Daphne, who was two months old and young enough still to sleep through a movie. Libby remembered her own brief motherhood, the subconscious instructions that had risen from within her body. Even now she unthinkingly held out her hand so that Daphne could grab her little finger. And there was the memory again, but softer this time—her own baby on the lip of death, as totally uninformed as a being could be, grasping her little finger, his mother's finger.

"So what are you doing?" Bobby asked her. "Are you going out with guys?"

"Bobby!" Kathleen said.

"Not really," Libby answered.

"I know some yardmen."

"I already know one yardman," Libby said, "and he's two weeks late cutting my lawn."

"Yardmen make better lovers," Bobby said. "Yardmen do it in the grass."

"I'm not at that stage of wild abandon," Libby said.

"Seriously though."

"I'll give it some thought."

"We don't want you to be morose."

"Am I acting morose? Really, I want to know."

"You're doing very well," said Kathleen.

They were driving to a theater in North Austin, which was filled with strip shopping centers and unconnected freeways and fresh roadcuts through the low western hedge of upthrust hills. But their windows were down—the windows in Bobby's old truck would not roll up—and she could feel the lingering humidity in the evening air and the strange combination of big city traffic and hill country repose. Austin was gentling down for the night.

It had seemed an amazing city to her when she had first come here from West Texas. She was used to the utter absence of scenery, and she had felt vaguely sinful just looking at Austin. You just knew something was going to happen to you here. Her mind, infected by Church of Christ dourness, had long since confused virtue with the subjugation of the landscape. The end-

31

less corrugated fields of her country had been put there not simply to grow cotton and milo but to reflect the glory of a drab and disapproving God.

And then there was Austin: so green, the slightly lusterless green of cedar and oak, the rich allergen-choked air, the calmness and lassitude at the heart of everything. It had dazzled her.

The baby was asleep by the time they arrived at the theater, and for the entire movie she lay on her back in Kathleen's lap while her mother swayed her from side to side and cooed under her breath, out of habit. The movie was astonishingly bad, much worse than even Bobby had hoped. She very nearly fell asleep herself, lulled by the cool dark theater, with her friends there beside her and the sleepy mewling sounds of the baby drifting under the harsh soundtrack. It alarmed her how deeply content she was; she knew she could settle for this.

It was eleven o'clock by the time she was home. Bobby gallantly walked her to the door. The phone was ringing, and she looked for her keys for quite a while in the dark before she realized she could just walk through the broken window.

Jack Powell, the head of the survey, was on the line. His formal, stately voice sounded tinny to her, and there were occasional loud whooshing noises that nearly drowned him out.

"I know it's late," he said. "I hope you can hear me. I'm calling from a pay phone in Dryden and there are all these semis barreling down the highway."

"Oh," she said.

"Libby, we had a little trouble here with Sam. Now let me preface that by saying that we're pretty sure he's all right."

She was thinking of a jeep wreck. She saw her husband tumbling endlessly down some arid slope with the jeep gaining momentum behind him.

Bobby had entered through the window, looking concerned. "What?" she said into the phone.

"I said we've had a little trouble..."

"No, I mean *what* trouble? What was it?"

"Well, a snakebite."

She took a seat.

"He's over on the other side of the caldera. Janet was with

him when it happened and there was no way she could get him out, so she had to leave him with some sort of herb healer over there while she came back to get help. But she stayed with him a while Libby, and she told us he's not that bad.

"Now listen. You still there?"

"Yes."

"We've got a jeep on the way to pick him up. It's going to take a while. When he gets here I suppose we'll fly him into San Antonio. There's a snakebite expert there. But I think the thing for you to do is to stay by your phone and I'll call you whenever I know anything for sure."

"Okay," she said dumbly.

"You're all right now?"

"I'm fine," she said.

"The point to be emphasized here is that, in all probability, he's fine."

"Was it a rattlesnake?" It was the first time she'd thought to ask. She saw Bobby's mouth fall open. It was his first hint about what was going on.

"Yes, Libby, it was a black-tailed rattlesnake. Janet identified it from the field guide."

"I'll be at home," Libby said. "You call me, all right?"

"You're first on the list."

"I'll be right here."

"I know. You hang on and I'll get back to you."

She remained seated, thinking. She knew little about snakes, but she envisoned a fierce countenance, fangs dripping with venom, and a hideous scaly skin.

"I'll take the baby home," said Bobby, "and Kathleen can stay here and sit up with you."

"Don't be silly. I'm fine."

"You're not, Libby."

Bobby went out to get Kathleen, and she did not stop him. But she insisted on getting out some sheets and making Kathleen a bed on the couch. It was not long before she fell asleep there, while Libby sat up with Dumptruck, waiting for the phone to ring.

She sat there all night, with the phone never ringing, while

33

her mind bounded back and forth between dread and a strangely exhilarating sensation caused by the possibility of having her existence torn loose from its moorings. As the night wore on she was overcome by a ragged, timeless feeling: she felt she could remain here waiting indefinitely, eternally. If she was calm now, if she concentrated and husbanded her will, if she recited her contraband mantra, perhaps time would lurch forward without her.

Chapter 3

THE first diver was wedged into the upper angle of a vaulted triangle of rock. His mask was still on, not even flooded. He had been very calm. His eyes, through the trapped air behind the faceplate, were enlarged, amazed.

Rick Trammel tightened his grip on the safety line and gave himself a moment to clear his head. He was a little narked at this depth. He was susceptible to the toxic effects of nitrogen even at shallow depths, and he usually enjoyed flirting with that spaciness, knowing through trial and error that his mind was essentially rated to a depth of 250 feet in open water. Here in the Well, in these dark chambers where the surface world was only the dimmest memory, he tended to get crazy sooner. At 120 feet now, there was some question in his mind as to whether he was in control—he was deep enough to be freaked.

The discovery of the body had not come as a shock; he had been looking for it, of course, and was prepared. But dead guys always brought the weirdness on faster.

He concentrated. He thought cleansing thoughts while he kept his eyes away from the body. In a few seconds he felt more in control. The thing was to get the job done and get out of here. They were losing bottom time.

Still holding the line Rick turned around to see if Gary had spotted the body. He looked much too placid, hovering there, respirating without a thought in his head. So Rick put his left hand in front of the light, where Gary could see it, and made the letters b-o-d-y in sign language. Gary nodded, and then Rick shone the light upward into the dead diver's face. Gary saw it, his eyes widened, and he reared, to Rick's addled mind, like a stallion. Easy boy.

Rick made the okay sign to him and he returned it, and then Rick made it again, which meant *are you sure?* Gary returned it emphatically. He was the sort to get it all out of his system like that, in a rush.

Rick took out his slate. He signaled to Gary to take up a little slack with the reel, since he knew that great loops of the dead diver's line were floating around somewhere in this room and if they got their own line tangled with it they might never come up themselves.

He tried to be as meticulous as possible in his notes, but unless he hurried they would have to decompress on the way up. He was cold, and it was difficult to hold the pencil through the thickness of his neoprene gloves.

He noted the mask was still in place, tank and backpack still on, weight belt still on too but the B.C.—the buoyancy compensator—was filled with air, which was why the diver was so buoyant. He had good equipment: Scubapro, SeaQuest. Most of it was even color-coordinated.

His regulator was still in his mouth. His pressure gauge showed that he had no air left whatsoever. Rick admired the guy. He had kept on breathing until his air was all gone, then he had gone looking for a place to die, wedging himself into this crevice like a lobster. No panic.

When he was finished with the notes he shone his light around the room. He had been here, the final room of Jacob's Well, many times before, and he knew it was just large enough to get lost in. But his light penetrated all the way to the ceiling, and it wasn't long before he saw the other one up there, tangled in the line, his mask off and his face looming forth from the black wetsuit hood like a pale moon.

He signaled to Gary for still more tension in their own line and then pointed up so that they would rise together. They both let a little air into their B.C.s and drifted to the ceiling, keeping their fins as still as possible so they would not stir up any silt.

Rick came closer to the diver than he wanted to, and he was

36

a little too buoyant. He had to hold himself off the ceiling with one hand while he looked the diver over. He was well equipped too, but he had not held up well. His fingertips were bloody from trying to claw his way out, his regulator floated behind his back, he still had 300 psi of air left in his tanks.

Rick could guess what had happened. This guy had kicked up a lot of silt and caused a whiteout. It had not rained for a long time and there was very little flow in here, and so the guy had probably panicked while waiting for the silt to clear, tangling himself in the line, kicking up still more silt, and spoiling it for both of them.

When he was through with his notes he checked his gauge—two thousand pounds left. Gary had less—the startle response had cost him maybe three hundred pounds—but they were in good shape. They had fifteen minutes to make it to the surface without having to decompress. He told Gary they were leaving.

As soon as they were out of the final room and cruising along the upward gradient that would lead them out, Rick's head cleared, and he felt relieved. This part of the Well was so familiar he knew every overhang and flue as well as he knew the furniture of his living room. But he missed the bad part of the cavern already—the cool gloom back there, the sense of urgent purpose.

He decided to take ten minutes of decompression anyway, just to be safe. They stopped at thirty feet, inside the long straight entrance shaft, and hovered there, bathed in sunlight, watching their bubbles drift upward to the gorgeous blue ceiling. Rick could see faces looking down at them from the rim, from where the great artesian well burst forth into the shallow water of Cypress Creek.

Below them the yellow line ran down into the absolute dark where they had left it tied off in the final room. Rick felt confident about following it down on the next dive to recover the bodies. He felt he had done well, that he had been in control, and that his intimacy with the Well had deepened.

The ten minutes passed sooner than he wanted them to. He and Gary glided upward, the water so clear above them that there seemed to be no definable moment when they rose into the element of air.

The banks of the creek were crowded with people, and Rick

37

was aware of the expectant silence among them when he and Gary surfaced. He took off his fins and stood up in the knee-deep water surrounding the Well, ignoring the crowd as best he could.

Thornton was waiting for them a few yards downstream, standing in the creek wearing his powder blue wetsuit with its County Sheriff's Deputy patch sewn prominently over the heart.

"What have you got?" he asked Rick.

"It's not too bad. There'll be a couple of tight places, but I think we can get them out."

"You can confirm that they're dead then? There's a TV crew here, and one of them's wife."

"Christ."

"Someone has to say so."

"Come on, Bill, they've been in there eight hours. It should be pretty obvious to anybody."

"Somebody told this guy's wife that there might be an air pocket. I'll tell her, that's no problem. I just thought she might rather hear it from you."

Rick unbuckled his tank and laid it and the rest of his equipment in the shallow water, and then stepped out of the creek and began walking along the bank to the wife. He could hear the trapped water squishing in his neoprene boots as he approached her. The woman was bony, with long straight blond hair and granny glasses, and she regarded him with a great, awful warmth. She knew what he was going to say to her. Rick remembered the overpowering tenderness he had felt toward the world when Jean died. There had been no bitterness, just the hard shock and the feeling that every animate and inanimate thing he encountered was surging with her presence.

He knew the woman was feeling something like this too. There was a powerful intimacy between them, and he took her hand and held it as if it were the most natural thing in the world. She gave him a hurt little smile.

"I'm sorry," he said, "we found them both."

But he had hardly gotten it out before she began speaking, rapidly, as if she meant to brush this information aside.

"I want to thank you so much for risking your lives," she said.

38

"We need to wait a few hours to decompress," he explained. "And then we'll get them out."

"That would be so nice of you."

People were supporting her on either side. She sagged a bit and seemed to pass out of consciousness for a beat or two.

"I'll write you a thank-you note," she promised, alert again. "I want to make sure I have your names and addresses."

She opened her purse to search for something to write with and then abruptly fainted in a heap. The people who were with her caught her before she hit the ground and bore her away up the hillside.

"It means a lot to us," said somebody, shaking his hand, then trotting along to catch up with the group that was carrying the woman.

He turned around and saw that the TV crew had gotten it all on film. The correspondent approached him. She looked harsh and strung-out in a particular way that could be read, especially over television, as glamorous.

"How many people thus far," she asked, "have died searching for the mysterious final passage in Jacob's Well?"

"Twelve, I believe," he answered as plainly as he could.

"Once there, what would they have expected to find?"

"I wouldn't want to speak for them. They're dead."

"Where do you think the final passage leads?"

"I don't believe there is a final passage. If there is, it leads to more rock."

"What about the scene down there today, Rick," she said. Where had she gotten his name? "Can you describe your feelings as you came upon the bodies?"

"My feelings today are geared toward getting the job done," he said.

"Do you think the Well will be closed after this latest incident?"

"I don't know. I'm not an official. I'm just a volunteer."

He wanted to go back down there again now. He didn't care if there were bodies floating around. It was possible to hold the bodies away from the vital centers of the imagination, to pay no attention to them. It was so still and so absolute down there.

39

The Well could contain the living and the dead in perfect harmony.

The woman thanked him and gave him a hard, indifferent handshake. There were some print reporters around too, and he had to talk to a few of them as well. The word had spread fast this time. These things reached a certain flashpoint. All at once the press was all over it, and he could tell from the tone of the woman's question that there would be some sanctimonious editorializing about closing the Well.

He walked back down to where Gary and Thornton were, and the three of them moved up the creek a little, away from the crowds.

"Have you got some food coming?" he asked Thornton.

"Something'll be here in a minute. You feel like eating after going down there?"

"I try never to lose my appetite," Rick said. "I'm trying hard today."

Gary took off his wetsuit top and spread it on a rock, and then lay back in the sun to give his burly torso a chance to dry.

"Where were these guys from?" he asked absently.

"Houston," Thornton said.

"They weren't joyriding," Rick said. "They had good equipment. And this one guy's sitting there with his regulator still in his mouth like he's still in control."

"The other guy screwed up, though," Gary said.

"The point is, they had all the right equipment and they did all the right things except die."

"We found their logbooks on the bank," Thornton said. "Maybe they'll tell us something."

"Where are they?" Rick asked.

"The sheriff took them back to the office. I'll get them for you later."

"I think they found a passage," Rick said. "I think they were trying to shoot the moon."

"Well," Gary said, "they managed that."

Rick took out his slate and his tables and began making notes on the recovery. They would need a backup team and safety tanks at intervals on the way down. Once they had the lines

40

attached the bodies should come out all right, as long as there were enough people pulling on the surface and he and Gary were below guiding them through the squeezes.

He had done this kind of thing before. He had been in charge of the last two recoveries at Jacob's Well, and a dozen others in Florida. All of the dead divers he had pulled out of caves had overextended themselves—as these two apparently had—and usually he found them without half of the equipment they needed: no backup lights, no line to guide them if they were suddenly plunged into darkness, tanks without pressure gauges. It was the fact that these two were so well equipped that intrigued him and told him they had been looking for something specific.

Rick got up and waded over to the edge of the hole. Looking down there, he could see the false floor at thirty feet, the place where swimmers and snorkelers thought the Well bottomed out. The water was clearer than any water he had ever seen, clearer than Palancar or Rhas Mohammad. It came from far below, from the vast aquifer, the place where runoff and rainwater were held and burnished into a pure state and then allowed to spring forth from the earth again. He could not wait to get back down there. This was his place; it had been assigned to him.

In another hour they were ready. They descended quickly, sure of where they were going this time and sure of what they would find. Rick thought clear simple thoughts: step A, step B, step C. There was no wasted mental energy. This time, when they reached the bodies, Rick noticed that Gary was all business, and he was glad that his dogged, workhorse mind was back in form. It was a search and recovery problem now.

They took the tanks off the bodies and let them fall to the floor of the room. Then quickly, efficiently, they tied the line around the first diver with a good solid bowline under the armpits. They pulled twice on the line and he began to drift across the room, his expression unchanging, his body coasting out of the room as if by its own volition. A flurry of silt particles followed him, a false light that blinded them for a while.

They followed the second diver out. Pulled along by the volunteers manning the rope on the surface, the body reminded Rick of one of those inflatable cartoon characters that float above

41

the Macy's Thanksgiving parade. Now and then the body would snag at a sharp angle and they would each take an elbow and, with a strange gentleness and regard, escort it around the obstacle. At sixty feet they found Thornton and the other diver holding open a body bag, waiting to wrap the dead diver underwater so that the ghouls waiting on the surface would be disappointed.

When the body was inside the bag Thornton took the regulator out of his mouth and let air flow into the bag to give it some buoyancy. Rick stayed where he was, watching the wrapped form float up the entrance shaft, in the glorious light, as if it were ascending into heaven.

For a long time he did not want to follow.

Chapter 4

HE was traveling back in time. It was nine years ago, long before he and Libby had met—that miserable summer she had told him about so often, when she had worked as a waitress in Maine while Hudson lolled about all day purifying his system with his mucus diet.

Sam saw himself there, standing on the hard, ragged Kennebunkport shore. He made his way by instinct, by dead reckoning, to the restaurant just outside of town. It was all so clear to him: the homemade pastries and souvenirs by the cash register, the cheap paintings of storm-tossed ships, the tables set with condiment racks and peg games. He took a booth. He was filled with such tenderness and wistful, rueful strength that he felt like an angel.

She came through the swinging doors, balancing her tray on her shoulder. She wore boat shoes, a white uniform with "Libby" embroidered in red thread at the slope of her breast. She was twenty-one years old. Her hair was longer, sunbleached and straight, and her gray eyes held the light like glass. When she set down her tray and began sorting out orders he recognized the glum, put-upon look that came over her when she was deep in thought.

He saw the polite smile she gave her customers. It was radiant to him. Beneath the white uniform her summer body was burnished and taut. When she walked through the restaurant carrying her empty tray, she glanced at him as she passed his booth.

She seemed to see nothing extraordinary. He wanted to walk up to her and tell her plainly who he was, what they would mean to each other in the years ahead, and why she should trust him.

There was a strong surge of pain and the pretty illusion fell away. He snapped awake and found himself looking into the flat yellow eyes of a goat. The goat was staring at him with the neutral, incurious look of a disturbed child. Sam shooed the creature away with his left arm and realized as he did so what a mistake that was. The pain pulsed up and down the whole limb like a berserk electrical charge. He held the arm still, took a series of shallow, even breaths, and in a moment the pain gave ground and retreated back to its source.

The room where he was lying seemed familiar to him from long ago. It was an adobe room, a shack, and beneath him he felt the form of his sleeping bag and the bare springs of the metal bedframe on which it rested. Across the room, running against the entire length of the wall, was a kind of trough, filled with clear, slightly agitated water. There were steps leading into the trough, as if it were a baptistry, and on the wall above it were crude wooden shelves loaded with canning jars that were filled with herbs.

The door of the shack was open and outside was the cruel midmorning sun. He could see other goats wandering in and out of a flimsy corral made of sotol stalks. The *curandero* sat out there in a folding chair, basking in the fierce heat like a reptile and now and then running a hand over the top of his head to wipe off the sweat. His hair was as gray as stone, cut close and unevenly against the side of his head.

The old man was familiar too. He was a fixture in this universe of pain and nausea and delirium. Sam remembered him coming into the room sometime in the dim past and, by the light of a lantern, slicing a prickly pear pad like an English muffin and laying the cool, succulent flesh of the cactus over the two fang marks in his arm.

The *curandero* sat out in the yard with his back toward Sam, but all at once he lifted his head like a startled deer and turned around to look into the shack. He saw Sam and smiled, then stood up and walked through the door to his bedside. He was wearing an old pair of double-knit slacks whose ragged cuffs trailed on the ground, a faded T-shirt advertising the Terlinqua Chili Cook-off, and a pair of half-glasses that hung from his neck by a silver chain.

"*¿Mejor?*" he asked Sam.

"*Mejor.*"

He went over to one of the shelves and took down an egg and a jar of water.

"*¿Como se llama?*" Sam asked.

"Ignacio Benavides. Don Ignacio, if you like."

Don Ignacio sat down on a stool next to Sam's cot, made the sign of the cross, and dipped the egg in the jar of water.

"If you would please lie still," he said.

"Are we speaking in English or Spanish?"

"English. Your Spanish is not that good."

"What are you doing?"

"*Barrido.* It won't be painful."

He began to sweep the egg over Sam's arm, starting where the snake had bit him and stroking upward. Sam lay still and closed his eyes, ready to tolerate anything that did not hurt. He saw no reason to put any faith in what the old man was doing, but he found the ritual strangely comforting. He could feel the egg soaring above his skin and could sense his blood rising in its wake, like ocean water being pulled by the moon.

"*De las doce verdades del mundo,*" the *curandero* was muttering, "*dígame cinco, las cinco llagas.*"

The feverishness he felt seemed to have some beneficial effect on Sam's poor Spanish. The meaning of the words came to him effortlessly, insistently. Of the twelve truths of the world, tell me five, the five wounds. Of the twelve truths of the world, tell me six, the six candelabra...

...tell me eleven, the eleven thousand virgins. *Las once mil vírgenes.* The egg floated above his skin, calling to him, purging him. He wondered briefly if he had been hypnotized, but he did not want to resist. He let himself fall into a soothing delirium, and he could feel the egg grow heavier above his body as it absorbed the impure spirits within him. When Don Ignacio stopped, Sam's reverie changed pitch and all at once he felt a spasmodic urge to vomit. He was more or less in his right mind as he hung over the side of the cot, his chest contracting violently and a thin line of spittle running down his chin. The old man sat there, watching him.

"How do you say dry heaves in Spanish?" Sam asked, falling back onto his sleeping bag.

Don Ignacio smiled without answering. He wiped Sam's mouth with a washcloth that he had dipped in the trough. The water was warm and sulfurous.

"I don't suppose you have any Gatorade?" Sam asked.

"No. I was making you some tea."

He stood up and removed a battered saucepan from the burner of a camp stove, then poured the hot water into a cup. He stared into the cup for a long time as if entranced, while the tea steeped, then he took a spoon and skimmed the twigs and shredded bark off the surface.

Don Ignacio brought the cup to Sam and held it for him while he took a sip. The tea was dark, but it tasted weak and flowery.

"If you can keep the tea down," the old man said, "you should eat some crackers."

The fingers holding the cup were thick and blunt. Sam looked up to meet the old man's eyes, which were staring at him with a serene blankness.

"What about Janet?" Sam asked, feeling suddenly lucid under the pale, languid gaze of the *curandero*.

"She left last night."

"In the dark?"

Don Ignacio nodded. "She was very anxious about you. She wanted to call a helicopter as soon as possible. I told her it wasn't necessary. In a week you should be able to walk out of here yourself. But she insisted."

"She shouldn't have done that in the dark."

"I prepared her."

"How?"

"With water."

He touched his forehead and then the base of his skull. "Here...and here. That will give her protection. And now you should take a bath before the helicopter comes."

Don Ignacio helped him to his feet and supported him while he made his way across the room to the trough. Sam made a point of not looking at his arm; it seemed to hover beside his body, a heavy floating thing like a gas balloon. Don Ignacio helped him with his clothes and then guided him down the steps.

Sam felt his body blissfully evaporate in the warm water, and almost immediately his awareness dimmed to a shadow. He stayed there a long time, and then, half-conscious, he saw that he was being led back to the bedframe.

He lay in a dull reverie, focusing on the ornaments that were tacked onto the adobe walls: a cheap religious calendar that showed the Virgin ascending into heaven; a picture of the famous boy folk healer El Niño Fidencia; a 3–D postcard of the crucifixion.

It was late afternoon now; he could gauge that by the ferocity of the heat. The old man sat in the center of the room. He had set up a small, rickety table whose surface was covered with cards. On the cards were pictures of various objects—swords, coins, cups—printed in vivid colors that danced in the sere overburden of light.

Don Ignacio glanced over at Sam and then back at the cards.

"I'm learning about you," he said. "Have you been asleep or awake?"

"I'm not sure."

"Would you like something to eat now?"

Sam nodded. Don Ignacio handed him a box of crackers, and then poured him a cup of canned alphabet soup from the same saucepan he had used to heat the water. Sam waited until the soup cooled a little and then drank it quickly, feeling its strength sluice through him. He ate half a dozen crackers while the old man poured him another cup.

"I want to thank you very much," Sam said.

"*De nada.*"

Sam glanced toward the cards. "What did you learn about me?"

Don Ignacio sat down again and looked over the cards.

"You're a scientist. Of course your friend told me that before she left. You have a wife and her name is Libby."

"Janet told you that too."

47

"No. I learned that from the cards."

Don Ignacio shuffled the cards and then dealt them out into little groupings on the table. For a long time he tinkered with them, changing the configuration of each group, never satisfied with how they lay. He was like a man playing solitaire with more rigor than the game deserved. Sam felt compelled to believe in the *curandero*'s powers, if only out of politeness and gratitude.

"What else?" he asked.

"The death of a little child."

"She shouldn't have told you that."

"She didn't."

Don Ignacio shuffled the cards again and began the process of dividing them into the groups.

"I'm concentrating now on the future," he said. He peered at the cards through his half-glasses. His thin legs were crossed beneath the table and one foot swung slowly back and forth as if the old man's torpid mental concentration were driving it. He began muttering in Spanish to himself. Sam heard Libby's name, but that was the only word he could make out. The mutterings seemed to take on the rhythms of an incantation, and in his own hazy state Sam saw that Don Ignacio was in thrall to some greater awareness; he had tapped into the vein. Sam clung to his skepticism, what he perceived to be his sanity, but it gave him no pleasure to do so. He was so close to tapping into that vein himself.

He felt the room begin to vibrate. The water in the trough started to roil, the herb jars clattered on the shelves, and a great shuddering noise descended upon them. The goats ran for shelter into the shack and huddled next to Don Ignacio. The panic they felt did not register in their dull yellow eyes.

The *curandero* hardly noticed the commotion. His own eyes were on the cards, darting from one picture to the next, his hands constantly moving cards to alter the design of the individual groups. As the noise grew louder, his attention grew more focused, the motion of his hands more urgent.

Sam gripped the edges of the bedframe, feeling if he let go he would be swept out of the room. It seemed alarmingly natural to him that such pandemonium could break loose, such devils could be released, as a result of the old man's intrusion into the vaster world.

Through the open door of the shack came a driven cloud of dust. The grit filled Sam's eyes, and in a teary blur he saw the cards gust away from the table. Don Ignacio watched them go, then turned to the doorway. A man in an orange jumpsuit was standing there.

"Anybody home?" he asked.

The man walked over to Sam while Don Ignacio picked up the cards from the dirt floor.

"You ready for a chopper ride?" he asked. He peeled the bloody cactus pad off Sam's arm and held it up with distaste.

"What is this? Voodoo?" he asked.

Another attendant came in and took Sam's blood pressure from his good arm while Don Ignacio shuffled his retrieved cards carefully and placed them in a cigar box that he kept secure with a thick rubber band.

"Where are we going?" Sam asked the first attendant.

"San Antone. Some pretty good snakebite people there."

When they had him on the stretcher and were taking him out the door he held out his good hand for Don Ignacio to shake.

"Thank you," he said.

Sam extracted his wallet from his back pocket, took out two twenty-dollar bills, all the money he had, and handed them to the old man.

"No," he said. "You'll need money in San Antonio."

"Take one, then."

"All right. *Para los niños*." He indicated the goats.

The helicopter waited outside with its blade swiping the air in lazy, idling strokes. Sam was struck with what a production the whole business was, how out of scale with the intimacy of the disaster. But he felt compliant, homesick, and the helicopter was a machine of deliverance.

Don Ignacio followed with Sam's backpack and sleeping bag and tossed them inside.

"What was in the future?" Sam asked.

"Your wife. But not as she was before. You will be together in a very beautiful and dangerous place, and you will need each

49

other there. Keep an eye out for the snake, also. He wasn't trying to kill you, only to get your attention. He's your ally."

As Don Ignacio stepped back from the blade, Sam suffered a brief hallucination. The *curandero*'s bland eyes appeared to take on warmth and color and beam out to him like a comic book illustration of x-ray vision. Then the helicopter blade caused the dirt to swirl and dance around the old man until he looked as if he were being consumed by a dust devil. Suddenly Sam felt keenly aloft, as if it were some mechanism within his own body that was causing him to rise.

"We'll get you started on some fluids here," the attendant shouted, slapping Sam's good forearm to raise a vein.

"You're lucky. I don't think that guy did you any harm. What was he anyway, a witch doctor?"

But it was too much effort to answer. When the helicopter banked, Sam looked down at the desolate landscape and saw a lacolith, a circular bastion of rock that was an immense knot in the smooth plane of the desert.

The attendant was chewing gum. His hand rested on Sam's shoulder. He was singing, but his voice rose above the noise only on the chorus—"Ooh ee ooh ah ah, ting tang walla walla bing bang"—while the copter hacked its way through the thin fabric of air ahead.

Chapter 5

"I THINK it was fate," the doctor said. "It was definitely fate."

The doctor had failed to introduce himself, but the name on his tag said Pancho Ahearne M.D. He was Sam's age, more or less; he had a thin little jawline beard and a pair of wire-rimmed glasses whose lenses he was rubbing against his pants leg, presumably with the idea that this would clean them off. When he returned them to his face they were covered with lint, but he did not seem to notice. He peered down at the wound on Sam's forearm.

"This is just so fantastic. You're sure about the black band across the eyes?"

"Yes."

"And the black tail?"

Sam nodded.

"It checks out with the symptoms," the doctor said admiringly. "Talk about fate. When I heard we had a blacktail bite I almost wet my pants. You lucked out, man. If I hadn't been here—I, the world's greatest authority on blacktail rattlesnake venom—they would have done a fasciotomy on you by now."

"What's that?"

"That's when they trim out a lot of tissue to keep the necrosis from spreading. You were smart to pick a snake with hemotoxic venom. I see very little tissue loss here. You may have a little more swelling, some clotting problems, but no dead meat."

51

"It still hurts," Sam said.

"That's why God gave us codeine. We'll slip some of that through the IV and you can zone out for a while. Very few people have been bitten by blacktails, you know. Look it up. There are only two case histories. You'll be happy to know they both lived."

Under the influence of the drugs Sam felt his perceptions thinning out, and he suspected the doctor was let down because he could not keep up his end of the banter. He wanted to care more about his condition, but could not. After a while he found himself in a hard, needling sleep that he finally had to pry off of his consciousness like a shell.

Janet was in the room, seated beneath the wall-mounted television. Next to her stood Jack Powell, still dressed in his field clothes, which included khaki shorts and a belted safari jacket with epaulets. Sam was reminded of a famous photograph of Powell, in which the head of the survey stood at sunrise on the east rim of the Chisos Mountains, the most spectacular scenery in Texas, picking his nose.

"You don't look so terrible," Powell said.

Sam reached for the water glass on the bedside tray, overcome with thirst. Janet rushed over and filled the glass from a pitcher, then waited to fill it again as he emptied it. She smiled at him; they were united in their adventure.

"You two shouldn't have come all the way here."

"We needed some good Mexican food," Powell said.

"How much was the helicopter?" Sam asked.

"My treat."

Sam looked over to Janet.

"Thanks."

"No problem," she said.

"Janet was heroic," Powell said. "She drove all night back to base camp. How she found it in the dark I have no idea."

Powell reached up to turn on the television. There was a brief image of a group of men in a motorboat chasing somebody on a sailboard and shooting at him with high-powered rifles.

"The TV works," Powell said, turning it off again. "That's good."

"Libby's here," Janet said.

"Where?"

"She's at the hotel now, sleeping. She was here all night watching over you. She was pretty nervous. In fact, I should probably call her now."

"Let her sleep. You two should get some sleep too."

"We can't," Janet said, "we have to go to Mi Tierra and get twenty-six number four dinners to take back into the field. Maybe we could sneak one up here on the way out of town."

"That would be nice. And a margarita."

"Coming up," Janet said. She kissed him perfunctorily on the cheek, and then squeezed his hand, a gesture that he understood was meant to convey significance.

"Think of us out there in the boondocks," Powell said, as he closed the door.

He lay there for a long time not knowing what to do with himself. The time spent with Don Ignacio had a dreamlike persistence in his mind, and its hold increased as his mental dullness began to dissipate. Only now was he beginning to understand the strangeness of what he had experienced, to feel alive to it. He waited anxiously for Libby to come. The *curandero's* prophecy had given his imperfect longing for her focus and range. He wanted to appear in her future as he had appeared deliriously in her Kennebunkport past.

When she arrived that afternoon she slipped in through the door so quietly that for a moment her appearance did not quite register with him; he thought he was back in the world of light-play and hallucinations.

She walked up to him, smiling tentatively, clutching her purse.

"You got your hair cut," Sam said.

She kissed him and pulled up a chair.

"You lost some weight out there, I think," she said.

"You look exceptional."

"I'm a little haggard, to tell the truth. Wondering if you were alive or not."

"Let me see it from the side."

Libby turned her head in profile. Her hair fell just so against her neck.

"How are things?" she said, when she turned again to face him. "Pardon me if I'm a little teary."

53

He touched her hair and drew her head down onto his chest. There was a faint smell of chlorine.

"You've been swimming."

"In the hotel pool."

"I dreamed I was with you in Maine that summer," he said. "I walked into the restaurant and you didn't recognize me."

"I wouldn't have then."

"No. But I wanted you to. I thought we could have taken it from there."

"That's a nice thought."

"That's what I thought about at death's door," he said. "Us."

Pancho Ahearne walked in, after rapping spiritedly on the door with his knuckles. He was carrying a Polaroid camera.

"What would you think if I took some pictures of your arm?" he asked.

"For your scrapbook?"

"For the annals of medical science. You can show your grandchildren."

"Go ahead," Sam said.

"Do I want to see this?" Libby asked as Ahearne began removing the bandages.

His arm was still swollen and discolored, but he did not think it looked so bad anymore. Libby was staring at it, chewing on her lip.

Ahearne used up a full roll of film, handing the pictures to Libby to hold while they developed.

"I wish you could have taken some pictures right after you got bit," he said.

"I don't know why I didn't think of that."

Ahearne stood on a chair to get a high-altitude shot of Sam's arm. He gave Libby a conspiratoral grin as he handed her the picture.

"The paparazzi are everywhere," he said.

"When do I leave?" Sam asked.

"You want to leave?" Ahearne asked. He put down the camera, looking hurt, and peered at the wound. "Let's see how far the swelling goes down in the next day or two. How's the pain?"

"Better."

"We'll get you off the hard stuff today. Back to Excedrin number three. If you're feeling perky enough I don't see why you couldn't leave day after tomorrow."

Ahearne replaced the dressing, folded up his camera, and then lined the photographs up on the bed.

"Which one do you like best?" he asked Sam.

"That one."

"It's yours. You can dine out on that picture for weeks."

He offered one to Libby, but she shook her head.

After Ahearne left they heard his jogging shoes squeaking on the linoleum in the hall.

"Is he a real doctor?" Libby asked.

"He's just excited. You have to realize that not many people are bitten by blacktail rattlesnakes."

"How nice for you."

"Here," he said, handing her the picture, "put this in your purse."

She made a face but did as she was asked, zipping the purse firmly shut.

"How are you planning to get back to Austin?" she asked.

"No idea."

"I could come back when you're released and drive you home."

"Would you?"

Libby nodded, but avoided his eyes.

"I'll get us a hotel room," Libby said, looking out the window. "It'll be the weekend by then. There won't be any hurry to get back."

"Libby..." He was overcome with gratitude.

"Don't say anything about how it'll be just like old times, okay? It won't. It's just that I don't think that one night will hurt."

"What's there to hurt, anyway?" he asked.

The next day, though he was dull and trembly, he felt his strength returning. His arm was down almost to its normal size and it was no longer so awful to look at, merely puffy and bruised. His parents flew down from Oklahoma City after he had tried to convince them over the phone not to bother. They were dis-

55

traught when they arrived; they entered his hospital room holding hands, as if preparing each other for the worst, and found him watching a game show on TV and drinking a warm Dos Equis from a six-pack that Janet and Powell had dropped off on their way out of town.

Sam's mother hugged him and deftly removed the beer from his hand at the same time.

"You shouldn't be drinking this," she said. "They're bound to have you on all sorts of drugs."

"Just aspirin."

"No cortisone?"

"No."

"That's just as well. I don't like the side effects. Let me see, honey."

She began to unwrap the bandage on his arm. Sam didn't protest. His mother had been an army nurse in World War II and whenever she was around illness she reverted to a quiet air of command.

Sam's father came around to the other side of the bed and shook his good hand, while his mother inspected the wound.

"You don't look so bad," he said. "I don't know what we expected."

"I told you not to come."

"Nonsense."

Sam watched him hitch up his pants at the knees when he took a seat at the windowsill. It was gesture his father retained from the fifties, when men's pants had been much baggier. Even in the tropical heat of San Antonio he was wearing a tie, and the sweat beaded up on the clipped gray hair above his collar.

Sam felt warm and weary with his parents there, his mother in her trim beige pantsuit double-checking his medical care, his father sitting at the window timelessly attired. It would be so easy just to slip away into their care again.

They still lived in the house in Oklahoma City in which he and his two sisters had grown up, though they were at that point in life when they were talking about retirement and condominiums and island-hopping cruises on ships with big-band orchestras. But for now Sam felt reassured by the fixity of their world.

56

His father was still general manager of Will Rogers Chevrolet ("Where you'll never meet a deal you don't like") and still went to work every day and sat in his office above the showroom, his desk bare except for the usual executive appurtenances and a sleek ceramic model of a 1957 Impala. Sam saw his father as a normal man: quiet, dutiful, fair; confiding in no one, confessing no secret desires, out of simple regard for propriety. Sam had always admired this demeanor. He thought of his father as a man sure enough of himself to live his life without comment.

Their house in Oklahoma City looked out over a municipal park, with a clubhouse and tennis courts built by the WPA. As a boy Sam had roamed through the park as if it were his own backyard. There was a sandstone boulder in one corner of the park into which kids etched their names with sharp-edged rocks. His mother had stood over him when he had put his own name there, scraping and scraping for hours, painfully forming the combination of letters he knew by heart but could not yet read.

"Your name will be there forever," his mother told him when he had finished.

"It will?" he had asked.

"Sure it will. It's rock."

But when he had brought Libby there, the first Christmas she had come home with him, he saw how the sharp edges of his name had begun to erode; the letters were disappearing as if he had written them in a mound of rising dough.

He had not yet told his parents about him and Libby. He had put it off, hoping that at some point in the future it would not be necessary to tell them at all. But they were clearly aware that something was not right, and they took pains now not to ask too much or too little about Libby.

They spent that afternoon with him, Sam's mother filling him in on family gossip and quizzing the nurses as they came in. His father talked about the new models, filling Sam with an echo of that strange excitement he had felt as a child, when it had seemed to him that the world was beginning over again each year with the annual modifications of tail fins and grillwork.

Finally he talked them into leaving and having a nice dinner on the river. They spent that night in a hotel nearby and then came to see him in the morning with a stack of magazines and a Rubik's Cube. They flew back home a few hours later, finally persuaded that he would be well and that Libby would soon be there to take care of him; leaving him with their unspoken confidence that his marriage would be healed by this new crisis.

When Libby came back she was carrying a suitcase. "It occurred to me you wouldn't have any clean clothes," she said. "So I raided your house. Also I bought you a new shirt." She tossed the shirt nonchalantly on the bed.

"You shouldn't have done that," he said.

"You're always so low on shirts," she said. "And I felt like being nice."

Before Sam was discharged, Ahearne stopped by with a graph he had made on which he expected Sam to chart the progress of his recovery.

"So that others may benefit," he said, "and so that I can cream the competition in the *Journal of Hemotoxicology*.

"Stay in touch, okay?" he exhorted Sam, as Libby wheeled him out. "Report back to me. You should have some tingling in that arm for a long time, but you won't have any permanent aftereffects. If anything interesting happens—say, if your arm turns black and falls off, pick up the phone."

In the open air Sam was seized with a staggering optimism and freshness. It was overcast and humid, and beneath the elastic bandage on his arm the sweat was beginning to bead up. But he felt as if he were in mountain air. Walking to the car, with Libby supporting him lightly at the elbow, he was enthralled by his unsteadiness. He liked the way the earth shifted under his feet.

"Let me drive," he told her.

"Are you sure?"

"Positive."

He guided the car aimlessly through downtown San Antonio. The streets here were laid out in a crazy manner—they turned back onto themselves, or disappeared for blocks at a time—that usually enraged him, but today he was unconcerned. He simply cruised along, observing the clusters of Lackland airmen and

Incarnate Word nuns, the citizenry in whose mestizo features the ancient Indian blood was dominant. It was a splendid, dark, spectral city, and Sam felt that only a precarious restraint kept its people from tearing down its office buildings and erecting gessoed Aztec pyramids in their place.

"Where are we staying?" he asked Libby finally.

"The Menger. We should check in, unless you want to drive around in circles for another few hours."

"I'm lost," he said disinterestedly.

"You're not lost. Take a left."

When they walked into the hotel he felt a surge of nostalgia. He and Libby had come here on their first two anniversaries, poor enough then that the idea of driving the eighty miles to San Antonio and staying in a hotel had seemed a reckless and exotic thing to do. He remembered a mesh cage containing live alligators that used to sit beneath the palm trees in the lobby. The cage was gone now, but the hotel's fusty and eccentric elegance persisted.

In their room he felt disengaged and very happy, and he watched blankly as a prim little bellman bustled around the room, opening drapes and turning on lamps and fine-tuning the television. He gave him five dollars.

"That was a large tip, don't you think?" Libby asked him.

"I'm feeling large."

Libby put her arms around his waist.

"In your bracket I guess you have to get rid of it somehow," she said. "You want to go for a swim?"

"Not now."

"Then take a nap," she said. "I'll wake you for dinner."

He did not realize until he lay back on the bed how drowsy he was. He lay motionless in the clean, frigid air from the air conditioner as he watched Libby change into her bathing suit. A powerful, easy desire engulfed him; nothing urgent. When he fell asleep he could feel like a heartbeat the stroking of her limbs in the luminous water of the hotel pool.

The pool was dominated by a group of Mexican kids who were performing cannonballs. The kids were fair-skinned and over-

59

fed, border scions whose parents had come north to shop. Their horseplay was curiously orchestrated: they lined up on the side of the pool and leaped out and grabbed their knees in sequence, like members of a water ballet.

Libby judged that she was likely to receive a direct hit if she attempted to swim laps, so she just slipped into the shallow end to get wet and then sat in a deck chair, feeling the water on her skin evaporate almost immediately in the extravagant midday heat.

She was feeling good about Sam and that bothered her. She wanted things to be clear, but the snakebite episode had muddied the waters. Here she was, behaving like a wife. At the same time she felt strangely illicit in violating the unspoken terms of their separation. She liked being with Sam again when common sense proscribed it.

She closed her eyes in the bright sun and thought about the summer before they had married. Sam had been working for the Bureau of Economic Geology then, studying erosion rates on the Cap Rock and living with oilfield workers in a forlorn little trailer park outside of Post. Libby had moved for the summer to her parents' house in Picture Bluff, and twice a week Sam would come down and they would sit in the darkened living room, watching cable television and listening to her father grumble about the windfall profits tax. Her parents drove into Midland on Wednesday night to play bridge, and that was when she and Sam made love in her old room, listening to Beach Boys records. Sometimes she would go with him up to the Cap Rock and sit in the car reading Willa Cather. At dusk they would eat a picnic dinner with their legs dangling over the eroded rim of the escarpment and the red-tailed hawks soaring beneath them. Behind them were the beginnings of the high plains, the horizon as clear as a tabletop in the brilliant sunsets and the landscape as vast as the unmarked field of a dream.

Her grandfather had been alive then, though it was his last summer and he complained of backaches that were the first signs of the cancer that would kill him with an unusual swiftness and decorum.

She and Sam visited him several times in the unpainted frame

60

house where he had lived since before her birth. He had sold
the ranch in a careless and heartbroken period after his wife's
death. He had not consulted anyone else in the family, and after
the new owner got rich off the mineral rights when oil was discovered, her grandfather imagined himself to be an outcast, despised by his children for his profligacy.

He was not despised, although Libby's parents were forever
nursing the hurt of that close brush with real wealth, and from
time to time they ran out of patience with him. He was a type,
she saw now: one of thousands of silent, displaced cowmen; skit-
tish with his own children, surrounded by a few poignant possessions and memories.

When Libby was a little girl he had taken her to every drive-
in movie that came to town, and driving back home he had let
her sit in his lap and steer on the flat, vacant streets. His presence
had always calmed her. Picture Bluff was a town of cinderblock
country clubs and cleared, monotonous land where televisions
flickered day and night, as if monitoring some profound weari-
ness of spirit; where dust rose in swirling updrafts from vacant
lots; where God's petty, wrathful mind roved like a parched
wind.

Somehow, through some companionable body chemistry, she
had come to understand in her grandfather's presence what was
beautiful about the landscape, and the claim it had on her. For
a long time a burrowing owl had lived in a hole in his backyard,
its eyes and its smooth, rounded head peering above the ground.
As she watched it she realized that a creature so mysterious would
not live in an environment as plain as the one she imagined
Picture Bluff to be. Her grandfather was like that owl for her,
someone silently connected to the deeper emanations of the
earth.

She took Sam one day to the little pictograph site her town
had been named for. The pictures had been painted on a brow
of sandstone that loomed above a dry creekbed. They were few
and of poor quality, and the place itself had long since degenerated into a make-out spot. But it was a serene location, the
sky overhead an unending shelf of blue, sharp and undiluted.
The paintings on the rock were drab stick figures—a Spaniard

61

with what looked like a saucepan on his head, a group of men lying on their sides, indicating they had been captured—but Libby and Sam were moved. They sat there on a boulder in each other's arms, feeling as if the stream of history had found them and accepted them. She remembered feeling the rise and fall of Sam's chest as he breathed, and watching a prairie dog on a mound not far away cluck and throw back his head in comic alarm as a hawk rode the thermals above him. She had been happy and felt as if all the mortal things around her were irradiated with eternal light.

It was a long way back to that efflorescent landscape, but she was feeling a little charged now, and her body was alert with simple desire. The Mexican kids had stopped their cannonball routine and were playing with an electronic toy that featured a panel of colors that lit up and beeped. One of the kids tried to take it away from his older brother and it was not long before the toy fell into the pool. Libby and the boys watched it settle to the bottom, still blinking.

When the hard heat had passed and it was near dinnertime, Libby went upstairs to wake Sam. She found him already up, wearing his new shirt and threading a belt with his good hand through the loops of his jeans.

"You ready?" he asked her.

"For what?"

"Dinner."

"You shouldn't be going out. We can order room service."

"No. I feel good. I want to take a walk. We can eat on the river."

"Sam."

"Seriously. I feel fine."

They walked outside, Libby hovering near him, expecting him at any moment to collapse onto the pavement. But Sam felt enlivened, steady on his feet, the nausea gone and the pain in his arm only a feeble, hesitant note.

Across the street was the Alamo looking squat and ancient. Libby followed Sam as he headed for it without consulting her. There was the usual knot of tourists at the doors and a girl in a coonskin cap handing out coupons. Sam walked up to the building and touched the cool limestone.

"I know where they quarried this," he said.

"Do you want to go inside?" Libby asked, a little indulgently. It was not a place of beauty to her but the site of some grisly catastrophe she understood only imperfectly. It had scared her as a girl—the cool, hushed, dank interior ripe with the romance of death.

Sam shook his head. "Let's eat."

They walked together toward the river, taking a shortcut through the lobby of the Hyatt-Regency and emerging onto the cool concrete banks between which the water sloughed along with charming unreality.

San Antonio itself she found exotic, sometimes appealingly so and sometimes not. As they walked along the river, its shallow water dyed a blue green and its surface crowded by mariachi barges and pedal boats, Libby decided the festiveness was too much for her, it was a burden.

Sam walked slowly but with enthusiasm, and his excitement was beginning to make her nervous. He was going to want too much.

They stopped at one of the mediocre Mexican patio restaurants along the river walk and drank a margarita apiece before ordering.

"Things are starting to seem real again," Sam said.

"Disappointed?"

"I approve of reality," he said, a little glumly.

"Any minute now you're going to topple over. How will I get you back to the hotel?"

"Stop worrying. Guess how much less lethal blacktail venom is than western diamondback."

"I couldn't possibly."

"Twenty-one percent."

"So you were almost twenty-one percent less dead."

Sam smiled and called the waiter over. When they had ordered he looked around at the sky.

"It's clouding up," he said.

Libby looked up and saw a lugubrious front moving in among the office buildings, a great load-bearing cloud that slowly suppressed the light. The water in the river seemed to grow more opaque, and by the time they had finished their dinner the sky

63

was tight and dark. The rain came angling in beneath the aluminum umbrella as the waiter was removing their plates. They took refuge beneath a footbridge and watched the little river buckle and swell under the mass of rain.

"It's going to flood," Libby said. "Maybe we should leave." She noticed that others were climbing up the steps of the footbridge, headed for higher ground.

"Let's wait," Sam said. He crouched there, fascinated. The mariachi boats tossed at their moorings, and one was shoved up onto the bank. The water was wild and muddy now, but the concrete trough still contained it.

The rain stopped all at once, but it was a while before the river was calm. It still threatened to crest, even as its energy was drawn away. When the front passed, a radiant evening light fell onto the wet streets, and Sam felt touched by the strangeness and harmony of this light, as if it had settled willfully on them. Libby's face was flushed with color, sunburned from her afternoon by the pool, and her eyes were as clear as quartz.

He took her hand. That was rare. They walked back to the hotel in the warm, sodden atmosphere.

"It's a shame about us, Libby," he said.

"I know."

"I don't think you're particularly happy."

"No, but I wouldn't be particularly happy with you again, either. I'm looking around, Sam. I want to be blunt about that."

"That's to be expected."

"And you've got something going with Janet."

Libby saw from the hurt look he gave her that she had guessed right.

"Not so far," he said.

"But possibly."

He wouldn't answer. He squeezed her hand.

"Just don't hold back on me tonight," he said.

"No," she answered, "I'm committed to tonight."

When they got back to the hotel, the extraordinary light was gone and the mild summer darkness had settled in. Their room looked out over the Alamo. They watched as the floodlights came on at its base, spotting the ruin with such intensity it seemed unnatural. It was like something from the unconscious mind, some grim memory.

It was all the light they needed. He could see her across the room, removing her clothes with a deliberate air. When she had finished she walked over to him at the window.

"Oh, Libby," he said, drawing her to him, "I'm so high."

It had been months since they had made love, but the absence did not matter. There was no novelty to it; it was a confirmation of the old, deep, familiar things. He was so used to the feel of her body that touching her was like experiencing again some half-forgotten, pestering sensation of childhood.

"You're burning up," Libby said, touching her hand to his forehead.

"Right."

"No, really. You've got a fever."

"Don't worry about the fever," he said. They lay on the bed. The sheets were already damp from the stagnant night heat. It hurt when she touched his bandaged arm, and he saw that she was trying to avoid it. But he was heedless of the pain. Perhaps the pleasure outweighed it, he was not sure. He was not conscious of pleasure, only of the need of her.

They lay there a long time, long enough to fall asleep though neither did. Libby could feel Sam's fever all along her body.

"Shouldn't you take something?" she said.

He stood up and took two of the high-potency aspirin from his pants pocket. Libby went into the bathroom to fill a glass from the sink and brought it to him. The hotel water was flat and warm. Libby lay back down in bed, not bothering to cover herself with the twisted sheets.

"Why didn't it work out?" Sam asked.

"Want to hear my theory?" she said, studying him now. "We didn't love each other enough."

Sam wondered if this were true. He could not help admiring her for saying it. Lying naked on the bed, her body righteous and taut, she reminded him of the way she had been in labor, testing herself to some higher standard that was not even in sight for him. He remembered how her pain had frightened and enthralled them both, and how at some point she had broken away from him, reaching another level. She had thrown off all the breathing techniques they had laboriously practiced in the weeks before, thrown them off as if they were trivial and took away from the awesome message of the pain. She lay there adjusting to the force of the contractions, accepting them with a wild, imploring look in her eyes.

"Sam," she had said, nearly out of breath, "help me. Please help me."

Help her how? He had failed her for not knowing how. He tried to get her to start the breathing again, but they both knew that such feeble encouragement was not worthy of him. Even now, he did not know what he had lacked in that moment. Perhaps it was courage, empathy. Perhaps she was right and it was love itself that he lacked.

There had been meconium in the baby's lungs, the first and most obvious of his many problems. He was rushed to intensive care before either of them really had a chance to see him. Sam noticed that he was the color of clay, and that as the nurse ran away with him his clenched fists opened like buds.

It had been static for a while between him and Libby, static as in any marriage, and they had been looking forward to this birth, to their great moment as husband and wife. When it had come they were left breathless and afraid and isolated in a way that neither could recognize. Then the baby died, and finally he knew what each of them could not forgive: that in that awful time they did not look to one another for comfort.

Libby could not look at him afterward, or talk to him, but he had guessed wrong that this was a sign that she held him responsible and did not want him around. Sam went camping alone in the Guadalupes, realizing at the time it was a melodramatic gesture, but desperate for some sort of movement, for a solitary purge in the wilderness. He had stayed there for four days, willing himself into a neutral, accepting mood. He stared at the great ancient reef of El Capitán as if it were a vision. The mountain was welded together from the skeletons of billions of tiny sea creatures, and it was in itself no more purposeful than any one of the coral polyps that had formed it. Sam was filled with nihilistic reverence: everything died, and nothing mattered.

66

He had come home to find her in control, not wrathful or wounded but consciously possessed with the idea of getting the marriage through this. It hadn't worked. He knew that she found him in some vague way ineffectual, without the heat to guide himself to her and make her love him.

But now, watching her lying naked on the bed, staring levelly at him, he felt that heat beginning. He felt strength in his blood, in his intellect, in every part of him, as startling as the light that had broken from the clouds after the storm. He wanted to find the dangerous and beautiful place Don Ignacio had told him about, the place they could be together.

He sat down beside her and trailed his fingers along her breasts and along her sweat-beaded flank. She raised herself to kiss him, and suddenly all his confidence left him and he was stricken with the knowledge that this was the last time and he could not have her again; that only these extraordinary circumstances had brought it about, when he had been wounded deeply enough to be worthy of her.

Chapter 6

RICK was indulging himself; he was thinking of Jean. He remembered the time, years before, when they had gone diving together at the Flower Gardens, a little remnant strip of coral reef a hundred miles out into the Gulf from Galveston. The coral was in eighty feet of water and stunted by the climate so that the coral heads did not rise more than five or six feet above the sea floor. But the water had been clear that day, and the tidy little reef was pretty and welcome after the long drop through the blue void of the open ocean.

They had been idling in the sand flats, following the trails of mollusks and watching the eagle rays and amberjacks cruise over the shallow coral beds. Rick had at one point backed away and watched Jean as if she were part of the fauna, admiring the perfect trim of her body in the water, the neutral buoyancy she achieved so effortlessly. He envied her because she seemed so much less an intruder than he did.

Suddenly they were aware of a great shadow passing above them. Rick looked up, cool and unafraid, thinking that whatever it was it would be good. Eighty feet above him he saw a megalithic shape paddling along with two outsize pectoral fins. He calculated, by the way the thing dwarfed the hull of the dive boat, that it was forty-five feet long. He had never seen anything so immense, and for a moment its presence shook him and he thought about grabbing Jean and looking for cover in the reef until it passed.

It was Jean who calmed him. He saw her looking up at the shape steadily, with serene appreciation, as if it were a vision she had been expecting. He took a moment and ran through the list of possibilities, until he realized that it was a whale shark, the largest fish in the ocean. It was a plankton feeder, of no danger to them, but Rick's breathing was still a little deep and ragged. He did not like things of that size sneaking up on him in the middle of the ocean.

But there had not been even momentary concern in Jean's eyes. She swam up to the shark without consulting him or looking below to see if he followed. Rick ascended after her, sighting her small form against the great outspread silhouette.

Jean swam above the shark and cruised along its back from its tail fin to its head, stopping to peer into its mouth. Rick cautiously fingered the dentricles on its skin and looked into one of its tiny eyes for some token of recognition on the fish's part that he existed. There was nothing there—the creature was uninhabited. It was pitiless, bland. He had been filled with a strange revulsion, but on the boat afterward he had never seen Jean so excited, her dark, wet hair close against her face and her eyes shining.

As he sat now on his little apartment porch, that was the image of Jean that came to him. It came accompanied by a murky, unpleasant sensation that he recognized from his earliest childhood. This feeling had nothing to do with his normal senses; it used some different path and rose from deep within him, deadly and full like a tide.

He thought that perhaps this feeling had come to him before any of his conventional senses had even developed, when he was lying unformed in the warm salt bath of his mother's womb and she had been given the news of his father's sudden death. What he felt, he thought, was the simple essence of grief. Now when he thought of the whale shark, which had seemed so malevolent to him in its torpor, the dark, insistent message that had been encoded into him swelled into prominence and then subsided, leaving him unable to recall it.

Across the street in the park a knock-kneed young woman was jogging, with her thumbs pointing into the air. She was passed by a middle-aged man whose legs were intricately muscled but whose upper body was emaciated. In the center of the park trotted a dog with a Frisbee in his teeth. The dog apparently owned the Frisbee. He wandered into the park this time, every time, looking for a pickup game of catch.

Rick got up from his ratty deck chair and turned his wetsuit over on the porch railing so that the inside would dry. He unzipped his dive bag, took out the slate on which he had made his notes on the body recovery the day before, and began transferring them to his logbook. He wrote:

JW 7/22/80 10:25 AM — 11:02 AM
BT 27 m PSI 2200 — 400 10 m decomp

JW 7/22/80 3:05 PM — 4 PM
BT 55 m PSI 2600 — 400

Near each of the entries he placed an asterisk, indicating they had been recovery dives. He didn't need to write anything more. He would remember. When he paged through the logbooks and saw asterisks, the events they represented leaped out vividly from his memory, and he could not help picturing the milky white bodies caught in the cypress roots beneath an impounded bass lake, or ceaselessly spinning in the turbulence of a waterfall, or scudding along with the current on the clean, pebbly bottom of a river. He was used to these things. Some part of him welcomed them. The dives without asterisks were pleasure dives. He remembered them too, but they seemed hollow beside the urgent errands that were noted in the logbooks.

When his gear was dry he packed it carefully back into the bag and hung his wetsuit up on a hanger, then fixed dinner and set a place for himself at the table. He ate his salad and broiled meat slowly, tranquilly, staring at a photograph he had framed and hung on the opposite wall that showed a diver soaring over a mountain of brain coral. When he was through eating, he immediately began washing the dishes, then dried them and put them away.

On the news there was a follow-up report on the Jacob's Well drownings. A county commissioner, with studied outrage, called for the Well to be closed, and there was footage from yesterday of the body bags being loaded into the ambulance. Rick saw himself and Gary at the corner of the screen, watching the bags as they pulled off their wetsuits.

He left the television on, watching one of those maniac sports-casters who had recently come into fashion put a loving cup on his head and cross his eyes. There were commercials for denture cream, tires, and jinsu knives. Rick pumped one leg up and down impatiently on the ball of his foot, feeling slack and torpid and vaguely afraid.

He got into his van and drove to the dive shop. It was in a little strip center in North Austin, sandwiched between a soft-ware store and a restaurant that served upscale chicken-fried steak. The front door was unlocked, and Rick remembered that Gary was teaching a class tonight. Eight or ten people were sitting at the edge of the training pool that adjoined the sales floor, hunched over by the weight of the tanks on their backs. They were looking up at Gary, who was lecturing them on something. Emergency ascents. That was what Rick would be teaching his class next session.

He went into the back of the shop and began filling tanks and overhauling regulators. The repair work demanded from him a certain modest concentration, and as he replaced O-rings and cleaned off corroded parts, his restlessness began to go away.

He had been working for an hour when Gary came into the back room, drying his ear with a towel.

"Finished with your class?" Rick asked him.

"Yeah. I didn't know you were working tonight."

"I felt like it."

Gary picked up the second stage of a regulator and peered at it, then attached it to a tank and turned on the valve. They could hear the compressed air rushing without interference through the mouthpiece.

"Free-flowing," Gary said.

"I was getting to that one next."

"I'll do it." He went into the office to change out of his bathing suit and came back wearing a polo shirt and corduroy shorts. Rick watched him disassemble the regulator. Gary was not much

71

of a mechanic, but he was competent and painstaking and good company. He and Rick were partners in the shop. Gary had bought the shop three years before with the insurance money that had come to him after his father had been killed in a refinery accident two weeks before his retirement. Rick's investment was substantially smaller, but Gary had always waved that matter aside, and so Rick made up the deficit where he could, working longer hours and leading the less exotic dive trips. Meanwhile, the business ambled on quite successfully, as an extension of Gary's unflappable good nature.

"How's the class?" Rick asked him.

"Not bad. There's one character in there who wants to go into underwater demolitions. He's got a T-shirt that says 'Happiness is a confirmed kill.' All the rest of them are pretty normal."

Gary held a tiny screw up to the light and inspected its threads.

"I got a call from the county commissioner today," he said. "Guess what he wants to do?"

"Close the Well," Rick said. "I saw him on TV."

"He wants us to do it. He said he can either put a lid over the whole thing or we can put a barricade underwater to keep people out of that final room."

"What did you tell him?" Rick asked.

"I told him I'd talk to you. He's up for reelection; he's very serious. I figured it might as well be us who did it."

"Maybe," Rick said.

"Maybe the guy's right. Twelve is a lot of dead people."

Rick hooked up the regulator he was working on and began to calibrate the air flow with a screwdriver. It was a delicate adjustment. If he made it too easy to draw a breath through the mouthpiece the whole mechanism could become high-strung and undependable as the pressure of the water increased. It was better for the air to come hard and steady than too smoothly.

The adjustment required his close attention, but he was aware of Gary watching him, waiting for an answer.

"Let me think about it," he said.

"I told him we'd call back tomorrow afternoon."

"All right."

Rick took a breath through the mouthpiece. The harsh, dry

72

air came out reliably but not without a bit of an effort. He was satisfied.

"By the way," Gary said, "Thornton brought those guys' log-books by."

"Anything in them?"

"Not a whole lot. One of them was a hydrologist. The other one was a realtor. The hydrologist had done a lot of cave diving."

"Where are the logbooks?"

"In the office."

"I'll take a look."

The realtor was a casual note-taker, and judging from the water-stained entries in his little spiral-bound notebook he had maybe forty hours of bottom time. "Great reef. Saw moray eel. Incredible dive!" That was the level he was on.

The hydrologist had recorded his dives in a hard-bound book filled with sheets of graph paper. His hand was exact, and his observations were terse and scientific. He had been through a lot of caves in Florida, and he had a habit of diagramming them on the page opposite the entry. Rick recognized most of the caves from the configurations: Peacock Spring, Devil's Eye, Archway Sink, a good bit of the Hyacinth system that Rick had been the first to map. There was one early entry for Jacob's Well, two years ago, and the diver's sketch corresponded accurately with reality. Beyond the final room he had put in a question mark. The last entry was for a dive on the Stetson Banks, out in the Gulf. There were no data for the fatal penetration into Jacob's Well. Probably he had intended to write it all up after he came out.

"Thornton also brought this by," Gary said, tossing an underwater slate with an attached pencil onto the desk. "He found it in one of the wetsuit pockets."

The pencil marks on one side of the slate were old and faded. Rick guessed they were from an earlier dive and the hydrologist had failed to erase them. The marks on the other side were fresher. There was an odd little sketch there. It looked like doodling—a dense mesh of spirals and concentric circles. What they referred to he could not guess. They had been done hurriedly, with a blunt pencil, in cold water at a depth not conducive

73

to rational thought. Whatever the hydrologist's eye had seen, his hand had not caught it well. Below the sketch, in big dense letters, were the words, STAY CALM!

"He should have left the realtor at home," Gary said.

"When does Thornton want this stuff back?" Rick asked.

"The next few days."

"I want to make a copy."

"You still think they found something?"

"Possibly." He tossed the logbooks and the slate back onto the desk.

"I think we should close it off, Rick," Gary said. "I don't want to pull any more bodies out of there."

Rick nodded distractedly and left it at that. He helped Gary grade the decompression problems on the test he had just given his class, and then they closed up the shop. The diving knives and chrome gauges in the display cases shone in the moonlight, and outside the air was soft and warm. There were fireflies in the parking lot.

When he left the shop he meant to go home, but he stayed there only long enough to collect his equipment, and then he set out on the thirty-mile drive to Jacob's Well.

He was seven when he first saw it.

His father had been an air force test pilot who, while plunging to his death in an experimental aircraft, had coolly given the manufacturer some useful hints on how to improve its performance. Rick was born six months later and the brotherhood of pilots closed in around the little broken family and did not relax its embrace until his mother had married one of its members. He was a widowed colonel with three children of his own, a solid administrator who was frequently reassigned to other bases. In his infancy Rick lived in Dusseldorf, Goose Bay, Abilene, Biloxi.

Austin was the first place he really remembered, though he saw very little of it beyond the base. Once when his stepfather and his three children were visiting his dead wife's parents, Rick's mother took him along on a picnic that some of the air force wives had organized, to a place called Jacob's Well.

74

He remembered the crowd that sat at the banks of the creek, which was so shallow except for the dark blue chasm of the sinkhole. He waded out to the center of the stream and stood at the edge of the circle where the creekbed had given way. The Well was about thirty feet in diameter, and thirty feet below he could see what he thought to be the bottom. The water that filled it was so clear that it frightened him a little to stand this close to the edge, imagining that if he lost his footing he would simply fall as if the water were not there.

But he watched the children jump off the rock ledge that overhung the creek and plunge into the hole, and after a while he got his courage up. He was a good swimmer, the beneficiary of two summers of spartan instruction at the Officers' Club pool, and he sensed that once he was submersed in the water he would feel at home. Walking back out to the edge again, he stepped forward and felt the water cradle him as he hovered in the void. Against all expectations he felt his childhood dreams of flight suddenly realized.

Older children dived deep into the Well, carrying rocks back with them to prove that they had reached the bottom. All day Rick tried to follow them, but he could never get closer than halfway. The water was cold, it took away his energy, and it flowed powerfully upward, shooting him up like a cannonball whenever he gave up straining against it. His vision was blurry underwater, but he could make out the tiny fish feeding on the algae that covered the rock walls. And his hearing was acute. Far below him he heard the pebbles on the bottom, rattling like bones in the current.

When they left that day he begged his mother to take him there again. She did so, over and over, sometimes venturing to the lip of the Well herself and performing a clumsy breaststroke around the circumference of the hole.

One afternoon a burly, fit man with a crewcut and a handlebar mustache came up to peer into the Well. He stood there with his hands on his hips, the muscles in his cheeks tense with concentration as he looked into the water. He wore khaki shorts, his knees were tanned and knobby. Rick knew he was there to do more than look.

The man walked over to the trunk of his car and removed a brace of gray cylinders that Rick thought at first was a bomb. The children who had been swimming in the Well all stopped to watch the man as he solemnly went about putting his old double-hosed regulator on the tanks. He pulled a few other pieces of equipment from a laundry bag—a mask, a pair of stubby fins, and a huge Bowie knife in a fringed leather scabbard that he attached to his weight belt.

The man hoisted the tanks onto his back, fastened the canvas straps, then put on the fins and waddled over to the edge of the hole and jumped in without ceremony. Rick looked down from the rim and watched him descend, his bubbles trailing upward and bursting on the surface.

The figure of the diver grew more and more abstract as he descended, until finally his image seemed illusory, like a rainbow in a puddle of water. Rick wanted to jump in and watch him from beneath the surface but he was afraid the man might somehow be endangered by this act, that the apparatus on his back was so fragile it would explode if the water were disturbed.

So he merely sat and watched, and when he was sure that the diver had reached the bottom, that plain of rattling rocks where he himself so longed to be, an astonishing thing happened: the diver disappeared.

"Something grabbed him! I saw something grab him!" one of the boys yelled, but Rick had seen nothing of the sort. The man had simply slipped away—he had gone somewhere, and Rick was stunned with the idea that what he had thought all along was the end of Jacob's Well might only be its beginning.

He believed though, soon enough, that the man was dead. He had been down there forever, and Rick did not doubt that there *were* things far below that could grab him. But after a very long time during which Rick did not move from the rim of the abyss, the bubbles reappeared, slowly gaining in intensity until the surface was boiling. Finally he saw the diver's refracted figure saunter from the darkness into the bottom of the Well.

The diver's head broke the surface in a froth of bubbles. His handlebar mustache drooped down along both sides of his chin, his ruddy face was blue, and when he shoved his mask onto his

76

forehead it left a red indentation in the skin around his face.

The man was shivering, but as he pulled himself out of the Well he retained his nonchalant bearing. In a little mesh sack tied to his belt was a load of rocks.

"Where does it go?" Rick asked him.

"It goes all the way," he answered heartily, "all the way to the center of the earth."

The man made a point of repositioning his mustache and then walked to the car. Rick followed him.

"Was there anything down there?" he asked him.

"All sorts of stuff." The man laid his tank on the ground and then reached into the mesh bag.

"See that rock?" he said, holding out a fist-sized sphere that looked like a piece of dried mud. "That's a geode. I'm gonna take that to a rock shop and have them cut it in half just like a cantaloupe. You know what's inside?"

"No."

"Diamonds." He reached back into the bag and tossed Rick a piece of whitish rock with a swirling, cone-shaped design etched into it. "That's for you."

"What is it?"

"That's a fossil. That's from a little animal that lived a long time ago."

Rick thanked him as the man hoisted his equipment into the trunk of his car.

"You kids be careful playing in there," he said, and then drove off without another word.

Rick kept the fossil. He learned from a book that it was a component of an ancient reef, a crinoid stem that once made up part of a sea lily, and so he imagined that there was an ocean at the bottom of Jacob's Well, a vastness filled with whales and sharks and giant squid.

His stepfather was transferred soon after that, but they came back to Austin three years later. He was ten, a moody, absorbed boy with an overriding errand. He had a face mask now, and when he dived into the Well again, wearing it, he saw so clearly that his heart began to pound. He could see every little rock on the bottom, see their ratchety movement under the power of

77

the current. To his astonishment, he was able to swim easily to the bottom, surging downward with even, powerful strokes. When he arrived at the bottom he let out a little bit of air so that he would be heavier, and then he looked to the side. There was a great tunnel he could not have seen from the surface, the means by which the diver had penetrated deep into the Well. It was a riveting sight to him, and without considering he swam into it. It was a vault of polished rock, and as he moved through it he could feel the surface light diminish. All at once he noticed that the tunnel's floor had dropped away, and that he hung suspended above a black chasm with a blue window of light behind him.

He was out of breath. When he turned around to go back he missed entirely the big tunnel through which he had come and began to follow a smaller passage that grew darker and darker. His lungs bursting, he turned around and saw daylight and heard the rattle of the stones at the mouth of the tunnel. When he shot out of the dark passage he could feel the change in temperature, and though his breath was completely gone he felt confidence and not panic. He let the flow take him up. An eel swam in front of him, its face pinched and narrow, its body moving in the clear water like a banner in the wind. It was heading down.

For just a moment, before he broke through the surface, he blacked out. Then he was aware again, feeling the current lovingly hoist him into the air.

When he was thirteen he took scuba lessons at the base, but before he had a chance to explore the Well his family started moving again, to Japan and Arizona. In high school something violent and resentful came out of him, and he did not try to quell it. He worked on projecting a superior, unconcerned demeanor, and he succeeded so well in this that he had no trouble finding people to pick fights with him. He saw physical violence as a way of honing his mental authority over his opponents. He could feel the power of his personality, he could feel it working on people. They wanted his attention.

He had a year at a junior college in Central Florida and two years at Florida State. He liked to get drunk and walk with exaggerated correctness, to get stoned and listen condescendingly to the witless babble around him. He liked to steal the

78

batteries out of fraternity boys' GTO's and throw them into the ocean.

He was rather comically enrolled in premed. All of one summer he worked as a diving guide at Pennekamp Park. He got to know the reef better than the campus, and with more empathy, and he hated returning to those classrooms where the nervous teaching assistants and untenured professors embarrassed him with their craven attempts to win the students' approval. Rick fell in with antiwar people, although he had no clear feeling of right or wrong about the war. He merely thought, Of course there's a war. In any case he wanted no part of it, and after a short time he wanted no part of the sociopathic ideologues he was hanging out with. He ignored the war, and it went away. Without much interest he watched the draft lottery on television. They picked a high number for his birthday. He was in the clear. He thought, What assholes.

He could feel himself going slack, losing it. A rich great uncle offered to let him stay at his cabin on the Illinois River outside Tahlequah, Oklahoma, and Rick spent that summer disciplining himself, purging away the hurtful and sloppy side. He read Gurd-jieff and Joshua Slocum and William Beebe with a monastic intensity. On the bluff above the river he set up an exercise bench and did situps while coeds drifted below him in canoes.

He was preparing himself. He wanted to burn with a pure, purposeful flame, to accomplish something. He did not know what he wanted to accomplish, only that he must be worthy for the task.

When the summer was over, he enrolled at a commercial diving school in Houston and spent three months learning rigging and gases and chamber operation. After he graduated he got a job with a company that serviced wellheads in the Bay of Cam- . peche. He worked in the equipment shop first, and then as a tender, but after a year he had broken out as a diver and was doing simple four hundred foot bounce dives. It was easy work, mostly observation of the rigs or guy-wire replacements, but he was restless and kept shopping around.

The money was in saturation diving, working in a bell during the day and then sleeping in a pressurized chamber at night.

Several times he stayed under pressure, in those cramped quarters, for thirty days, doing isometrics to keep in tone. The idea of sat diving was to avoid the pressure differentials that gave you the bends, but he got hit once anyway, not bad, but enough to get his attention. He was making $50,000 a year, would be making easily twice that when he became a pipe-line welder. But he was already beginning to feel the effects of all that pressure on his bones; it was just too much of a squeeze, day in and day out. One day something cut the umbilicus of a diving bell that had been down at 850 feet, and Rick saw what the guy looked like when they brought the bell up.

The money wasn't enough. He was in his fifteenth day of a saturation dive, nauseous and sweaty in the constrictive space of the bell, looking out at the ocean in which his tiny vessel hung like a star, when he thought about Jacob's Well. He realized that he was homesick, not for any of the dozens of airbases he had lived on, but for that hidden place, that submerged crevice whose unexplored passages still taunted him. All at once he felt frenzied with longing, and it took every bit of his powers of concentration to ride out the two remaining days of the job.

He left the rig, quit the company, and lived on his savings. He became a pilgrim, not daring to approach the Well yet; he felt too agitated, too impure. He dived in the Red Sea and then went to Australia, to the Great Barrier Reef, and then lived for a time with a girl in Byron Bay.

From Australia he drifted back to Florida, down to the Keys and up and down the Atlantic coast. He had his instructor certification and he did some free-lance work, teaching tourists how to dive. A friend talked him into attempting to set a world depth record for scuba. Rick was not much interested but he agreed to go along, and soon he was looking forward to the thrill he would experience if he survived such a suicidal feat.

The standing record was 390 feet. Rick and his friend would attempt 410. As a commercial diver, using mixed gases and umbilical rigs, he had gone to much greater depths, but he could expect the compressed nitrogen in a scuba tank to begin pinching off his awareness very early on. In this dive, his mind was the critical instrument; it had to be strong.

They were to sign their initials onto a slate tied to the end of the down line. The arrangement was that if either had any difficulty at that depth, the other was to leave him. This was a solemn pledge. They would be so crazy with nitrogen sickness that if one tried to help the other they would both surely drown.

They descended rapidly when the time came, with lots of thumbs-up signals and head nods, and Rick noticed, as they went deeper, that his friend began to look less and less familiar to him, that there was a sinister edge to his appearance. That was the zone of paranoia. He passed through another zone of hilarity. Rick found himself smiling, still clenching his mouthpiece, and the eyes of his partner were bright. They were sharing a secret.

Then he felt his consciousness ebbing away. He rallied every few feet, making himself think, *Yes, here I am, here is what I am doing,* but these efforts became less and less frequent. Most of the time he had no more sense of himself than a mollusk, but that very dimness was somehow familiar and reassuring.

But a piece of his conscious mind was still embedded in this vagueness. He was guarding it. When he reached the end of the line, he took out that awareness like a treasure and used it to write a wobbly RT on the slate. The effort exhausted him. His friend took the slate from his hand, studied it, then took the regulator out of his mouth and tried to write with it. Rick watched, wondering if he should have used his regulator as well.

Some amount of time passed, during which Rick hovered there respirating. He noticed his friend was gone. He looked up, and then down, and saw him ten feet below, with air escaping in a rush from his regulator and his body hanging limp. Rick dropped to where he was, replaced his regulator, and studied his air bubbles to determine which way was up. It took them forever to reach the rope. Rick remembered the promise they had made to each other; he felt bad about breaking it. But they came up together, intelligence washing over them and the sea blackness falling away.

He was famous for that incident. When he drifted into the interior of Florida to learn cave diving he found that the people there knew his name and were eager to dive with him. The underwater systems were vast: they went much farther and deeper than the laws of physics and chemistry would allow a diver to follow. Rick was humble in this environment; he was obsessively well equipped and cautious. He learned mapping, and picked up the practical lessons of geology, how to recognize the good cave-forming limestone, to spot dissolution zones, collapse features, trunk passages. Sometimes they would take scooters and cruise through the wide scalloped corridors, in water so clear it was almost an abstraction. Rick carried four lights always, a big hundred-watt primary as bright as an automobile headlight, and three backups. He used double tanks with redundant valves. He carried two knives and two razor blades and a reel filled with bright yellow line.

Jean was one of the people he dived with. She worked as a mermaid at Weeki-Wachee, wearing a sequined fishtail costume and vamping for the patrons of the underwater theater. She was older than the rest of the girls there—she was twenty-four— and had a certain savvy and irony that set her apart from them. She didn't care about the audience, the stupid routines in which she was called upon to drink a bottle of soda pop underwater, but it was a point of pride to her that she made her living submerged.

She and Rick ranged together through the vast cavern systems, steeping in the isolation and secrecy. As near as he could tell, he loved her. He loved her body in the water.

Divers were always dying in those caves, college boys from Tulane or Georgia Tech who went in, four or six at a time, without adequate lights or a safety line or enough air to get back and died all together, flitting in panic in a black cave like trapped birds. Rick volunteered for the recovery dives; it was a way of keeping in touch, of maintaining the tension. If he was lucky he would find them soon after they had died. He would catch the chromic gleam of their equipment in his light, and the distressed looks on their faces. The longer they were there the more the catfish would have gotten to them. He learned to take extra weights down with him, to compensate for the bloating.

Once after a bad season in which he was called upon to make three recovery dives in the space of several months, he and Jean got into his van and started driving west. The dead, silent forms of those divers haunted his imagination all along U.S. 90. They stopped in Austin, intending to stay only a few weeks, but the place drew them in. Without ever really discussing it, they began to make their home there.

When he first took her to the Well she waded out into the creek and circled the fissure, appraising it like a connoisseur. She bent down and stroked the surface with her hand. The water responded, so clear and transparent it was like air vibrating in response to a tone.

"You were right about this place," she told him. "It's gorgeous." It seemed to Rick that Jean's face glowed with the reflected radiance of the water.

"Who was Jacob?" she asked.

"I don't know. Some guy."

"There's a Jacob's Well in the Bible. 'Whosoever drinketh of this water shall thirst again.'"

Rick looked at her admiringly.

"Didn't I ever tell you I won a hundred dollars on 'Bible Bowl'?" she told him. "Daddy bought me a bunch of those learn-while-you-sleep tapes with the New Testament on them."

They put on their gear and entered the Well, and it struck him after Jean's remark that it was indeed like some biblical place; ancient and sacred, a place where one went in search of visions.

Dropping down through that room in which he had almost drowned as a child, Rick felt the beginnings of a powerful adult fulfillment. He thought giddily that the Well would open for him at every constriction, that every room would yield a clear passage that would lead him deeper and deeper to the place he wanted to go.

But there seemed to be an end to it. There was a final room beyond which there was no passage. He hovered with Jean in the center of that room, the two of them with their buoyancy expertly controlled, neutral and motionless in the water. He accepted that he could go no farther, but at the same time, in the rich deep-water haze that affected his thinking, he could feel something. He could feel more.

Gary often dived with them in the Well. Rick had met him

in Florida a year earlier, when Gary had come down with a group of Texas divers to explore the Peacock system and had engaged Rick as a guide. They had hit it off, especially underwater, and when Rick came to Austin Gary took him on as an instructor. But after a month of that Gary said he was embarrassed to be his boss, that he would rather Rick were his partner. Rick took the remnants of his savings and bought into the shop, helping to finance the training pool and upgrade the rental equipment. He was settled, and for a time he was happy.

Then Jean. It had been a routine traffic fatality. She was on her way to her parents' home in Beaumont when she was hit head-on by a drunken state senator on his way to Austin two days late for the start of the session. The senator was killed too, and though he was clearly responsible for the accident the press was sympathetic. He had been a good state senator, a man of principle, and had turned to drink because his wife was dying of some sort of muscle-wasting disease. "Sadly," the newspaper had said, "these things happen."

Her parents did their best to be kind to him, but their sympathies were limited. He stood a little apart at the funeral, like a spy in a movie, wearing a suit he had bought for the occasion. Afterward he had settled in and let the tide of grief swell and suck around him while he clung to his right mind like a scallop to a rock. When the grief was diffuse enough he was back, leaner and colder, with nothing in his way.

The moon was full, and by its light he could see the pebbly bottom of the shallow creek and the deep shadow of the Well. He parked near the bank, opened the back doors of his van, and began organizing his equipment. He put his wetsuit on first, pulling the stubborn neoprene over his calves where it invariably bunched up. The rest of his equipment he donned in an orderly, efficient way, and in ten minutes he was in the Well, feeling the chill until the wetsuit warmed the trapped water against his skin.

The first rule of diving, he told his students incessantly, is never dive alone. It was a rule he broke frequently. Sometimes the whole point was to dive alone.

Underwater, the rock gleamed in the moonlight, and for a long time as he descended he left his own light off and felt his way like a sleepwalker among the half-lit formations and passageways. He dropped to the first level at thirty feet, then slipped into the tunnel and swam out into the first deep vertical room. He let some air out of his buoyancy compensator and began to sink. There was still a pale light from the surface, and as he descended Rick looked up behind him and saw the entrance through sixty feet of water, a circle in which the full moon was centered like a wavering white flame.

When he reached the bottom of the room he stood there flat-footed in his fins and turned on his light, spotting a crayfish and a large bullhead catfish. There was another tunnel ahead that narrowed to a constriction at about seventy-five feet. Rick fly-walked along the ceiling of the tunnel, pushing off with just his fingertips to avoid stirring up silt, and inspected the constriction. The opening was a semicircle, about four feet wide by three feet high. It would be easy enough to close it off and keep divers from going any deeper. He would think about that.

For now he slipped through the constriction, feeling the increased flow of the water as it squeezed through the small-bore opening. In a little while the cave opened out again, and then constricted once more before it led into the big final room where he had found the divers two days before.

Rick swam to the center of the room and slowly revolved, illuminating the walls, which were fluted and whorled by the water. It was so quiet. He hung upside down; there was no difference. Barely kicking, he soared across the room, letting out line from the reel. He turned off his light and felt the total darkness rush in instantly, aggressively. The exquisite blackness was like a weight; it seeped into his body and made it heavier. If he had been on Mars he could not have felt farther from the familiar world above him.

Rick turned his light back on and inspected the room one more time. The ceiling was high, and there were a few chimneys in it that he had explored thoroughly a long time before. They both pinched out thirty feet or so below the surface. The bottom of the room lay at 128 feet, though it was irregular, filled with breakdown boulders that were massive and so evenly broken they looked as if they had been quarried.

The walls of the room were polished and white—good cave-forming cretaceous limestone. Near the bottom, though, was a layer of red sandstone eight or ten feet thick and below that a bed of conglomerate. The sandstone was the problem, the reason the cave went no farther. It was a type of sandstone that was resistant to the chemical aggressiveness of water. It did not dissolve out like the limestone, it repulsed every assault the water had made upon its structure. The sandstone was a barricade. He liked the word the geologists had for it: aquaclude.

There was no apparent way the cave could go deeper, and he was convinced, after long explorations, that there was no passage leading laterally into the limestone. He had to accept that there was an end to it. Yet, as he swam along in the solitude of the cavern, he could not help believing that somewhere in this room there was a passage that would take him farther, that would take him all the way, deep into the heart of the aquifer, deep into the center of the earth.

There was the fossil, the crinoid stem that that diver had given him when he was a boy. He knew that fossil came from Paleozoic rock, millions of years older than the cretaceous formations around him. Where had the diver found it?

He could not shake the instinctive certitude that the two dead divers he had pulled out of here two days ago had been on to something. The cave went somewhere, he knew that.

He checked his watch and his pressure gauge and saw that he was running a little long. He took one last, long, sweeping look, as if with that gesture he might at last discover the way, but he saw nothing new, only the bone-white limestone and the impermeable sandstone beneath it, the aquaclude that denied him passage.

It took four divers, working in relays, the greater part of a day to install the barricade. Rick had designed it, a simple steel grid that the divers brought down in two sections and welded in place.

When the job was finished, Rick swam down to inspect it one

last time. It was a good barricade. He shone his light through it and saw the beam disappear in the darkness on the other side. He took hold of the bars and shook the grid hard, but it was firmly in place. The barricade would do what it was meant to do. For someone to get through, he would have to want it bad.

Chapter 7

A PATCH of dead, blackened skin sloughed off his forearm in one piece, revealing the flesh beneath it, pink and aching to heal. Sam noted this event for Pancho Ahearne and also something less tangible, a constant crawling sensation in the ends of his fingers. He thought of this as a ghost message from the snake, still alive out there in the Trans-Pecos, still yoked to him by the poison they shared.

Like the snake, he holed up and narrowed his focus. His isolation was a kind of shelter, and he tried not to think of the order and comfort of his life with Libby, the bright little fixed-up house where she still lived, surrounded by plants and books and cooking utensils hanging from the kitchen ceiling. Sam did his best to feel at home here, in his shabby little rented house beneath the airport flight path. He put the moonstone he had found in the Abuelos on the mantelpiece, next to random chunks of rock and fossils toward which he had obscure sentimental attachments. He had tacked geological maps onto the walls for ornamentation, along with a faded print of a Bierstadt landscape and a small framed photograph of Libby. He was doing his best, but only Dumptruck was there to remind him that he was still in some degree a family man.

He spent his days in the survey office, writing his report on the Abuelos. He would have liked to go back there, to look in that creekbed for more moonstones, but the field operation was winding down. People were coming back now to bask and laze about in the air conditioning and to lethargically assemble their data.

Janet came in one day like that, in pressed corduroy jeans and a flowered Mexican blouse. She walked into his office and kissed him on the cheek and sat down in a lopsided chair.

Sam looked at her. He thought of that perfect Austin day they had talked about in the Abuelos and somehow he wanted it very much.

"I saw the zone-tail again," she said.

"Good."

"Powell's real happy. It was a very successful trip. Miranda found a bunch of Indian mounds. The zoologists found some new subspecies of mouse. You should see all the carcasses they brought back. The body count was very high."

She asked to see his injured wrist. Sam held out his arm and Janet took it in her hands. He could feel her breath on the tender skin, and when she ran the tip of her finger across the two fang marks, it struck him as a gesture of provocative intimacy.

"Let's take a walk in the gumbo," she suggested.

It was early afternoon. The heat was not as fierce as it would become. But as they walked out of the air-conditioned survey office they found the parking lot shimmering with heat mirages, and the white light of the sun bore down relentlessly. It was only a short distance to the shaded running path that bordered the lake, but they were both drenched with sweat by the time they reached it.

Neither of them minded. The immersion felt good and strangely bracing. There were few joggers on the path, and the lake water was still and bright.

They crossed the lake on a pedestrian bridge that had been built beneath a highway overpass. Cliff swallows had fastened their mud nests below the supports. Janet stopped halfway across the bridge and pointed at a small V-shaped wake in the water.

"Know what that is?" she asked.

"A dog."

"Huh uh. A nutria."

"Nutrias aren't that big," he said.

89

"They're the world's largest water rat. They're as big as Shet-land ponies."

Sam smiled and continued walking. Despite the heat they were keeping a good pace.

"Have you changed?" she asked, with some seriousness. "After the snakebite business?"

"How?"

"I don't know. Are you convinced of mortality, or whatever?"

"There are lots of good arguments for mortality," Sam said.

"I'm serious."

"I haven't seen God during my convalescence, if that's what you mean. Mostly I've seen reruns of 'Mary Tyler Moore.' It's funny how extraordinary things like that just blend in. It's the normal things that stand out for me."

"Like what?"

"Going to the laundromat with Libby. Going to the movies. All that seems so exotic to me now."

"You sound like you're still moping to me."

"You know what the Aggies say? 'Hunker down and squeeze.' That's what I'm doing."

They stopped to watch a boy with a bamboo pole pull a stubby little perch out of the water. It looked like a toy fish.

"Who or what," she asked, "are you planning to squeeze in the near future?"

Sam laughed quietly and continued walking. Janet slipped her arm through his. A group of adolescent boys on balloon-tired bikes in single file soared by them on the path.

"I know what you want," she said.

"What?"

"You want to be safe."

Sam looked ahead without answering.

"I didn't mean that as a criticism," she said. "I think it's a touching trait."

It was almost six o'clock by the time they arrived back at the office. Sam left his car in the parking lot and rode with Janet to a trendy barbecue restaurant on Bull Creek. The place was jammed with students and white-collar barbecue snobs. Sam and Janet sat on the terrace overlooking the water while they waited

90

for a table. There was a dock where boats could tie up. The people in the boats had spent the day skiing on Lake Travis before idling up this tributary to the restaurant, and by the time they pulled up to the dock they were badly sunburned and loudly drunk.

Janet pointed out a ringed kingfisher to him as it hovered above the waterline, a small, gorgeous, industrious bird. On the other side of the creek rose a stairstep cliff of Glen Rose limestone, hard solid rock alternating with eroded marl beds. So much limestone. It had been deposited in such a calm, endless fashion—just the eons-old lapping and settling and receding of the sea. No intrusions or eruptions like out in the Abuelos, just the constant little quiet deaths, the departing souls of coral animals and mollusks.

Twilight settled over them while they sat on the terrace, and in the stillness the sounds of the powerboats seemed to be muffled.

"Part of the deal between you and me," Sam said to Janet, "is that I haven't given up on Libby."

Janet reached out for his hand and smiled in the dusk.

"Of course I know that. You think you have to be so goddam honorable, that your cards always have to be on the table."

She withdrew her hand and looked out across the water, slightly testy.

"Just let things be a little ambiguous," she said. "For my sake."

After dinner they drove back to her house in the dark. Janet lived near the university, in a little house her father had bought for her after it became clear she was never going to leave Austin. She had recently begun, in a fit of independence, to make the payments.

Sam and Libby had been here often, and now as he entered the house with Janet he was comforted by its familiar appearance: the bird prints on the walls, the macrame plant hangers, the bookshelves filled with dilapidated paperbacks by Carlos Castenada and Margaret Mead. There was a picture of Janet's parents on the mantelpiece. They were standing on either side of Lyndon Johnson, shaded by his massive ears.

Sam felt the impulse to actually shake his head to clear his mind of Libby. Janet turned on the air conditioner, and when the house was cool he crossed the room to kiss her. He was very deliberate. Holding her, he understood for the first time how depleted he had been by loneliness.

Certain things are not complicated, he told himself, as he went with Janet into the bedroom. This is one of them. It is only as complicated as I make it. He was inspired by how lightly Janet took the whole thing. They lay with their clothes off in the cool air, her body so startling and unexpected. The very strangeness of it was provocative.

"Are you feeling good about this?" she whispered, as she backed up against the headboard, opening her legs.

"Yes," he answered.

"I'm glad. I want you to."

They lay as torpid as lizards afterward, feeling the cool air on their exposed skin. After a time Janet got up and walked into the kitchen, returning with a pitcher of iced tea and two glasses. She poured with one leg cocked, the pitcher level with her naked flanks. She squeezed a wedge of lime into each glass.

"High tea," she said, handing him one, and then sat down next to him on the bed, playfully touching her cold glass to his bare thigh.

"Tell me what you think," she said. "Now that we've achieved boyfriend and girlfriend status."

Sam lay back and balanced his iced tea glass on his stomach. "I don't know what I think," he said. "I like you."

"Did I tell you what Don Ignacio did to me before I set out on my epic journey to find help for you?"

"He told me. He said he rubbed water on the forehead and on the back of your skull." He touched the places on her head as he recounted them.

Janet nodded. "That was to attract the spirits of light to me. *Los espíritus de luz*. Oh, Sam, I felt so good that night, wandering around in the desert. I felt like I couldn't take a false step. And I felt so close to you. We were really on the same team that night."

"We really were," he said.

"I know this is a casual thing," she said. "But we're not just

92

working off our lust here, are we? I mean, there's something."

"There's something," he said, but it came out sounding cold and perfunctory, and he saw how she was hurt. She stood up and grabbed the pitcher and went into the kitchen. Sam followed her. She stood in front of the open refrigerator door, her body outlined by the light so that she looked like one of those arty, delicate nudes in photography magazines.

"I'm just an ordinary person," she said. "I want the ordinary things."

She laid her head into his chest and closed the refrigerator door.

She dropped off easily when it was time for them to go to sleep. He stayed awake, feeling a disoriented excitement, and feeling beleaguered by some new weight of responsibility.

He remembered he had not fed Dumptruck. He had not been home all day. In his half-sleep he began to worry—rather absurdly—that the dog would feel abandoned. He imagined Dumptruck in the backyard, dumb and frantic, because Sam had not come home to give him food.

This unperformed responsibility loomed larger and larger in his mind until finally he ran his hand up and down Janet's bare spine to wake her. She turned to him, embracing him drowsily.

"I have to feed Dumptruck," he told her. "Let me borrow your car."

"Sam, it's three o'clock. He's asleep. You can feed him in the morning."

"He doesn't know where I am."

"He's a dog."

"Let me have your keys."

"I can't believe you."

"Believe me," he said, kissing her. "I'll be back before you wake up."

He dressed in the dark and walked out into the early morning air. It was fresh and temperate. The car was Japanese and encrusted with state-of-the-art technology, and he had trouble for a moment finding where to put the ignition key. The dashboard was piled with notes, books, and a melted Elvis Costello record. He felt uncomfortable, driving a strange car, sleeping with a strange woman, entering new territory. He could feel himself drifting. He suddenly wanted very much what Dumptruck wanted from him: the signals and gestures that told him things were in order, that life went on and on.

Chapter 8

IN those weeks Libby attempted to shake down her life to its plain and observable elements. She went to work every morning with an odd feeling of anticipation, a keen desire for the dark cocoon of her office where the hours passed one by one, all accounted for.

But she had her lapses. Cranking the handle of her adding machine while Bancock dreamily pulled the price tags off books, she would often feel herself slip away helplessly in an undertow of reverie.

She remembered the first time she had met Hudson, at a peace rally she had gone to with some girls from the dorm. One of the girls had a boyfriend who had converted his van into a Sno Cone truck, and they rode to the rally with him, crouching next to the crushed ice machine.

"You wouldn't believe how much money I make at these things," he told them. "Peaceniks love Sno Cones."

He was right. As soon as the truck pulled up to the fringes of the crowd, the whole focus of the event shifted away from the strident little man with a goatee and proletarian cap who was holding forth from a bandstand.

"Capitalist bloodsucker!" the man shouted, as his audience drifted away toward the Sno Cone truck.

One of the girls from the dorm introduced her to Hudson, who was standing by a park swing set, casually leaning against one of the supports. Bart trotted nearby, a bandanna around his neck. Hudson distantly acknowledged the introduction, his eyes resting on Libby for a second and then going back to sweeping the crowd.

"You girls want to smoke a joint?" he said.

They agreed, and followed him past the ring of police in riot gear to his car, and then on to his house. There were some other people there, hangers-on. Libby would come to know and detest them.

She was not sure how much she disliked Hudson as they passed the joint around. She did not like his narrow, compelling eyes, his sense of self-importance, but she could feel his power and he had moments of charm. He had dropped out of Harvard, defying a powerful family tradition. He and his parents were savagely estranged. She knew he made a lot of money selling grass—he supplied her whole dorm—and looking around the apartment she could see how he frittered it away, supporting this spacy retinue, which included an untested writer whom Hudson imagined would one day write his biography. His fellow dealers were slow-witted and full of themselves. A few of them carried guns. They used their profits to buy double-necked electric guitars or custommade cowboy boots with marijuana leaves tooled into the leather.

No, she did not like him very much. He was vacant and hard. But she was attracted to him, and young and naive enough to think that her dislike was somehow a failing in her. Later that day, in the bright afternoon, she slept with him on a bare mattress set in a bay window. She could not help feeling privileged. The heavy metal music he played contrasted amiably with the sunlight. The acrid marijuana smell was everywhere, and in the two years she was with him she never escaped it.

She lived for those brief moments of the day when he was straight. They would eat breakfast together sometimes, and talk, before he would light up a joint and slip away into the cruel waking dream of his workaday life.

But it was her life as well, and some part of her responded to its chaotic, depraved texture. She attended her classes, a little stoned, a little dislocated and bored. She found it easy to disapprove of the concept of higher education. She was a history major, for no particular reason other than that she had received good grades in that subject in high school. She had no idea what historians did in the real world and was not eager to find out. This was at a time when it was thought cowardly to look ahead. She was no different from anyone else: she trusted in the present moment, not in any grand existential way, but because nothing she saw or heard suggested to her that there was any value in projecting her mind forward.

Looking back, Libby saw that she had been an ordinary girl: not political, not profound; just wanting the power and guidance of love. She could not be blamed for thinking she had found it in Hudson. One small part of her attention went to her classwork, and she was smart enough to slip by with average grades and to graduate with a degree made doubly useless by the mediocrity she had displayed in pursuing it.

Later she wondered how different her life would have been if her mind had been enlivened in those years instead of dulled by her time with Hudson.

She had graduated by the time they left for Maine. Hudson had recently weaned himself off speed—she had to give him credit, even now, for a certain strength of character—and was so proud of himself he was motivated to put the rest of his life in order. So they went to Maine, where he had friends, former clients who had bought land and gone into the business of peddling lunatic food theories. With a moody, portentous air, Hudson began his mucus diet. He and Libby sat on the sea cliffs at sunset; she watched him tremble with hunger, growing remote from her as a way of trying to snare her into the diet.

She refused. As he weakened physically she began to feel strong and sure. Once or twice she left him at home thinking she was at work, and drove by herself to Ogunquit Beach, lying on the firm sand and watching the perfect rollers come in, or strolling around the tide pools. Her eyes teared up from loneliness, from some unaccountable fear, but she was strong in the knowledge that what she felt for Hudson was pity.

If Sam had come to that restaurant, as he had dreamed, she would have left with him. She would have left with him in a minute.

Now she didn't want to think about Sam. She was resolute about that. It was over. Leaving Hudson had been an escape finally, a delirious escape. But the break with Sam shattered her somehow. It had been so easy to believe that they were securely in love when they were only, perhaps, a relief to each other. That love had been tested with the death of the baby. Sam could not deal with the helplessness. He had retreated. But then she knew that she had shut him out as well. It was nobody's fault. It was just broken, finished. It would take forever to sort it out. The proper therapy was to move onward.

Bobby and Kathleen arranged a date for her. She prudently, fatalistically, agreed. His name was Terry. Bobby mowed his lawn. Libby knew from the moment he picked her up in his Mercedes how it was going to turn out. He was a restaurateur in his late thirties who was thinking about opening a video bar. He had a catamaran. Toward Libby he was deft and solicitous. He ran totally on charm, and then on maudlin intensity, so that when the inevitable approach came she could see, as he gazed ferociously into her eyes, the beveling of his contact lenses.

She stammered and backed away and acted neurotic to save his feelings—"It's not you, Terry, it's me. I'm just not ready for this yet"—and he had enough of that macho graciousness to act concerned and sympathetic. While he drove her home he held her hand as if she were a child.

That episode only made her irritable. After work the next day she went grocery shopping at a toney natural foods supermarket filled with chic Westlake Hills matrons buying preservative-free meat, and grain freaks carrying tiny bags of millet to the checkout counter. Libby bought some gorgeous fruit—just the sight of it cheered her a little. The boy who rang up her purchase wore baggy white pants with a drawstring at the waist, and was so languorous and blissful he seemed to float on a carpet of air. Libby realized, as he smiled vapidly at her, that this boy's awareness had a ceiling, just like Dumptruck's. She felt a twinge of raw superiority; of unashamed arrogance. It seemed to her at that moment she was capable of almost anything, of great understanding and great change.

She drove through town in an agitated mood, feeling that awareness spin around inside her, disengaged. She passed a miniature golf course filled with plaster dinosaurs. Abruptly she stopped the car, paid the fee, and began playing the course in the heat. She moved through the hazards with concentrated energy, her game improving with each hole. The dinosaurs were shoddy and dilapidated. She could see the wire mesh inside them where the plaster had been chipped away. She saw them truly as obstacles, as oppressive presences, and when she made her final hole in one on the eighteenth hole she walked some distance away and began to cry.

She was like that all day, shaken, manic, with nowhere to go. She felt an intolerable need to do something abrupt, and that night as she sat alone drinking a third beer and watching Jacques Cousteau descending through a curtain of blue water, she thought to herself, Why not that? It appealed to her suddenly, and very strongly. She had always felt at home in the water; as a child she had loved to sink down to the drain at the deep end of the swimming pool and flatten herself against the bottom while the sandstorms raged on the surface.

Cousteau's divers wore yellow tanks accentuated by yellow stripes that ran down the seams of their diving suits. They descended rapidly, silhouetted by surface light, propelling themselves with lazy, even strokes of their fins. They looked so at home there. They looked like different creatures entirely. That appealed to her.

She filed that desire away, and after a few weeks it seemed like a very droll notion. She was driving around one Saturday when she passed a portable sign in the parking lot of a strip center that said "Scuba lessons," and before she could talk herself out of it she walked through the door.

A mannequin stood in the center of the shop, dressed in a blue wetsuit and completely covered with various diving encumbrances whose uses she could only guess. There were posters on the wall: Bonaire, Cayman Brac, Cozumel, Roatan. They showed divers soaring in the water, their arms outstretched like birds, with the reef in the foreground like an alien landscape.

A man in the corner was filling air tanks. Libby heard a hollow

99

whoosh as he turned the grips on a bank of cylinders. She took a step back.

The man saw her and smiled. "It won't explode or anything," he said. "Trust me."

He had a stocky, powerful body and an appealing round face. He wore a T-shirt that featured a sad-eyed picture of a baby harp seal. His name tag read "Gary."

"I was wondering about diving lessons," she said, when he was finished with the tank.

"For you?"

She nodded, realizing suddenly that there were probably few women who came in here without being prodded by their husbands or boyfriends.

She was disappointed when she heard how complicated it would be. It would take four weeks, with a lecture session one night a week and then a full day in the water on Sunday. And it was expensive. Three hundred dollars.

"Of course the price includes some of your basic equipment," he told her. "Mask, fins, snorkel, a pair of gloves."

He showed her these things. They hung by hooks from a pegboard wall. She held a mask up against her face, noting the little glass panels at the edges that gave her a distorted peripheral vision. She had a little money saved, and she felt like spending it on just these objects. She let Gary fit her with fins like a shoe salesman and sign her up for the classes.

That night Kathleen and the baby came over and Libby brought the equipment out as Daphne made a few tentative creeps across the floor.

"You know this is textbook behavior?" Kathleen said, holding the mask and giving it an uninterested look.

"What?"

"This stuff. Classic substitution."

"You mean what I really need is a man."

"Yeah."

"I want this. I'm not substituting."

"Terry told Bobby he liked you, but you were a little too unsettled for him."

"How kind."

"I don't like him either, but he's rich." Kathleen handed the mask back to Libby. "Being underwater gives me the creeps."

"What do you know about Sam?" Libby asked.

"I don't know. I think he's had a torrid night or two with Janet."

Libby took off her watch and dangled it in front of Daphne's face. The baby's eyes locked onto it and tracked it as Libby moved it from side to side.

Kathleen picked up one of the fins and examined it.

"I have nothing against hobbies," she said. "Stained glass, macrame, whatever."

"This isn't a hobby," Libby said as the baby reached out her hand for the watch and, miscalculating, closed her fingers on thin air. "It's something more."

What it was she couldn't have said. But she wanted to believe it was more. Already she pictured herself drifting, descending. She looked up at the ceiling and imagined what her living room would be like if it were flooded with water. She would allow herself to float out of her chair and drift around weightlessly. It was a strangely comforting thought. She noticed she was not thinking about Sam and Janet.

Daphne was now chewing on Libby's shoestrings. Libby picked her up and the baby smiled broadly, twisting her head to the side as if in shyness. The weight of the baby surprised Libby. She was solid. There were two raw places on her lower gums where Libby could see the milky subsurface gleam, like forming flowstone in a cave, of her first teeth.

"I want to have a baby," Libby said, surprising herself.

"Of course you do," said Kathleen.

Before it got dark, Kathleen left to pick up Bobby, who was down the street mowing the lawn of a big Methodist church. Libby's spirits sagged a little after they left. She decided to look forward to, to live for, the diving lessons that were to start next week.

She hated the solitude and the static time that came with it. Summer in Austin was not a time to be alone. The heat in itself was enough to make you seek refuge in another person. As an element it seemed unfair and vengeful; it was like something

101

that sought her out alone, cutting her out the way a pack of predators will take the weakest from a herd.

She gathered up her little store of diving equipment and drove to Barton Springs. It was dusk when she got there, but there was still a crowd of idle college kids on air mattresses in the middle of the pool, floating on a slick of suntan lotion. The pool was two hundred yards long, a deep creekbed reinforced with concrete and filled by clear spring water. She could see where the spring discharged, near the diving board, by the constant bubbling on the surface.

She spit into the mask to keep it from fogging—she had learned that somewhere. She was not sure how to use the snorkel so she left that on the bank.

The water was frigid. To warm up she took off swimming as fast as she could, with the stiff fins on her feet cramping the arch of her foot. The clarity of the water through the mask enchanted her. She saw the broad rock terraces beneath the lifeguard stand, the waving fields of water plants through which the turtles swam with their heavy strokes.

Libby swam to the point on the surface where the water was riled by the turbulence of the springs below. Treading water there, she could feel the force, the urgent outward flow. Through the mask she could see a rock shelf, like the lintel of a door, ten or fifteen feet down. Below it was an opening of some kind.

Awkwardly she pushed herself toward it, but soon the pressure began to squeeze her eardrums and she could get no deeper than halfway.

What would she do about that? Surely there were techniques. She submerged again and fought down to as far as she could stand it. She could hear the clacking of the little stones at the mouth of the spring as the outrush of water moved them. Hovering there, she forgot about the necessity of holding her breath. The moment was eternal. There, she thought, looking down at the spring opening, there is where I want to go.

On the first night they were taken into a small classroom with cheap plastic school desks and shown a slide show titled "Welcome to the Underwater World." Moody, rapturous music, accompanied by gloomy whale songs, played on the synchronized soundtrack.

"Since earliest times," said the reverent narrator, "man has been fascinated with the sea."

Libby shifted impatiently in her chair. She was not sure anymore that she wanted to be here. She noticed that their instructor left the room during the slide show. He came back just as the music swelled climactically, waited politely for the narrator to wrap it up, and then turned off the machine.

The instructor's name was Rick, and to Libby he seemed very sober and dignified. He wore a nice sport shirt and a pair of khakis with a dry cleaner's press. His brown, slightly receding hair was trimmed close. His appearance made her think that he took his duties seriously, and she was heartened by that.

That first session they did not go into the pool. Instead, Rick brought out the equipment they would be using—wetsuits, tanks, regulators, submersible pressure gauges, buoyancy compensators. She wrote down their names in her notebook.

He talked about the things that could hurt them: the bends, embolisms, nitrogen narcosis. He said that all of these things could be prevented by common sense. She found herself watching him more, observing the clarity with which he demonstrated Boyle's Law, which she dimly remembered from high school physics.

The pace of the lecture was slow and deliberate. She enjoyed taking her notes, although she noticed that she was the only one doing so. She was older than the rest of the students. Most of them were college kids, on their way to the Caribbean or Hawaii before school started again, and their air of indifferent privilege made her feel awkward and isolated.

But she was cultivating that detachment, wanting him to notice. So that was it. She was disappointed in herself, falling for a diving instructor and his stricken air of authority.

When the class was over several students came up to her to introduce themselves, and she was embarrassed by her rash judgments of them and by her studied reserve. Nevertheless, she was glad to get away. At home she poured herself a glass of white wine and put on a record, and while she listened to the music she thumbed through the workbook Rick had given them. It was like the workbooks she remembered from grade school, with true and false questions and incomplete sentences that ended in blanks. "Air at sea level has a pressure of _____pounds per square inch." She remembered that and wrote it in—14.7. She took a sip of wine, amused that she was such a good student, and went on with the lesson.

He thought she was one of those women who had been pushed into a scuba class by a husband who wanted her to share his hobby. He imagined that her husband was a doctor with some manly specialty like orthopedics, whose waiting room was filled with color photographs of wrasses and clown fish that he had taken himself.

He found himself playing to her, to her intelligence. She lent the class gravity. For a while he did not allow himself to notice the blunt desire he felt in her presence. She sat in the back of the class taking notes, wearing jeans and a sleeveless blouse. Her body looked strong and capable. He wondered if people considered her beautiful.

In the first pool session they practiced flooding their masks underwater and then clearing the water out. She was good at that. She did not panic, as some of them always did, when the water flooded in, obscuring their vision. She had trouble clearing her ears until he took her aside and practiced with her on the surface, having her hold her nose and blow with her head cocked first to one side and then to the other. He heard the tiny inrush of air into her eustachian tubes.

When the group broke into buddy teams she was left over, the only one in the class who had not enrolled with a friend. So he assigned himself to be her partner and helped her don her weight belt and tank and buoyancy compensator. She swayed docilely under this weight while he checked and tightened her straps.

"God, it's so heavy," she said.

"That's why we like to be in the water."

104

That first time they only went five or six feet into the pool. There were problems with leaking masks, ears that wouldn't clear, too much or too little weight. He attended to them all, with an eye on her. Libby. Her buoyancy control was impressive. That was the hardest part to learn. All over the pool he heard the sounds of the student divers pressing the buttons on their power inflators that let air into the B.C. jackets. Invariably they let too much in, and their B.C. ballooned out and lifted them toward the surface while they fumbled for the dump valve. Usually they would then let too much air out and become negative, sinking like a weight.

But she just hovered there, slightly above the bottom of the pool, seeming to know by instinct just how much air she needed to stay neutral.

"Did you like it?" he asked her when they surfaced.

She wiped the wet hair from the front of her faceplate and took the regulator out of her mouth to speak.

"Sure," she said.

The next week they went in the late afternoon to Lake Travis, where Rick had them put on their wetsuits in the sun. Libby tugged hard at the sleeves and legs of this bizarre garment, and before she was dressed she was exhausted.

They stood on the shoreline with their fins in their hands, like frogmen waiting for inspection, while Rick put his own gear on. Libby watched him, feeling the weight of the tank, its straps cutting into her shoulders. Rick put his arms through his own straps and slipped the tank over his head in one movement. There was a kind of grace in that, the grace of the refined gesture.

He led them into the green water; it was warmer and murkier than she'd expected. He stayed near her as they descended and swam at ten feet, cruising among the silt-covered boulders where little fish, guarding their young, snapped futilely at Libby's fingers.

She was disappointed. The underwater landscape looked like rubble, like the aftermath of a nuclear war. It was bare and covered with silt and tinted a bottle green. They saw a tire, and farther on, a pay phone that someone had tossed into the lake.

Rick led them deeper, and she felt the cooler water of the

105

thermocline as her ears cleared automatically. She liked it better here: it was darker and cleaner. She wanted to go deeper, to follow the sloping blocks of limestone, but Rick guided them upward and back toward the place where they had put in.

"I thought it'd be prettier," she confessed to him on the surface, as she helped load the empty rental tanks into his van.

"Not under here," he said. "It's pretty dull. You want to be in the Caribbean."

"Thanks. I'll save my pennies."

"Listen," he said, with careful inflection.

"What?"

"Would you like to stop off on the way back to town and have a drink?"

"Yes," she said, proud of her forthrightness. "I would."

They met at a little bar with a deck that looked out over the lake. She got there before he did and saw him drive up in his van. When he got out she noticed he had changed out of his bathing suit into jeans. He also wore a heavy blue cotton T-shirt and sandals.

"Have you ordered anything?" he asked her.

"Not yet. I'd like a margarita, I think."

Rick waved over a waitress and ordered it for her. He ordered an iced tea for himself.

"You're not having a drink?" she asked him.

"No."

"Don't you drink?"

"Not really."

"Why not?" she asked.

"I don't know," he said. "At some point back there it just got to seem trivial."

When the waitress arrived with her margarita, Libby lifted the glass to her lips, tasting the salt for a moment. The foliage below the deck seemed to gather texture in the evening light.

"Are you having a good time?" he asked. "With the course?"

"Yeah," she said. "I am. I feel comfortable in the water."

"I hope you keep it up."

"Why wouldn't I?"

"Most people don't, not really. They'll get into skiing or windsurfing or something after a while. They have no will power."

"Will power, huh?"

He smiled and looked out over the landscape.

"That's a little harsh, I guess," he said.

"Some might say so. But then you come across as pretty devoted."

"What do you do?" he asked.

"I have a crummy little job."

"You have a wedding ring."

"Yes," she said.

"Do you have kids?"

"No. Well, one. But very briefly. He died."

He nodded his head without offering the usual sentiments. She wished she hadn't told him that. She looked over at him. He was nervously stacking coasters. He had the appearance of someone in very tight control, someone who was constantly shoring himself up inside.

"I don't mean to be coy about the wedding ring," she said. "My husband and I are separated."

He put his sandaled feet on the railing deck and set his face to catch the subsiding sun.

"Thank you for not being coy," he said.

"It's pretty here," she said.

"Where are you from?" he asked. "Lubbock? You've got the accent."

"Picture Bluff. Just below the Cap Rock."

"Not much diving there."

"That seems to be all you think about."

He didn't answer. They watched the deepening night in silence, the fireflies above the live oak leaves and the running lights of the boats far out on the lake.

"I think about you," he said, so softly that she was not sure she heard it. She looked down at her hands like a schoolgirl. She could see the pulse beating in her wrist. Something told her she had to let it all pass, to pretend, in fact, that she had not heard. After a time, he spoke again, asking her if she wanted another drink. She said yes, another margarita.

It grew so dark that they could barely make out each other's

107

features, and they lingered so long without coming to terms that in the end they had no option but a civil parting. Driving home on the dark winding road, she hated herself for her primness. But it was her courage that had failed her: she saw how deep she would go with him, and how fast.

Chapter 9

THEY drove at night through the brush country, along a farm-to-market road littered with the remains of small animals. Sam was driving, and Dumptruck, from the rear seat, rested his chin wearily on Sam's shoulder.

The dog growled at the fleeing white tail of a deer, waking Janet, who looked out into the cone of light the car cast on the road.

"Forty more miles," she said, yawning.

There were snakes on the road, absorbing the last bit of the sun's heat that was still trapped in the asphalt. They were rattlesnakes mostly, and Sam kept a keen watch for a blacktail like the one that had bit him. But the snakes and their fieldmarks vanished quickly, moving with a liquid flourish across the surface of the road.

"See our friend out there?" Janet asked him.

"I don't think our friend hangs out in the chaparral. I could be wrong."

Sam looked up over the headlights at the night sky. The stars were vivid.

"That's nice," he said. "Up there."

"Remember Astral Dominicus?" Janet said, watching the sky now too.

"Vaguely."

"This is his kind of sky. He'd get so worked up. He ever do your chart?"

Sam shook his head. "Never was gaga enough for that."

"He was fun. A little undernourished. Did you ever notice how guys like that don't like to eat? You should have heard him when he got going on Baptists. He hated Baptists more than anybody in the world. He said they were irrational. This was from a guy who had to sweep the spirits out of his van every night with a broom."

Janet lay down again, her feet in Sam's lap and her head against the passenger door.

"There's Mars," Sam said.

"Hmmmm."

Sam remembered the Martian photographs from the Viking Lander. The pictures were all of the same swath of wasteground, a desert floor stippled by rocks and dominated by a boulder the analysts had named Big Joe. It was all so dead. What was the point of a lifeless world? The point was that life was not the point.

On the side of the road he saw four squat forms trotting with surprising speed before veering off into the brush.

"Javelinas," he said to Janet.

"There's a lot of them out here. Daddy and I used to hunt them. We'd eat the meat, too. You know where the turn-off is?"

"I remember."

He and Libby had been to Janet's father's ranch before, not so long ago, when Janet had hosted an elaborate party on some questionable pretext. He recalled that drug use at that party had enjoyed a revival. He and Libby had remained straight, but when they walked out into the brush in the gloaming, they felt the country's hallucinatory edge all the same. Everyone else staggered around aimlessly, up and down the hummocky creeks, the drugs they had taken only serving to add the correct amount of psychic shadow and shade to a landscape that was already spectral.

Now here he was with Janet. He was not entirely comfortable, aware of the ground he was losing with Libby, but he was lulled by the night air and the star field above and the dusky, mysterious shapes that darted forth from the scrub.

They turned off the farm-to-market road onto a caliche road that ran for miles and miles through the brush. He couldn't remember how many sections Janet's father had, how many head of Brahmas and Beefalo and Charolais he ran, but he guessed that you could drive all day on this road and never leave the property.

"Daddy really ought to get a helicopter," Janet said. "He keeps threatening to."

After a few miles he saw in the headlights a dense stand of cottonwoods and oaks. The pale sheen of the ranch house showed up just beyond them. The house was built like a mission church, with an adobe wall guarding it. There were cars parked outside the gate.

"Uh-oh," Janet said. "It looks Like Daddy and Mother are here."

Sam slowed to a stop before they reached the house.

"Janet, you said nobody was going to be home!"

"I guess I should stay in closer contact with my parents. I thought they said they were going to Port O'Conner to take the boat out. Come on, it won't kill you to meet them."

He was not ready to perform for anybody's parents, especially Janet's, but he allowed her to talk him out of the car.

"You're a good sport," she said, kissing him.

Dumptruck jumped out of the car and began sniffing around the driveway.

"Oh Christ!" Janet said, noticing a limousine parked on the other side of her parents' car. "Phil's here too."

"Who's Phil?"

"*Phil*. The Governor."

"No, Janet."

"Afraid so, kid." She walked on through the gate, crossed the courtyard, and waited patiently for him at the front door of the house. Sam told Dumptruck to stay and then steeled himself as well as he was able before joining her.

Janet opened the door without knocking. The entrance hall was dominated by a spangled Mexican saddle displayed like a museum exhibit. There were also a small bronze of a vaquero and a Porfirio Salinas painting of some idealized hill country glade.

Janet's father and the Governor were seated in the living room, which with its high beamed ceiling and white adobe walls looked like a New Mexican ski lodge.

"Hello, Daddy," Janet said. "Hello, Phil."

The two men rose in surprise. Janet's father looked much more casual then he did in the Gittings business portrait that hung over the mantel, which depicted him with his head soberly cocked at an odd angle and his index finger keeping his place in a forbidding leather-bound book. He was thinner in real life. He wore tortoiseshell glasses, a *guayabera*, and jogging shoes. Sam knew the type: the cultured land baron who prided himself on his ranch Spanish.

"Well, will you look at this!" he said as he put his arm around Janet's shoulders and shook her like a comrade.

"This is Sam, Daddy," she said. "Sam, this is Phil."

Sam shook hands with Janet's father and then with the Governor. The Governor was tall and sixtyish. He kept his hair swept back and polished, but it ended in an untended little ruff at the back of his neck. His eyebrows were immense and his eyes were suspicious. He studied Sam frankly as he shook his hand.

"Glad to know you, sir," the Governor said.

"Your mother and Velma are upstairs watching 'Dallas,'" Mr. Sullivan said. "They'll be down in a minute. I'll have Jaime get you a drink."

Jaime wore a white jacket and moved with stealth and admirable bearing. He greeted Janet with just the proper amount of warmth, and then took their drink order.

"I thought you were going to the Deep Sea Roundup," Janet said to her father.

"I was," he said, "but this character invited himself down for the weekend."

The Governor gave a gleeful little smile.

"What are you hunting?" she asked.

"Doves," the Governor said.

"It's not dove season, Phil."

"Well, whatever. Whooping cranes." The Governor turned to Sam and gave him an appraising look. "What do you do to stay out of trouble?"

"I'm a geologist."

"The hell you say. Know old Curly Fentress up at College Station?"

"Know the name."

"That old bastard's got me into more dry holes. Nice fella, though. He's working up in that Austin Chalk now."

The Governor took a sip of his drink and closed his eyes as if in reverie. Sam watched him; he had a fondness for such blustery democrats. Phil Throckmorton was a former oilfield tool-pusher who had been shrewd and lucky and perhaps ruthless enough to expand his Tonkawa Well Service into one of the largest corporations in the state—exactly the sort of man the Texas electorate, in its collective unconscious, wanted for governor. He had been in office for six months and was not doing badly. He was a redneck liberal who kept the ideologues on their toes.

Janet's mother came in, a tired-looking woman in a velour jogging suit. Janet's presence did not seem to please her all that much. She gave her daughter a prim kiss on the cheek and shook Sam's hand with the same amount of enthusiasm, he imagined, with which she had once greeted Astral Dominicus Marvin. The Governor's wife, Velma, was with her, a composed, likeable woman who took a seat next to her husband on the couch and held his hand in her lap.

They talked about the arcana of state government: interest-rate fights, redistricting battles, old alliances and betrayals. The more the Governor drank, the more maudlin and defensive his talk became.

"Let me ask this man here something," he said, indicating Sam. "You don't think there weren't a lot of people who wanted this job?"

"No. I mean yes."

"Damn right."

"Phil," said Janet's mother, who had taken an atlas down from the bookshelf and was holding it open on her lap, "see if you can answer this. What is the state tree? What is the state tree of Texas?"

"Goddammit, I'll tell you what the state tree of Texas is. It's the live oak."

Janet's mother doubled up, wheezing with laughter.

113

"It's the pecan," she said. "Some governor. What is the state gem?"

"They don't have state gems."

"It gets sort of silly from here on," Janet whispered into Sam's ear.

They were about to stand up and make their excuses when Sam heard Dumptruck whining softly for him outside.

"That your dog?" Janet's father asked him.

"Yeah. I'll go out and calm him down."

"Hell, bring him in. He won't be the first dog that's pissed on the carpet."

"That's not the problem. He's housebroken, but he sheds in the summer."

"A little dog hair never hurt anybody."

"We'd be delighted to have him come in," said Janet's mother.

When Dumptruck trotted in, the people in the room rose to greet him, as if he were an honored guest. The Governor tottered a little, then bent down and scratched him behind the ears.

"I like the look of this dog," he said. "He's a damn fine dog." He turned to Sam. "You've risen in my estimation for owning such a dog."

They stayed a little longer to be polite, and then Janet ushered Sam and Dumptruck out of the living room and down a long hall filled with guest rooms. She chose one at random.

"Should we be in different rooms?" he asked her.

"No. They haven't been shocked for a long time. Phil couldn't care less, either. He's had a few escapades here without Velma."

In the corner was an earthen fireplace. Sam wondered if it ever got cold enough this far south to use it. The walls were hung with bluebonnet landscapes and the bookshelves lined with *Reader's Digest* Condensed Books. Sam felt a little wave of homesickness. Here in this house with Janet he felt that he was only a curiosity for the wry observation of her parents.

"I'm sorry they were here," she said. "I wanted this to be sort of idyllic."

"Don't worry about it."

"It can be idyllic tomorrow," she said, lying on the bed. "We can make a picnic and ride horses down to the creek."

114

He lay down beside her on the Indian bedspread, too tired to remove anything but his shoes. Dumptruck collapsed at the foot of the bed, and Sam and Janet both fell asleep without meaning to, the overhead light still burning above them.

Dumptruck's whining woke him. It was almost dawn. The dog urgently paced in front of the door, looking back at Sam expectantly. Sam got out of bed, put on his shoes, and splashed some water on his face, then led Dumptruck outside. The light was just up over the brush, and it softened the flatness of the land, giving it relief and subtlety. There were big cat tracks in the mud around a water faucet that had dripped all night, and after Dumptruck had relieved himself he circled the tracks, sniffing excitedly.

Sam noticed the Governor standing on a little rise, wearing a safari jacket and scanning the horizon with a pair of binoculars.

"Morning," Sam called.

"Well, good morning there," the Governor said. "You're up as early as I am."

"The dog woke me."

"I'm an early riser myself. I'm what you call a workaholic. See, right now I'm improving my mind. I've got one of these goddam bird guides and I'm learning to spot birds. I've already seen a scissortail flycatcher."

The Governor showed Sam the picture of the scissortail in the book.

"I got an idea," he said. "Let's take old Ted's jeep and drive around some. He keeps the keys on top of the refrigerator."

The jeep had been outfitted as a hunting vehicle. There were a pair of seats elevated high in the back and a spotlight for startling game. Sam and the Governor sat below the platform with the Governor behind the wheel.

"Janet's the one who got me interested in this bird-watching business," the Governor said as they took off along the caliche road. "I thought, hell, I'm open to it. A man in my position, Sam, has to have a breadth of knowledge. Knowledge for its own sake. I make it my business to know a little bit about everything: western art, quantum physics, cake decorating, you name it."

He pulled the car abruptly over to the side of the road.

115

"See that bird up there?" he asked, looking through the binoculars.

"It's a hawk. A red-tail."

"Look it up in the book to be sure. Let's don't get ahead of ourselves."

The Governor peered at the picture in the book, then shot his eyes up to the hawk.

"You're about half smart," he said, handing the field guide to Sam. "Check that one off for me, will you? There's a place in the back where you do that."

Sam found the list at the back and made a check next to the red-tailed hawk. The Governor peered over the steering wheel as he drove, with his eyes sweeping the landscape.

"Okay," the Governor said. "You're a geologist. Give me the lay of the land here. What are we looking at?"

"Alluvial stuff. Tertiary shale. You'll get some sandstones a little farther west."

"Ted's got some wells here."

"I'm not surprised."

"Who do you work for? Exxon?"

"I'm not a petroleum geologist. I do field work for the Wilderness Survey."

"So you work for the state. Like me. I hate to say it but if you had any sense you'd be out there looking for oil. You and Janet serious?"

"We're old friends."

"She needs to settle down. That's what the Governor of her state thinks."

"I'm not the one," Sam said.

"So what the hell are you fooling around with Janet for? You're wasting her time."

"She seems to have it to waste."

"Well, now, I'll grant you that."

The Governor drove on, accelerating. Sam could see he had forgotten about the birds. The breaking light was intense and concentrated, groping for purchase. A jackrabbit skittered just ahead of them, causing Dumptruck to almost jump out of the jeep. Sam heard a mourning dove not far away.

"Let me ask you this," the Governor said. "What is your purpose in life? Be honest. What is your perceived goal? You want to be the world champion geologist?"

"Why not?" Sam said.

"I'm just trying to get a handle on you. You interest me. How does a man like you think?"

Something ran out onto the road in front of them, something huge with small, driven eyes. The jeep struck the creature at an angle, the front fender ripping into its flank. Sam heard it squeal as the Governor slammed on the brakes, throwing them into the dash.

He looked back and saw the animal moving away into the brush, dragging its hind legs, its exposed entrails trailing in the dirt. Dumptruck was already after it.

Sam jumped out of the jeep, running after Dumptruck. The dog was circling, baring his teeth at the animal, which lay in a clearing only a few yards from the road, guarding itself by pivoting on its crushed legs, swiping futilely at Dumptruck with its tusks.

Sam worked around Dumptruck and grabbed him by the collar, then pulled him back to the jeep and tied him up with a piece of rope.

"That ain't no javelina," the Governor said, standing over the animal.

"No," Sam said. "It's a boar hog."

The hog glowered at them. Its face was narrow and wild. It looked like a man trapped in some hideous costume.

Dumptruck was howling, maddened by the sight of the boar's exposed intestines and furious with frustration. Sam went back to the jeep, looking for a gun, but there was nothing except a posthole digger. He lifted it out. It was unwieldy, like a giant pair of scissors, with two killing blades at the end.

"What are you gonna do with that?"

"He's in pain."

"Those tusks can slash you to ribbons. We'll drive back and get a shotgun."

"That'll take too long."

"He can stand it."

117

Sam tried to get behind the boar but the animal kept turning, eyeing him with such hate and fury that Sam did not know if he could tolerate it. Toward the creature itself he felt a dreadful tenderness. He held the posthole digger and tried to concentrate on the narrow ridge of the boar's head. As he swung the twin blades, winding up for the blow, the animal rooted furiously in the air with its tusks, mucus flying from its snout. When the blades hit he heard Dumptruck howl in excitement, or terror. The blow fell badly on the boar, but it was enough to stun it, and Sam brought the blades down twice more, cracking the skull while the broken rear legs twitched.

"Good God, son," the Governor said.

Sam threw the tool back into the jeep and then made Dumptruck jump in while the Governor got back behind the wheel. The Governor said nothing on the way back. Sam still felt the weight of the weapon in his hands. He could not keep himself from trembling.

The day had lost its crepuscular edge by the time they were back at the ranch house, the half-lit brush brought into full light. He felt drugged, slow, ghastly.

The Governor examined the front of the jeep in the driveway. There was a streak of blood and hair at the edge of the fender, but the damage was slight.

"Just a little fender-bender," the Governor said. "I'm gonna go see if Jaime knows how to make *migas*. You interested?"

"Maybe in a minute," Sam said.

He went back to the guestroom and found Janet still asleep, lying on her back with her arms at her sides, as serene as a figure on a sarcophagus. He closed the door softly and walked outside onto a patio surrounded by a low stone wall. There was a rusty folding chair and he sat in it, resting his feet on the wall and looking out at the endless waist-high carpet of brush. It was filled with every imaginable sort of furtive and cautious creature, everything that needed cover.

"Mr. Marsh?"

Jaime had appeared on the patio, less formally attired this morning in a pale green sport shirt and slacks.

"Yes?"

"Could I fix you some breakfast?"

"I don't think so. Thank you."

"Just some coffee?"

"Yes," Sam said, rising to go in, "I'd like some coffee."

"No. Please. I'll bring it out."

Jaime brought the coffee out on a little tray and set it on the stone wall. Sam noticed that when he lifted the cup to his lips his hands were still shaking. He set it down for a moment and took a few deep breaths.

It disturbed him that he had been so ready to put the boar out of its misery. In his heart he did not know if he had acted honorably, out of mercy or compassion, or if he had been moved by the same simple, righteous cruelty that had seized Dumptruck. The desire to finish it, to see it end.

But he felt the power of what he had done, he felt the blood still high in his veins, and in thinking of the boar he found himself confronted with the memory of another suffering creature, his baby son. He remembered the IVs in his chest wall and ankle, the plastic breathing tube shoved down his open throat and taped to his mouth, his arms waving and his legs back-pedaling in pain. All of it added up to a fierce silent scream that Sam heard in the cold arythmic beating of his own heart: *Help me*.

Sam remembered Libby, looking to him, her face red and dry, asking the same thing: *Help him*. The awful look in her eyes was challenging him, asking him if he had the courage. He did not. The moment passed as if it had never appeared, and the baby's suffering, as it turned out, did not go on much longer, but he knew now that that was the moment that had counted.

Mercilessly, out of mercy, he could crack the skull of a boar, but he could not end the other things that truly needed ending.

Janet came out to him wearing her robe. She had taken a shower. She leaned over to kiss him, and as he cupped the back of her neck with his hand, he could feel the quickened pulse beat of his cowardice. It was something weak and craven in him that needed her; he needed this casual, pleasurable feeling that was not love almost as badly as he needed love itself.

Janet talked him into breakfast. In the dining room they were all there eating, while the Governor told about the boar hog.

119

The place that awaited him had a bright yellow napkin artfully folded into the shape of a cockle shell. There were fresh flour tortillas, dishes of chorizo and eggs, and bowls of hot sauce. Sitting down next to Janet he could feel the terrible conviction that had seized him earlier begin to subside. He was not shaking anymore; he could not feel the reverberation of the killing blow in his hands.

Chapter 10

THE class continued for two more weeks, with Rick, solemn and professorial behind the podium, instructing them in how to use decompression tables, how to plot a course underwater with a compass, how to put your fist up against your chest to signal to your buddy that you were low on air.

Libby liked plotting hypothetical dives, looking up repetitive groups and bottom times on the laminated decompression tables, and more and more she liked the actual dives in the lake. The boring topography bothered her less as she began to warm to the familiar feel of the equipment, to understand better how it worked, how it supported her and allowed her to roam in the green viscous depths of the lake.

The final session was a free dive. She was paired with Rick, as usual, and he led the class deeper than they had been before, to sixty feet, well out of sight of the surface. He took her hand once, to lead her down a few feet and show her the morose countenance of a huge catfish peering out from under a ledge. He held the hand for a while. She did not pull it away. He turned over on his back, sculling along facing the surface. She did the same, marveling at how little difference it made. Looking up, she could see the nutrients and clouds of silt they had dislodged swirling above them. There was light, but she could see no detail. It was as if she were looking through a gauze blindfold.

He suggested to her, after that final session, that they dive together sometime. She agreed, but as she drove home alone she did not think it would come about, and in the weeks that followed he did not call. But he did not recede in her thoughts; he began very nearly to dominate them, and in a calm, patient way she waited for him. She sensed the intensity of the attraction between them, but it was tentative now, hesitant, finding its level.

She drove to work in the August heat, so muggy that at eight in the morning she ran the air conditioner, and she noticed when she stopped at lights how many of the drivers, thinking themselves unobserved behind their rolled-up windows, were singing. She moved the radio dial back and forth as she watched them through the rearview mirror, trying to find the song they were singing along with. When she found it everything would snap into synch. One day she detected four people singing "Born to Run." She sang with them.

At work she daydreamed about diving as she pulled the lever of her old adding machine. She thought of herself soaring through the medium of the lake, gaining depth with just a tilt of her body and a lazy waggling of her fins. There was an erotic filigree to these daydreams that she noticed and accepted.

Life seemed fluid, benevolent. It was quickening its pace. If she was not quite happy she was sensate and fit, and when she thought of the bad things it was in the context of the awesome richness of life.

One day, behind her desk at work, she thought of the baby for the first time without that deadfall sensation at the center of her body. How mysterious that had been, really; what a lesson. She remembered looking down at that little body in the incubator after all the instruments had finally gone flat. The nurse touched her arm and whispered, "It's all right to hold him now," and then went about disconnecting the tubes, pulling them from his throat and chest. She wiped him off and wrapped him in a blanket and handed him silently to Libby. She remembered how, quaking with grief, she held the tiny form to her breast, fingering the limbs, the fetal creases where the last of his body's heat still resided.

Holding the baby, she had felt a sudden dull panic. She was struck with the knowledge that the baby, in his death, was alone

122

and uncared for, lost. She was aware of his plaintive, bewildered spirit wanting to connect with her. She felt her body trying to die. Then something happened. She saw her grandfather, whom she had loved and who had been dead for several years. She saw him in the room; he was there. And as she held the little body in her arms her grandfather made her understand that the baby was with him. He was accounted for. She could live.

She never asked herself whether she believed that moment or not. She knew that in times of grief, of stress, the mind did things like that. She was grateful that it did. She never told Sam, though she had wanted to. She wanted to give him that moment like a gift. But the time for giving it never seemed to come, and after a while the knowledge seemed to be hers alone.

Now she did her work, and her daydreams of diving in the lake merged with the remembrance of her grandfather's appearance, as if in some way beyond her understanding they were part of the same fabric.

Bancock had a little portable Pac-Man game now, which he took up whenever he finished detagging a pile of books. Though she was his boss, responsible for his behavior, she did not mind if he spent an hour of his working day playing Pac-Man. That was fine.

"Everybody's scrambling their signals now," he was saying. "Cinemax, HBO, the Movie Channel. Where does it leave these people with their four-thousand-dollar satellite dishes? Mark my words. In less than a year there will be a revolution in this country."

"Over satellite dishes?"

"Mark my words."

She heard the beeping of the game as he manipulated the levers. It was not, he had told her, "arcade quality."

"You shouldn't make light of all this stuff," he said. "Your life is going to be changed by it."

"How much?"

"More than enough. You'll be a happier person, Libby. Eighty-four channels."

"What about you?"

"Maybe I'll be content. Not happy."

"Why on earth not?"

"I'm not the happy type. But that's all right."

"You know that's not all right."

"I'm not attractive to women."

"That's not true."

"What's the case in point? You? You're separated from Sam and you're not putting any moves on me."

"Jesus, Bancock."

"No hard feelings. Just a statement of fact. I don't mean totally unattractive. It's just that the girls I could get are the kind that hang out at fantasy cons and Mensa conventions. They're not like you. They're not real women."

He put out his tongue and panted to try to make a joke of this last point, but she saw the unconscious hurt she did him, day after day, just by being there. She gave the lever a hard crank.

"I don't know how to respond to this bullshit," she said.

"Remember Jimmy Carter?" Bancock said amiably. "'Life is unfair.' You've got to hand it to that guy. He spoke the truth."

"I can't handle this," she said. "I'm going on a break."

She walked up the stairs to the first floor on her way to the break room, and there was Sam. He was buying drafting supplies. He had not seen her, and for a moment she wondered if she should just go on. But things were not that bad. She stood where she was and watched him.

He was inspecting notebooks, turning the blank pages slowly, as if he were reading. Then he walked over to a bin of felt-tipped pens and ran his hand through them. There must have been two hundred pens there, all of them the same, but he lifted up several individual specimens and gave them an appraising look. She remembered how serious he was about the tools of his trade.

Libby had not seen him since San Antonio, a month and a half earlier. She had wanted it that way, once she was convinced that he was recuperating from the snakebite with no ill effects. They had talked on the phone once or twice, joking about Pancho Ahearne and his follow-up forms, but they did not search each other out.

He looked good to her. His hair was longer, and his color had returned. When she walked up to him his back was toward her,

124

so she touched his elbow and said, "Hi, Sam."

He turned around, and she saw he was trying not to smile too broadly.

"I'm drawing maps this week," he said. "It's funny, but I didn't even think about seeing you when I came here. I just came for some odds and ends."

"Does that mean we're really estranged?" Libby asked.

Sam selected a pen from the pile and popped the cap on and off.

"What's all this I hear about diving lessons?" he asked.

"I took some. No reason. It was just something to do."

"I took lessons in high school," he said. "For P.E. We used to go up to Lake Tenkiller."

"You never told me that."

"Yes, I did."

"I don't remember ever hearing it."

"It doesn't matter," he said. "Let's go next door and get a cup of coffee."

The place they went was filled with students slouched in plastic booths, blearily looking at textbooks whose pages they had covered with yellow highlighting. Sam sat on his side of the booth with his back against the wall and his feet up, a posture that had always subtly irritated Libby. In the booth behind them sat a morose-looking boy with a Mohawk haircut.

"You have a lot to fill me in on," she said.

"You mean about Janet."

"Whatever."

"When we're a little more estranged," he said, "we can sit here and chat amiably about Janet."

Libby took a sip of her coffee. "It does hurt," she said. "It's not a bull's-eye, but it hurts a little."

"We'll have to get used to that," he said. "I'll have to get used to it about you."

"I wish it were five years from now and all this was over and we didn't resent each other."

"You wish we were friends."

"No, more than that."

"You wish we were in love."

Libby gave him a rueful smile and settled back in the booth like Sam, absentmindedly stirring her coffee. She did not know what she felt about the thing with Janet, what she deserved to feel or was entitled to feel. She knew that even such a casual affair as this one would have come as a body blow when their marriage was together.

They had been faithful to each other, at first because they were fulfilled and then more and more because they were disciplined. They expected it of one another, of themselves. It was the adult way to be. Libby began to see that Sam's fidelity was based less on love and concern for her than on his own self-respect, his image of himself as the honorable husband. So when she thought now of him being faithful she thought of him being merely careful.

Sam was tearing the edges off his Styrofoam coffee cup and making a little pile with the bits. He saw her watching him.

"How's that for a nervous habit?" he asked.

"That's a new one."

"Tell me about you. Bobby said they set you up."

"I think they did it to show me how good you looked by comparison."

"Did I?"

"I would have married you in a minute."

"Somebody's going to turn up, though," he said in a hurt voice. "I can feel it."

"You want to read my palm?"

"Somebody serious."

"Not like Janet?"

"No."

"Then where will we be?" Libby said.

Sam swept up the little pile of Styrofoam and poured it back into his torn cup, not answering.

"I have to get back," she said.

"I've decided to rise above self-pity," Bancock said when she returned.

"Thank you."

126

"Also I'm sorry."

He settled silently into the corner, nestling up to a four-foot-tall stack of biology books.

"I'm sorry too," Libby said. "I'm sorry I don't have the hots for you."

"That's all right. *Puedo exhumarlo.*"

"What?"

"*Puedo exhumarlo.* That's Spanish for 'I can dig it.'"

Bancock was in a talkative mood. He wanted to compensate for his maudlin display. She engaged in the usual banter with him for a while, but she was distracted, thinking about Sam. She wanted to feel more secure about the failure of their marriage, she wanted dead certitude, a quick kill.

That's the way it had been with Hudson, hate finally, and fear. She had left him one day and stayed with Dumptruck in a motel room for a week, afraid of reprisals.

She heard later that he had gone a little crazy, that he had thrown a vulgar three-day drunk, sent his minions out combing the houses of acquaintances for her, shot a hole in the ceiling with his .22, and all but frothed at the mouth. But then the storm passed, and soon he was living with a woman who played pedal steel for The Lukewarm Catholics, a strange band that had been voguish at the time for its country-western version of "O Salutaris Hostia."

Libby left Austin soon afterward, wanting to be someplace fresh, someplace not tainted with her memories of Hudson. She packed up her car and left town with a hundred and fifty dollars, heading for Houston, feeling like she needed the charge of a big, sprawling city. But when she got there she impulsively drove on through, suddenly panicked by the idea of stopping anywhere.

She drove along the coast, heading south, with her dog beside her. Sometimes she felt good and solitary, but most of the time helpless and unfocused. She liked the coast because it was different from Maine—flatter and duller. It was another nothing place like Picture Bluff. She found an apartment in Corpus Christi and grabbed the first job she could find, an assistant to a podiatrist who had a pink stucco office on Ocean Drive. The podiatrist had rococco tastes which included elephant's foot planters and live macaws. It was her duty to swab the hideous ingrown toenails of the clients before the doctor came in with his instruments. She lasted a day and a half.

She started waitressing again and learned to tend bar and began to hang out on the beach with her coworkers, who were surfers mostly and permanently stoned, too old to be in junior college and too hip to be in the Navy. Libby refused to get high with them, and she did not bother with the surfing since the waves were so laughably poor and she did not think she could stand doing one more thing that did not have at least the possibility of excellence about it. She held herself remote from the surfers; they were the context in which she imagined herself finding the secret of her own wants and capabilities.

She liked the beach, but she was afraid and lonesome, desperate to put herself to some use. She did not know where to begin. At night in her apartment she read books about shells, and while the surfers floated on their boards, waiting hours for a decent wave, she walked along the swash line, picking up cockle shells and sharks' eyes with the neat little holes that had been drilled into them by predatory gastropods. She studied the shorebirds, the terns and herons and the occasional roseate spoonbills she would see in the marsh when she drove back to Corpus in the dusk. In that way she began to piece together her self-respect, and as a result to hold herself less aloof from her companions.

One Saturday morning she was walking along the beach, stamping her feet to fool the tiny, pastel-colored coquina clams into thinking that a wave had passed and it was safe for them to rise from the damp sand. A man came up to her and asked her what she was doing. His name was George Fullbright. He was her age, a landman from Tulsa, just starting out. He had never been to the beach before.

Libby drove him down in her car almost all the way to Little Shell, telling him what she had learned about shells and birds, feeling excited by the mere fact of his sensible, intact mind. They had a companionable two weeks together; nothing in particular ended it, and she felt no regrets when it had run its course.

Soon after that her sojourn had run its course too. She and Dumptruck drove back to Austin. She found an apartment, a

128

bartending job. It had been a year since she had left, and she thought to herself that she had accomplished just what she had unconsciously set out to do. She had broken off all her associations with Hudson, renewed her sense of worth, had an inconsequential love affair, and in some unidentifiable way had taken control of her existence.

Hudson came to see her at the bar where she worked. He looked tan and trim but with the coldness still in his eyes. His clothes were a little more stylish than they had been before, and that suggested to her that he had raised the stakes. She assumed he was dealing in cocaine now, working in the dangerous leagues.

They talked for a while, very civilly, while she made frozen margaritas for a group of Junior Leaguish matrons out on the town.

"You really seem to me like you're getting it together," he had the nerve to tell her.

She said nothing. She did not want to score any points with him, to impress him or hurt him or fill him with shame. He seemed confused by the polite distance between them, off his guard. In the end they parted like old friends, almost sweetly, though she took pains to avoid ever running into him again.

She made a few friends on her own while working at the bar. One of them was a garrulous and overweight young lawyer known as Barf Mooney. Libby was never clear where he had gotten the nickname, only that it referred to a legendary college indiscretion involving the Chairman of the Board of Regents and a Bluebonnet Belle.

Barf showed her how to make a drink called a hairball and several times a week he would come in and down two or three of them and talk to her about city politics, which he had just entered with a thud by running a losing race for city council. Just when Libby thought he was going to make a move for her he brought his wife, and the two of them decided in her hearing that she should meet a friend of theirs named Sam.

She agreed. She was twenty-three years old and already thought of herself as far too adult to participate in a ritual like a blind date. But she didn't want to be cynical.

When Sam arrived at her door she remembered him, a name-
less presence from a half-dozen casual encounters over the years.
She liked him for being familiar. His arms and his face were
tanned, and later she was pleased to see that the tan on his arms
ended at his biceps. That made her think he was not vain. They
went to see a spaghetti Western and laughed together at the
dubbing, and when they came back to her house they went
silently and deliberately to her bedroom.

She was so relieved to like him, to want him. He seemed to
her to be a man, a grown man of consequence and bearing, as
solid as the rocks he studied. It was as if fate were handing him
to her in compensation for Hudson.

She passed silently into his life. Some of his friends were
familiar to her and they had a few in common, and she felt with
him that a circle was closing. After a strange, errant time she
was entering into a period of tranquillity.

Sam had worked in the Co-op briefly as an undergraduate and
he still had friends there who had risen to patronage positions
and were eager to offer her a job. The pay was respectable and
at first she liked being near the campus, whose presence had
been so dim and unreal to her when she had been enrolled there.

She and Sam lived together for a year. They traveled a little
within the state when it was feasible for her to go along on his
bureau assignments. More often he would be off by himself, and
she felt his absences with an intensity she did not want to admit
to herself.

Looking back, she realized she missed him with such fervor
because she was compensating for some kind of lack when they
were together. It was something very subtle, some half-forgotten
part of herself that his presence did not address. There was a
caution, a propriety, a goodness in him that over time could turn
tiresome, and yet she needed to believe in those very qualities.
She could sense a power in him that she did not yet understand,
but she trusted him as she had never trusted anyone in her life.

When it seemed time they were properly and discreetly married. She remembered being very content indeed, and taking it
on faith that she would be happy. She could feel the potential.
There was something there for the two of them. It lay deep,

further than either could reach, waiting for them to find the strength in each other.

They hadn't found that strength, and she thought now that they had come together too easily, as too much of a relief for each other, to deserve it. She often wondered what it would have been like if they had met at a less convenient time. What if one or both of them had been married, had children? Would they have had the unassailable predatory instinct to come together anyway? Would they have hurt and shocked others for love and looked back on the damage without regrets?

Chapter 11

A BOY had drowned. He had been playing on the bank of a creek, near a place where the water pitched over a limestone overhang. The drop was only three or four feet high, and it would have been stretching the definition to call it a waterfall, but the water was swift there—it had worried a little trough into the rock that concentrated and powered its movement. Though the water was only five or six inches deep, it had swept the boy off his feet when he stepped in and thrown him over the falls. No one ever saw him surface.

Rick got a call at the shop asking him to help out, though the county divers had been working the creek for half a day and had found nothing.

He arrived there late in the afternoon. People were still searching the banks, and snorkelers were cruising the shallow creek. They had searched for two miles downstream and the boy's body had not turned up.

"He's got to be caught in the falls," Rick told Thornton, who was shivering in his wetsuit and eating a sandwich.

"That's what we thought," Thornton said. "But he's just not."

"How old was he?"

"Four."

"Shit."

"I've got a four-year-old," Thornton said. He was starting to cry.

Rick put on his gear, trying not to look at the boy's parents, who stood some distance away, their faces blanched. He put on a lot of weight and left his fins in the gear bag.

He got in just below the falls. The water was thigh deep and as he waded upstream, fighting against the force of the water, it did not get much deeper. He calculated that it was about shoulder deep at the base of the falls. The resistance was almost total; he could not move against the churning water. He put his regulator in his mouth and sank to his knees, just underwater, and moved over to the side until he felt the rock and then began to advance as best he could around the falls. Even here it was like proceeding against a hurricane. There was no visibility, just a dark green froth.

He pulled himself a foot closer to the turbulence and then the mask was ripped off his face and the regulator pulled out of his mouth. He replaced the regulator and forgot about the mask, though he felt peculiar and vulnerable without it.

He was behind the waterfall now. He could feel the extra weight holding him down as the water tried to lift him and pound him with its spinning force against the rocks. He moved on his knees, like a penitent in a gale. He probed the limestone with his hands, looking for a place big enough to hide a body. It was clear to him that the boy had never made it out of here. He had been caught in this circular tide and held here, in turbulence so great it seemed like even the boy's soul was trapped here in the darkness.

He was very close. The rock behind the waterfall was smooth and slippery. He swept his hand up and down in parallel lines, looking for the place. Finally he detected a little pocket, not much more than a few feet in circumference. He told himself it was too small. Do not make me put my hand in there. But he knew that was where the boy was, and as he put his hand in he could feel the water pushing his arm forward until he touched the boy's hair. For a moment the suction held his arm there and it seemed he could not move it, it seemed he could be sucked into that space himself.

He took several deep breaths, then removed a coil of rope from his weight belt. He was able to get both hands in the crevice and work the rope through the boy's shoulders, though the force

133

of the water kept kicking him against the rock and his knuckles were rubbed raw in the narrow passage. He pulled on the rope, but as he expected, the body would not budge. He worked his way out from the falls, trailing the rope, then surfaced and let the current take him downstream where Thornton waited. He told Thornton to get the parents away. When they were gone the rescue personnel stood on the bank holding a rope. At a signal, they all pulled.

On the way home he had to pull his van over to the side of the road. I lost too much body heat, he thought. That's why I'm shaking so much. I need to eat.

He pulled into the drive-thru lane of a McDonald's, but his teeth were chattering so much he could not order. He parked the van on the far edge of the parking lot and walked out into a vacant lot, staring at a half-finished bank of condominiums. He realized he just wanted to cry.

Why this one had hit him so badly he didn't know. It was as if the boy's frightened soul had possessed him, and he suddenly saw the world with the plain terror of a child.

In the McDonald's bathroom he washed his bleeding knuckles, then ordered a hamburger and milkshake and ate in his van. When he was through he walked back inside and found a pay phone and looked up Libby Marsh's number.

"This is Rick Trammell," he said.

"Yes."

"Could I see you?"

His voice sounded shaky to her. She thought perhaps he had been in a car accident. Or maybe he was drunk. If he was, she thought, what gall. But then she had never expected a courteous call asking for a date. She knew that when he called her he would be in need.

She gave him directions to her house, then turned on the air conditioner and began picking up a little. It was almost dark. The air was humid, a tightly woven fabric that clung to her as she moved about.

When she answered the door he stood there, hesitant and sweaty. His hair hung limp against his head and his knuckles were torn and abraded.

"It looks like you need about ten Band-Aids," she said. "Have you been boxing or something?"

"No," he said. "Working. A body recovery."

"A dead body?"

He nodded. "I'm a little moody. This is probably not very smart of me, to come here now."

"Why not?"

"I don't feel like I'm putting my best foot forward."

"Who needs your best foot," Libby said. "I know you don't drink but do you want a drink?"

"No thanks."

"I've got a can of orange juice in the freezer. How about that?"

"That sounds good."

He followed her into the kitchen and stayed while she made the orange juice.

"How do you recover a body?" she asked.

"Different ways."

She handed him his orange juice and poured a glass for herself.

"Should I encourage you to tell me all about it?" she asked.

"No."

"I'm glad."

"Have you been diving?" he asked.

"No. I thought you were going to take me."

"I wasn't sure if I should."

"I'll let you worry about that," she said. "I'm ready."

On the wall behind him was a poster illustrating herbs. She focused on this as she talked to him, afraid to meet his eyes.

"I'm leading a tour to Cozumel in two weeks," he said.

"Dream on."

"You can afford it."

"How do you know?"

"I'm guessing. I'm hoping."

"Try paying."

"I'll pay," he said.

"Just kidding."

She took her eyes from the herb chart and looked at him.

135

"Come into the living room," she said. She touched his elbow, ushering him.

They sat for a time facing each other, and then he set his orange juice down on the coffee table and walked toward her. She saw that he was not compromised by doubt or a stray thought.

He kissed her with restraint, drawing him up to her. She could feel the tension in his body that kept the whole mechanism operating. He was lean and full of purpose.

She turned out the overhead light and they undressed in the living room. She saw him watching as she took off her clothes. He laid his own clothes neatly on the couch, and when he came to her the shock of his bare skin thrilled her. There were goosebumps on her arms, a chill in her spine.

"You feel so new," she said.

"I am new."

They went into the bedroom and lay down without pulling back the bedspread. She heard the hum of her electric clock. He kissed her deep in her mouth as their bodies conformed and grew perfect for their task. It seemed to her that her whole life's experience was compressed into those moments he was inside her, into that final spasm when she did not hold herself above any sensate thing on earth.

They turned down the bedspread afterward and slipped beneath it.

"You have a picture of your husband on your bureau," he said.

"Do you want me to go over and turn it face down?"

"It doesn't bother me," he said.

"Whose picture do you have on your bureau?"

"I don't have a bureau."

"Come on. Whose?"

"Jean's."

"Were you married to her?"

"No. We lived together a while."

"When did you split up?"

"She died in a car wreck. A year ago."

"How hard was that?" she asked.

"Pretty hard. There's still a little shock. The part that hurt was not really being there as a participant. I was in her apartment

136

when her parents came up to clean it out. I felt like such a jerk. She'd left all these notes to herself about me, how moody I was, what sort of things she could fix me for dinner. Her mother comes up to me and says, 'Would you like something to remember her by?' Real cold. So I took one of those little notes."

He ran his hand along her leg.

"She was a good diver," he said.

A dog was barking outside. Libby heard one of her neighbors, out for a late stroll, shushing him. Rick sat up a little and adjusted the pillow beneath his head.

"We should have gotten married, I suppose," he said. "That might have helped. The way it is now the whole thing just lingers."

"Marriage might have helped that way," she said. "Maybe not."

"Probably nothing helps," he said.

He turned to her, and she felt herself rushing to the comfort of his strangeness. They made love again and then they slept, her open hand spanning his chest, monitoring his presence.

In the middle of the night she woke up alarmed, hearing something next to her.

He was sitting up in bed, facing the wall, talking in an urgent voice but unable to form anything but nonsense syllables. She moved away from him, terribly frightened for a moment. Half asleep, it took her a beat or two to remember his name, to accept him. He was like a madman, speaking in tongues. She listened, shaken, until her head was clear, and then she touched him and said his name.

Rick was dreaming he was in the Well, facing the barricade he had put there. He thought he heard his name and looked upward at the blue circle of light and at the figure suspended, silhouetted there.

It was a naked woman. He watched her drift down to him. Neither of them was wearing a tank or regulator. They could breathe underwater. This was a revelation to him like the discovery of love.

He rose to her, to Libby. She opened her arms to receive him, and they floated that way in the middle of the Well. He spoke to her, as plainly and lovingly as he could, and heard his words so garbled by the water that he could not even remember what he had meant to say.

He looked down at the barricade, and it seemed his vision took him beyond it. He felt within his body that nauseous, deadly pulsing he remembered from his childhood. It led him inward, into the earth. He could sense the aquifer, deep below, a region of light, the place where the dead waited for release. Their souls were like the water that had seeped into the bedrock and filtered through the porous strata until it was brilliant and ready to issue forth again. Jean was there, he knew, and the little boy he had pulled from behind the waterfall. They were in that region of light.

But he floated far above it now. He had ceased trying to talk. He felt a touch on his shoulder, a soft voice saying, "Rick? Rick?" and then he came awake enough to lie back down and move close to the form beside him on the bed.

Chapter 12

SAM went to visit the baby's grave. This was one of his adult
duties. He got out of the car and walked over to the recessed
marker that looked like a flagstone. "Patrick," it said. That had
been Libby's grandfather's name. He tried to remember either
he or Libby ever referring to the baby by name. There hadn't
been time for that.

Still he thought that in those few hard days he experienced
the full force of fatherhood. Even now he did not quite think of
the baby as dead. He thought of him as someone who had missed
the first pass but would be around again.

Sam and Libby had come out here once together. He had
thought it would be a maudlin thing to do but it had been strangely
comforting. They had gone home afterward and taken a nap
together.

He looked over the field of tasteful markers and the flowers
lying beside them, vulnerable in the fierce heat. He bent down
and idly pulled a St. Augustine runner off the marker, feeling a
little derelict for not bringing flowers himself. He stopped short
of grave-tending, but he understood the impulse. It was a signal,
a little probe into the ineffable.

Fifty yards away a burial was in progress. The open grave was
bordered in green fabric like a surgical incision. The wind rippled
the vestments of the priest as he read the service.

Sam fingered the letters of his son's name, cut into the granite
of the marker, feeling hesitant and witless; feeling the baby's

greater knowledge. He stood up and reached into his pocket for his car keys.

It was Saturday. He would not work today nor would he see Janet, who was gone this weekend, leading a birding tour to the border. They saw each other about four times a week now, rarely more, and that was fine. He was glad to see her but was hardly bereft in her absence. When he was alone he felt concentrated, steadily applied to some unformed goal.

He drove back from the cemetery through downtown Austin. Near the state capitol his car overheated, reminding him of the hole in his radiator he had never fixed. He found some shade and parked the car for an hour while he toured the rotunda of the capitol, waiting for the car to cool down. He had a full canteen in the trunk, and when he returned he poured it into the radiator. But now when he turned on the ignition the engine would not turn over.

Bobby came to get him, bringing his tool kit, and insisted on crawling under the car to have a look.

"I think it's your starter," he said from beneath the car. "You'll have to get a new one in the morning."

"What will it cost?"

"Fifty dollars. I'll put it in for you. You'd better come home and have dinner with us. Kathleen's making chili. There's always plenty."

"Cars are weird that way," Bobby said as they drove to his house. "Something goes wrong, then something completely un-related conks out. Sympathetic response. If you want to know the painful truth you were sending it thought messages and they weren't healthy."

"So if I think happy thoughts my car will run better?"

"This is my belief. Things are integrated. You use the same psychic circuits as your car."

"I wasn't using any circuits," Sam said.

"You're on cruise control. I've been watching you lately. You've relinquished the wheel, Sam."

Kathleen did not appear surprised to see him. She must have assumed that Bobby would bring him back for dinner. Sam could smell the chili, the cumin and peppers simmering on the stove while Kathleen patted out flour tortillas like a Mexican housewife.

Daphne sat on the living room floor, her back propped up against a pillow. When she saw Bobby and Sam she waved her arms in circles like a hummingbird.

Bobby brought him a beer, and they sat on the worn couch in silence, smiling while the baby peered at them and Kathleen slapped tortillas in the kitchen.

"How's your arm lately?" Kathleen called out.

"Fine," he said, aware of the faint web of sensation that still overlay the skin of his forearm.

Sam tilted his head against the couch and looked up at the water-stained ceiling. Bobby slid down to the floor and gave the baby a sip of beer. A new Neil Young record was playing on the stereo. The languid domestic pace made Sam almost drowsy.

He and Bobby had been roommates their first year at college. Bobby had been a specialist in bogus courses; he once found them a survey of popular culture taught by a professor in a Nehru suit who lectured on Blue Cheer albums. One semester he hitch-hiked to Palenque, somehow managed to smuggle back a laundry bag full of psilocybin mushrooms, and stayed in his room for three weeks. When he emerged he enrolled in the film department and promptly made the rounds of the banks, trying to talk loan officers into financing an epic Super 8 movie about World War II, told from the point of view of animals.

The craziness had worn off a little by the time he met Kathleen, and over the years their casual, hit-and-miss marriage had more or less stabilized itself, with Daphne providing a great deal of the ballast.

At dinner, Bobby toyed with his food and fed the baby little strips of tortilla. He held a spoonful of chili up to her mouth.

"Don't," Kathleen said.

"It won't hurt her."

"Bobby," she said. "Don't be an idiot. There's too much red pepper in there. She'll go into shock."

Daphne leaned forward in her high chair, straining to reach the spoon that Bobby held in front of her.

"What do you think?" he asked Sam. "She's a Texan, right?"

"She eats strained peas," said Kathleen.

141

"Don't give her chili," Sam said.

"Thank you," Kathleen said.

Bobby looked playfully at his wife, in mock deliberation, and put the spoon down.

Sam leaned back in his chair and took it in: the friendly bickering, the worn, comfortable home crossed by columns of air from the oscillating fan. This is what he and Libby would have had, perhaps, if the baby had lived.

He helped Bobby wash the dishes while Kathleen put Daphne to bed. Looking through the kitchen window he saw that the yardman's yard was unmowed. In one corner of the yard was a heap of old lawn mower parts, rusted two-cycle engines, and stray miniature wheels. Darkness was coming down on it all like a press, forcing the color out.

"How's work?" Sam asked.

"It's the height of the season. All these women are giving parties. Suddenly I'm more important to them than their gynecologist."

Sam held a bowl under the faucet, spraying his shirt with deflected water. An anole lizard walked sideways on the window screen.

"Let's do something after we wash the dishes," Bobby said. "Let's drop some acid and go hear some music."

"No thanks."

"We'll check out some of those eternal truths."

"Name one eternal truth," Sam said.

"Easy. Jesus was an astronaut."

Sam laughed indulgently as he rinsed off a handful of silverware.

"I shouldn't have to beg you," Bobby said. "This is very good acid."

"What would the point be?"

"I'm tired of hearing you talk like that," Bobby said, with a sudden bitterness that surprised Sam. "I'm tired of you being so cautious. Why don't you show me a little courtesy?"

"All right," Sam said. "For friendship."

"Damn straight."

Bobby went into the other room and returned with a small square of paper.

"Lick," he said, handing it to Sam.

Sam licked the paper and finished drying the dishes while Bobby went in to clear things with Kathleen. Coming on to the acid, Sam felt ridiculous; his mature mind resisted. The last time he had done such a thing was with Libby, at Enchanted Rock. Years ago. That had been strangely deliberate and solemn, and he thought of that huge barren mountain now as a shrine.

This was different. He was going on a journey for which he had not prepared, for idle reasons. He took a few deep breaths—"cleansing breaths" they had called them in childbirth class—and tried to give some order to the teeming thoughtlessness in his mind. He needed to be ready, if there were something worth understanding.

The fading flush of daylight hit him at the same time as the drug, and Sam felt a pang of love for it, an easy swell of euphoria.

He looked through the window into the big yard and saw with the sharpness of a hawk the overgrown grass, each blade visible to him in the splendid failing light.

"Your lawn needs mowing," he said to Bobby when he returned.

They did not speak again but walked purposefully outside. Sam helped Bobby get the mowers out of the truck. He noticed Kathleen standing at the door, a hard, disappointed look on her face. Was he responsible for that?

"You take this half of the yard," Bobby was saying. "Keep your feet away from the blade."

Sam felt a twinge of fear at the mention of the blade, and began to form elaborate and dark scenarios in which the lawn mower sliced off his feet like a scythe. But the engine, sputtering when he pulled the cord and then evenly humming, caught some identical frequency in his own body and he aimed the mower into the wilderness as if he and the machine were possessed with one desire.

Bobby worked the other side of the yard where the grass was sparse and filled with debris. A rock, faceted by Bobby's mower, sailed past Sam's face, and he identified it in midair, a quartz cobble far from its origins in the granite hills of the Llano Uplift.

Beneath the mower the grass submitted, wanting to be tamed. Grasshoppers struggled in the piles of clippings, which held them

143

like quicksand. Life and death. Like some great celestial reaper he cut a new swath, unable even to guess how many minute organisms, how many communities of creatures had been torn away through the exhaust. It seemed to him that there was nothing but life, nothing but awareness. Everything was in on the secret.

Bobby was mowing with an idiot grin on his face, pushing his mower forward and then running to catch up with it. Sam noticed that the day's brilliance had disappeared. It had grown dark, and he felt the loss as if the darkness were an indication to him that a blessing had been withdrawn. He was humbled. The motor's sound came from somewhere else now; not from within him. The noise was ragged and threatening. It seemed to take him hours to cut the last few strips of grass. They kept reappearing.

When he turned off the mower the noise shot away, and he heard the muted castanet sound of cicadas, thousands of them announcing their presence to an indifferent world.

Sam became vaguely aware that he and Bobby were somewhere else. They were driving in Bobby's truck, and then they were in a bar, listening to music that was so frenzied and witless he could distinguish it from the cicadas only by its volume. The band wore string ties and metallic jumpsuits. They were into that robot stuff. Their name was written on the drum set: The Excrementals.

There were punks on the dance floor, engaged in their solitary, spasmodic posturing, and there were ordinary people too, drawn here out of curiosity, out of some secret allegiance to the death force.

But from somewhere he could feel life, its tremors, its goodness. He put his hand to his neck, feeling for the carotid artery, and when he found the pulse he left his fingers there.

He began to hallucinate a little. The eyes of the band spiraled out toward him. He could read the evil in those eyes. They were paying particular attention to him. He felt as if he were in a cavern, far from light and air.

He managed to get Bobby to move torpidly, incrementally toward the door. The moon was full outside, and Sam saw the craters clearly. The Sea of Tranquillity. The Ocean of Storms.

144

"Look hard," he told Bobby, "you can see the moon buggy they left up there. You can see the grain in the rock."

The music followed them down the street. Sam could feel it perched on the back of his neck, riding him.

But they drove west, out of town, into the cleansing night. When Sam looked out the windshield he did not see motion before him but a series of still scenes, sequentially arranged like a slide show. Under the moonlight the live oak leaves were as gray and soft as moss and the clouds bounded across the sky like gazelles. He thought of Libby in the most tenderhearted and carnal way.

They were in a place he recognized, a state park on the outskirts of town. A river fell through a series of limestone shelves. The rock was smooth and beveled and in the deep holes the water lay still. Across the river he could make out the darker shades of sandstone and conglomerate.

He and Bobby sat down on a little river beach. For the first time that night nothing seemed to be pursuing or crowding them.

"That's better," said Bobby.

"Yes."

Something moved at the edge of the beach, silhouetted against the water. It looked like a miniature dinosaur with a long neck and a serrated back. It moved very slowly, dragging a thick tail.

"Are we for that thing or against it?" Bobby said cautiously.

"We're neutral," Sam answered. "We're prepared to communicate."

The creature turned away a bit from its perfect profile and Sam saw what it was, an alligator snapping turtle.

"It must weigh forty pounds," he told Bobby.

The turtle slipped soundlessly into the water. They saw the jagged midpoint ridge of its shell cutting through the surface as it dived.

"It chose not to communicate," Bobby said.

"Apparently."

Bobby lay back in the sand and stared at the sky.

"I'm starting to believe it all," he said.

"What?"

"Everything. The I Ching. Sasquatch. Astral travel. The Shroud

145

of Turin. Findhorn. It's easier to believe all that shit than not."

"Then go ahead and believe it," Sam said.

"Thank you. I will."

"There was a woman in the paper the other day who said that the image of Christ appeared on her Corning Ware."

"I believe her. It's a package deal. You believe everything or nothing. You can't let your guard down. You can't doubt. I will now start your car with mental energy."

Bobby made low rumbling sounds as Sam looked up in the sky and saw a meteor, a brisk little taunting image.

"I'm taking a walk," Sam said. He stood up and walked along the shoreline, not bothering to take his shoes off as he stepped into the cool water. A tributary came in not far downstream and he turned to follow it. It deepened into a narrow stone chasm, and the stream that had carved it was almost dry. The limestone bluffs gleamed like chalk. Sam took a big rock and broke it over the sharp edge of a boulder and looked at it in the moonlight. Dull, sedimentary rock. Cement. All along the stream bed, as dense as gravel, were fossils, Pelecypods. Their whorled shells had lithified, turned to rock; a hundred million years ago their lives had been as transitory as that meteor he had seen in the sky, but he could sense their ghosts in these fossils, sealed in the spiral casts.

The bluffs were steep on both sides of the river. Sam had the urge to climb, and then felt a cold, familiar thrill. It was a place like the gulch in the Abuelos. He felt his arm tingling, and he felt the will of the blacktail, its stewardship, its guidance. The fire of the venom was in his veins again. The snake was his ally, his dangerous ally. He stepped away from the bluff and stared at its sheer height; and just like the housewife who had seen Jesus in her casserole dishes, he saw his own face in the rock.

146

Chapter 13

LIBBY felt the searing burden of morning light on her bare back. She woke and kicked loose of the sheet that had knotted at her ankles during the night, then looked out the window, at the fierce whiteness, bright as a star. Cozumel.

The shower was running, a thin drizzle of water that sputtered against the metallic shower stall. She heard the loud squeaks of the handles when Rick turned it off. He walked out of the bathroom with a towel wrapped modestly around his waist.

"Have you seen the water this morning?" he told her. "Look."

Libby got up and walked to the window, standing beside it because she was wearing no clothes. She looked past the square to the ocean. It was taut as a bedsheet, and flushed with radiant turquoise light. For a moment it was a shock. It surpassed her understanding of the beauty the world had to offer.

They had not seen the water last night. Their plane had been late and they had come in in the dark, with Rick herding his tour to the hotel, trying to keep track of their luggage and equipment. The streets had been jammed with drunken Americans on Mopeds.

Looking at the water now, she was entranced. It was like some gorgeous dream image that had delivered itself like a gift to her conscious mind.

"I've never been anywhere before," she told Rick.

"This isn't really anywhere," he told her. "The real part's underwater."

She turned to him and took his towel away, drawing him to her side of the window. He was already sweating, even though he'd just had a shower. She laid her head against his chest and felt his perspiration on her cheek.

"I've got to wake those bozos up," he said. "The boat leaves at nine. You'd better get ready."

Rick went down the hall to rouse the other divers. Libby lay back down for a moment, lazy with happiness. She looked across the room where they had stored their things. Her big hand-me-down American Tourister suitcase towered above Rick's canvas carry-on bag. Next to it was his gear bag made of a faded blue rip-stop fabric. When they had arrived last night he had promptly unzipped the bag, unpacked his wetsuit, and hung it on a special hanger he had brought himself. She liked that about him. He had a few simple things, of the best quality, that he cared for devotedly.

Most of her own equipment was rented, but she had brought the mask, fins, and snorkel that she had purchased for the course, and a pair of gardening gloves that Rick had recommended to protect her hands from the coral. She pulled on her bathing suit and rummaged through the gear bag that Rick had loaned her, looking for the Sudafed she had brought along. That would help her to clear her ears. She was nervous. She wanted everything to go well.

She took two of the tablets and then checked through her bag once more to make sure everything was in place. When Rick came back they went across the street and had breakfast.

"Don't eat anything greasy," he said, looking at the menu.

"I'll just have toast."

"Are you worried about the dive?" he asked, though at that moment his keen eyes were not addressing her. They were looking at the water.

"I can handle it," she said confidently. "If you don't leave me floundering there. If you'll be my buddy."

"I'm your buddy," he said.

The boat was an old fishing schooner that had been fitted with an engine and robbed of its mast. It was a narrow, sharp-nosed craft, much different from the stable broad-beamed dive boat

148

that Libby had expected. The crew consisted of two teenage Indian boys and a man Libby took to be their father, a fleshy, deep-chested man who wore polyester cut-offs and a Utica Blue Sox baseball cap.

Rick spoke to the man in passable Spanish, planning the itinerary, as the other divers came aboard, groaning under the weight of their equipment. Libby helped lash the tanks to the sides of the boat, looking over into the water as she did so. Even here at the dock, near where the effluent from the power plant was discharged, the water was heart-stoppingly clear. She could see black sea urchins below, an occasional brilliant fish, and the dark green knobs of isolated coral heads.

Besides her and Rick, there were seven people in the group: three engineering majors from Rice, a wiry, humorless man from Houston who sold and trained what he called "protection dogs," a North Dallas dentist, and two college girls from Austin with deep, dangerous tans.

As the boat left the dock, the two girls took a position on the bow where they could catch the most sun and lay face down with their bikini straps untied. Libby noticed how the Indian boys watched them, how disturbed they seemed by the girls' heartless desirability.

Rick sat with her for a while, propped up against the dive bags, as the boat left the little town and coasted along the lee shore, angling out a little into the deeper water where the reef lay. The luxury hotels on the island reared up out of the foliage like jungle temples.

"The guide says Fidel Castro was here last week," Rick said.

"Doing what?"

"Diving the reef. Just like us."

Libby saw a dolphin's fin break the water near the placid beach, and then a flock of bright green birds flying over the boat on their way to the island.

"What are those?" she asked him.

"Parrots."

"Not really."

"Really."

Libby took his hand, feeling gratitude, as if he were respon-

149

sible for the sudden flight of the parrots across the blue sky, or for the formidable, unattainable beauty of the ocean.

There was a slight wind now, and the boat rocked in the low swells. Libby could feel the first whispers of seasickness but she made them go away by an act of will.

"How long till we're there?" she asked Rick.

"Thirty minutes."

"Should I start getting ready?"

"Not yet. I'll tell you."

He stood and walked to the stern to consult with the guide.

"You ever seen water this clear?" the dentist asked her. He was standing a few feet away inspecting a foam-lined suitcase that held his underwater cameras and strobes. The suitcase was plastered with decals.

"Sure haven't," she answered kindly.

The dentist closed the suitcase and moved closer to her. He was wearing a panama hat and a pair of striped swimming briefs and smoking a cigar.

"I have," he said. "Right here. I've been to Cozumel three, four times. Then I was in Caicos once working with Jean-Michel Cousteau. We were taking an inventory of the local dolphin population. To be honest with you I wasn't really on his staff. It cost me three thousand dollars and I had to work eight hours a day. But that's the kind of vacation I like. I don't like to be inactive. How about you?"

"I like to be inactive sometimes."

"Not me. I like to be active."

The dentist looked out to sea, satisfied. In the stern Rick was talking with the guide, gesturing with his hands when his Spanish failed him. The guide and one of the boys were fishing with a handline.

Two of the engineering majors were playing a game with an electronic chess board. The third sat there and watched, waiting to take on the winner. Libby noticed how all three of them would glance forward to the bow, keeping tabs on the two girls who seemed so remote and self-absorbed.

The boy who was watching the game had a weak chin and a pallid, freckled complexion, but it was he, and not his better-looking companions, who finally worked up the nerve to go to

150

the bow and talk to the girls. They looked up at him and smiled, propping themselves on their elbows without bothering to fasten their bikini straps.

Libby watched as the other two boys looked on jealously. They had to play out their game for form's sake before they could wander up to the bow.

"Check this out!" their friend called back. He was looking over the bow into the water. Libby followed the two boys forward, along with the dentist and the dog trainer. There was a dark, moving slick on the water.

"Manta ray," the dentist said.

"Can you ride them?" one of the girls asked.

"Hell yes. That's what they're for."

Libby watched the manta ray until it disappeared, the muscular tips of its wings rising in tandem above the lovely water and then the whole mass sinking and drifting off as a submerged shadow.

The girls lay back down on the deck, their faces to the sun. They had their own cooler, filled with cans of Tab, and they sipped the drinks flat on their backs while the engineering students took a seat at the bow railing and stared at them, looking for an opening in the girls' self-possession.

Libby returned to the center of the boat and found Rick there, checking a clipboard.

"Why don't you start getting ready?" he told her.

"Just me?"

"I'm giving you a head start."

Libby pulled on her wetsuit top and then attached her regulator to her tank, seating it backward the first time but correcting it before Rick noticed. He was walking up and down the length of the boat, notifying the rest of the group that they were closing on the reef.

Libby opened the valve and took a breath of the dry air. It was working. Then she strapped her knife to her calf and buckled on her weight belt and then spit in her mask and rinsed it out. Rick hoisted the tank onto her back and stood beside her, supporting her, while she adjusted the straps, working to balance herself on the unsteady deck.

Rick waited until everyone was ready before he began putting

151

on his own equipment. The boat slowed down as he did so, as if following his lead.

"This is a drift dive," Rick told the group. He was standing at the gap in the rail, wearing the bottom half of his blue Farmer John wetsuit and holding his mask and fins in his hands. "The guys on the boat will watch our bubbles and follow us down the current. I don't want anyone surfacing with less than six hundred psi."

He sent them into the water two by two, checking their pressure gauges as they walked past him. He waited until everyone else was overboard, strung out along the line of the current, and then he signaled to Libby to jump over the side.

She did so heedlessly, holding her mask against her face so she would not lose it when she hit the water. But she did not feel the impact she was bracing for. It was an easy transition, like passing into a denser layer of air. She put her face into the water and looked down at the ranges of coral and at the other divers letting themselves drift to a distant underwater landfall. She hovered in the thin troposphere of the ocean and wondered how water so clear could be dense enough to keep her from plummeting.

A swell passed over her head as she was putting the regulator into her mouth and she swallowed sea water. She gagged and all of a sudden felt lost and vulnerable. Then Rick appeared in the water beside her. He took her elbow like an escort.

"Take a moment to let yourself get used to it," he said. "Then we'll go down."

Libby took a few deep breaths of natural air and then put the regulator back in her mouth. She made the okay sign to Rick and they let the air out of their B.C.s together, sinking steadily. She took a moment to clear her ears and he waited patiently for her.

The current was much stronger on the surface than below, and by the time they got underwater it had carried them past the other divers, who were now a hundred feet below them, wending in and out of the coral rifts, the bright primary colors of their equipment vivid against the muted shades of the reef.

She held onto Rick's gloved hand as they descended, not for

comfort but to be in touch with him in this beautiful moment. The reef topography below them loomed larger; they came teetering in on the current like birds. Libby saw a huge eagle ray below them, surging along on languid wing strokes.

They came to rest in a valley, digging their heels into the sand for purchase against the current. The coral rose forty feet above their heads, and in the clear water she could see the waving anemones at its summit.

Rick guided them into a shallow coral cave and they stayed inside for a while, looking out the opening at the water and the blue sky above it. A huge turquoise fish, with incisors like a rodent's, swam into the cave and began coughing up the bones of its latest meal.

Rick looked at her. He let air out of his B.C. so that he would settle more securely on the bottom, and she did the same, seeing that he meant to stay here. She looked at her pressure gauge and saw how every breath she took diminished her time here with him. Outside they saw the rest of the divers drifting by in the current and carried onward. It was as if a wind had come up and was sweeping the earth clean of everyone but themselves.

They made one other dive that day. After lunch the boat took them to another part of the reef, to a coral wall that dropped straight as a cliff face deep into the abyssal haze. Libby drifted along the wall, letting herself go deeper and deeper until her gauge said a hundred and thirty feet and she felt cheated by her own prudence. Rick swam beneath her, looking up into her eyes, urging her back. They ascended together, and as they rose to the sunlight, she felt the deep pull of the wall loosen its hold.

Sunburned, tranquil, she walked with Rick back to the hotel. They left their tanks and weight belts in the dive shop near the dock, but they carried the rest of their gear through the streets. The town was filled with astringent European divers, Houston singles on their eternal Happy Hour tour, and *helado* vendors pedaling heavy bicycles with coolers attached to their handlebars.

Back in the room he set their equipment under the shower, then turned on the water to rinse off the corrosive salt.

"We might as well get in too," he said.

When Libby stepped under the stream she felt the purgative

heat of the water on her sunburned back. He drew her to him. She looked up and saw the peeling skin at the ridge of his nose.

"I wanted to make love underwater," she said, "in that little cave."

She turned in his arms, feeling the water on her spine and her breasts peacefully enclosed in his hands. They dried off and lay down once more on the rumpled, abused bed. She felt an overall soreness—part sunburn, part muscle stress—that only added to the joy of welcoming him once more into her body.

At dusk they rented a Moped and took off down the highway, following the perimeter of the island. The machine was so small it was like a toy, and Rick drove it unsteadily at first. It was only when he had humbled himself and accepted its scale that he drove it well. Libby sat in back, wearing a sundress over her bathing suit, her arms gripping his torso. Iguanas raced across the road ahead of them, the reptiles' meaty legs bowed inward like bulldogs'.

They stopped at Chancanab Lagoon for a swim. It was nearly dark. The *refresco* stands were shuttered closed, and the track of the rising moon was visible on the water.

Rick watched Libby swim. She moved in a firm, even crawl, leaving a good wake. Beneath her, in the sand flats, he saw the shadow of a big ray keeping pace with her.

Libby felt like swimming forever. She knew that Rick's eyes were on her. Although it was growing dark and the sea was full of things she did not understand, she felt safe under his gaze. She was his guest in the ocean.

When they got back to town they ate at one of the overpriced steak-and-seafood restaurants that had sprung up to capitalize on American tourists, then they strolled through the square, looking into the curio shops filled with onyx chessmen, wedding dresses, huaraches. The villagers were gathered in the square, the children running back and forth, the old men with their straw hats in their hands, exposing their heads to the warm darkness. Sound carried over the island with magical fidelity. It seemed to Libby that not a word, not a note was lost.

Later, in the room, they lay against the headboard of their bed. They had not taken another shower, and the salt from their

154

swim still clung to them. Libby was leafing through a field guide.

"That's pretty," she said, showing him a picture.

He bent to look at it. "It's a tube worm."

"Will we see one?"

"I'll point one out to you tomorrow."

"Will we see a barber pole shrimp?"

"Yes."

"An elegant fanworm?"

"Yes."

"A blue chromis?"

"You've already seen a hundred blue chromises. You just didn't notice them."

"What I really want to see," she said, "is an octopus."

"We'll look. They're secretive."

She went back to her reading. He could tell by the growing intensity with which she regarded the book, the way she moved back and forth from the text to the color plates, that she was truly learning. He admired that, as he admired her stroke in the water, yet it made him restless, afraid to interrupt her.

The walls of the room were bare. There was a television in the lobby outside. It was tuned to a program featuring retrograde disco music: "El Show de Ricardo Suarez." A group was singing in falsetto imitation of the Bee Gees.

> *Cuando estoy bien otra vez*
> *Yo te amaré.*

He wanted to be away from her for a while. It bothered him that her concentration on the book kept him rooted there, idle. He could feel himself losing the vital distances between them.

"I'd like to take a walk," he told her.

"I'm a little beat."

"That's okay. I'll go by myself."

Libby shut the book. "I'm boring you," she said.

He stroked her hair. "I like to watch you read."

"But not that much," she said.

"Not that much."

He sat up and put on his sandals.

"Am I hurting your feelings?" he asked her.

155

"Don't think that," she said. "I'd tell you if you were. Or I'd sulk."

Outside the night was rich with the fumes of motorbikes and heavy with their sounds. The bicycle vendors still circled the plaza, the motion of their legs unvarying and tireless. The moon was high now and the water lay out of sight in the darkness. The night revived him. It was fresh and sound. It was like some fine crystal that could be tested, rung by the tap of a fingernail. He regretted that Libby was not with him. It had not been the solitude he needed, just the air.

"Rick!"

It was the dentist, trotting across the plaza. Keeping pace with him was the dog trainer.

"Where's the disco?" the dentist asked.

"Two blocks over," Rick said.

"Is *that* it? There were no women there. We thought it was a gay bar."

"That's the last place I wanted to be with this joker," the trainer said. He was taller than the dentist, and less coordinated. He wore a gold chain around his neck with an ankh attached.

"So what are you doing?" the dentist asked.

"Just walking around."

"Hell, we'll come with you."

They wandered along the waterfront, passing a movie theater whose last feature was just letting out. The movie was called *Perro Loco*. The poster showed a Doberman pinscher with blood dripping from its bared fangs.

"Maybe you could find a part for one of your killer dogs in a movie like that," the dentist said.

"I have explained this as patiently as I can," the trainer said. "They are not killer dogs. They are protection dogs."

"Bullshit," the dentist said. "License to kill."

They settled in at a bar with ceiling fans and louvered windows that were opened to the sea. The trainer talked about the dog business. It was recession-proof, he said. For instance, it was cheaper to buy a guard dog than hire a night watchman.

"Maybe I could train one as a dental hygienist," the dentist said. He turned to Rick. "Is this your line of work, pretty much?"

"Pretty much. I'm partners in a dive shop."

"Good business or not?"

"I can get by," Rick said. "I'm not stashing it away."

"What are you? Thirty-four? Thirty-five?"

"Thirty-three."

"No family?"

Rick shook his head.

"Hell, I don't blame you. The simple life. You get out of that real quick, though, when you start making a little money. If anyone ever asks me for a piece of financial advice, I've got it."

"What's that?"

"Never buy a boat. Never buy a boat and you're set for life."

"Chiclet alert," said the trainer, staring at two unescorted women who were just entering the bar. They took a seat at a nearby table. One was blond, with layered hair in a mane meant to distract attention from the thickness of her face. The other one was trim, with shorter hair and a headband.

"You girls divers?" the dentist asked, calling across the room to them.

"Snorkelers," the woman with the headband said.

"You should try diving."

"There's a resort course at our hotel," the other woman said. "We're thinking about it."

"Talk to this man right here," the dentist said, indicating Rick.

"Oh?"

"He's an instructor."

"Is he certified?"

"Grade A."

The dentist started telling the women about the dive on the wall. They were ready to be impressed. They picked up their drinks and moved over to the table, and no one offered anything other than token objections when Rick excused himself.

Outside he could see phosphorescence in the water. A boy was replacing the poster at the movie theater. *Ochenta Piedes a Felicidad*, starring Wayne Newton. It was late. Not many people were out now. The tourists were either in the bars or asleep in their hotel rooms, dreaming their autonomic underwater dreams. He walked through the dark *calles* behind the square where the

157

houses fronted the curb like shops. In an open window he saw an old woman plaiting her grown daughter's hair.

It was two A.M. by the time he got back to the hotel. Libby was asleep. He turned on a little bedside lamp, removed the sheet that covered her, and stared frankly at her nude body. The sight of her weakened him.

"How was your night on the town?" she mumbled, her face buried in the pillow.

"I was gone a long time," he said. "It's late now."

"I know."

"Are you angry?"

"Yes."

He did not apologize. Instead he turned off the lamp and lay beside her on the bed, waiting for her to turn to him, to draw him back. The island was quiet. When he closed his eyes he saw a solitary whip-tailed ray cruising through the sand flats, and felt the surge of water through the coral rock.

Chapter 14

IT was early October now, and the vague Texas autumn was almost detectable. The heat was measurably less intense, and there were days when the air had a little lilt and the oppressive atmosphere rose like a curtain waiting to drop again.

Sam's car was fixed. He was well. Hay fever season had not yet set in. He knew from Bobby about Libby and Rick but he was proud of the way he was able to force his attention elsewhere to the consolations of his work: the quad maps tacked to the walls, the lead dinosaurs he kept on his desk, the sarcastic camaraderie with which the people in his office communicated.

Janet was working only part-time for the survey. She had started a free-lance bird guide business. There was some demand for that. People would pay her a hundred dollars a day for a guaranteed sighting of a Colima warbler in Big Bend.

"It's really the world's most boring bird," she told him. "If it weren't endangered it'd just be another trash bird."

Her clients tended to be elderly couples who had a few more birds to check off on their life lists before they died. The women had an eccentric, attractive demeanor that must have seemed like coarse rebelliousness when they were young. Some of the men were on walkers. They had snow-white hair and flannel shirts with the collar buttons fastened against drafts.

When Janet was in the office they would usually have lunch in a sandwich place across the street, and after work they would stay together or not, depending on their moods. When she was out of town he tended to stay later at the office, and he had to work harder to keep his lassitude at bay.

Janet came back from the Big Thicket one day with a shoe box containing a tortoise the size of a baseball.

"Did you find him on the road?" Sam asked.

"No," she said. "He's a present from my friend at the Houston zoo." She set him down in her backyard. "There you go, kid. Scoot."

They watched the tortoise negotiate its way through the tall grass.

"You don't recognize him, do you?" Janet asked.

"Should I?"

"He's an aldebara. From the Indian Ocean. He'll grow almost as big as a Galapagos, but right now he's just an infant."

Sam crouched down and peered into the turtle's face. It was wizened, scowling. The mouth was gumming a leaf.

"He may live three hundred years," Janet said. "Of course by that time he'll be the size of a boulder. You and I will be dead before he's two feet across. He won't even come to sexual maturity for eighty or ninety years."

"What's his name?"

"Fluffy."

"What's going to happen to him after you've passed on? Is he going to be a ward of the state?"

"I was hoping I'd have children who would feel a sense of obligation. He'll be an heirloom by then, Sam."

The tortoise craned his neck forward until it seemed he would wrench it out of the shell. Sam marveled at the perfect replica the creature was of himself as an adult, three centuries hence.

"Isn't it touching?" Janet said.

Sam agreed, watching the tortoise breast a fallen tree limb.

"He's pretty much maintenance-free, too," Janet said. "He just wanders around the backyard."

"For three hundred years."

"It's a long haul for old Fluffy, that's for sure. Let's get me something to eat. I've got a weird craving for fragrant chicken."

They drove to a Chinese restaurant and ordered the chicken, and something called Delicate Flavor Prawns. Janet practiced with her chopsticks before the food came, but when it came down to it the technique failed her and she reverted to her fork.

"How were things in the Big Thicket?" he asked.

"This millionaire hired me to help him find an ivory-billed woodpecker. He said if he saw one he could die in peace. I told him I was of the opinion it was extinct, but he wanted to forge ahead. Now I feel guilty. I shouldn't have taken the guy's money."

"Why do I feel like I need to go out and run around the block?" Sam said.

"It's the MSG. They're very big on it here."

Sam put down his fork for a moment, feeling a cyclonic whirl in his chest.

"Eat rice," Janet said. "That's what I do. Look over there. Is that Hudson?"

Sam looked across the restaurant. Hudson was seated with another man and two women who looked like models. It had been a while since Sam had seen him, but he looked the same, maybe a grade more advanced on the outlaw scale. His blond hair was professionally cut, and he wore designer jeans and a belted leather coat.

Hudson noticed Sam and waved.

"That's him," Sam said, waving back.

When Hudson finished his meal he stopped by their table on the way out, motioning his companions ahead. He kissed Janet on the cheek and shook Sam's hand.

"Janet and Sam," he said, pulling up a chair and sitting on it backward. His mustache turned down slightly at the corners in a discreet Fu Manchu. He stared at them as if they were his long-lost children. He had a way of courting people, flattering them with a few moments of his undiluted attention. It was not quite charm, more a parlor trick, Sam thought.

"I hear you and Libby have broken up," said Hudson. "Or is this a sensitive issue?"

"Some might find it sensitive," Janet said.

"Well, she's a phenomenal woman," Hudson said. Sam guessed this was meant as a note of sympathy. He did not think of Libby as "phenomenal," and understood that Hudson used the term as a way of hyping his own past. He remembered how Hudson had come to their wedding, uninvited, wearing a white suit and carrying a gift-wrapped box that turned out to contain a toaster—a gift that Sam knew was offered with irony, maybe even contempt for the mundane life that Hudson imagined henceforward for Libby. He had come up to Libby and kissed her with a wounded, *C'est la vie* expression on his face, then departed before the reception.

"Who's the guy she's going with now?" Hudson asked. "Some deep-sea diver or something."

"I haven't met him," Sam said, feeling the MSG accelerate his metabolism.

"What do you guys think of the food in this place?" Hudson asked. "It's up for sale."

"You could do worse," Sam said.

"God, things are hectic," Hudson said suddenly, shaking his head as if in disbelief. "Not only do we have to make a decision about this place, but we're closing on a big piece of commercial property out on Loop 360 next week. Whatever happened to laid-back Austin?"

"It's just a gleam in our eyes," Janet said.

"I was really going crazy there for a while. Then I went to this entrepreneurial workshop up in Colorado Springs. Really fabulous speaker there. Know what he said?"

"No," Sam answered.

"He said, 'Good business planning *is* good tax planning.' Talk about staggering simplicity."

Hudson took Janet's hand.

"Look at how far we all go back," he said. "When you go back that far you can not see somebody for years and just pick up where you left off. It's like family. What we should do is have a big reunion out at my place. I'm serious. I'd love to see Libby again, for instance."

Hudson gave Janet's hand a squeeze, said his good-byes, then hurried out to catch up with his friends. Sam could see them through the window; they were leaning against the fender of Hudson's Suburban. The price sticker was still taped to the window.

"Are you going to the big family reunion?" Janet asked, when he'd gone.

162

"I hardly knew him back then. He forgets that."

"Yeah," Janet said, "but any friend of Libby's.... I still think he's a charmer, in his way."

"He's ruthless," Sam said, "in his way."

"I know, but still. Did Libby love him, really?"

"Maybe."

"Not like she loved you."

"That's nice of you to say."

"I had a little thing with him once. Before Libby. You remember?"

"Dimly."

"We did it on somebody's roof. There was a party going on downstairs and I remember the Incredible String Band was playing."

Janet sang softly, playing with her silverware.

> Dust of the rivers doth murmur and weep,
> Hard and sharp laughter that cuts like a stone...

She broke off and looked up at him, smiling.

"The old rip-roaring days," she said.

Sam smiled back and finished his rice. He could feel the MSG rush dissipating, and driving home he felt a moody lethargy in its place. What had he learned during all these years; what did he have now, to keep?

He remembered the first time he ever saw Libby, one of those casual, soporific gatherings in which no one was making introductions and strangers walked in and out of the house unquestioned. They were sitting on somebody's living room floor, playing Mexican poker. It was a winter night. He wore a peacoat in those days whose buttons had long since fallen off. There was the smell of grass, of some nauseating incense, and feverish nightmare blues playing on the stereo. He did not remember Hudson but he must have been there, watchful and proprietary. In that room filled with white noise and vacant minds, Libby's face had drawn Sam like a beacon.

He saw her a few more times in similar circumstances, but they did not know each other and never spoke. With Hudson himself Sam had only a nodding acquaintance, through friends like Bobby and Janet and Barf Mooney who made regular trips to his house near the campus to buy marijuana and smoke a ritualistic joint in his black light room.

Sam was on the sidelines in those years. His own cautious instincts ran against the heedlessness of the times, but he saw no other place for himself. Holding himself above the general posturing, he developed a posture of his own, that of the solemn, studious observer. He took a kind of theatrical comfort in this role, and he began to think if he could not be a full participant in all the nervy fun he could be steady and grave and attract people to himself the way that rocks and earth—his highly irrelevant and even suspect field of study—attracted him.

So he waited for things to come to him, but they rarely did. His college romances were tentative and brief. He spoiled them somehow. Girls came to him out of trust instead of ardor, wanting to talk, to confide.

He had grown out of that isolation somewhat by the time Barf Mooney had given him Libby's phone number and told him to call her. He was no longer too proud or too distant to follow through, to admit he needed someone, and he saw in Libby's eyes that first night just how much she needed exactly the sort of person he was. It was as if he had been subconsciously preparing himself, molding his personality so that it would be of use at this crucial moment in his life.

The decisions they made—to live together, to marry, to have a baby—stood out in his mind now not as milestones but as part of a process of completion and symmetry, part of the flow. Neither of them was caught off-guard, neither of them ever doubted or thought to pull apart from the other to gauge what it would take to bring them back together.

But slowly, unconsciously, cumulatively, the way people lose their faith in God, they had begun to lose the excellence of their marriage.

"I want to be away from you for a while," Libby had said to him several months after the death of the baby. They had been sitting up late at night, watching a Japanese monster movie on television.

Sam stared at the screen. The monster was a flying turtle that spun in a circle like a pinwheel and shot rockets from ports beneath its shell.

He gave the slightest possible nod and she turned her eyes from him and looked at the screen. He knew what she was thinking, he agreed with her: if tragedy had not brought them together, had not tapped them into that deeper vein, what chance did ordinary life have of doing so? He saw their domestic comforts—the cozy late-night viewing of a creature feature—as a sham.

She had offered to move out but he had instead, taking Dumptruck and moving his things bit by bit, hoping that during the protracted transition something would occur to them, some reason that they should still stay together. That never happened, but at the same time he never felt it ending between them. He could not foresee the moment when it would be proper and healthy for him to go on with his life. He felt that the vital link between them was still waiting to be discovered.

When they got back to Janet's they wandered around her backyard until they found Fluffy; he was stationed at the base of a tree, perfectly content. Janet coaxed him out of his shell with a piece of lettuce.

"What were you thinking about in the car?" Janet asked Sam.

"Libby."

"I'm not going to nurse you through these moods," she said.

"I know."

"I have my little friend here. If necessary we can do without you."

Sam sat down in the grass next to Janet and Fluffy. He touched the tortoise's bony beak with his finger, thinking how this moment would pass into the reptile's awareness, encoded there but never to be considered or recalled as Fluffy wandered through his immense life span. Next to the tortoise Sam felt evanescent, a shadow passing over a rock.

Chapter 15

LIBBY did as Rick told her: descended quickly through the opening flue onto the shelf thirty feet below. She was accomplished at descents by now. The pressure equalized in the canals of her ears automatically. They had learned their lesson in the Caribbean.

When she reached the shelf she looked up and watched Rick come down, moving through the water with perfect trim except for the gauge console that trailed behind him by a thick rubber hose.

So far she liked it. The water in Jacob's Well was clear beyond her imagination, and already she could sense the enclosing presence of the rock and the absolute darkness farther on.

She unhooked her light from the D-ring on her weight belt, wrapped the cord around her wrist, and turned it on, shining it into the passage that branched away to her side. A catfish swam across the beam.

Rick appeared beside her and she swiveled to see his face. Their eyes met and they stared at each other without embarrassment, something she knew they would not do on the surface, in the real world. He showed her more of himself when they were underwater where no one could watch.

He pointed down and made the okay sign. She returned it and followed him into the passage, swimming with one hand on the line that he let out from his reel. They had not gone far when the bottom of the passage disappeared and she saw she was hovering above a deep chasm. Rick let out some air and dropped; she sank after him, descending with exquisite slowness to the bottom of the chamber. The beam of her light skittered across the smooth face of the rock and she was aware, now that they were deep inside the cave, how deeply she relied upon that light.

At the bottom of the chamber she checked her depth gauge: seventy-two feet. She rose to the center of the room and performed a languid somersault, feeling as exhilarated as a child.

Rick watched her from below, hovering a few feet off the bedrock in a standing posture, his arms limp at his sides. She came to him, her arms spread in a swan dive, an acrobat released from the bonds of gravity. He held her waist, adjusted his buoyancy to hers, and the two of them floated in tandem around the circumference of the room.

At the bottom of the room was another passage, a low sloping tunnel that led to the constriction where the barricade had been placed. In this passage Rick demonstrated the swimming techniques he had told her about on the surface. The most dangerous thing in a cave, he had told her, was silt. In a narrow passage one improvident wave of a fin could dislodge enough silt to cause a whiteout. The best cave divers hardly used their fins. They walked along the floor on their fingertips, like crayfish, or hung upside down on the ceiling, pulling their passive bodies along with their hands.

Libby watched Rick delicately making his way in this fashion, and then tried it herself, floating upward to face the ceiling. As she moved along, her air bubbles collected against the rock. They were trapped, with nowhere to go, and as she watched them she felt her first twinge of fear at how very deep and far away she was.

Her gauge read seventy-five feet. She had gone deeper than that at Cozumel, but here in Jacob's Well she felt she was on another planet. A little wave of forgetfulness and unconcern passed through her. She attributed that to nitrogen narcosis, and with the full force of her conscious mind, she rallied and drove it away.

They arrived at the grate. The flow was strong through the

bars. She held onto them and the current almost picked her up like a flag in a breeze. A crayfish passed in front of her mask; one of its claws was gone.

Rick asked to see her pressure gauge. She had plenty of air left, more than he did. Women were more efficient that way, he had told her. So they stayed at the barricade a while longer. Libby was cold; her fingers were beginning to go numb through her neoprene gloves. And she missed the sunlight, the air-breathing world that she seemed now to have such inadequate memories of. But she shone her light past the bars into the void and wanted to go on, beyond the point where the beam vanished.

He turned to her. There was a look of welcome in his eyes, of pride. He gave a little shrug, which she read as a gesture of apology that he could not take her farther.

From a wetsuit pocket she pulled out her slate and its tethered pencil and wrote, *How deep does it go?*

Libby held the slate up to Rick. He read her question, then took the slate from her and began to write. When he handed it back she read his answer, *Deep*.

Chapter 16

"I WAS just curious," Sam said over the phone. "Are we getting divorced?"

Libby was standing at the kitchen window, watching a mockingbird swoop in and out of the limbs of a live oak tree. It was a clear November day—a Sunday. It was good to hear Sam's voice.

"I was half hoping that subject would never be broached," she said.

"My attorney feels that this matter should be cleared up."

"You don't have an attorney," Libby said.

"No."

"What are you doing now?"

"Reading the paper."

"Why don't you come over? Bring Dumptruck."

He arrived twenty minutes later. She watched his car pull up, with Dumptruck sitting absurdly upright in the passenger seat. Libby had resolved to kiss Sam lightly on the lips when he came to the door. This she did. Dumptruck nuzzled her calves and squeezed his body between them.

Sam looked the living room over carefully.

"Rick's in Bonaire," Libby said. "Anyway, we don't live together."

"The word out on the street is that you're going steady."

She gave him a pained look. "I've gone to the trouble of making you a Bloody Mary," she said, "so don't be sarcastic."

Sam sat in the good chair. He was wearing a corduroy shirt and jeans.

"Where's Janet?" Libby asked. "As long as we're delving into these matters."

"Down at Falcon Dam. Looking for brown jays."

Libby went into the kitchen to get their drinks. "You want something to eat?" she called.

"Are you offering to make biscuits?"

"No."

"Let me."

"Only if you clean up the mess."

He followed her into the kitchen and began taking down bowls and measuring spoons and ingredients. He knew the recipe by heart.

"How many times," she asked, "did I ever make you biscuits?"

"Not once," he said, measuring a vile-looking heaping table-spoon of Crisco. "But I remember that after my grandmother died you made me a chocolate pie."

"That was sweet of me."

"How many biscuits do you want?"

"Just one. Maybe two."

"I'll make them large then."

Libby leaned against the counter and watched him work. Clouds of flour rose up from the cutting board and dusted his shirt. She watched his brown eyes narrow in concentration as he cut the biscuits from the dough with a wide-mouthed glass.

"Tell me about your travels," Sam said. "I've only heard about it secondhand."

"I really took to it, Sam."

"The diving?"

Libby nodded.

"And the company too, I bet," Sam said.

She didn't answer him. He set the biscuits in the oven and while they were baking he and Libby stood by the stove. Every so often Sam peeked through the greasy oven window to see how they were browning.

"I never noticed that you were such a compulsive cook before," Libby said.

170

"Tell me about Rick."

"I'd really rather not."

"That's fair," Sam said, sweeping up the flour on the cutting board with his hands.

While he cleaned up Libby set out raspberry preserves and butter and laid down two rather formal place settings. When the biscuits were done Sam set them down in the center of the table. He and Libby ate in an easy silence with Dumptruck looking up at them, salivating. Sam tossed him a biscuit.

"Your dog is shedding on my linoleum," Libby said.

"Send me a bill."

"I thought he only did that in the summer."

"He prefers to shed year-round now."

Sam reached for a fourth biscuit.

"I like being in this kitchen again," he said. "With you."

"Let's not comment," she said after a pause.

Sam put down his biscuit. He stood up and kicked her refrigerator, dislodging a strip of chrome.

"Don't do that," she said.

"How come it has to be this way?"

She could not answer. He knelt down and replaced the chrome, snapping it carefully back into place. She wished suddenly that he would leave it on the floor, and that he would kick and flail at the refrigerator until he was bloody and it was half-destroyed.

She walked into the living room and put on a record. Schubert's *Trout* Quintet. It was Sunday brunch music, a balm for the searing brilliance of life. When she sat down Dumptruck wandered over to her and collapsed at her feet like a skittery foal. There was a passage in the music she was listening for. She did not want to be disturbed. Sam came out of the kitchen and sat down next to her on the couch, not too close. He did not speak, and when the passage came it calmed them both.

"I went diving in Jacob's Well," she told him, when the music was over.

Sam looked up in surprise. "When was this?"

"A few weeks ago."

"That's a dangerous place, Libby. People die in there all the time."

171

"Rick thought I was ready for it. I was, too."

"Well, if Rick says you're ready, then by all means."

"Come on," Libby said, taking his hand, "no ironic asides. I just wanted to tell you."

Libby got up to turn the record over, and when she came back to the couch she laid her head on his chest.

"How come it seems like we were happy?" Sam said. "How come it seems so much that way?"

Libby rubbed his knee with the palm of her hand, an idle, consoling gesture. She listened to the music.

"If we got divorced," she asked him, "would you still remember my birthday?"

Sam drew her closer and kissed the top of her head.

"If we made love now," Libby said, "I'd feel that I was cheating on Rick."

"We can just sit here."

"Yes."

Dumptruck stood up and wandered into the hallway. They could hear the clicking of his toenails on the hardwood floor. Sam remembered how they had pulled up the old carpet and spent weeks plucking away the fabric strands that clung to the floorboard nails. It had taken Libby a long time to talk him into helping her, but once she had they worked together on the floor as allies, happy and invulnerable in their labor.

He heard Dumptruck stop at the door of the second bedroom. Libby had put them to work there, too, painting and outfitting a nursery. Once Sam had come home with a postcard, an Ansel Adams photograph of Yosemite Valley, and taped it at the foot of the cheap, thirdhand baby bed they had bought, where the baby could see it when he woke.

Dumptruck came back in and stood in the center of the living room, as if putting himself on display. He was graying at the muzzle, and there were calluses at all four legs where for reasons of his own he had chewed the hair away.

"How old is he now?" Sam asked.

"I thought you were keeping track."

Sam leaned his head back on the couch and felt the sharp November sunlight on his face. He was thinking about the trip he and Libby had taken after their wedding. Neither of them, at the time or since, had called it a honeymoon, since it had been a vigorous, punishing agenda, an endless drive from Austin to New York, across the continent to Los Angeles and back home again.

It had been his idea, but she had gone along cheerfully, sitting in the car while he read the landscape to her, pointing out upthrust zones and lava domes, feeling as if he had to account to her for every change in sea level, every variation in rock.

They had very little money, but the car was nearly new; he had made the down payment only four months before. They camped out most nights and drove all day, through the buckled Ozarks, where syncline and anticline were as apparent to him as the furrows of a plowed field; through the rills and dikes of the Missouri karst country; up the morainal plain to the New York schist.

They had saved their money for Manhattan. It was the first time either of them had been there and immediately they saw what a touchstone it was, the origin of so much unthinking cultural fealty back home in Texas. Because they could not afford theater tickets or expensive restaurants, and because they felt themselves to be so alive and beyond the reach of such stolid entertainments, they gravitated to Little Italy. It was the time of the San Gennaro festival, and they strolled through the endless arcades, eating sausage-and-pepper sandwiches and ices, holding on to each other so they would not be separated in the crowd.

In a hotel on 45th Street they sat at the windowsill looking below at the awesome street life, at more pedestrians than they had ever seen in one place, all of them fixated, impelled, some of them mad. Sam and Libby lay in bed listening to the ambiguous shrieks and cries from the streets; they felt the city's density driving them together.

They drove west along the grim turnpikes; they crossed the great rivers. They crested the Rockies, traveled through the basin and range country, subjected themselves to the aggressive power of the California surf. In that great surge of movement across the country, he thought the two of them had been fused together, like two minerals in the same protective matrix.

173

Sitting with her now in their old house, he could neither dislodge that feeling nor, on the evidence, trust it. He thought the best thing to do was leave.

When he disengaged himself and stood up to go, Libby followed him to the door and hugged him there.

"This was good for us," she said.

In what way it was good she did not yet understand. It was clearly over; she was convinced of that. And yet the thought of divorce made her so nervous and sad. Things had not quite bottomed out between them. That was another level, one they had not explored.

Chapter 17

THE palmetto swamp looked as false as a stage set jungle, and Sam wandered through it with distaste. A norther had come through the day before, but the air was thick and warm in the swamp and he worked in a T-shirt. The smell of sulfur was everywhere, and the green palmetto fans that rose from the banks of the scummy bogs seemed to track him like radar antennae.

Robins as large as pigeons rooted noisily where the undergrowth was dry, and Sam could see the shadows of buzzards on the ground and hear the tapping of woodpeckers and rustling of squirrels. Vines were wrapped around the trunks of the trees like giant constrictive snakes.

The botanists would have fun with this bog, and Janet was excited about the bird life, but Sam was bored. There was little observable rock, few straightforward outcroppings. Beneath the loam and peat was a thick shelf of ferruginous sandstone, but it did not present itself. Everything was sodden or rotten, in a state of accelerated decay.

He felt as if he had been set down in some hostile, far-removed place, but he was only three hours away from Austin in an anomalous scrap of boggy terrain the survey was considering for a park. The acreage belonged to the brother of the state Land Commissioner. He was willing to swap it for some coastal real estate, and Sam knew that Powell was under some pressure to see that it appraised well.

Sam walked out of the bog and came across a channel of the

Mirasol River. The banks were eroded clay cliffs, twenty feet high. They had turned the water a khaki color, though it was not stagnant like the water in the swamp, but rough and fast. He watched it dislodging the banks, and he could measure, by the piles of blanched driftwood on either shore and the exposed roots of trees still clinging tenaciously to the slopes, its power in flood.

There was bedrock lying exposed by the river, more of the dark iron-rich sandstone. He wandered along the bank, looking for a contact with an older formation. It was cold here, and he took a corduroy shirt from his backpack and put it on. He walked for an hour without finding anything, but he was happy in the rhythms of his work, happy that his mind was focused on the secretive rock.

When he left the river terrace he was in the bog again. There were mud boils along the path, and he could hear as well as see the syncopated bubbling they made on the surface. At the edge of a large stagnant pond he sat down to rest from the moist air. His head was hammering, full and engorged, and his breathing was fast and shallow.

A shape rode the still surface of the bog, a long thick animal shape coated with the same larval scum that covered the water. It did not move at all. He thought it was a branch that had fallen from overhead and steeped in the dark water until it glistened. But it seemed to draw his attention like an animate thing, to appraise him with camouflaged eyes. Sam stared at it; it compelled him. He could feel the ghostly movement in his snake-bitten wrist.

It was late in the day and the forest canopy overhead had already choked off a good deal of the available light. Sam stood to go, still watching the shape in the bog. He could not decide if it was alive or not. He thought about throwing a stick at it to see if it would move, but before he did so the thing riffled the thick surface of the bog and disappeared beneath it.

Sam stood there for a long time, waiting for the creature to rise again. But soon it was nearly dark. He did not see it again, and he was not sure he trusted his original sighting. He walked with deliberate slowness away from that place, the mysterious creature, real or not, lingering in his mind like a vision. When he reached the caliche road that led to the ranch house where they were staying, he stopped to remove a sweater from his backpack.

The ranch house was three miles away but he did not mind the walk. He felt light-headed, his energy restored, his attention focused on the darkening road.

From behind him he heard a horn, and he turned to see the survey jeep lurching over the gouged road, with Powell behind the wheel and Janet sitting in the passenger seat.

"Want a ride back to HQ?" Powell asked.

Sam threw his equipment into the jeep and jumped in behind Janet, who handed him an open box of vanilla wafers.

"How's the geology?" she asked him.

"What stories these rocks could tell," Sam said, taking a handful of cookies, "if they could only speak."

"What kind of rocks have you got around here?" Powell asked. "Crustaceous?"

"Cretaceous," Sam said, smiling privately at Janet. Powell's ignorance of the natural world was legendary.

They watched the sides of the road, where the armadillos were rooting with their lethal-looking front claws. The light was failing in a rich, invigorating manner, giving the armadillos' armor a rose cast like the pastel sheen on the insides of seashells.

Powell reached back for the box of cookies.

"When I was a kid I used to make vanilla wafer sandwiches," he said. "Want the recipe?"

"I don't think so," Janet said.

"You take one and chew it up real good until it's nice and mushy."

"Definitely not," Janet said.

"Don't swallow it, though. Spit it out and mash it between two more vanilla wafers. Serves one."

They stopped to pick up Miranda, who was walking along the side of the road in a pair of Maine hunting shoes and a straw cowboy hat.

"Where's the rest of your crew?" Powell asked her.

"I sent them back early," she said, taking off the hat and letting two long braids fall onto her shoulders. "There's nothing to see here, no mounds or anything. This place has been Nowhere USA since the dawn of man."

Janet sat in Sam's lap and recited the day's bird count.

He listened to it contentedly, sharing in the high spirits of the day's end. The road improved, and they cruised serenely through the dark pecan groves near the river, and Sam almost forgot about that creature in the swamp and its nagging claim on his attention.

That night the Land Commissioner's brother threw an elaborate barbecue for the members of the survey. They lined up at the barbecue pit, holding their paper plates, paying no great mind to the subtle bribery of the landowner. The bracing mesquite smoke stung their eyes as they sat down to eat on the porch of the stone ranch house.

There was even a band, a self-conscious outlaw group whose posturings Sam found offensive, but whose music swayed him a little under the clear night sky. The lead singer's name was Faron Pearsall, a local luminary of medium wattage. He was a trust-fund hippie from upstate New York who had come to Texas to assume the role of a world-weary and slightly sinister cowboy.

While Pearsall played his bogus blue-collar laments the members of the survey danced on the patio. Sam danced with Janet, and then with a small frail botanist named Charlene. She had stuck a white tube-shaped flower in her hair.

"What do you call that?" he asked her.

"It's a wild orchid. It's called 'nodding ladies tresses.' Isn't that nice?"

"That's nice."

"I probably shouldn't have copped it but there are lots of them out there."

The steel guitar cut right through them; it seemed an eerie but natural manifestation of the environment, like foxfire or the northern lights. The effect was spoiled a little when Pearsall started to sing, but the mood was set. Sam felt unsettled in some rich, vibrant way.

After the dancing he went over to the beer keg, where Powell was speaking with the host. The Land Commissioner's brother was a raucous friendly man named Crenshaw, an oilman from

178

the larger-than-life school. When Powell introduced them, Crenshaw took Sam's hand and clamped him hard on the elbow with the other hand.

"How do you like our land here?" he asked Sam. "Goddam pretty, isn't it?"

"It has its charms," Sam said.

"That's well put. Jack and I were just saying that it's the kind of land the state ought to take an interest in."

"That's not exactly what we were saying," Powell corrected.

Crenshaw ignored him. "Some people," he went on, "say they don't like the way it smells. But that's the way God wanted it to smell. This land is part of our heritage, and I just want to make sure the people of Texas have an opportunity to see it. Of course I wouldn't want to influence y'all one way or the other. That's just my opinion."

Crenshaw shot Powell a challenging look, but Powell did not flinch. He was a true-believer bureaucrat and could not be bought.

"I'm gonna slip up there to ole Faron and see if I can get him to play 'Blue Eyes Cryin' in the Rain,'" Crenshaw said, breaking away. "You boys eat some more of that barbecue."

Sam obediently picked up another paper plate and piled it with brisket. The sharp cold air made him hungry. As he ate he watched Janet on the patio. She was attempting to perform the cotton-eyed joe with a drunken zoologist who finally pulled away from her and began dancing the twist by himself in the darkness.

Janet noticed Sam and smiled, a smile so easy and sure it startled him with the strength of its claim. Had they come that far together already?

Janet walked over to him, leaving the dancers behind her in the yellow patio light.

"Kevin says he found some quicksand today," she said, indicating the zoologist, who was now doing his silent twist with such absorption it could have been a Zen exercise. "He says that a little later a bunch of them are going to go skinny-dipping."

"In quicksand?"

"Supposedly it's not deep."

Sam leaned against the ranch house and looked up at the silhouette of the treetops against the sky.

179

"This place isn't so bad at night," he said.

Janet stood before him, drawing a pattern in the dirt with the toe of her hiking boot and swaying to the music.

"I saw something weird in the swamp today," Sam said.

"Animal, vegetable, or mineral?"

"Animal. Right on the surface of the water. I thought it was a limb until it moved."

"Alligator," Janet said confidently.

"Maybe."

Janet grabbed his belt and pulled herself to him. Sam put his arm around her and they walked away from the house, following a slight upward grade that ended at a bare promontory, a thick shelf of exposed rock looking out over the blackland prairie. There was a town below them, a few miles away. They could see the Dairy Queen sign and the milling headlights around the square. It reminded Sam of Picture Bluff.

Janet lay back on the boulders and picked out the constellations. Her eyes were very sharp. Orion was brilliant in the eastern sky, and Polaris hung over the little town like the Star of Bethlehem. She pointed out the lopsided W of Cassiopeia.

"You've been studying," he said.

"No. I've always known this stuff. There are the Twins."

With her finger she traced a pattern in the sky. She did this silently, for herself.

"I see a bat," Sam said.

"Yes. Lots of them."

They watched the dark, frantic shapes against the star field. He wondered if in the bats' radar he and Janet were distinguishable from the rock on which they sat. Lying next to Janet, he could feel the baffled warmth of her down vest.

"What's going on with you?" she asked him.

"What?"

"Your thought waves are bouncing all over the place."

"I'm thinking about us." He said it without planning to.

Janet did not answer. She picked up her binoculars and scanned the town below them.

"What's your position on that subject?" she finally asked.

"I don't know."

He kept thinking of the creature he had seen in the swamp. Its image loomed in his mind, a challenge to his ordered perceptions, to the extraordinary contentment he felt with Janet. He was safe with her, but like a fever that had risen in him he felt the dangerous compulsion to leave her, to divest himself of the idle comforts their relationship provided.

"I can't help thinking of Libby," he said to Janet. "And that's not fair to you."

"You're right," she said. "I'm only about one-sixth masochist." She looked through her binoculars at the sky.

"There's Sirius coming up," she said.

"Where?"

"The really bright one."

They could hear Faron Pearsall's voice drifting up the slope to them. He was singing a song about a cowboy who wakes up in a drunk tank and finds a note in his pocket from his little girl that says "I Love My Daddy."

When the song was over Janet made a fist with one knuckle raised and hit Sam hard in the arm.

"Take a look in the morning and see if I raised a bruise," she said.

"Janet..."

"I have no hard feelings, Sam. I just feel that I have the right to frog you."

Sam watched the headlights in the town moving back and forth between the Dairy Queen and the square. The air was so clear there seemed to be no atmosphere at all. He could think of nothing to say to her, nothing that would not trivialize the pure hurt he knew he had done her. In a little while she kissed his arm where she had hit it and laid her head alongside. In the cold air her hair smelled as fresh as ice.

"I'd like to make it really cut and dried," she said. "I think that's healthy."

"Okay," he said numbly.

"What if we say that it's over at midnight tonight?"

"Fine."

"I can go get my double-wide sleeping bag and bring it back up here. We've got time."

181

"It wouldn't hurt if we ran a little over."

"You're a flexible son of a bitch," she said.

He watched her go, feeling cruel, and feeling that cruelty as a strength. He believed he was ready to begin leading himself back to Libby.

Chapter 18

ALL that winter Libby and Rick dived in the Well. It did not matter to them if it was cold, or if it was day or night. The water temperature, the darkness there, were constant. It was very much their place, she thought, and she imagined their presence somehow bringing that cold rock into a kind of fulfillment, as if it yearned to be seen and swept with light.

Always they would swim down to the barricade and look ahead, and Libby would imagine what was beyond the reach of her light. Rick had described it to her, the passage that led to the final large room where he had found the two dead divers. That was where the Well ended, a hundred and ninety feet deep in the earth, perhaps a quarter of a mile back from the opening. Those who believed it went farther, he told her, were only subscribing to a legend.

Occasionally, they would see an eel swimming upward, on its way, Rick told her, to the Sargasso Sea. It had been born there fifty years before and swam for months across the Gulf and up a network of inland waterways to this place. Now, ending its life, it was ready to go home. It would swim back to the Sargasso Sea, snaking overland if the creeks were dry. Its sex organs would develop on the journey. It would stop feeding; its awareness would fuse into the urgent impulse that drove it onward. Finally, it would reach its goal, and dive down a thousand feet to spawn and die.

She marveled at that, and at times it seemed to her that her own life had been pared down like the eel's to a simple desire. She wanted to be with Rick. But she was not ready to give herself over entirely to that desire; she held herself back from it just a little. They saw each other every day when he was not leading a diving trip to Cozumel or the Caymans, every night when he was not teaching a class. But they did not live together, or take any satisfaction in the idle domestic routines that she and Sam had finally come to depend on. If the mood between her and Rick was not charged or significant, they were liable to fall away from each other, to return to their separate houses.

One Saturday in March she rebelled against this state of affairs. They had made love late in the afternoon, and afterward she could feel the restlessness in him, the anxiety that he always courteously denied. She wanted the two of them to stay together, to join in a meaningless project. She decided she would cook a really complicated meal. Leaving him in the bedroom, she got up and leafed through her cookbooks until she found a Middle-Eastern fish recipe that called for fresh pomegranate seeds and a sesame sauce made with garlic and tahina paste.

"I think I can pull this off," she said, showing him the recipe.

He studied it seriously and then nodded his assent.

"I don't know where you would get pomegranate seeds," he said.

"The pomegranate seeds are not a problem," she answered. "Are you on the team?"

"Count me in," he said.

They drove to the natural foods supermarket in Libby's car. There was a strange, ruddy wall of cloud moving in over the escarpment, bearing down on the clear sky. The light inside the cloud was reddish and turbulent, and for a moment she did not recognize it.

"Isn't this your kind of weather?" Rick asked.

"What do you mean?"

"It's a dust storm."

"God, you're right," she said. "I've never seen a dust storm in Austin before."

"It's a real one, too."

"Now I'm homesick," she said. She peered over the steering

wheel to look up at the sky. She felt exhilarated. She could see the irradiated dust inside the cloud. It was like some malevolent, confined spirit. Joggers ran along the lake path, dallying with the razor-sharp edge of the weather mass. There was a group of people, wearing antigravity boots, hanging from a series of chinning bars like a colony of roosting bats. Libby could see the dulled concern on their blood-heavy faces as they craned their necks to watch the approaching storm.

"Oh boy," she said to Rick. "I'm really getting into this."

He smiled, and she reached out to take his hand as she drove.

Classical music was playing inside the supermarket, and near the front door a woman dressed for jazzercise was talking to a sallow man in white about kefir, and writing down a recipe in a plush vinyl notepad.

She sent Rick off for the fish while she pushed her cart to the produce department. A little girl in a turban walked by her, popping carob stars into her mouth. She found the pomegranates next to a weird, mottled variety of melon that cost fourteen dollars a pound.

Sam was standing not far away, his arms filled with groceries. He was trying to rip a plastic bag off the spool with one hand. She went up and did it for him.

"What do you want to put in here?" she asked, holding up the bag.

"Apples," he said. "About four. I thought you were going to keep your hair short."

"I'll have it cut before summer," she said, as she picked out his apples.

"All your clothes are new."

"Just the ones I have on. How's Dumptruck?"

"I think he has arthritis. It takes him a little longer to get his mojo working in the morning."

Libby handed him the apples. He freed one of his hands to take the bag.

"Here," she said, moving her pomegranates to the back of the shopping cart. "Put your stuff in my cart. We can sort it out at the checkout counter."

She watched him as he unloaded his groceries, watching for

a hint of the bereft bachelor, but he seemed to her to be in control.

"How do you like the dust storm?" he asked. "I remember that time your father and I went fishing up at Lake Floyd Atwater. One came up then and we couldn't even see the shore."

Libby made her way along the rows of produce, stopping at the garlic cloves.

"Guess who's in the store," she said.

"Uh-oh," he said, exaggerating a bit.

Libby shrugged and pushed her cart ahead. Sam fell in with her. She remembered the way they used to shop—Sam roaming ahead of her through the aisles, picking up things on impulse until his arms were full and then coming back to her to unload them and go out foraging again. She looked down now at his things in her cart: shrimp boil, hamburger, a box of something called Nutri-Nut Bars that she suspected he would never eat.

"The business with Janet ran its course," he said.

"I heard that."

"She's going with one of those Mr. Duckett people now."

"Who are they?"

"You've never heard of them? There was this nineteenth-century chemist named Mr. Duckett. He was a big healer or something. Anyway, these people claim he never died. They go into trances and he speaks through them."

"Janet believes this?"

"I don't think she believes it. She doesn't mind hearing about it, apparently."

Libby saw Rick at the end of the aisle, looking for her. When he saw her he was hesitant. He knew it was Sam. She waved him over with a tilt of her head, and when he came up to them, cradling the wrapped fish in the crook of his arm, she said to him, "This is my husband."

They shook hands with a firm, forbearing politeness, a masculine conduct that strangely warmed Libby's heart.

"Everybody knows this is awkward," Libby said. But she felt oddly at ease, even at peace, with the two of them there. Rick was uncertain, wary; she knew he would not know how to play this. But she could sense the confidence in Sam and knew that

186

he had been imagining this moment, practicing for it. He had decided long ago that he would like Rick for her sake, out of regard for her.

"It's not so awkward," Sam said. He looked at Rick. "What do you think?"

Rick tossed the fish into the cart. "I'm no judge of these things."

"Why don't you come have dinner with us?" Libby said to Sam.

"Now I think you're overcompensating."

"Maybe so," she said. "Who cares?"

Sam looked at Rick.

"I'm all for it," Rick said.

When they went outside they saw that the eerie radiance of the approaching storm had degenerated once the storm had arrived. Dust was whipping off the curbs and drifting up onto car windshields like snow. People were running around in it, laughing, their eyes stung by the grit.

Sam followed them in his car. Libby watched him in her rearview mirror. He drove with both hands on the steering wheel, a little tense. When they stopped in traffic she noticed that he looked out his side window to avoid catching her eye.

"I'm sorry about all this," she said to Rick.

"Why? Don't worry about it."

"I just blurted out this invitation without consulting you."

"It's not such a big thing," he said. She could not tell if he really meant that or if he was just retreating from the complications, harboring himself in some neutral, distant place.

The dust storm had passed by the time they got home, and the light that it had been suppressing flared up again before nightfall. The weather kept Libby's mood high, and she convened the three of them in the kitchen and set them to work. Rick cut open the pomegranates for the seeds while Sam crushed walnuts with a rolling pin. The two men, as they would, talked cordially about their work.

She listened to the straightforward shoptalk between them. Sam told Rick about the survey. Rick answered Sam's questions about commercial diving, what the food was like on the rigs, the economics of running a dive shop. Libby held the big sea bass

187

she had bought under the tap and rinsed out its body cavity. They were getting on well enough, she thought; it was not just politeness.

"I used to dive a little," Sam told Rick. "I learned back in the 'Sea Hunt' days."

"It's changed," Rick said. "Not so many maniacs with spear-guns."

"Now I don't even recognize the equipment."

"You should get back into it," Rick said, taking a sip of mineral water.

"I've thought about it," Sam said. "What do I do with these walnuts?"

"They're going into the sauce," Libby said. "Put them in a bowl for now."

"Libby says you've taken her into Jacob's Well," Sam said to Rick, taking a cereal bowl down from the cabinet.

"That's right."

"I keep hearing about what a dangerous place that is."

"We don't go down very far. And Libby's very good."

"Okay, Sam?" Libby said.

"Just the natural concern of the husband," Sam said.

"There's an example of the sort of remark we don't need," Libby told him. She poured some oil into a frying pan and stared at it, waiting for the oil to heat up.

"Sauté all ingredients," she read out loud. Her mood was dropping. What was she trying to accomplish here?

Sam was good enough to mend the little rift.

"I'm sorry," he said to Rick.

Rick answered with a wave of his mineral water bottle.

"How far down have you been in Jacob's Well?" Sam asked him.

"To the bottom. About a hundred and thirty feet."

"What do you get there? Sandstone?"

Rick nodded. "That and conglomerate."

Sam opened the refrigerator to get a beer. "Sounds like a dead end. I'd like to see it sometime, though."

Libby set the table, putting out the three place settings of china she had accumulated in the five years of their marriage.

188

She laid down the plates silently, wondering who the company was, Sam or Rick. The two of them walked out of the kitchen to join her. They were still talking about the Well, about phreatic zones and fault blocks. Rick liked to talk geology. He was proud of what he had picked up, the odd bits of information that were of use to him underwater. Listening to him talk to Sam, who knew how all the bits fit together, Libby saw how deliberately constrained Rick's knowledge was, how dedicated, as if he would be thrown off course if he were to learn too much.

His mind seemed to her to be as lean and disciplined as his body. There was a kind of scholarliness about him, but it was streamlined and selective. Libby thought of how he read the newspaper in the morning, impatiently turning the pages and scanning the headlines rapidly, looking for some fact, some story, that did not seem to him extraneous. By contrast, Sam had a leisurely breadth of knowledge that she missed.

Libby went into the kitchen and set about stuffing the fish with the sautéed ingredients, sewing it together with dental floss as the recipe suggested, and then placing it in the oven, where its inert, uncomplaining face stared out at her through the window. Then she filled a plastic tumbler with white wine and went back out to the living room and listened to Sam speak, as exotic cooking smells filled the house.

He was explaining to Rick how that sandstone barrier had formed. Once it had been a beach, fringing a granite island in a vast carbonate lagoon. The water had risen, covering the sand, and under the steady pressure of unimaginable years turned it to rock. The water above it had deposited out as thick-bedded limestone, its joints and cracks widening into caverns as the chemically aggressive rainfall dissolved the rock, searching for passage.

His voice lulled her; she liked to hear him speak familiarly of these ancient events. And his talk about Jacob's Well seemed to support the intimacy that she and Rick felt for that place and for each other.

Once or twice over dinner Sam caught Libby's eye, and some unreadable nuance passed between them. The fish was a success. They toasted their expertise over its remains. Sam helped with the dishes and then, as if his dignity required a swift exit, made a point of not lingering.

She walked with him out to his car, her arms folded against the chill. Dust was still drifted up on the sidewalk, and it seemed to her there was still a detectable charge to the weather.

"I thought that went all right," she said.

"I'd say so."

"Thank you for your understanding, or whatever."

Sam got into the car. Libby bent down to the window.

"Are you sad?" she asked.

"Yes," he said. "I'm sad."

Rick wanted to leave, to spend the night at his own place, but she talked him into staying. They went to bed and lay chastely beneath the covers, holding hands.

"Great moments in history," she said.

"It wasn't bad," Rick said. "He's a good guy. I wish I felt a little less like a homewrecker."

"The home was already wrecked."

Rick turned to go to sleep and she moved in close to him. She was used to the feel of him now, dependent on the shape and contour of his body for some vital sustenance. She kissed him behind the ear and murmured, subaudibly, that she loved him. She was still in shock from loving him. But it was Sam's voice she kept hearing as she fell asleep, Sam's careful recounting of the story of the earth. She had a final half-lucid thought that night—a fear that she and Sam may have given up too soon. She could still feel the slow accumulation of something solid between them. But it was too slow; it was as slow as rock forming from the sea.

Chapter 19

SPRING arrived slowly, tentative and subtle, like an island rising out of the ocean. Sam slept better; he had long, clear dreams that reverberated in his mind throughout the rest of the day.

The dreams involved water, and Libby. Water was the medium through which he pursued her with a forlorn perseverence, a thoughtless longing like that of some migratory bird or spawning fish. Once he dreamed that Picture Bluff itself was underwater, and that he was swimming down through the sky to the overhang where the pictographs were painted. Libby was there already, and together they looked at the symbols and saw some agreeable message there.

He had a friend named Tom Schafer who worked for the Water Quality Board and was a free-lance diving instructor. One day Sam called him up and asked what it would take to get recertified.

"An afternoon," Tom said. "Assuming you haven't forgotten everything. I'll send you a book and you can bone up on all the technical shit. We'll whiz right by that. Then we'll get you in the water and see what happens to you."

Sam tried not to dwell on his motives; in any case they were not clear to him. It just seemed to him all at once that it was a practical necessity to renew his diving skills, as it was to keep his passport up-to-date against all reasonable expectations of foreign travel.

Sam studied the book that Tom sent him. It all came back. He was pleased to see how much sharper his mind was than it had been in high school. He remembered the decompression problems as daunting, but he grasped them clearly now, almost intuitively.

They met at a small cove on Lake Travis, whose placid surface was crowded with windsurfers who shifted their sails with the grace of matadors.

Tom was overweight. He had put on twenty pounds since the last time Sam had seen him, and he had outgrown his custom-tailored wetsuit. He was unable to fasten the beavertail, and it flapped uselessly behind him.

"The truth is I haven't been underwater in a year," he said, gazing out at the lake and drinking a beer. "It used to be I'd go out every weekend and then head down to the Caymans or someplace at least twice a year. Then the baby came and now I'm lucky to get out of the house at all."

They hauled the equipment out of Tom's car, and they reviewed how to attach the regulator to the tank valve and where all the buckles and straps went. The buoyancy compensator was new to him, as was the extra regulator mouthpiece, the "octopus" that was meant to be passed to a diver low on air.

Once they were in the water Sam had trouble clearing his ears, and it was difficult to adjust to the bulky buoyancy compensator, which caused him to loll around awkwardly in the water. But once he had filled the B.C. with the proper amount of air he saw the point. Achieving neutral buoyancy was like achieving harmony with the water itself. Sam hung still at thirty feet along the slope of the lake, rising a few inches when he took a breath and then sinking back to his original position when he exhaled.

Tom looked bored in the colorless lake, but Sam was entranced by this new skill. Tom had him do an emergency ascent and a few other maneuvers that gave him no problem, that were a joy to perform.

Afterward they went to a chicken-fried-steak place, and before they ordered Tom handed him several loose-leaf pages filled with his handwriting.

"What's this?" Sam asked.

"Your quiz."

192

He was through filling it out before the food came. Tom looked it over casually as he ate.

"You pass," he said, sopping up cream gravy with a piece of Texas Toast. "You aced it. I'll get your C-card in the mail to you."

"That's it?"

"That's it. You're at the head of your class."

"What do I owe you?" Sam asked.

"You get dinner."

"Thanks, Tom."

"No problem. How come you decided to start diving again?"

"I'm not sure." Sam set his plate aside. A waitress came to refill their big sixteen-ounce glasses with iced tea. "Have you ever done any cave diving?"

"A little. You're not ready for that, though. That's not something you just go and do."

"What's it like?"

"Scary as hell. Some people like it."

"I think I might."

"Get a little open-water experience first, Sam. Then you want to find the best people you can to teach you cave diving."

"Who are the best?"

"Rick Trammell. Gary Falk. There're a few others around. Count me out, though. Marlene said she'd divorce me if I ever went back into a cave."

Sam joined an underwater club at the university so that he could keep his new skills sharp. The first meeting he went to was held in a small auditorium in the physics building whose blackboard still contained an underlined message from the last class: "In the quantum universe, all things are possible."

The club had perhaps twenty members, most of them undergraduates, though Sam was introduced to a forty-five-year-old American Studies professor who wore a bolo tie and three or four turquoise rings, and who sat in the back of the classroom staring with undisguised longing at a sprightly girl in pigtails.

"Okay, minutes from the last meeting," the president said.

193

"Last meeting we had a report from Eric who just got a job at the Party Barn and said he could get us kegs at a discount. Then we had a discussion about whether the club logo should be a megamouth shark or a sawfish crushing a can of beer in his fist."

"Sawfish don't have fists," someone observed.

"Duly noted."

Sam was asked to rise so that he could be introduced as a new member. He did so hesitantly, wishing now that he had not come. He felt the eyes of the club members on him, silently questioning his motives. He assumed they thought he was like the professor, that he was searching out lecherous diversions.

It embarrassed him a little that he had gone to such blatant lengths in pursuit of Libby, but once he had acknowledged to himself that he *was* in pursuit the embarrassment seemed insignificant. It was a price he was willing to pay, a little dip in his manly pride. Perhaps she would feel pity for him; that was a risk. He would not dwell on that. His immediate purpose was to become a good diver, to satisfy his pride in that way, and to bring himself that much closer to her orbit.

So he went diving with the club at every opportunity. The membership preferred night dives. They liked to drink a lot of beer and drift through the moonlit coves. Once Sam, having lost his bearings underwater, surfaced next to a large flat boulder where the professor was making out on a groundsheet—not with the girl in pigtails but with a broad-shouldered Petroleum Land Management major named Vonetta McGee.

"Humanoids from the deep," the professor said, giving Sam a poker-faced look.

"I saw that movie," Vonetta volunteered, as Sam slipped beneath the water.

He drifted down to about twenty feet. He had been with two other divers when he had surfaced to reconnoiter, but they had gone on without him. He stayed there for ten minutes, happily violating the rule against diving alone, secure in his abilities and peaceful in the environment. The moonlight fell on the silt-draped rocks, making them look like primitive life forms that were rooted to the lake bottom.

Over the weeks he acquired confidence in the water, a sure

194

bearing that provided a satisfaction he found mysteriously significant. He bought a good mask and fins—from a dive shop that competed with Rick's—and picked up a few secondhand pieces of equipment here and there until he was more or less outfitted. He kept a log, noting the depth and duration of his dives, the amount of air expended.

One weekend the club sponsored a dive in the Gulf. Sam drove down to Freeport on his own, leaving at three in the morning so he could be there at seven when the boat left. When he arrived the converted crew boat they had chartered was already warming up its twin diesels. The rest of the group had driven down the night before in a van and had spent the night on board. They were hung over, still in their sleeping bags, as the boat pulled out into the Gulf.

They were headed for the wreck of a drilling platform fifty miles out. Vonetta was the first to crawl out of her sleeping bag. She opened the cooler next to her and got a beer just as a fish plopped into her lap.

"What is this?" she asked Sam.

"A flying fish."

"Please remove it."

Sam picked up the fish. Its long, flat, aerodynamic fins reminded him of the wings of a dragonfly. He tossed it out of the boat like a model airplane and it submerged only for a moment before it bounded out again, coasting above the waves and disappearing beyond the bow of the boat.

They had not gone far when they encountered a front, a massive steel-gray barrier of cloud. Sam thought they would turn around, but the captain wanted to check the weather on the other side of the storm. The blue water turned opaque and rough. The boat plowed on through the swells, slipping over the crests at first and then plunging off them, landing with shattering impact while the rain and spray washed over the deck. The rest of the divers carried their sopping sleeping bags into the crew cabin, but Sam preferred the open deck to the stagnant quarters below. Once when a wave smashed them broadside the tanks came loose from their storage racks and rolled across the deck. Sam planted his feet wide for stability and lashed them back into place.

All at once they were overwhelmed by sunlight as the boat came out of the storm. Sam watched it recede toward the coast, dragging its whitecaps and leaving clear blue swells behind. Soon even the swells were gone, and the divers looked out onto the mild tableland of the Gulf. Seagoing dolphins followed in the wake of the boat, and Sam saw a lone sea turtle, its great head peering mournfully above the waterline, as if it had surfaced to look for bearings, for any kind of mark in the void.

They suited up on the deck while the boat angled in and tied off to the exposed jack-up leg of the oil rig. The rig had blown up and sunk a year before, and it lay now on its side in over two hundred feet of water. They could see it beneath the surface from the boat: a latticework of thick, corroding pipes.

Sam was teamed with Vonetta, who was haggard and a little drunk from the wild trip out. He helped her with her tank and watched nervously as she swayed unsteadily on the deck. Vonetta was big-boned and had a native voluptuousness that was obscured by her wetsuit. In the water she was so buoyant that she had to wear twenty-two pounds of weight.

Sam maneuvered her to the railing and let her jump in first. He followed, his inflated B.C. catching him and holding him at the surface.

"So it's your first ocean dive," Vonetta said.

"Right," Sam answered, spitting out sea water.

"Nothing to it," she said, but then a look of concern appeared in her eyes and she put her faceplate in the water and began turning around in circles.

"What are you doing?" he asked.

"Looking for sharks. I've seen them here before. Maybe we should have brought a bangstick."

Sam put his regulator in his mouth and descended ten feet and waited for her to follow. That was all he needed, to be teamed with a paranoid drunk. But she came down and made the okay sign to him and he felt allied with her. It seemed to him that the deepening pressure of the water cancelled out her inebriation as it took the edge off his own surface acuity. They were equals here.

The sight before them was like a Jules Verne fantasy: an immense skeletal city, a web that stretched far past the horizons of their vision. Barracuda cruised in the foreground, their bodies gleaming like chrome, and in the deep water below, Sam could make out schools of amberjack and snapper.

He let go of the descent line and swam down along one of the cantilevered legs of the rig to the great capsized platform. Vonetta followed him, stationing herself a few feet below, so that he could see her heavy body drifting like a cloud over the girders.

Other divers were swarming over the platform, peering into the quarters, the machine shops. He could hear the clanging of the metal doors as they were ceaselessly opened and shut by the surge. They swam up the wall of the upturned helicopter pad and looked up at the shadow of the dive boat. Sam let himself drop to a hundred feet and then went down twenty more, and still the bottom was a hundred feet below him. He felt the first symptoms of nitrogen narcosis—a mild amusement that centered on Vonetta and her fear of sharks—and he stayed at that depth just long enough to experience the feeling, to be able to know it.

When he looked up he saw that she had gone in through one of the open doors. He followed her reluctantly into a long room with a silt-covered blackboard on one wall and a Coke machine lying on its side, still plugged in. Vonetta was hovering over the Coke machine, pulling the knobs. A surge passed through the room and knocked her sideways, against the ceiling. She made the okay sign to Sam, somewhat shakily, as he swam to her. He pointed toward the door but before he himself left he hovered in the middle of the room, liking the definition it gave to the nothingness of the open water. They kicked up a lot of silt as they left the room, so much so that the doorway was almost obscured.

Outside there was a shark, a small one, no more than four or five feet long. It swam before them, focused in on itself, listening to some inner voice. Vonetta pulled on his arm and when she had his attention put her hand on top of her head and flapped it up and down. He remembered: that was the sign for shark.

She pointed back to the room they had left, but he shook his head. They were low enough on air, and the boat was close. He

197

had confidence the shark would not bother them. Sam pushed off from the rig and coasted through the blue atmosphere. He was bathed in the element, strong in it, ready for whatever might come.

Chapter 20

BACK from the Gulf, Sam found an invitation in his mailbox, a postcard of a fur-bearing trout with a typeset announcement on the back. Bobby and Kathleen were house-sitting for the summer at the lake place of one of his lawn-mowing customers, and they were throwing a combination housewarming and birthday party for Libby.

Sam set the postcard on the dining-room table. It hurt him that he had reached the point where he could be notified of his wife's birthday in such a distant and formal manner. But of course he would go. He drove to the mall that evening, looking for a birthday present. He considered buying her a lavender blouse, a big picture book about elephants, a record of Brenda Lee's greatest hits. These were the sorts of things he had bought her in the past. But they seemed charged with significance now, calculated to produce some emotional effect. He could find no object that was neutral, that did not comment or wound. Everywhere he looked he saw nothing but gifts he was no longer allowed to give her.

Rick was waiting for her when she got off work. He was standing in front of the Co-op, peering idly into a display window filled with pastel backpacks. Libby was surprised to see him, and he looked out of place there, standing so still and firm among the slack college students, egg-roll vendors, and craftspeople selling stained-glass trinkets and winsome paintings of unicorns and hobbits.

"I thought you were going to come by for me at home," she said.

"I changed my mind." He took her arm and walked her through the dense pedestrian traffic. A train of silent roller skaters glided past them. A street corner musician was playing the theme to "The Andy Griffith Show" on a balalaika. A derelict smelling of spray paint staggered toward them, but Rick turned him away with his eyes.

"There are a lot of pathetic people in the world," he told her. "How do you put up with this every day?"

"It's not as bad as it used to be," she said. "At least you don't get the Jesus freaks anymore."

"What happened to them?"

"They're assimilated. Part of the mainstream. Unlike you."

Libby eased her arm around his waist; she could feel him stiffen for a moment, and then yield to this public affection. They were almost knocked down crossing the street by a pack of bicycle racers, who flashed by on their expensive machines like a single organism with a single will. Libby saw their skin-tight black shorts that looked like nineteenth-century bathing costumes, the pockets at the backs of their jerseys bulging with bananas and granola bars.

"Where are we going?" she asked.

"Here."

They stopped at a tiny jewelry store she had hardly ever noticed. Behind the counter was an anemic-looking man with a ponytail and long, bony fingers.

"It's finished," he said, when he saw them come in. He opened a small manila envelope and took out a necklace and laid it on the counter.

"What's this?" Libby asked.

"It's for you," Rick said. "For your birthday."

Hanging from the necklace was an aquamarine stone framed in a triangle of gold. She picked it up and held it to the light. The stone shimmered like water.

She wore it out of the store, so conscious of it that she thought

200

she felt the heat of the stone against her skin when the sunlight struck it for the first time.

"This is just the thing," she said to him, touching it. "I'm all choked up."

"Good."

He removed a parking ticket from his van and tossed it into the trash, and then he drove her to his apartment. They rarely went there together, and she always liked seeing it, what it said about him: the bed made, his shoes side by side in the closet, the bathroom soap resting in a seashell.

"I bought some beer for you," he said, opening the refrigerator. He brought the bottle to her.

"Are you hungry?" he asked.

"No. There's going to be food at the party anyway."

"Is Sam going to be there?"

"He's invited. I don't know if he's coming."

Libby set down her beer and kissed him. He seemed distant, in need of her. It was as if the gift of the aquamarine had exhausted him, depleted the store of his emotional energy. They moved to the bed, where she removed everything but the necklace, feeling its contained light at the base of her throat.

She glanced through the window and saw a squirrel sitting on a branch, peering inside with an intense, curious look, as if the sight of them had stopped him in his tracks. Libby smiled. She whispered to Rick that she loved him, and she heard him murmur it back. She believed him, she felt that it was true, but she could sense a final indifference in him, an attention that was focused beyond her. She did not mind. She loved what he withheld, admired his power over her. They lay there for a long time until he consulted his big diver's watch, with its red buttons and rotating bezel, and told her it was time for her party at the lake.

The house Bobby and Kathleen were occupying for the summer was built of cedar and glass and was reached by a private and prestigiously unpaved road. When Sam pulled up to the house, Dumptruck shot out of the car as soon as he opened the driver's door, headed for the dark water that was visible in the moonlight off the rocky beach.

The party seemed to be mostly outside, so Sam followed Dumptruck. There were other dogs around, swimming or pacing nervously on the shore. Sam found Bobby basting a *cabrito* over an open fire, a headless, spindly creature whose exposed musculature glistened as it turned on the spit.

"We're having German shepherd for dinner," Bobby said, indicating the *cabrito*. "There's beer in that washtub."

Sam pulled a beer out of the ice. Daphne toddled up to him and began to rub her head against his knees. He picked her up and she pointed to his nose and said "Doh."

"That's right, doh," Sam said.

"She's a real party animal," Bobby said.

"Who lives here?" Sam asked, looking up at the house.

"Crawdad Mabry."

"No kidding."

Crawdad Mabry was a former Dallas Cowboys running back who had been suspended in 1965 after he called a press conference to announce that he had smoked banana peels and seen God. He later graduated to real drugs, served time in prison for conspiracy to sell, and emerged as a youth evangelist. He was now the host of a Christian talk show and the owner of a sports-club franchise.

"He and Jeanine are in Maui," Bobby said, "witnessing to the faithful. You seen the house yet?"

"No."

"The birthday girl's up there. Kathleen's giving her and Rick the tour."

"I'll wander over in that direction unless you need help with this beast."

"Naw. Nothing to it. Everybody gets a knife and we're just going to slice off hunks of meat like in some Kirk Douglas movie."

Sam set Daphne down by her father and went to the house. On the front steps a round-faced, barrel-chested guy was sitting and cranking an ice-cream freezer, staring dreamily out at the lake. He offered Sam his hand as he went by.

"Gary Falk."

"Sam Marsh."

"Libby's husband?"

"That's right."

"I work with Rick," Gary said. A look of concern came over his face. "You know Rick, don't you?"

"Oh, sure," Sam said. "We've met."

Gary sat there turning the crank, helplessly trying to think of something to say.

"You want me to take a turn at that?" Sam asked.

"Thanks," Gary said. "I'm fine. You might pour a little rock salt in there for me."

Sam sprinkled some of the salt into the bucket and stood there for a moment out of courtesy, watching the ice revolve as Gary turned the crank, and then excused himself and went inside.

The house was filled with interior decorator art: anonymous, trendy bronzes and wall hangings. There was a Universal Gym in the living room that faced a semicircular panel of mirrors, and along one wall a huge, narcissistic painting that showed Mr. and Mrs. Crawdad in their designer workout clothes, their faces contorted in righteous exertion as a heavenly beam of light shone upon them.

Libby and Rick were on the other side of the room, talking to Kathleen and to another woman that Sam didn't know. Libby saw him and smiled, and he mouthed the words "Happy Birthday," and kept moving, stopping in the dining room to look at her birthday cake. It was a big bakery cake crowded with plastic figures: baseball players, spacemen, ballet dancers, circus animals, bowlers. The words "Happy Birthday Libby" wound across its busy surface, and someone had taken the time to put in all thirty-one candles.

Barf Mooney walked in from the kitchen, eating *ceviche* out of a paper cup. He was wearing a suit.

"I didn't know you were coming," he said to Sam.

"I was invited. What are you dressed up for?"

"I was up seeing some honchos this afternoon. I'm thinking about running for state representative."

"That's a big step," Sam said, watching Libby and Rick in the other room.

"I've got a political analyst and an astrologer both telling me to go for it."

Barf put his cup of *ceviche* down on the table next to the cake. "Should I apologize for introducing her to you?" he asked Sam, looking at Libby.

"No."

"That's good. I'm going to play some music." He went over to the elaborate stereo and put on a Sons of the Pioneers record, turning the volume up high. The first cut was "Tumbling Tumbleweed."

Sam walked outside, carried like a wave on the high-decibel chorus of the song. People were gathered around the *cabrito*, holding paper plates, while Bobby carved. Sam saw Bancock and a few other people Libby worked with whose names he could not remember.

Dumptruck ran up to him, soaking wet from the lake, and leaped, leaving paw prints on his shirt. As if that had been his sole purpose the dog then raced back to the water.

By the light of the cooking fire Sam saw Janet. She was looking at him, holding a paper plate. They had been true to their agreement; he had hardly seen her since that night on the bluff above the Mirasol Swamp. She had been avoiding the office, concentrating on her free-lance guide business.

"I'm here with a date," she said when he walked up to her. "FYI."

"I've heard about this guy."

"He's around here somewhere. His name's Clifford."

"You're not into this Mr. Duckett business yourself, are you?" Sam asked.

"No, but if I were I wouldn't seek your approval." She picked off a piece of meat from the fibrous chunk of *cabrito* on her plate. "A little bitterness creeping in there," she said.

"No problem."

"Anyway, Clifford's not a flake. He makes sixty thousand dollars a year at Texas Instruments."

"Good for him."

"I met Rick earlier. The bad news for you is that he has sex appeal."

"I've got a little stored up," Sam said.

Later, inside the house, where they gathered to sing "Happy Birthday" to Libby, Sam made a point of walking up to Clifford and introducing himself. Clifford was tall and well groomed, with soothing colorless eyes and a square jaw.

"So you're the famous Sam," he said.

"That's right," Sam said, while Clifford stared at him in an unembarrassed, expectant manner that seemed designed to make Sam blurt out some profound revelation about himself.

Fortunately, they were interrupted by the singing. Sam joined in, barely moving his lips. He noticed that Rick stood apart from Libby, staring at the cake. He seemed uneasy and distant.

Libby noticed it too, but it did not bother her. That was the way Rick was. He would not press his claim to her here, in this crowd, with Sam on the other side of the room making an effort to mouth the words of the birthday song. She saw Sam's eyes fall on the aquamarine stone as she leaned down to blow out the candles.

"Well," Bobby said by way of a toast, "here we all are."

Daphne's hands appeared at the table edge. She was trying to pull herself up to the cake. Libby lifted her and held her while Daphne pulled up the plastic figures and licked the icing from their bases.

After the cake everyone drifted outside. There was a good moon, and the goat carcass shone in its light like the evidence of some ritual murder. Gary finished cranking the ice cream and held the dasher out to the dogs.

Sam went down to the shoreline to inspect the boathouse. A big Ski Nautique hung above the water on belts. Bobby didn't have the use of that, but there was a rowboat and a crimped aluminum canoe lying nearby. Sam felt the urge to set off across the lake.

He was looking around for a canoe paddle when he saw Rick walking down to him.

"I was hoping you'd be here tonight," Rick said. "I wanted to show you something."

He reached into his pocket and held out a fossil. Sam took it, peering closely at it in the darkness.

"It looks like a crinoid stem," he said.

"Know where it came from?"

"No. Where?"

"Jacob's Well."

Sam looked at the fossil again. "That's not very likely," he said. "It's too old."

"I know, but that's where it's from. When I was a kid a guy dived down there and brought it up."

"Maybe it washed in," Sam said, giving it back. "This is Paleozoic, from way down deep. Even if you didn't have that sandstone aquaclude you couldn't get down that far."

Rick put the fossil back in his pocket.

"Maybe it was planted," Sam said.

"Sure," Rick said. "By the CIA."

Sam sat down on the prow of the rowboat and listened to the Sons of the Pioneers.

"Is Libby having a good birthday?" he asked Rick.

"I think so. She's glad to see everybody."

"Are you guys about to have a fistfight or anything?" Bobby called from the direction of the fire.

"No," Sam called back.

"Good. We've got a contingent here that wants to go for a cruise."

Bobby came down to the boathouse pulling Libby along by the hand. Gary was with them, and soon Janet came down with Clifford. They found the oars and paddles on top of the rafters in the boathouse, and then they parceled themselves out into the two boats. Sam ended up in the stern of the canoe, with Bobby and Gary. Rick took the oars of the rowboat, with Libby in the prow and Janet and Clifford in the stern.

The dogs followed them into the lake, Dumptruck straining and panting as he paddled along, trying to keep pace with Sam in the canoe. Sam ordered him back, and eventually the dog turned around, suddenly cognizant of the deep, limitless water ahead. Sam watched over his shoulder until Dumptruck reached shore.

The two boats stayed together, with Sam keeping the canoe in the wake of the rowboat, almost touching the stern. He noticed the way Rick feathered the oars, moving the boat ahead without a wasted stroke, the blades pulling deep and even.

"How deep is this lake?" Bobby asked. His voice carried with an eerie intensity across the water. They could still hear the music from the house. Somebody had put on a Van Halen record.

"Three hundred feet," Rick answered from the rowboat. "There are whole towns at the bottom."

The music from the shore grew fainter as they moved farther into the lake. The water was very calm and warm. Sam noticed Janet trailing her hand in it.

"Everybody who believes in the Loch Ness monster," Bobby said, "raise your hand."

Clifford raised his hand; so did Janet, laughing.

"What do you think, Clifford?" Bobby asked. "Is it that kind of night?"

"I'd keep my eyes peeled," said Clifford.

"You guys," Libby said.

Rick altered his course, turning the boat parallel to the shore so that they would not stray too far out into the lake. Sam, at the stern of the canoe, followed without comment. Rick picked up the pace a little, to keep the rhythm of his rowing steadier. He could feel Libby's eyes on his back, watching him.

"Do you want me to row for a while?" Clifford asked him.

"I'm fine," Rick said.

"Where are we headed?" Gary called from the canoe.

"Nowhere," Janet said.

"I know a good place to swim," Gary said. "Over in that next cove."

Rick moved in closer to shore, following Gary's directions. The water was fairly clear, and he could see the blades of his oars as they stroked through the water and the big limestone boulders that sloped down into the lake.

"It's along here somewhere," Gary was saying. "It's about six or eight feet underwater. A nice little tunnel that you can swim through."

When they got to the place Rick lifted the oars and set them inside the boat. Sam brought the canoe up alongside.

"You can see it down there," Gary said. They peered over the side of the boat and could make out a pale archway beneath them, formed by two huge boulders leaning against one another.

Bobby stood up in the canoe, nearly capsizing it, and began to take off his clothes. Sam held the canoe steady against the side of the rowboat as Gary did the same. He watched Janet and Clifford slip off the stern of the rowboat.

"Come on!" Gary shouted to Rick from the water.

"I'll stay with the boats," he said. He looked at Sam and Libby. "You two go on."

"We can put the boats in at the shore."

"That's all right. I'll stay."

Fixing her eyes on Rick, Libby pulled off her blouse, then her shorts and underpants. Sam was blinded by his wife's nakedness, a sight that had once been such a casual pleasure, a gift.

Sam followed Libby over the side and swam with her to the others, who treaded water above the submerged archway, waiting for them.

Rick watched them from the boat. He was not sure why he felt so remote, so morose. But he did not feel like one of them. He watched their bodies beneath the water, their skin the same shade as the limestone in the moonlight. With one oar he trolled along behind them, holding the canoe alongside with his free hand. His love for Libby, his true regard for her, seemed suddenly tedious, unequal to some solitary calling within himself he could not identify and that perhaps he feared.

Underwater, the swimmers surged through the rock tunnel, in the muffled light that filtered down to them. They moved single file through the brief corridor, the long muscles of their thighs shuddering with propulsion. They felt free and long on breath, but something bothered them all. They could feel Rick's presence above them, his commitment to something darker and graver. When they swam back to the boat they felt chastened somehow by his apartness.

He held the boats steady as they pulled themselves over the sides, and while they sorted out their clothes and dressed he sat with the handles of the oars in his hands, ready to pull away from the cove.

Clifford left his clothes off. He sat next to Janet in the stern, staring out over the water.

"Are we ready?" Rick asked.

"Ready," Libby said.

The boats glided away from the cove, Sam still nudging the stern of the rowboat with the bow of the canoe. After a while he noticed that Clifford was shaking.

Libby, from the front of the rowboat, was watching Clifford too. The muscles in his cheeks had gone slack, as if in fear, as if he had indeed looked out onto the lake and seen the Loch Ness monster.

"Are you cold?" Libby asked him. He did not answer.

"I don't think he's cold," Janet said. She handed him his shirt just the same, but he pushed her hand away.

"This is Mr. Duckett speaking," he said then, in the voice of a kindly, middle-aged man.

"Uh-oh," Janet said, "I thought so."

"I'm happy to be here with you," he said. "Is there anything you would like to ask me?"

"What's the square root of pi?" Bobby asked from the canoe.

"Bobby!" Janet said. "He's serious!"

Rick stopped rowing and boated the oars. Sam brought the canoe up alongside.

"It's somebody's birthday," said Mr. Duckett. "That's nice. I feel much love here, but I feel other emotions too. Would you like to know what they are?"

"Sure," said Janet, looking at Sam.

"Okay. I feel resentment. I feel loneliness. I feel sorrow. There are three people here who are not in harmony. They are not satisfied. They are looking for something, but the way is not clear to them yet. They have to be patient. They have to be observant."

Clifford paused for a moment. His teeth were chattering. Libby noticed that he was getting an erection.

"You can all find the same happiness here on earth," he went on, "as I have found on the other side. Send for my booklet, *The Soul in Turmoil*. When Clifford returns to his body he will give you information on how to order it."

"May the force be with you," Bobby said.

"Here, kid," Janet said gently, spreading Clifford's shirt over his lap. "Come back to earth now."

The boats drifted apart a little on the way back but they reached shore at the same time, the dogs swimming out to meet them and Kathleen standing there with the baby in her arms like a whaler's wife staring out to sea.

Bobby helped Sam drag the canoe onto the shore and then went up to Kathleen.

"Is she asleep?" he asked, tenderly stroking Daphne's fine hair, which rose in tufts and swayed in the almost imperceptible breeze.

"God knows how," Kathleen said.

Bobby put his arms around his wife and baby and the three of them walked back up toward the house. The rest of the group followed, except for Sam, who sat down in the beached rowboat, feeling some warm, pervasive regret. He looked up at the sky, searching out the constellations that Janet had taught him. But it was no longer a winter sky, and the stars had shifted.

Libby came walking back to him, holding a beer for each of them. She stepped into the boat and sat across from him in the stern, her still-wet hair framing her face.

"I came down so you could tell me happy birthday," she said. "You haven't done that yet."

Sam leaned forward and kissed her. He did not care if Rick was watching.

"I don't have a present for you," he said. "I was looking for something meaningful but not pushy, and it doesn't exist."

"I remember all the things you've given me," she said.

Dumptruck ran up and lay wearily beside the boat. Libby swung a foot over the gunwale and nuzzled the dog's stomach with it.

"I've done some diving," Sam said. "I got recertified since the last time I saw you. I've been to the Gulf."

She gave him a disappointed, exasperated look.

"You're tailgating me, Sam."

"I admit it."

"It's not worthy of you."

210

"I like the way you speak to my best self. I don't care what's worthy of me."

Libby took a sip of her beer. She was a little awed at this new step of Sam's. She felt that she should be more put out by it than she was; that would be her own best self's reaction. But tonight she had her heart set on being the self-absorbed birthday girl. And in this mood she was glad—irresponsibly glad—that he was there in pursuit, in support.

Sam looked up over her head at the *cabrito* fire in the background. He could see Rick there in silhouette, standing by himself.

"Rick showed me something earlier," he said.

"What?"

"A fossil from Jacob's Well."

"Well, that's natural. You're a geologist."

"I thought it was a nice gesture."

"That too," Libby said.

"Does he know you're down here talking to me?"

"Do you think I should get a permission slip from him?"

"I just don't want him to feel left out."

"He doesn't. Should I ask him to come over and sit in the boat with us?"

"That's the question. Should we all be friends or not?"

"You be the judge, Sam."

"Go get him."

Rick was standing with his back to the lake. It was a warm night, too warm to be standing by a fire. He was sweating and the smoke from the cedar logs was burning his eyes. Everyone else was inside, or on the second-story deck, idly dancing or looking up at the stars. He felt Libby behind him, and turned to face her.

"We want you to come join us," she said.

Rick reached into the washtub and pulled a canned Coke out of the melted ice. He rubbed its cold aluminum against his sweaty forehead before he pulled the tab.

"What are you talking about down there?" he asked.

"This and that. You."

He walked with her down to the boat.

"We were wondering," Sam said, as Rick took a seat next to

211

Libby in the stern, "if we should all be friends."

"You two need to work that out."

He was impatient with them. He resented the deep texture of experience and affection they shared, and the fact that they would not let go of it. He wanted to wrench Libby out of that texture; he knew that in a way she was waiting for him to do just that, and yet he held back. The situation interested him. He felt an unlikely warmth toward the two of them, along with the impatience. It was apparent to him that their marriage was desperate to heal itself, whether it deserved healing or not. Rick did not know his role in all of this, he only knew his want, which was for Libby.

"We've worked it out," Libby said.

"Fine, then," Rick answered. He raised his Coke can in salute. "I'm sure Mr. Duckett will be pleased to hear it."

"Don't talk about that," said Libby. "That guy is creepy."

"Catch!" Bobby called from the deck of the house. He sent a Day-Glo Frisbee sailing over their heads, coasting along as pale and silent as the moon and landing in the water beyond them. One of the dogs went to retrieve it, but by the time he set it down by the rowboat it was no longer luminous.

Sam tossed it out again, to indulge the dog. Dumptruck roused himself and leaped into the lake as well, and Sam watched the dogs paddling around in the dark water, searching for the lightless disk.

Sam leaned backward, not minding the discomfort of the boat's prow pressing into his back.

"Don't go to sleep on us," Libby said.

"I'm wide awake," he answered, but under the deep sky he felt eerily receptive, as if with just the slightest relaxation of his will he could fall into a trance. He was on the verge of feeling the way he had in the Abuelos, in the *curandero*'s hut, under the sway of that thrilling fever. In this mood he thought of the tunnel that he and Libby and the others had swum through tonight while Rick had brooded above them in the boat, and suddenly he remembered what Don Ignacio had told him, that there was a dark and dangerous place where they would be together.

"Let me see that fossil again," he said to Rick.

Chapter 21

A FEW days after her birthday party Libby drove home to Picture Bluff for her parents' fortieth wedding anniversary. She detoured a bit to the west so she could pass through the hill country. The scraggly meadows were solid with wildflowers, their colors so startlingly vivid they gave a cartoon brightness to the landscape. The water in the creeks was high, washing over the low-water crossings as deep as her hubcaps.

She had recently had her car tuned and a worn tire replaced and so she drove with confidence. As she left the scenery behind and hit the open country around Brownwood her head felt as clear as the horizon. Her troubles with Sam seemed to have entered a new and more complicated phase with his announcement that he had taken up diving again. She did not know what to make of that, but she felt peculiarly unruffled. Behind the wheel of her car, cruising through a landscape that God had made for driving, she was too content to worry about Sam's motives. That was his job.

She tuned in one preacher station after another on the six-hour drive, imagining the presences—the mean, pig-eyed faces fleshed out with baby fat—behind those weak, hysterical voices. She saw the cotton gins and truck stops that were the first harbingers of Picture Bluff long before she was ready to stop. She could have driven all the way to Colorado, the way she felt.

Before she went to her parents' house she stopped at the pay phone outside the K-Bob's Steak House and called Rick. Dialing the number, she glanced across the street at the old drive-in theater where her grandfather used to take her. The silhouette painting on the back side of the screen—a Commanche on horseback raising his arms to the Great Spirit—was faded now, and seemed as archaic as her own past.

"Dive shop," Gary answered.

"Gary, this is Libby," she said. "Is Rick there?"

"No. He's gone to the bank. Where are you?"

"Picture Bluff. Tell him I'll try—"

"Wait a minute. He just drove up."

She felt her whole body sag in relief. She was as desperate as a teenager to hear his voice.

"Did you make it?" he asked her.

"Yes."

"What's all that noise?"

"I'm calling from a pay phone. I didn't want to call from my parents'. I'm not ready to fill them in yet."

"Okay."

"I feel so far away from you. It seems like I imagined you."

"You didn't, Libby."

"I love you, Rick. You don't have to say it back. I don't want to embarrass you in front of Gary."

"He's in the other room now."

"So you can say it?"

"Yes. I love you."

"That makes my day."

When she pulled up to the house she saw one of the neighborhood kids running along the top of the cinderblock fence, with his dog behind him snapping at his pants' cuffs. Libby's mother heard her car and came outside to meet her.

"You look fit," she said, hugging her and running her fingers through the hair at Libby's temples.

"So do you," Libby said. "Where'd you get the glasses?"

"Do they make me look old?"

"No, of course not."

"The man at the optical said you can see like a hawk for only so long."

They did make her look old, and she looked thin as well. That

214

could be worry. Picture Bluff's economy was at a crisis point. The secondary recovery boom was over and now with the oil glut the rig count was lower than it had ever been since Libby's birth. Her father owned a small oilfield construction company. Two years ago he had been talking about selling it and retiring; now he was maneuvering to stay ahead of bankruptcy.

Libby dropped her suitcase off in her old bedroom and then sat down at the kitchen table with her mother, facing a corkboard collage of family photographs. She noticed Sam's picture was still there, along with her younger brother and sister.

"You shouldn't have come just for our anniversary," Libby's mother said. "That's not something you kids need to celebrate."

"I'm just here to see that you and Daddy celebrate it."

"Tell me how things are with Sam," she said, after a silence.

"Not much different."

"You see him every now and then, though?"

"Sure I do."

Libby's father came home early and the three of them got into his Buick and drove to Lubbock, to a franchised crêpe place that had just opened in the mall and enjoyed an unchallenged claim to elegance.

"I better get a double order of these," Libby's father said, looking down at a pitiful portion of something the menu had called *la crêpe bifteck*.

"We should have stopped at K-Bob's and gotten you a rib-eye," her mother said.

"Ah, hell no, I'm fine." He raised his wine glass. "Here's to number forty. And here's to our daughter. I hope you and Sam will turn out someday to be as happy as we are."

Libby touched glasses with her parents, not minding her father's heavy-handed version of a subtle hint. She could feel the warmth in it, the true feeling; the acceptance of the hurt she was doing them.

She had been, in their minds, an errant daughter—not wild, but inexplicably unsatisfied, always wanting something better but finding something worse. There had been some bad scenes during the time with Hudson. She was still not sure if they ever knew what his business was, but she remembered her father's

215

instinctual and undisguised dislike of him the first time they met. Hudson had taken pains, for her sake, to be straight and charming. He had asked her father thoughtful questions about his business, listened patiently to his right-wing harangues, but it had not done any good. Some callow, unconcerned, contemptuous note kept emanating from Hudson's politeness, a silent, alarming signal that her parents had heard at once.

With Sam they had plainly thought she was safe and settled. But when she told them that she and Sam had separated, they took the news with a calm disappointment that surprised her in its restraint. Perhaps they had stopped judging her. She knew she had been an agent in making their own lives, which had once been so rigorous and sure, now more aware and accepting of the shifting ground beneath them.

"Anybody want to see the pictographs?" Libby's father said, as they drove back in the evening light. He had been saying that since Libby was a girl. Whenever the family would perform that quaint and long-dead ritual of "going for a drive" Libby's father would drive to the pictograph site and sit in his car while the family went down to look at the rock paintings.

It was no different this evening. "Y'all go ahead," he said, pushing a button of the console that made the car seat inch backward. Libby and her mother obediently walked down to the bluff. She could not help thinking of Sam there, though she wanted her mind to be preoccupied with Rick.

"Why does Daddy always stay in the car?" Libby asked.

"He likes the view from there."

"Did you and he ever come here to make out?"

"Once or twice." She peered with her new glasses at the faded colors. "I never did understand why those Indians couldn't draw any better than that."

Libby leaned back against the rock. It was still warm, even though the light was nearly gone.

"June Claymore called right before you got here this afternoon," her mother said. "She said she'd seen you making a call from a pay phone."

"I was calling somebody in Austin," Libby said, feeling suddenly defeated. "It wasn't Sam."

"You still could have called from our house."

"I know."

When they walked back to the car they found her father asleep. Libby woke him up and persuaded him to let her drive back into town. When she was behind the wheel she felt good again and tried hard to think of nothing but Rick. Her parents sat there compliantly as she drove them, helpless to do anything for her but wish for her happiness. In the darkness, out of the corner of her eye, she thought she saw her father reach into the backseat and touch her mother's hand.

Rick felt uncomfortable with Libby gone. His focus was scattered. He resented how much he had grown addicted to her presence. She was only gone for four days but it was enough to disrupt things. He could not seem to fall back on his old solitary routines, he could not seem to get through the day without a quaking physical want of her. That was strange, because there were times enough when they were in town together that he was glad to get away from her, from her silent, forceful demands. But now when she was gone, inaccessible even for a brief period, he could not find that core of reality he needed.

It had not been that way with Jean. He remembered them as being in perfect equilibrium until her death had so drastically altered the balance. She did not want so much from him, or excite a corresponding hunger in himself. They were just good together, with an easy affection that he knew—from the shock he still carried—had deepened into love.

With Libby it had been love right away, and they were now busy filling in the easy comradeship, making things work on a normal plane. There was the complication with Sam, and the further complication that Sam had opened Rick's eyes to Jacob's Well again. He had seen the interest in Sam's face when he showed him the fossil, an unspoken acknowledgment that there might be something more beyond the final room. It was a hunch they both shared. That made them allies, Rick thought, not antagonists.

There was something else. Jagged as he felt now without Libby, his instinct told him to keep his distance. There was something uncompleted between her and Sam. He was not a part of it. He was outside, watching; and within himself, at the profoundest level his conscious mind could reach, he felt a strange, neutral fascination in the outcome.

Libby was to come home late that night. Rick went to a taco place after work and sat down with his burrito at a small wobbly table. No one else was there except for a tired-looking woman in a Walt Disney World T-shirt who had driven up with her little boy in a candy-apple red '66 Mustang.

Rick tapped his foot as he ate, anxious to get it over with, anxious to see Libby again. He held one awful thought at bay: that she was driving alone on the highway, the way Jean had been. He hated this restlessness he felt, this nervous desire.

"They put sour cream on it," the little boy said to the woman in the Disney World T-shirt as he examined his taco. "I hate sour cream."

"Well just wipe it off," she said.

"I can't get it all off," he whined.

Rick watched from the corner of his eye as the woman grabbed the boy's arm and shook him.

"You see that man over there?" she told the boy, looking toward Rick. "He's a detective. And if you don't start behaving he's gonna pop you one!"

Rick stood up, leaving his half-eaten burrito on the table, and walked out the door without looking at the woman. He took out his pocket knife, covered the blade with his hand so she wouldn't see it, and scraped the tip along the side of her car as he walked by it, leaving a long gouge a quarter inch thick in her nice paint job.

In his van he felt not remorse but disappointment in himself. He still had a lot to work out of his system.

He drove around town for two hours, circling back to Libby's house every thirty minutes until at last he saw her car parked in the driveway.

"I let the cat out of the bag to my parents," she said to him in bed that night.

218

"About what?"

"About you. So that's sort of a milestone for us."

Libby put her hands behind her head, drawing her breasts out from beneath the thin sheet.

"Do you talk to your family?" she asked him.

"Not much. I send them something at Christmas."

"But you don't hate them?"

"Why should I?"

"I don't know. Hudson did."

"I'm not Hudson," he said.

"I didn't mean that. I'm sorry."

"It makes me angry to think about you with him."

"I don't feel that way about Jean," Libby said. "I like thinking about her."

"Why?"

"Because I have this feeling she made you happy."

Rick took her hand and absentmindedly threaded his fingers through hers. His hands were large, the fingers long and beautifully formed, like a pianist's.

"We used to pack a lunch and go snorkeling in Crystal River with the manatees," he said.

"What color were her eyes?"

"Brown. And she had brown hair, longer than yours. What else do you want to know? Her sign?"

"While you're at it."

"Taurus."

Libby hesitated for a moment, then ventured another question.

"How do you feel when you think about Sam and me?"

Rick was silent for a long time while she assumed he was thinking.

"I want to take him into Jacob's Well," he finally said.

"Why?"

"To see what he can see."

"I don't like any of this," Libby said.

"He's smart. I think that if there's a way through that sandstone he can find it."

"That's all I need," she said, "for you two to team up. For

your information, he's hot on my trail. He's your adversary."

"Are you worried about that?" Rick asked.

"Well, no," she said. "I suppose not."

"Good. Then I'm not either."

Chapter 22

THE crinoid fossil had begun to intrigue him. Out of curiosity Sam spent an afternoon in the geology library at the university, checking stratigraphic reports and well divers' logs. The crinoid was very old, from paleozoic limestone, and all the exposed limestone around Jacob's Well was much younger. The old rock was buried deep; the nearest outcropping was fifty miles to the west. Sam supposed it could have washed into the Well from there, but fifty miles was a long trip for a little limestone fossil, and it was more likely that it would have dissolved before it ever went that far.

Shortly after Libby's birthday party he was in the field again, camped out for a miserable week in the Monahans sand dunes. He and Janet were careful to enforce a polite reserve between themselves as they trudged ankle-deep through the dunes. It seemed their canteens were always empty and their eyes always filled with grit. The sheer hostility of the environment threatened to drive them together again.

They drove home in the survey van. Picture Bluff was on the route, and they stopped there at a Pizza Hut for dinner.

"Are you going to call the in-laws?" Janet asked him.

"I think not."

"That's a shame. I bet they like you."

"That's nice of you to say."

"I can still be nice," Janet said, shaking the sand out of her hair.

When he got back to the office there was a message on his desk asking him to return a call from Rick Trammell.

"Have you got any free time this afternoon?" Rick said, when Sam called. "Maybe I could come over to your office and talk."

Sam said sure, and thirty minutes later Rick showed up. They shook hands—some odd propriety still demanded that—and Sam removed a stack of books and maps from the drafting stool that served as his visitor's chair. Rick sat down and looked around the room before he spoke, as if he was waiting for some disturbance to subside that only he could detect.

"I was wondering," Rick said. "You told Libby you'd been doing some diving."

"A little bit."

"Much open water?"

"Some. I think I've got about twelve hours logged. Most of it in the lake but some in the Gulf."

"You feel pretty comfortable underwater?"

"Sure. Why?"

"I was wondering if you might want to take a look around in the Well. Just see if there was anything that interested you."

"I'm already interested. I've been doing a little research on your crinoid. It definitely doesn't come from any of the surface rock around here."

"I know. It came from the Well."

"Maybe. The problem is the Well doesn't go that deep. It bottoms out at the sandstone."

"That's what everybody seems to think," Rick said. He stood up and put his hands in his jeans pockets and looked out Sam's window, staring at an old woman waiting for the bus. Sam watched him, trying to break his confused feelings down into their component parts. Jealousy, he decided. Hope. Excitement.

He saw that Rick was using him, using his need for Libby and his professional curiosity for his own ends. And yet that seemed such a small part of what was going on. He liked Rick; there was something solemn and clean about him which he approved of, which he did not begrudge Libby for wanting. At the moment it did not seem to matter that they were all engulfed in such a welter of motivations; it mattered only that they were moving toward the same goal, looking for the same place.

"I'd like to take a look," Sam said.

Rick turned from the window. "Good," he said. "Are you free this weekend?"

"Sure."

"What equipment do you need? I can bring it from the shop."

"I suppose I'll need a light. I've got just about everything else."

Rick nodded and then hesitated before he spoke again.

"Libby's a little uncertain about this," he said.

"Let's not worry about her," Sam decided.

Chapter 23

SAM arrived at the Well early on Saturday morning, a half hour before the time they had agreed to meet. At that hour there was still mist on the creek and the furtive rustlings of small animals in the brush on the near bank. He had not been here since college, when he had come on a field trip to see a specimen of a natural artesian well.

Jacob's Well had been a recreation spot with a campground then, but the amenities had languished over time, and now it was merely a half-hearted county park, with a few scrappy acres and four or five picnic tables in need of weatherproofing.

The Well itself was much smaller than he remembered it. He waded out now into the cold water of the creek, wearing his secondhand wetsuit booties, and stood at its edge. The opening was only ten or twelve feet across, a wide-bore hole in the bed-rock filled with water as bright and brilliant as a precious stone. He saw the point; it was like the portal to another dimension, a world of unnatural vibrance and mystery.

On the far bank were bluffs of the same thick-bedded, massive limestone in which this opening section of the Well had formed. The shallow creek was filled with gravel, and he waded down-stream, sorting through it. It was ordinary alluvium—bits and pieces of the resident limestone, as well as the detritus he would have expected to see washed down from other drainages: quartz, feldspar, pink dolomite, chert, pieces of hard flint jacketed in dull gray rock. The fossils he found were entirely in order—

Cretaceous clams and gastropods that had once lived in the bed of the ancient sea.

He saw Rick and Libby drive up. Rick turned the van around and backed it up almost to the edge of the creek, so that they would be close to the water when they donned their heavy equipment. Libby emerged from the passenger side, wearing a pair of gym shorts over her bathing suit. She walked into the creek, not bothering to take off the old pair of jogging shoes she wore. She was carrying a box of doughnuts. "Want one?" she asked Sam, holding the box out.

Sam put his hands in the water to wash off the gravel mud and then took a doughnut.

"Do you like it?" Libby asked, tilting her head upstream in the direction of the Well.

"So far," he said. "It's pretty."

Rick came down to them with a quart bottle of orange juice, which they passed around while they waited for the early morning lethargy to disappear.

"We're not going very deep," Rick said. "Just down to the barricade. We won't ever be far from surface light. The thing to remember is to try not to kick any more than you have to. Just use your B.C. to stay neutral."

"It's a snap," Libby told Sam. "Isn't it, Rick?"

"The other thing," Rick said, ignoring her. "You get narked pretty quick down there, faster than you do in open water. You'll probably start to feel a little goofy about fifty feet. But don't worry. I'll be watching you."

The three of them finished their orange juice and began to suit up. Sam struggled with his wetsuit, leaning against his car and pulling the heavy neoprene up his legs until his fingers were sore. He noticed that Rick put on his own wetsuit as casually as a pair of pants. Sam supposed that must come with practice.

He watched Libby, taken with the brisk, efficient way she dressed for the dive, a private ritual that excluded him. She looked good in the form-fitting wetsuit, full of purpose.

Sam added two or three more pounds of weight than he normally used, to compensate for the flow, and he slipped his hammer through his weight belt. The flashlight that Rick had loaned him weighed even more than the hammer. It had a clear Plexiglas housing and a pistol grip.

Rick checked Sam's straps as they stood at the lip of the crevice; he checked to make sure that Sam's air valve was open and that the various hoses and gauges were connected and functioning. He did the same for Libby, but in a much more perfunctory way. He knew her better; he could count on her to be prepared.

"Keep an eye on your pressure gauge," Rick told him. "I want to know when you're down to a thousand pounds of air."

Sam nodded his head. He spit into his mask, washed it out, and then sealed it over his face. Rick went into the water first, and then Libby.

Sam let Libby submerge about ten feet and then followed her, descending feet first, and wishing he were wearing even more weight. He had to fight against the flow, and it spoiled the rhythm of his descent.

But he was comfortable enough as they swam through the cave. It was a place of beauty to him, and he trailed his gloved hand along the polished rock, appreciating how clean the water kept it. It was a solid cave, with good lines, and the walls of its main channel had a sculpted, fluted look from the ceaseless action of the water.

He watched Libby swim before him, the slow, subtle stroking of her legs that kept her in balance with the dynamics of the water. There was a sureness there, a purpose, that he had never seen in the years of their marriage.

He followed her white, long-bladed Plana fins into the darkness. He saw the beam of Rick's bright light below, and when they were all gathered at the floor of the chamber Rick held out his hand, wanting to see Sam's pressure gauge. When Rick handed it back, Sam read it himself and saw that he could be doing better on air, so he tried to breathe calmly, to inure himself to this marvelous place.

Rick made the okay sign and Sam and Libby returned it. The three of them made their way into the tunnel that led to the barricade. Sam watched how Rick and Libby moved delicately forward on their fingertips and was suddenly aware of the mess he was creating with every stroke of his fins.

At the barricade they simply stopped and looked ahead. Sam shone his light ahead, momentarily confused about what he was looking for. That was the nitrogen narcosis starting to work, he told himself. He turned around, wanting to explore the large vertical chamber they had passed through on their way down. He saw the absolute darkness behind them, like something that had been following, waiting for its moment to swallow them. For a moment he could not find the broad and well-defined corridor through which they had descended. He thought a blind passage had been substituted for it. He swept the heavy flashlight back and forth until finally his fear subsided and the tunnel began to look familiar to him.

Libby was beside him, kneeling on the bedrock, and joining the beam of her light with his. He turned to look at her, marveling at how assured and handsome she looked, how effective. Then she rose into the clear water above them like a spirit gliding upward.

Sam looked at his pressure gauge. He was breathing a little better. He began to reconnoiter around the big vertical room, spiraling upward around its circumference and looking for interesting things in the rock. Rick stayed planted below them, keeping watch.

Sam felt an overwhelming affection for the three of them, comrades in this buried place. The affection was almost equal to the solitary longing he felt for Libby, and the wariness he still harbored toward Rick. But he was happy as he scanned the rock, inspecting the little domes and solution pockets he found here and there, the crevices filled with alluvium or lithified mud.

At about fifty feet below the surface he saw the opening of a small chimney, and he followed it up for five or six feet until it pinched out above him. Just at its apex, though, he saw something interesting: a piece of ancient, hardened coral, cemented into place by calcite deposits. He took the hammer from his weight belt and began to chip away at the calcite. At the first sound of the hammer hitting rock, Libby and Rick gathered beneath him, shining their lights up into the crevice. Sam looked down and saw Rick making the okay sign in the beam of his light. Sam returned it and motioned him upward, until the narrow crevice was illuminated and Sam was free to use both hands to free the rock.

It was a tight place to work, and he knew his air consumption was going up as he hammered at the cement, but he did not want to take the time to look at his gauge. Finally the rock was loose enough for him to pry it away with the hammer, and then it suddenly dropped into his lap, thunking against the lead on his weight belt.

When he came down out of the crevice he signaled to Rick that he wanted to ascend. The rock was the size of both his fists put together, but he felt he was still underweighted against the flow. He led the way out with Libby following and Rick behind her, winding up line on the reel. When Sam reached the opening flue he could feel the warm sun beating down to him, and looking up at the skylight above him he felt secure and thrilled. He let the flow take him upward, taking care not to rise too fast, wanting to give in to the dreamlike ease of the ascent.

He took off his fins and tank and stood at the edge of the sinkhole, watching Libby surface in a froth of bubbles. She swam from the Well into the shallow water of the creek, and then got up on her knees and let Sam help her with her tank. When she took off her mask he saw that her lips were blue from the cold.

"What did you find?" she asked.

"Something interesting. I want to get my hand lens."

Sam went to his car and got the lens out of the glove compartment, examining the rock as he walked back to the creek. Rick had surfaced in the meantime and had already ditched most of his equipment on the bank.

"It's a piece of coral," Sam told them. "Part of a reef."

"How old?" Rick asked.

"Paleozoic, for sure. Just like your crinoid. It could have been brought up in a flood and worked itself into that crevice."

"What does all this tell us?" Libby asked.

"I'm not sure," Sam said. He took the rock from her and looked at it under his lens again. The tiny rugose corals were huddled together in the remnant of a colony that had kept them safe during their brief lives hundreds of millions of years ago. Their circular forms reminded him of the undersides of mushroom caps.

They stopped in San Marcos on the way back to Austin and while they ate lunch in a café overlooking the river, Rick drew him a map of what the Well looked like beyond the barricade. It was a very precise sketch. Past the grate the passage widened, sloping downward, widened again into a medium-sized chamber, and then got tight again until it opened out into the big final room, which bottomed out at 130 feet into the basal sandstone.

"There's a lot of breakdown on the floor in that room," Rick said, sketching in a series of blocks at the bottom of the map. "And some smaller stuff—talus. Is that what it's called?"

Sam nodded. "No lateral passages?"

"One or two that don't go anywhere. A lot of crevices. I've checked them all out."

"I wouldn't mind seeing it myself," Sam said, folding up the map and putting it in his jeans pocket. "Anybody else want a piece of pie?"

"I'll just have coffee," Rick said.

"I'll have a bite of yours if you order peach," Libby told Sam.

While they were waiting for the pie the three of them looked out the picture window of the restaurant. San Marcos was the home of a teachers college that Sam had always heard was the greatest party school in the state. The river that ran through the town was spring-fed and clear, choked in places with riverweed and stocked with giant golden carp that someone had once introduced into the river on a whim. Some of the kids from the college were leaping into the river from a rope swing below the restaurant. Others were sunning themselves on the bank, using their textbooks as eye shades, or standing around in groups playing hacky-sack.

Libby took a bite of Sam's pie, as she had promised, and then went up to the jukebox and looked for something she might be able to stand.

It was all wimp rock or Hank Williams, Jr. She put in her money and pushed a button at random and the luck of the draw gave her Air Supply. She moved away from the jukebox a little to dissociate herself from the music, but she did not return to the table. Instead she stood there watching the two men and wondering how much screwier her life was going to get.

229

They were psyching themselves up, as men will, trying to give each other reason to hope that the cave went as deep as their intuition told them it did. She had seen Sam this way before, working a hunch, staying in the field while she waited for him at home, or when he did come home staying up all night with his quad maps and thick maroon-bound geology texts. In the end he would usually run his little theory to ground or see that it was unworkable. There would be an end to it.

With Rick, she knew, there was no end. It was a chronic yearning of some kind, powerful enough to pull her along, powerful enough to make her care. The truth was she wanted to find that passage too, to get beyond that final room, and sort it all out there.

Chapter 24

THE next day Libby had a sudden desire to hear some live music. She had been missing that lately. One night she talked Rick into going with her to a club over on Second Street, a small place with an adjoining patio—set in the remains of a lumberyard—where the band played.

They took a seat at a wobbly spool table under the warm night sky, and Libby stroked her foot against Rick's shin as she listened to the music. It was loud, progressive jazz, with here and there a little rumba or *conjunto* thrown in, performed by pale, drug-wasted musicians who could hardly hold up their instruments with their stringy biceps. But they were good, the music as intelligent and quirky as they were dull.

She found it soothing, but Rick sat there impassively, uncomfortable with the demands of the music. He would not let it enter his system.

"Don't you like it?" she yelled into his ear.

"It's too loud. I can't think."

"You're not supposed to think. You're supposed to listen."

She got a little drunk, just to pester him, while he sat there upright in his chair, holding his damn mineral water. Bats were flying out from under the bins of the old lumberyard and Libby could see them circling above, chasing insects that were drawn to the patio light.

Finally she gave up.

"Let's take a walk," she told him. "I can tell you weren't born to boogie."

They walked out into the street and let the music recede behind them. Even Libby found it peaceful. She held onto Rick's arm as they walked through the downtown streets, mostly vacant except for the raucous preppie circus on Sixth Street. That was where the rich fraternity boys now took their dates, buying them drinks in the fern bars, blackened redfish in the snooty restaurants, and then renting a hot tub to finish out the evening.

They walked all the way down to the State Capitol and went inside, into the hushed rotunda, and Libby stared with droll amusement at the portraits of the governors, and the stalwart statues of Stephen F. Austin and Davy Crockett.

"Texas, our Texas, all hail the mighty state," she began singing softly into Rick's shoulder. She noticed a security guard smiling at her, as if he wanted to join in.

"You want to go to the dive shop with me?" Rick asked.

"Now?"

"Yes."

"What for?"

"There's something I want to look at there. I can take you home first if you want."

"No thanks," she said. "Whither thou goest."

He apologized in the car for spoiling her evening. She saw that he was sincere, that he regretted not being able to hear what she heard in the music, to trust himself enough so that his body could go slack and listen. She forgave him out loud.

"We'll try again," he said. "I'll get psychiatric help."

The little shopping center where the dive shop was located was dark except for the interior lights of the stores, left on to deprive a burglar of the security of the darkness. Rick disconnected the alarm, then opened the door and followed Libby in. They walked past the mannequin, past the compressor that still scared her a little, and into the back office.

Rick opened a locked filing cabinet and sorted through the folders until he pulled out a piece of paper.

"What's that?" Libby asked.

"One of those guys we pulled out of the Well drew some kind of sketch on his slate before he died. This is a Xerox of it."

He set the paper down on the desk where they could both

232

see it. The photocopied marks there were very pale—little spirals and circles with radiating lines.

"Would you say that these look like the coral we found in the Well yesterday?" Rick asked.

"They're so faint," she said. "But yes, they do."

Rick folded up the paper and put it in his shirt pocket. "Let's go see Sam," he said.

The lights were still on inside Sam's house, and through the half-drawn curtains of the living room window Libby could see the milky glow of the television screen. A 727 passed low overhead as they knocked on the door, and the roar of its engines drowned out Sam's surprised words of welcome.

There was a big bowl of popcorn on the coffee table that he had made for himself. She glanced at the television before he turned it off; some World War II movie. The whole scene tore at Libby's heart a little.

"I've got something to show you," Rick said. "Do you still have that piece of coral?"

Sam got it down from the mantelpiece. Libby noticed that he kept it up there with his other rocks, the ones she knew.

Rick took the paper out of his pocket and unfolded it next to the rock.

"Do you see any similarity?" he asked.

"Sure, but what's this?"

"This was on one of those dead guy's slates. He saw this down in that final room."

"It could have been just another chunk like this one," Sam said.

"Then why would he go to the trouble of sketching it? Why wouldn't he just bring it up?"

Sam took a handful of popcorn and sat back in his chair, thinking.

"Doesn't this suggest to you," Rick asked, "that that guy found a way through the sandstone?"

"You're talking about a whopping unconformity," Sam said.

"What's that?" Libby asked.

"That's when you've got new rock lying on top of old rock with nothing in between, no transition. Here, for instance, you have a gap of more than two hundred million years."

"Is that impossible?" she asked.

"No," he said. "It's not impossible. It's thrilling."

Sam went into the kitchen and came back with a bottle of Cranapple juice and three glasses. He poured them each a glass, deep in thought, without bothering to ask if they wanted any.

"You said there was breakdown in that final room," he asked Rick. "What kind of breakdown?"

"Mostly sandstone," Rick said.

"Not limestone from the ceiling?"

"A little bit, but the big stuff is sandstone."

Sam walked across the room on the balls of his feet, putting one foot directly in front of the other like a tightrope walker. That was the way he concentrated, Libby remembered, as if he were trying to creep up on an idea.

"I'm starting to get excited now," he said, putting his glass down on top of the television.

"Some of us would like to know what you're thinking," Libby said.

"Here's what I think. That sandstone had to collapse into something. It didn't just fall into itself. There's got to be some sort of soluble rock directly beneath it."

"Limestone," Rick said.

"Not just any limestone either," Sam said. "If we can believe these fossils we've got a reef under there. A whole paleo reef that nobody knows about!"

Sam sat down and put his hands in his pockets. "Know what reef limestone is famous for?" he said to Rick.

"Caves."

"Absolutely. Jesus Christ. That place could go on forever!"

Libby watched Rick nod, slowly, soberly, already given over to the next step.

"Just because it's there," Libby said, "doesn't mean you can find it."

"Those other guys did," Rick said.

"Yeah, well they're happily dead."

"What about the barricade?" Sam said.

"I can remove the barricade."

"I bet I can find a passage," Sam said. "Will you take me down to that final room?"

Rick shook his head. "That's serious cave diving."

"You can teach me," Sam said.

Libby took a handful of Sam's popcorn and sat down in his ratty easy chair, watching them both warily, feeling she should disapprove of the whole scene but already sensing it had gone too far. She was excited too, she could feel herself being swept along, heedless of all the emotional logistics.

"Let me think about it," Rick finally said, after a long moment.

They left Sam alone. Libby knew he would not sleep that night. She was glad for him, pleased that his attention was centered on something besides her. But Rick's thoughtful silence on the drive home was troubling. It reminded her of the way Hudson would get before a deal was about to happen: clench-jawed and hostile, waiting for his chance to play cops and robbers.

He pulled into her driveway and turned off the ignition.

"I'd rather stay by myself tonight," she said.

Rick turned to her and reached across the gap between the seats to kiss her.

"You've got a lot on your mind," she said.

"Including you."

"Are you going to take Sam down in there?"

"I could use him."

"I'd be coming along in that case."

"I know that."

She got out of the door and walked around to the driver's window and kissed him again. She wanted him to come in, but she just didn't feel that she could take any comfort from him that night. He was too silent and distant.

She went into her house and put a Boz Scaggs record on the turntable—one of the good ones, before he went disco—and then undressed and lay in bed, remembering back to the old days when she and Sam used to go to sleep every night listening to music.

Impulsively she reached for the phone and dialed Sam's number. He answered on the first ring.

"I'm not sure why I'm calling," she said.

"Don't get nervous and hang up."

"I wouldn't do that. Do you really think there's a passage?"

"Yes."

"It's dangerous to go that far back."

"Maybe a little."

"I'm going too," she said, and in the silence that followed she felt that some crucial decision was being made. They were entering a place that was not safe, a place without light or air or warmth. Would he let them be together there, at risk?

"Sam?" she pressed.

"I want you to go," he said.

When she hung up she felt scattered, envious of Sam and Rick and their masculine focus. But she was not immune to the excitement about the Well. When she closed her eyes now she had a sensation of spinning, and then of vectoring in toward the alluring darkness. She snapped her eyes open, not knowing whether she was afraid or exhilarated. The music began to calm her. She closed her eyes again, listening to the final track of the record and wishing she could fall asleep before it was over.

Chapter 25

"THERE are a few things I don't like about it," Gary said. "One, we put that barricade there for a reason."

"We wouldn't have put it there in the first place if we'd known what we know now," Rick said.

"Maybe not." Gary was silent for a moment as he inserted a length of optical tubing through the open neck of a scuba tank and peered inside.

"Corrosion city," he said. "No sticker for this guy."

Rick watched as Gary unscrewed the tank from the vise and laid it on the floor.

"So what's your point?" Rick said.

"I don't know. Maybe that it's bad karma or something to take it down. Now you've got me sounding irrational."

Gary hoisted another tank up onto the counter and began to unscrew the valve. Through the open door Rick kept an eye on the customers in the shop's showroom. A high school boy that Rick had recently certified was there with his mother, picking out his graduation present while she looked on disapprovingly.

"And I'm not thrilled with taking Sam and Libby that far back," Gary went on. "They're still novices."

"I want you to help me train them."

"Why don't just you and I go?"

"Because Sam's the one who knows what to look for."

"Do you mind if I ask you something?" Gary said.

"What?"

"Isn't this whole thing a little messy? I mean with the inter-personal relationships and whatnot."

"I'm not thinking about the interpersonal relationships," Rick said. "I'm thinking about the Well."

"Are you still interested?" Rick asked Sam over the phone.

"Sure," Sam said.

"We'll need about three or four full days to train you. Libby says weekends are best for her."

"Fine."

"When I think you two are ready I'll take down the barricade. Then we'll see what we can find." Rick hesitated for a beat. "You have to realize how serious this is. If we remove that barricade we'll be going very deep and very far back. We can't make many mistakes.

"And," Rick added, "we all have to be on the same team."

"Don't worry," Sam said. "I'm on the team."

Rick and Gary supplied all the equipment from the shop, gear they had worked on personally and knew was in good shape. On Saturday morning the four of them unloaded it all from Rick's van and laid it on the bank.

"We're going to be using doubles all the time," Rick said, looking down at the yoked tanks, which were gunmetal gray, without a spot of paint or any kind of decoration. "Even when we're just practicing. We need to get used to them."

Libby had never worn a pair of doubles before. When Rick lifted them onto her back she had to lean forward just to keep them from toppling her backward. On dry land their weight and bulk unnerved her, but she knew that when she was underwater she would not mind them so much, and that there would come a time when she would be grateful for the extra air they provided.

With the tanks on her back, and the added burden of two backup lights in addition to her primary, she saw how casual her dives into the Well had been thus far. They seemed trifling, recreational. Now, whatever her misgivings, she felt in touch

238

with the Well's deeper power. She could feel the vacuum pull of that hollow rock as if it actually led somewhere, as if deep in the aquifer there was some willful presence that was drawing them in.

They made their first dive just to get the feel of the additional equipment and to give Sam a chance to practice some of the techniques that Libby had already mastered. She hovered with Gary in the center of the first chamber and watched as Rick showed Sam how to flywalk on the ceiling of the corridor that led to the barricade.

Afterward they waited on the surface for their bodies to purge themselves of the excess nitrogen they had accumulated during the first dive. Rick was always careful about surface intervals, never cutting them short. He had seen divers get the bends without doing anything wrong on dives where the tables told them there was no need to decompress. Against all expectations the nitrogen had come out of solution in their bodies, fizzing and bubbling like carbonated water and blocking the flow of blood. So it was better to be cautious. It was his responsibility, his cave. His people.

He gave them some decompression problems with which to occupy themselves while they waited to go in again. Libby sat up against a tree and Sam sat on the hood of his car, both of them dutifully working the problems. While they were occupied with that, Rick and Gary taped aluminum foil to the insides of their masks.

"What's that all about?" Sam asked, looking up from his notebook.

"You're gonna love this part," Gary said.

At the edge of the Well Libby pulled the foil-lined mask over her face and felt herself swallowed by the perfect darkness. She quickly pulled it up again and looked at Gary, and then down into the water, where Rick was already leading Sam out of the opening flue and into the first corridor.

"You don't like it?" Gary said.

"Should I?"

"You need to get used to it. That's what you see when the lights go out."

She slipped the mask over her face again, put the regulator in her mouth, and let Gary hold her hand and take her into the water. It was the oddest sensation, drifting downward in the blackness. She had the sudden awareness that this was the way the cave was meant to be experienced, that the play of a flashlight beam down here was such a transitory phenomenon it could not even be measured against the eternal darkness it disrupted. Here we are, Libby thought, with our flashlight batteries and our bottles of air, little brief specks of life in the great void.

Gary maneuvered her next to Sam, as he had told her he would do. They were to practice buddy breathing, to simulate an emergency in which their lights had failed and one of them had run out of air.

Libby felt along Sam's chest for his tank strap and then closed her fist around it as she had been told. She felt Sam doing the same. Then he took his extra regulator—his octopus—and tapped it against the glass of her mask. She removed the regulator from her mouth and replaced it with the one he offered. Floating there with him, holding him, breathing the air from his tank, she felt united with her husband in the dark wellspring of the cave.

Rick shone his light on them. They looked odd in their sealed masks, like troglodytic creatures that had never grown eyes. He watched how they clung to one another, sharing their air and circling aimlessly in the chamber. They seemed so helpless, so in need of him, and yet so complete on their own. Watching them, he felt like an intruder who had stumbled onto some private and unfathomable ritual.

The rest of the week Libby sat behind her desk, hardly aware of where she was. Her working life seemed so mild and inconsequential she could barely register it. She kept daydreaming about the Well, imagining the moment when they would swim beyond the barricade.

Bancock staggered in from the sales floor carrying a box of

books. He heaved them onto the packing table.

"What's that?" Libby asked.

"*Tristes Tropiques*. Water damage."

"Why don't you stash them for a while? You need to detag those *Soul on Ice*s first."

"You're really into giving orders these days," Bancock said, sitting on the packing table and picking up the newspaper. "It's all that macho cave diving.

"Listen to this weirdness," he said, and proceeded to read her an article from the paper about a man in Grand Rapids who had a special fondness for a granite boulder in one of the city parks. He used to spend hours daydreaming there when he was a boy. He proposed to his wife there. Last week he had died of a heart attack while driving and his car had crossed the interstate median, plunged down an embankment and landed on top of the boulder.

"A coincidence?" Bancock said in a Boris Karloff accent. "Perhaps. Perhaps not."

"*Soul on Ice*," Libby reminded him.

But before Bancock had made it halfway through the stack of books he had fallen asleep. He tended to do that now during the long afternoons. Despite his woeful assessment of his charms he had found a girl friend, a law student, and they stayed up together watching the late-night simulcasts.

Libby stood up and unplugged the heating iron Bancock still held in his hand. She did not want him to burn himself. Then she sat down again behind her desk and tried to concentrate on her work.

On Saturday they made a decompression dive, deliberately staying down long enough so that they had to surface in stages, giving their bodies the time they needed to absorb the nitrogen that had formed in their bloodstreams under pressure. Rick was meticulous about the stops, and with him there, monitoring things, she was not afraid of the bends.

That was their last training dive, and when they drove away from the Well that evening Rick left it unsaid that she and Sam had passed, that they were part of the team.

"What happens now?" she said to Rick in bed that night.

"We cut down the barricade," he said. "After that we go into the final room and let Sam have a look around."

"Am I good enough to go down that far now?" she asked him.

"Yes," he said, turning to her. "Now you're an expert."

She thought perhaps it was a dream. The acetylene torch flamed with a metallic brilliance as the unquenchable fire cut through the bars. She was with Sam and Gary, holding herself by her fingertips off the floor of the cave, and looking over Rick's shoulder as he worked. The glow from the torch made an aura around his body, and as he worked within that circle of white light it seemed that he had little to do with the rest of them, little to do with her. She saw the grate slowly fall backward when he cut the last support, and when it was down it seemed as if the water flowed faster and colder from the dark aquifer.

Chapter 26

THE dive plan Rick had worked out called for them to make a quick trip down to the final room, staying no longer than ten minutes to avoid having to decompress on the way up. If they found something in that time, fine. If not, they would keep diving for as long as it took.

Sam felt confident. He had a certain amount of anxiety, but it was a reasonable anxiety concerning his skills. He was not afraid, and he had been diving enough with Libby by now to know that he did not need to be afraid for her.

He was suited up before the rest of them, and while he waited for them to be ready he sorted through the alluvium in the creek with the point of his foot. He found a piece of worked flint, and bent over carefully with the heavy doubles on his back to pick it up.

"Here," he said, showing it to Libby.

"What's this?"

"Part of a scraper. For working hides."

Libby fingered its serrated edges and set the fleshy part of her thumb into the rock's smooth curve. She liked the way it fit her hand.

"Are we ready?" Rick asked.

"Ready Freddy," Gary said.

Rick pulled some line from his reel and tied it around the trunk of a cedar, then backed up, letting out line, and stepped into the opening of the Well. Sam followed him, so familiar by now with this part of the cave that he hardly noticed it as they descended. He took a moment to check the rate of his breathing: it was slow and even.

The grate lay on its side at the mouth of the constriction. Rick stopped there, turning to make sure that everyone was ready, and then sailed through. Sam followed, facing the ceiling and pulling himself along while the cold flowing water entered his wetsuit at the neck and rippled along his spine. The ceiling was filled with hundreds of circular depressions, the beginnings of domes that might someday dissolve out all the way to the surface.

The passage was narrow for about thirty feet and then it widened to a space about the size of his living room. They stopped there again to take stock. Sam looked back at Libby. She floated next to Gary, one hand touching the line. The beams of their lights crossed the room, and when one passed in front of her face he could see the color in her eyes. She nodded at him: *Here we are*.

Sam looked at his depth gauge. It showed eighty-five feet, only five feet deeper than they had been at the constriction. But the next passage took them down, and he felt the depth now. It made him a little hazy and concerned. Just a little. He was very aware of how dependent he was on the line and the air he carried on his back. He worried about Libby, and turned to look at her, but she seemed to be cruising along without concern and he felt better.

The passage ended like a chute in the final room. It was a large room, the largest yet. He followed Rick to the center and then down twenty feet to the breakdown boulders that made up the floor. He shone his light this way and that, feeling a little absent, almost forgetting why he had come. It seemed to him they had been gone a long, long time, but when he looked at his bottom timer he saw it had only been five minutes. He took a few deep breaths and studiously reeled his mind back in. Above him Libby floated in the emptiness of the cavern. He felt such warmth for her, such regret at losing her, that he could hardly bear it. But he turned his face to the rock at his feet, searching for the passage.

Rick waved him over and made the okay sign to him. He

looked concerned. Sam returned it and nodded. In slow motion Rick pointed to a pile of limestone talus that had fallen down one of the walls. It was smaller than the sandstone breakdown, about the size of bricks, and it was all concentrated in one corner of the room.

Sam shone his light along the wall against which the rocks had fallen. He could see no hint of the reef, but he guessed it was there, deeper, beneath the debris.

While Sam studied the cave wall Libby hung by herself in the center of the room, one hand on the line. Sam and Rick and Gary were perhaps ten feet below her, but she felt as if she were watching them from a great distance. Whenever she thought about how deep they were, how far removed from the opening shaft of the cave, she almost trembled with concern. It seemed hopeless to think they could ever return. But at the same moment she was entranced with the alien place where they had secreted themselves. Not even an astronaut on the moon, she thought, would feel so wonderfully strange.

A beam of light skittered across the wall in front of her eyes. That was Rick's signal, telling them it was time to go. Libby watched the three of them soaring upward toward her, as slow and as silent as fish. She let Gary take the lead, and then she followed him, kicking upward to find the narrow chute that led back to the surface.

"Did anybody have any problems in there?" Rick asked as they were laying their equipment on the riverbank. "Anybody get the creeps?" He looked at his tables and made a few calculations on a slate.

"We need about a three-hour surface interval if we want to get back into the water today," he said. "I'll go into San Marcos and get the tanks filled and bring back some chicken or something."

Sam volunteered to go along. Libby stayed behind with Gary, who spread a towel on the bank, pulled off his wetsuit top, and lay down with his deep chest exposed to the sun.

Libby left her wetsuit on and used its buoyancy to float without effort above the entrance to the Well. She looked up at the sky, at the distant cirrus clouds, and felt a corresponding vastness below her.

"Have you ever been to the Great Salt Lake?" she asked Gary.

"Never have," he said, sitting up on the bank, beads of sweat already rolling down his chest.

"Sam and I drove through there on our honeymoon. We lay in the water like this, hardly moving."

After a while she came out of the water, took off her wetsuit, and sat next to him on the bank in her bathing suit.

"Are you having fun?" he asked her.

"I suppose so. Fun seems like hardly the word for it."

Gary squinted into the sun. "That's the word I like to use," he said.

"What's your opinion?" she asked. "Are we going to find a way through?"

"Probably so."

"How can you tell?"

"I don't know. I trust Rick's instinct. I trust Sam's judgment too."

Libby studied Gary's face, moved by his uncomplicated, reliable presence. Rick had told her earlier that he had wanted Gary along to "anchor" the team, and she understood now that he meant the word almost literally. Whenever she happened to glance at him underwater she felt a little more secure, a little more in touch with the world that waited for them on the surface. Without him she imagined that their peculiar threesome might just drift away into the darkness.

They knew Rick at the dive shop in San Marcos where they stopped to fill the tanks. Employees came out of the back room to shake his hand and the manager refused to charge him for the air.

"You seem to be famous," Sam said as they were driving off.

A tired expression came over Rick's face.

"You might as well come out and say it," Sam said.

"What?"

"Aw shucks."

"Chicken all right?" Rick said, ignoring him and pulling into the drive-in window of a fried chicken place.

"Whatever," Sam said.

"Let me ask you something," Rick said, as they were driving back with the warm box of chicken sitting on the console between them. "Do you think Libby's got her eye on the ball?"

"What do you mean?"

"I don't want there to be any emotional static down there. Cave diving is stressful enough without all these vibes. I was just asking you about it because I think you know her better."

"That's thoughtful of you."

"Bullshit," Rick said.

"She'll do all right," Sam answered, after giving it some genuine thought.

"Good," Rick said. "That's one thing we don't have to talk about anymore."

Rick took a piece of chicken out of the box and ate it while he drove. It seemed to Sam that Rick was eating only for nourishment, for protein. He was driven by the thoughtless, indiscriminate hunger of a predator. But Sam admired that; he was beginning to share in that singlemindedness himself.

Were they, after all, friends? He told himself it was better to think otherwise. They were just elements, bound together by some powerful valence, some need. But he could feel the comradely bond between them, an affection grounded in respect and further secured in some strange way by the antagonism they felt toward each other.

When Rick and Sam returned they ate their lunch at one of the dilapidated picnic tables and then began to suit up again. Libby donned her equipment with an efficiency and eagerness that she welcomed because it told her she was not afraid. The familiar objects—her mask, molded through use to the contours of her face; her fins; even the impersonal knife she strapped to her calf—gave her comfort, as if they were not inanimate things but knew and understood their duty to support her in the alien environment.

When Rick lifted the heavy doubles onto her back, though,

she felt only their weight. They were inelegant, intrusive, the final proof that none of them belonged down there.

When they reached the final room the four of them congregated on the broken floor, looking at one another, checking in. It seemed very comical to Libby, as if none of them knew what to do with themselves. Then Sam pointed to himself and then to the wall where the talus was concentrated. He made a hand signal: *stay,* and then swam over there and began to probe through the debris.

The three of them shone their lights at the wall, spotlighting the working area. *Oh, I get it,* thought Libby. *He's looking for the reef.* She saw him move one rock at a time very carefully. She heard a few pieces dislodge themselves from above him, tumbling down the slope, and she was worried for a moment but it looked like the pile was stable. It was as if he was tinkering with the bottom row of a display of soup cans in a grocery store. It was humorous, but she could sense the danger too, just a vague little thrill.

That is my husband, she thought. She set her hand on Rick's forearm, for support, for contact, for whatever. He turned her head to face him. *Okay?* he asked with his hand. She returned the gesture but she kept her hand on his arm. He seemed very strange to her, very powerful, his diving gear like some primitive, shamanistic raiment. And yet he held back patiently while Sam worked through the broken rock, looking for the passage to the reef. In that moment Rick seemed helpless to her, useless.

Sam turned and wiggled his light in front of their faceplates. Then he pointed to Rick. Rick swam over and Sam showed him something. He came back and Gary went, then he came back nodding and pointed to Libby. It was her turn. She swam over to where Sam was waiting. She thought she heard him talking. *Look, Libby. Look here.*

She followed his pointing finger. Yes, there it was. The reef. It was whiter than the sandstone and conglomerate above it, pure and porous, crowded with tiny fossils whose riotous colors in life she could almost see in the bleached rock. She nodded her head. *Yes. Yes.*

• • •

"We've found the reef," Sam said, on the surface. "Now we have to dig the rock out of the passage."

"How do we do that without the rest of the talus falling in on us?" Rick asked.

"We'll start at the top and take down the whole slope. Just stack it over on the other side of the room. Then we'll dig till we find the opening."

"This sounds like a job for a steam shovel," Libby said.

"We can do it," Rick said. "It may take a few trips."

It took another weekend's worth of diving, with the four of them going down in teams: Sam and Rick, then Libby and Gary. They ferried each individual rock over to the other side of the room and laid it with the others in a neat, stable pattern on the floor. At first the task looked daunting to Libby, but she enjoyed it—taking the topmost rock off the pile and flitting across the room like a bird gathering material for a nest. And she enjoyed the silent working partnership with Gary, who was so stolid and reliable and with whom she felt safe.

It took a total of only four shifts for the pile to be reduced down to the base of the conglomerate where the contact with the reef lay. When Sam and Rick went down for the third time they could see the reef limestone exposed a foot deep along one wall. Rick felt they were getting close. He knelt down and began lifting the big pieces of talus and handing them to Sam, who swam them over to the other side of the room to be discarded. It was hard work, and the increased air consumption it demanded cut into their bottom time. Rick was worried that he would have to call the dive before they broke through. He knew they were very close.

He grabbed a piece of thick, flat rock the size of a dinner platter, and as he worked to dislodge it he could feel movement beneath it, an upwelling pressure. When he finally moved the rock a burst of water hit him in the face with the force of a fire hose, knocking off his mask and sending it high into the room.

Rick backed off from the column of water, waving with his hands for the mask. *I'm all right*, he told himself. *I'm breathing.* He kept his eyes open. He inhaled and exhaled, letting the process calm him. He saw Sam's blurry form swimming in the cave and then coming back to him and handing him the mask.

249

Rick put it on and cleared it, and then looked down at the ferocious rush of water that came from the passage they had opened. There it was. The thing it seemed he had been searching for his whole life: the way in, the way back, the way beyond. He offered Sam his hand over the column of turbulent water.

Chapter 27

THEY took a week off. Rick knew this was the prudent thing to do. He had to put on the brakes a little and work out the dive plan carefully, without regard to the urgency he felt to explore the passage they had opened. He owed it to them to be cool and disciplined.

Rick kept an eye on the wavering, inconclusive weather, the late afternoon cloud banks that left behind them only more sodden heat. He would not have minded a good rain higher up in the watershed, to power the flow in the Well so that it would sweep itself clean of silt.

Libby came over and cooked for the two of them one evening while Rick sat on the floor of his apartment, taking apart the diving lights and inspecting the Nicad batteries inside them. On the wall was a diagram of the Well he had drawn on posterboard, and pinned next to that were a series of decompression calculations.

"This place looks like command central," Libby joked, opening a cabinet. "Where do you keep your spices?"

"In the salt and pepper shakers," he said.

Libby looked over her shoulder at him with a sarcastic smile. "Who needs chicken tarragon anyway?" she said.

While dinner was cooking she sat on the couch and leafed through one of Rick's back issues of *Skin Diver*.

"What are you reading?" he asked her.

"An article about how to take better pictures of nudibranches." She put the magazine down and walked outside onto his ter-

251

race. The sky was overcast above the park, and there was the rumble of thunder, muted and distant.

Rick finished reassembling his light and went outside to join her.

"We'll be doing decompression dives from now on, won't we?" she asked him, still looking out over the park.

"Yes," Rick said. "Does that make you nervous?"

"A little bit."

"I wouldn't let you go if I didn't think you were capable of it. Sam too."

"But there's only so deep we can go, right? We're never going to get to the end of it."

"Right."

"So what's the point?"

"The point is to go as far as you can."

Libby sat down in the deck chair and folded her arms. Rick leaned back against the railing, facing her.

"You don't have to stay out here with me," she said. "Go back inside to HQ. Keep an eye on the chicken."

"If you're nervous you shouldn't go," he said.

"That's not it. I want to go. I want to be there with you."

Rick went inside. He took down a tackle box filled with O-rings and spare parts and sorted through the trays, looking for a spare bulb for one of the little Tekna lights.

"Here's the thing," Libby said softly, appearing behind him and slipping her arms around his waist. "I want you to love me."

"I do."

"I want you to love me more than you seem to."

Rick turned to hold her. She pressed her lips against the hollow of his throat and then turned her head aside. With her ear against his chest she heard his breathing, so even, so measured, as if even here he had to ration his air.

Powell had just returned from one of his many junkets and was in high enough spirits to be actually working. Sam found him in his office, gazing down through a viewer at a 3–D quad map of the Solitario.

"All I see is two dimensions," Powell said.

252

"Keep shifting it around," Sam said. "It'll leap up."

"There we go."

The Solitario was an immense lacolith in the Trans-Pecos. From the air it resembled a circular maze or the ruins of an immense ziggurat. The survey was scheduled to go there for two weeks later in the summer.

"I've got a line on some interesting geology," Sam said to Powell.

"Really? Where?"

"Jacob's Well. I thought it might be useful for me to do a little preliminary research there for the survey."

"In other words you want me to postpone your Monahans report."

"That wouldn't hurt," Sam said. He began to explain about the unconformity, but as soon as he began throwing out terms he noticed Powell's eyes glazing over.

"Tell me just one thing," Powell said, interrupting him. "Is it a special place?"

"It's a special place," Sam said.

"Then no sweat."

Sam went back to his office, cleared his desk of the Monahans notes, and began to sketch a cross-section of the Well, letting his imagination guide him in depicting what lay beyond the passage they had opened.

Janet came into his office and stood with her back against the opened door. She was holding a huge plastic tumbler of iced tea.

"We found the passage, Janet," Sam said, looking over his shoulder at her. She walked over to him and looked down at the sketch, chewing thoughtfully on her ice.

"So that's where you and Libby are headed," she said, picking up the sketch and sitting down on the drafting stool.

"I think you're going to dangerous lengths here," she said. "And if I were a two-bit psychologist I'd tell you why."

"It's not just Libby," Sam said.

"Maybe not," Janet answered. "Would you like to hear my announcement?"

"Yes."

"I'm leaving the survey after the Solitario. I'm going full time with the guide business."

"That's great," Sam said. "Congratulations."

"I'm taking our friend Governor Phil down to the Chiapas rain forest to see a horned guan, so I'll sort of be the bird guide to the stars."

"You can't miss."

"That's sweet of you to say. Mr. Duckett thinks it's a good idea too."

"I thought you were keeping yourself at arm's length from that."

"I'm not like you, Sam. I'm grateful for any information I can get. Besides, Clifford's an upright citizen. It's just that every once in a while he turns into Mr. Duckett. I can live with that."

Janet took a sip of her iced tea.

"If I may vent a little spleen?" she said.

"Go ahead."

"He's got a better grip on reality than you have. And he's better-looking, in my opinion."

Sam smiled at her and put his feet up on his desk, popping the cap on and off a felt-tip pen.

"How's Fluffy?" he asked.

"Fluffy's fine. He got out one day and wandered around the neighborhood. You'll never guess who found him."

"Mr. Duckett."

Janet nodded. "He told us to look under a crape myrtle two houses down."

She turned her attention back to the sketch of the Well.

"When does the expedition shove off again?" she asked.

"This weekend."

"I'd hate like hell for you to die in there, Sam," she said. "Having helped save your life in the Abuelos."

He saw her face clear suddenly of irony. She walked over to him and drew him up from his chair. Then she dipped her finger into the iced tea and touched him at the forehead and at the base of the skull.

"*Por los espíritus de luz,*" she whispered, and kissed him on the lips.

Chapter 28

SAM'S alarm went off before dawn, jerking him out of sleep but not fully into consciousness. He dutifully got out of bed and stepped into the shower, but the water rushing over his head seemed only to deepen his trance, to beat down whatever clear thoughts were rising in his mind. He was going somewhere, he remembered dully. Where?

As he was drying himself off he became slowly aware. Jacob's Well. The knowledge came to him as a burden. He recognized this anxiety and wondered if it was fear.

He was to meet the rest of them at the dive shop, where they would load the equipment in Rick's van and set out for the Well. Rick wanted to get there as early as possible in order to set the safety tanks at the decompression stops and still have a full day's diving. He didn't want to waste a minute of potential bottom time. He had even talked them into camping at the site that night, so that they could continue the dives the next day without driving back and forth to Austin.

Sam took down his sleeping bag from the top of the closet, stuffed a change of clothes into a small backpack, and threw all his gear into the trunk of his car. When he arrived at the dive shop he saw Rick's van parked in front, next to Gary's car. A thick band of cloud, flushed with morning light, framed the roof of the shopping center.

The doors of the van were open and when Sam looked inside he saw Rick there, lashing tanks to the upright racks he had built on either side of the wheel wells. He was wearing a T-shirt and corduroy shorts and thick braided Mexican sandals through which his feet showed, as gnarled and strong as tree roots.

"Morning," Rick said. "Libby and Gary are inside. There's coffee."

"You need any help here?"

"In a minute. When we load the tanks."

Sam went inside. Gary was at the compressor, filling tanks. There was a stack of doubles, already full, on the floor of the shop.

"Journey to the center of the earth," he said cheerfully, when he saw Sam.

"You look bleary," Libby said, walking in from the office. She handed him a cup of coffee in a Styrofoam cup. "What happened to your early-rising skills?"

She looked wonderful to him. Her hair was not quite dry from the shower, but it was full and as soft as that light-saturated cloud above them. There was a sleepy radiance about her that cut through the dolorous early morning air and made his heart sink.

Sam transferred his equipment into the van and then the four of them loaded the tanks and the rest of the dive gear.

They drove out the interstate, with Libby sitting up front with Rick and Gary and Sam behind. Sam looked out the window, sipping his coffee and feeling his spirits lift as the morning light hit the escarpment. It was hardly more than an upfaulted terrace, but it was a dramatic sight for such mild country, and he could feel the subtle power of the landscape. There were scissortails on the high wires and meadowlarks picking through the grass at the side of the highway.

Rick went over the dive plan as he drove. "These are going to be decompression dives from now on," he said. "They're a little more complicated but we're going to play it very safe. I've worked it out so we're way within the tables. We'll have decompression stops at thirty feet and ten feet. We'll put tanks there, just to be sure.

"Sam and I will go in first. We'll do the actual penetration. Gary and Libby will stay in the big room for backup."

"I'd like to have a safety tank there too," Gary said. "With an octopus."

Rick nodded.

"When do Gary and I get to go in?" Libby asked.

"After we've checked it out and gotten some idea of where it goes. Some of those passages may be too tight for four people."

Rick turned off the interstate and onto a farm-to-market road that led up into the escarpment. Sam watched as the marly limestone on the slopes gave way to the harder, more resistant rock farther up.

"One more thing," Rick said. "Anybody can call this dive at any time. If you're uneasy, if you don't think you're ready, let me know. We'll do it some other time."

Sam listened to Rick's textbook caution, not believing it. They were deeper than that now, too far in.

As soon as they got to the Well, Rick and Gary suited up and ran the line down all the way to the big room, tying it off on one of the big sandstone boulders so that it would be a permanent reference point. They set a tank down there as well, near the opened passageway where the water continued to flood forth with great velocity, and then they swam back up toward the surface and tied off the other safety tanks.

After that dive they needed a two-hour surface interval before they could go in again, so it was nearly noon by the time the four of them entered the Well.

Libby was used to the way her mind dimmed when they reached the floor of the big room. Because the sensation no longer took her by surprise, she felt comfortable with it. She took it into account.

Rick tied his reel line onto the permanent line he and Gary had set earlier, and then the four of them gathered together and compared pressure gauges. The plan called for him and Sam to take ten minutes exploring the passage. At the end of that time they would come up, and all of them would ascend, two by two, to the first decompression stop. If they were overdue Gary would pull twice on the line. Two answering pulls meant that they were all right and on their way. Four meant that they were in trouble.

Rick went in first. The passage was about three feet wide. It went straight down, perhaps ten feet. The pressure of the water against him was intense and he had to force his way down with strong kicks that caused the uprushing water to fill with silt. Libby held onto the permanent line as Rick's fins disappeared into the hole.

It was a good flue except for the resistance. It kept its width. Rick held the reel and the light with one hand and used the other to grab handholds to pull his body down against the flow. He felt the familiar sensation of his intelligence narrowing itself down, settling on one task.

Sam followed him, setting his face directly into the current so that the water could not have an angle to pull off his mask. He kicked but seemed to get nowhere, so he pulled himself down as well as he could, knowing that if he let go of his grip he would be shot back up through the flue. He saw Rick's light below him, and soon he had dropped out of the chimney and into a low hemispherical room where the strength of the water was diluted. Rick made the okay sign. Sam returned it, knowing he was a little narked. He looked up the passage he had just descended. He saw Gary's light up there, and the silhouette of Libby's face in the beam. She had never seemed so far away. It was as if she were on a star looking down at him.

Sam and Rick shone their lights in a circle around the room. There appeared to be two passages leading out of it, both of them good-sized. Rick looked at his compass and took an azimuth on each of them. One ran due south, the other a few degrees shy of northeast.

Rick decided they would try the south tunnel first. He indicated this to Sam, who, after a lag, nodded his head. Rick swam off with the reel, looking behind him to make sure that Sam followed and that he had his hand on the line. He seemed to be in good shape, only a little fuzzy. Rick sensed that Sam's mind would hold up against the depth, that it was as resistant to the effects of narcosis as the insoluble sandstone above them was resistant to the chemical assaults of the water. In that sense Sam's mind was better than his own; it made up for his lack of experience.

Rick shone his light along the ceiling, which was peaked slightly and marked by a good joint trend. The passage was wide and

258

easy, but after twenty feet or so it began to narrow, and Rick moved to the ceiling to keep from stirring up silt. Sam did the same behind him, automatically, pressing his faceplate against the fossilized rock, working his fingers along the pocked coral surface.

The passage was horizontal. That was good. It ran straight at about 140 feet and gave their heads time to get used to the depth. Sam knew if he dropped another ten or fifteen feet he would start getting silly and careless, but for now he was all right.

After about a hundred feet into the passage it narrowed considerably. They turned themselves around, their stomachs to the floor, their tanks banging against the ceiling. Sam shone his light ahead of him at Rick's waving fins, wondering how much tighter he would let things get before he turned around. Rick stopped and waved Sam up with his light. There was a little bulbous pocket at the end of the passage where they could both fit, and they inspected it with their lights. Sam found a few cracks, no wider than a drainpipe, where the water came in, but there was no way to get farther. Rick looked at him, and then shrugged. Sam took his index finger and moved it across his throat: *dead end*.

Rick nodded and gestured for Sam to precede him. He did so, shining his beam into the tight corridor through which they had come and which seemed to him now an endless black tube, the landscape of a nightmare. He swam forward, bumping along in the tight passage, while Rick reeled up the line behind him.

Suddenly he found that he was stuck, that something was holding him back. Instinctively, before he even checked to see what the problem was, he jerked forward, causing an explosion of air bubbles in the cramped space. Sam saw what had happened. His octopus regulator had become jammed in a crevice and had begun to free flow when he tried to dislodge it. He understood the problem and was not afraid, but as he tried to reach back and close the valve that fed air into that unit he became tangled in the line and it seemed that he could not move in any direction. The line pulled against him, like a spider web drawing in a victim, and the more he moved against it the more he felt himself ensnared.

He was close to panic. He looked ahead, at the dark endless tunnel before him that led out but through which he could not progress. In the beam of his light he saw something odd, a pale white creature about eight inches long with a shovel nose and two little useless pinpricks for eyes. It was resting on four legs, drawing in water through its external fern-shaped gills.

The creature was very calm, so pale and unmarked it looked unborn. Somehow its presence calmed Sam too. It seemed at home here. He watched its gills move and timed his breathing to that of the creature's and lay as still as he could. Soon Rick swam up to him and shut off the valve and then freed him from the rope. Sam felt two tugs from Gary. Time was up. He returned them, made the okay sign to Rick, and they swam on. Sam reached the hole in the ceiling that led up to Libby and Gary and entered it, letting the water propel him upward. When he rose out of the passage into the big room where they waited he felt as safe and relieved as if he were already on the surface.

Chapter 29

THEY made their decompression stops on schedule. As they hung in silence, within sight of the sky above them, Libby kept looking at Sam. She did not know what had gone wrong down there, but she could read the fear in his eyes. It was a residual presence, like the compressed nitrogen that they were purging from their blood, but it alarmed her. Once or twice she reached out, just to touch him, and he made the okay sign back to her.

"He got tangled up in the line," Rick explained when they surfaced. "He's all right."

"Are you?" Libby asked.

"I'm fine," Sam said, unbuckling his tanks and slinging them onto the bank. "I'm a little shaky but I'm fine."

"You didn't panic. That's the important thing," Rick said.

"I did too panic."

"Not enough to count."

"Great," Sam said, "I get to keep my self-respect."

"What's it look like down there?" Gary asked.

Rick took a slate from his wetsuit pocket and began drawing a sketch. "It forks at the bottom of this passage," he said. "We went this direction. It was a good level passage but it pinched out about a hundred and fifty feet back, so we can rule it out. Tomorrow we'll go the other direction. That's the way in for sure."

Libby watched Sam as he pulled off his wetsuit top. He was making a point of avoiding her eyes. He tossed the wetsuit onto

261

the roof of the van to dry and walked over to one of the picnic tables, taking a seat in the sun.

Libby followed him, leaving Rick and Gary to confer over the sketch. She took a seat next to Sam on the bench.

"I want to have a serious talk," she said.

"Not me."

"You almost died down there."

"I didn't almost die, Libby. It was just a glitch. Rick was right behind me."

Libby reached down and unstrapped the knife and its plastic sheath from her calf. She laid it on the picnic table, then unzipped her wetsuit, feeling the harsh late-afternoon heat settle on her shoulders like a protective cocoon.

Despite herself she felt her lower lip trembling.

"It really frightened me," she said.

"It frightened me too," he said, pouring water out of his wetsuit boot and avoiding her eyes. "But nobody ever said it was supposed to be safe."

They drove to San Marcos for dinner. Some sort of festival was going on there, with a river pageant and crafts booths and a *menudo* cook-off. The four of them bought *chimichangas* and *fajitas* from an Optimists Club booth and sat on the banks of the river, watching the floats drift by as they ate. The floats were manned mostly by students from the college, wasted from too much beer and sun, and their papier-mâché armadillos and oversized replicas of Budweiser and Lone Star cans were ripped and water-damaged.

There seemed to be no theme to the parade. It had a spontaneous, generic aspect, an all-purpose gesture of appeasement to the river.

As they were walking back to the van, they passed a high plywood corral with a sign that said it was the locale of the eighteenth annual Jaycees Rattlesnake Roundup. Inside the corral were hundreds of rattlesnakes woven into a thick undulating braid.

"That's primal as shit," Gary said.

262

The Jaycees were picking up the snakes behind their heads with tongs and stretching them out on a chopping block where they decapitated them with a machete. After that they hung them from a clothesline, gutted them, and ripped the skins from their bodies, leaving a ghostly, larval thing that still writhed and twisted.

Sam looked away, horrified and shamed, remembering the blacktail in the Abuelos and the ungraspable compact that still seemed to linger between him and the snake. He could feel the crawling sensation in the tips of his fingers. He was reassured to have it there, to feel the presence again. In some hazy, disquieting way he knew himself to be on course.

They were back at their campsite by dusk. Sam found a level spot of terrain and set down his foam pad and sleeping bag. Gary did the same farther downstream. He was wearing a pair of earphones and had a Walkman clipped to the elastic waistband of his gym shorts.

Rick and Libby would sleep in the van. Sam helped haul the extra tanks out of the cargo area and stack them on the ground; then he watched Libby lay down a pad and two sleeping bags inside.

"I want to have a look at your octopus," Rick said, when Libby was through. "Let's get that free-flow taken care of."

Sam brought him the regulator and followed him into the van where Rick took it apart on the sleeping bags. Libby sat next to him, crouched against the rear seats, her legs drawn up. Gary brought in a lantern when the light began to fail and crouched near the rear doors, rocking gently on the balls of his feet in time to the music he heard from his earphones.

"What are you listening to?" Libby asked him.

"Brahms. Want a hit?"

He passed the whole unit over to her by way of Sam. She listened for a moment, awed by the unnatural fidelity of the sound, perfectly contained within her head and yet as vast as the cosmos. It was a moody, gathering passage she was listening to, and it reminded her of the groundwater searching for release beneath them.

She handed the Walkman to Sam to pass back to Gary. Rick continued working on the regulator. The parts were spread out on the sleeping bag. Rick picked them up with his hands, inspected them, and inserted them into the housing without a misdirected thought or wasted motion. Sam watched him; they all did. There was an air of consequence about him that Sam resented and envied, that he admitted to himself he was trying to learn.

Sam had found the cave passage, but it belonged to Rick. He had the superior claim. And it worried Sam—scared him—that Rick had the superior claim to Libby as well, simply by virtue of his obsessive, sullen presence. He noticed the careful physical distance that Libby kept from Rick inside the van. This was for Sam's benefit, to keep from hurting him.

Rick finished with the regulator and hooked it up to a single tank they had left inside.

"Try that," he said.

Sam took a few breaths of air. The delivery was stable and precise.

"You just got it a little bit out of whack," Rick said.

"It and me both."

Libby took a beer out of a cooler and looked around for something to open it with.

"I don't think Sam should go in with you tomorrow," she said to Rick. "He should stay in the big room with me."

Rick shook his head. "I don't want the two least experienced people diving together. Besides, Sam's the geologist."

"You've dived without geologists before."

"I know, but it's nice to have one along."

Sam found a diving knife behind him in the van and handed it to Libby to open the beer.

"Libby's a little bit concerned," he said to Rick. "You know how married people get."

Libby gave Sam a hard look. With some difficulty, she opened the beer with the knife.

"Anybody want this?" she asked.

"I'll take it," Gary said.

"Pass this to him," Libby said to Sam. She pulled another beer out of the cooler.

264

Rick looked at Sam. "What do you think?"

"Do you mean am I afraid?"

"I suppose."

"I have a healthy fear. Enough to keep me on my toes."

"No problem with that," Gary said. He had put his earphones around his neck and they could hear, in miniature, the music swell and subside.

"I don't want to be responsible for you getting hurt," Libby said.

"I'm not getting hurt and you're not responsible."

Libby opened the beer and handed it to Rick. "Drink a beer tonight, all right?" she asked.

He accepted it and took a sip, then set it down by his feet and did not touch it again. He sat with his legs crossed. He was not part of this. He was somewhere else. Sam saw a large bird sweep across the open doors of the van as silently as a moth. An owl, he thought.

"I think if you're nervous about the dive we should make other arrangements," Gary said.

"No need," Sam answered, looking at Libby.

"I for one don't want any negative vibes down there," Gary said.

"Does jealousy count?" Sam asked suddenly, tired of the whole business now. All at once he felt deserted by whatever part of himself had been guiding him, confidently urging him on to the place the *curandero* had foretold. He should not have let the talk degenerate like this. He felt the self-pity and pettiness within him rising and swelling.

Rick was looking at him, not saying anything.

"I thought this whole thing was a demonstration of how you'd conquered jealousy," Libby said.

"I'm here before you in a spirit of candor," Sam said, watching Rick.

"We'll sort all this out later," Rick said.

Libby studied him. She saw the willful desire to shut them all out, the fatigue of dealing with them. It gave her a cold, fearful sensation. He was homing in on a signal that none of them could hear.

In the charged silence Sam's eyes drew her. In his face she

265

could read resentment, embarrassment, apology. She wished he would go away. She wished for some sort of violent confrontation, but Rick denied it to them somehow. He did not approve, or he did not care.

"Forget about the jealousy," Sam said after a moment. He removed his regulator from the tank and walked out into the darkness.

He lay on his back and watched the intermittent clouds coast across the summer sky. Sam picked out the stars he knew: Polaris, Vega, Aldeberan. But for every one he knew there were ten thousand he had no name for. The sky was rich with them, immense worlds as infinite as the coral polyps on the fossilized reef below them.

He could hear Gary on the bank downstream, snoring lightly. Twenty-five yards away was the van. Its lights were off, its back doors closed. His wife was inside. He made an effort not to think about her but about the dive tomorrow. He was shaken but not afraid. He had confidence in himself.

He had no plans beyond tomorrow, no clear idea why he was here tonight. But he understood that something had impelled him, and he was ready to listen to its silent, prodding voice.

Inside the van Rick lay on his back using an inflated B.C. for a pillow. A certain amount of light came through the windows from the stars and the negligible moon. Libby was beside him and he could see the dark, clear outline of her face in profile, looking up at the roof of the van.

"None of this makes you nervous?" she asked, not turning to face him.

"What?" he asked.

"Sam."

"Am *I* jealous, you mean?"

"Yes."

"I'm not interested in being jealous."

Libby was offended by his remoteness, and a little frightened.

266

She turned to kiss him anyway, one hand laid tenderly on his high forehead and the other on the flat plain of his stomach. She was naked, ready for him. She was aware of Sam's presence outside, and it confused and aroused her, made her understand for the first time how much she truly wanted to betray him, to finish it.

Rick was aroused too, but it was only that part of him. She pulled away and turned her back and he did not complain or draw her to him, but simply slid his arm around her waist and held one breast as if it were an object. Even so she craved the feel of his body and moved against him. He was a touchstone to her, some charmed but unfeeling thing.

Rick dreamed of the whale shark. He saw its form pass slowly and implacably overhead, as large and blank as a dirigible.

He opened his eyes. He could see nothing in the van, but Libby's face was close to his, saying his name.

"Are you awake now?" she was asking.

He looked at her, trying to make out her features, and at the phosphorescent glow of his diver's watch. 2:30. He slowly nodded his head.

"I want to call the dive," she said. "I want to call it off."

He kept his eyes on her dark face a long time before he spoke. "We're very close, Libby. We're almost there."

She sat back on her heels, saying nothing. He could not tell if she was deliberating, but after a time he saw her head move, nodding; then, without dressing, she opened the door of the van and walked outside.

She felt the warm night air on her skin, and after a moment she could see well enough to pick out Sam's reclining shape some distance from her on the bank. The Well was visible to her also— a deep shadow in the creekbed.

She slipped into the water and pulled herself down into the opening for as long as her breath lasted. When she surfaced Rick was there, and he wordlessly followed her down again to the false bottom where the clacking stones reverberated in the stillness. They were able to peer into the wide, fluted tunnel that

267

had so impressed Rick as a boy and that told him the Well went farther, that it went all the way down to the core, to the seat of his longing.

If the pressure in his lungs was not so great now he would have taken her by the hand and surged forward into the darkness, into the boundless caverns of the aquifer that he knew were there. Instead he turned to look at her. They embraced and let the flow carry them upward. They could see starlight through the water.

On the bank Sam sat upright on his sleeping bag. He watched them emerge into the shallow creek. They did not stand up but lay there, clenched and twisting against the pebbly bottom of the creek.

It hurt him. He turned his eyes away, to the pale, star-washed rock of the opposite bank.

Chapter 30

IT was as if they were wakened simply by the force of Rick's desire to proceed. They opened their eyes, feeling his unspoken insistence that they do so.

It was daylight. When Sam sat up in his sleeping bag the first thing he saw was Rick. He was already dressed in the bottom half of his wetsuit and was fitting their regulators onto the tanks.

Libby emerged from the van, her hair stiff from sleep, and walked down to the creek to rub her eyes with water. She looked at Sam only to nod good morning.

"Let's do it!" Gary cried from downstream, still recumbent in his sleeping bag.

They made coffee on a little portable stove that Rick had brought and passed around a carton of doughnuts, none of them speaking much or alluding to the awkwardness of the night before.

"Same basic plan today," Rick said, sipping his coffee.

After breakfast Sam put an extra two-pound weight on his weight belt, remembering the effort of forcing himself down through the narrow passage. He hoisted his tanks onto his back and asked Libby to check the straps, to see that they were not twisted or binding any of his hoses. She did this thoroughly, and then he did the same for her.

Rick and Sam entered the water first. When they had made the right-angle turn at the bottom of the first shaft and passed out of sight, Libby and Gary followed. She felt a little ear squeeze

269

this time and had to stop and ascend a few feet to clear them. While she did so, fifteen feet below the surface, she looked up in time to see a red-winged blackbird sweep across the sky.

When her ears were clear she followed Gary into the first tunnel, away from the surface light, and dropped with him to the bottom of the long vertical room. They flywalked along the ceiling, easing through the constriction where the barricade had been, where the Well had once ended for her. Her head felt clear, and she took pleasure in the sight of Rick and Sam ahead, ambling along in single file, hardly using their big power fins as they moved with authority and grace through the treacherous darkness.

She and Gary followed them into the big room and the four of them drifted to the bottom in unison. On the way down she could feel the turbulent rush of the water that forced itself— invisibly, unstoppingly—through the narrow passage. Libby looked around. This place was very familiar to her now, as familiar and mysterious as the bluff near her home where the Comanches had painted their pictographs, or that coral cave in Palancar Reef that had been hers and Rick's alone. This was enough for her. She was happy in this place, and her mind was stronger than it had been on the last dive; it dismissed at once the first tentative suggestions of narcosis. She hoped that Rick and Sam would find nothing in that one remaining passage, that it would pinch out after ten feet. That would be the end of it, and they would all be safe in this lovely room..

Rick signaled them together. They checked their watches and bottom timers. He held up the fingers of both hands to tell them they would be gone ten minutes. Then he looked at Libby, his eyes large and calm behind the faceplate, so absolutely sure. She nodded, as if in understanding or encouragement, and watched him pull himself into the passage. The powerful beam of his primary light flooded the narrow flue with a white brilliance whose heat she could almost feel. Sam waited for that violent intrusive light to diminish a little, and then he followed, kicking hard against the flow, the illuminated column of water that did not want them to penetrate any farther.

Libby and Gary hovered on either side of the passage until

the light from below disappeared. Libby rose a few inches from the floor and adjusted her buoyancy so she could stay there with as little movement as possible, just waiting.

At the bottom of the flue Rick stopped to wait for Sam, and then did not hesitate in swimming forward into the untried passage. He held the reel in one hand, letting out line smoothly, his light illuminating the rock corridor ahead like the headlamp of a train passing through a tunnel.

He did not notice the gradual downward slope until he realized his attention was beginning to slacken and he thought to look at his depth gauge—158 feet. He was surprised that they had dropped almost twenty feet in so short a time, but it was no problem. There was a ways to go before it became a problem.

Behind him, Sam felt the increasing depth as a gain in his confidence. He began to feel at home, disappointed that they would have so little time here. He gazed wonderingly at the remains of the coral polyps in the rock, thinking of the individual lives that had gone into the construction of this massive, hidden reef. They had had their instant of excruciating awareness and then had gained release from it, the way his baby son had, or the boar hog he had killed with his own hands on Janet's ranch. That was all fine; that was the way it was supposed to be. As he moved through the passageway it seemed to him he could feel the breath of the inanimate rock, which in some way was itself alive and efflorescent, aching to be delivered to some larger purpose.

He watched Rick as he unreeled the line ahead and moved with perfect buoyancy in the center of the corridor. Sam looked at his bottom timer, wondering how long they had been gone. *Not long*, he thought, forgetting to read the dial even as he stared at it. He was confident that Rick would know when to turn around. *If I get narked*, Sam thought, *there is no reason to worry, because Rick will know when to turn around*. His depth gauge read 160 feet. That seemed deep. Who was he to judge?

Ahead of him Rick came to a narrow downward chute. He shone his light into it and saw that the chute was not deep— perhaps four or five feet—and that it opened out into a large room with a long sloping floor. He looked at his watch. They

271

had been gone five minutes. It was time to go back.

But he hesitated. The necessity of turning around kept drifting in and out of focus, until he realized that he was narked. *If I'm aware of it*, he thought, *then I'm not narked*. That seemed to him to be an elegant observation. That it was not true, that experience had taught him otherwise, slipped his mind. What mattered, of course, was that he was functioning. And he felt himself operating at full capacity. He could recite the whole dive plan; he could revise it on the spot if he wanted, working the decompression calculations in his head.

He felt so close. He felt that beyond this next room was some central place, some vast cavern that was the heart of the whole system, where Jacob's Well had its origin. It was the place he had so longed to go as a boy.

He decided that he would take a moment and bounce down into this room, just give it a quick check and then swim back. That would take two minutes maximum, and they would easily make up that time on the way out, with the flow behind them.

He motioned for Sam to swim up beside him. Rick looked at him for a long moment, almost forgetting what he had to tell him. Sam looked back at him, then shrugged. *What?* Rick pointed to Sam and then made a fist. *You. Stay.* Then he pointed to himself and down the chute.

Sam in turn pointed to his bottom timer. Rick nodded. He understood Sam's concern. They would be leaving in a minute.

Some dull weight had settled on Sam's mind. He understood what Rick was telling him; he did not understand why. He put a finger to his temple and spun it in a circle. Rick nodded and made the okay sign. It was okay to be narked then. Sam decided his consciousness had not dimmed out quite as much as he thought, and with this encouragement he rallied. He had a moment of lucidity in which he understood with some alarm that he could no longer trust Rick's judgment, but the moment passed and left only a fretful tension, a desire not to be left alone in this dark, silent, impinging place. He was awash in confusion, but he told himself that there was some part of his mind that was not going to be affected by this, some part that was still going to operate, to take charge when the rest of his awareness evaporated.

272

Sam nodded. *Go ahead*. He watched Rick drop into the chute, and looked down after him as his powerful light illuminated the room below. He looked at his bottom timer, thinking hard. He was going to give Rick two minutes and then pull on the line, demanding that he come up.

The room Rick entered was large and deep, with a steep sloping floor. He hovered near the ceiling. He was at 172 feet, still good on air. He did not want to go any deeper, so he shone his light as far as it would reach, finding what looked like promising passages on two sides of the room. Far below him, at the bottommost reach of the cavern, he saw a constriction where the water came out with force, rattling the unstable gravel that sloped into it.

That was it. That was the way to go. He would never reach it. It was too deep, too far back. But that was it, for sure. Within himself he felt the old sensation, the strange primitive upwelling that was so urgent and diffuse and that tried to tell him... *something*.

With his attention focused on that place he did not notice himself losing his neutral buoyancy and sinking, descending so subtly and smoothly that his rational mind gave him no clue that it had largely departed. His fins touched the gravel bottom, which slid loosely for a few yards downslope. More out of habit than concern he checked his depth gauge. 250 feet. Was that deep? He had some task to perform: to sign his initials on a slate. Some other thought kept pestering him, and as the line jerked in his hand he almost understood what it was. But it passed like some ungraspable memory of childhood.

Something kept pulling on the line. This bothered him a great deal, as if there were some hook in his brain trying to wrench a thought from it. He let go of the reel and felt better.

Sam felt his fear and isolation as a loss of heat, a sudden quaking in the center of his body. He hugged his torso and yanked on the line again. There was still no response, and this time no resistance. Rick had let go. Below him Sam could see Rick's light, a stationary beacon that seemed hopelessly distant, as distant as a star.

Okay, think. There was some explanation for this, some reason that would patiently reveal itself if he waited. He looked at his pressure gauge and saw that he did not have enough air to wait long. He had to move, and the situation seemed to demand that he move downward to Rick's aid. He owed that to Libby. That was his responsibility. Just before he set out into the chute he felt two tugs on the line from behind him. That meant something. He could not remember what.

Libby watched as Gary pulled on the rope again and received no response. He shrugged, as if it was insignificant. She pointed to herself and Gary and then to the passage, asking if they should go down after them. Gary shook his head no, and held up two fingers. They would wait two minutes.

Rick kept his eye on the constriction as he swam toward it, convinced now more than ever it was the real thing, the real way in. He saw a beam of light flashing on the wall above it, moving frantically back and forth, and he turned to see Sam swimming down to him. He remembered Sam. He was glad to see him and gestured toward the constriction. Sam shook his head, but Rick headed for it anyway. Before he reached it Sam pulled on his foot and when he turned around held a slate in front of his mask. It said, in nearly illegible letters, *Too Deep*.

Sam watched as Rick stared at the slate, his brow furrowed behind his mask, his eyes narrowed. Sam had written the message at the top of the room and no longer remembered what it said or what it pertained to, only that it was important that Rick see it. Rick looked up from the slate to Sam. He nodded, and made the okay sign, and kept making it until Sam returned it.

Sam watched passively from a few yards above on the gravel slope as Rick explored the constriction. It was apparent to Sam that the opening was too narrow for Rick to get through with his tanks, and with what was left of his conscious mind he hoped that when Rick realized this he would turn back and they could leave.

274

Then he saw that Rick was taking off the tanks.

Sam shouted into his mouthpiece. *"Nnnnnh! Nnnnnh!"* He swam forward, but Rick's eyes stopped him. He saw in them what he had seen in the eyes of the boar hog, deep behind its fearful stare: the longing, the simple need to disappear.

Rick backed into the opening, hauling the double tanks after him by the valve. He kept his eyes on Sam, paralyzing his faded mind with one simple message: *Good-bye.* Then his face slipped backward out of sight, leaving his hand exposed to pull the heavy tanks through.

Sam heard a rumbling sound all around him and looked up-slope to see the avalanche of gravel that caught at his feet before he realized that all he had to do was rise above it. He managed to get out with his fins still on his feet and his light still in his hand, but he had lost the line. He ascended to the center of the room and saw what he believed was the chute that led out, but just as he set out for it he was engulfed by a massive rising cloud of white silt.

The silt traveled rapidly through the corridors of the cave, and when it rose through the passageway into the big room, Libby looked up at Gary and saw the dread in his eyes. That was all she needed to tell her to go. Out of the corner of her eye she saw him shaking his head and reaching out to stop her, but she was already well into the milky flue, one hand on the line and the other grabbing for purchase to propel her downward. She could see nothing, absolutely nothing, just the white void all around her.

She could feel her intelligence unraveling as she traveled, hand over hand, deeper into the whiteness. She could feel the unnecessary parts of her mind disappearing but knew that at the core there was some irreducible, diamond-hard awareness that she would not give up. She did not know whether she was rushing toward Sam or Rick; she had lost the distinction.

She felt herself moving constantly downward, but she did not think to check her depth gauge or to monitor her air supply, or to consider how deeply she was narked. She just followed the line, and soon it made a nearly right-angle turn that was, she assumed, straight down. Her conscious mind had thinned out considerably by the time she felt the line embedded in a pile of gravel. She let the line go. She no longer had any use for it.

Libby had the impression that the silt had lessened somewhat but she still saw nothing. It seemed to her that she was in the center of a large space and that she was not alone. Something, some thought-figure, was with her there.

Sam, forty feet away from her on the other side of the room, felt the same. His wild, wasteful breathing came more carefully now. He had spent the last few minutes in an almost pure state of panic, revolving aimlessly in the center of the room, and he mistook this sudden calm for the moment of his death. He could feel himself approaching someone, some thing, and he was ready to relinquish himself if only this peaceful instant would last.

They drifted toward each other in the impenetrable whiteness. They were touching, embracing, before the silt cleared enough for them to see.

The constriction had opened out into a good-sized passage and Rick followed it, stroking hard with his fins, wanting to reach his place before his strength was exhausted. The heavy tanks, which he had not bothered to strap back on, were dragging him down, holding him back, so he took the regulator out of his mouth and cast them aside. He did not miss them, and he smiled to himself, thinking how humorous and sad it was that he had lived all his life without realizing that he could breathe underwater. He wished Libby were here, so that he could show her. For a moment he missed her sharply, painfully, as he missed his air now when he thought about it. But he would bring her to this place sometime.

There she was now, just ahead in the beam of his light. She was naked, and he dropped his weight belt and began to unzip his wetsuit, to get rid of all these absurd and unnecessary encumbrances. He wanted to join her, just his plain flesh against hers in this distant place.

But then the corridor opened out and he was no longer thinking of Libby. It was there before him, the great thing, the place. It was a cavern that he knew stretched for miles, a vast hollow in the earth. He could feel the muted pulsing at the heart of its

276

stillness, the thing that told him it was alive, that it was the greater life and therefore entitled to his. He shone his light all around him and the beam did not touch anything solid, just kept traveling into the darkness.

He let the light go too now, dropping it and watching it fall; it seemed to take an infinite time to drift downward, the bright spot growing smaller and smaller until it was finally just a brilliant, unmoving speck. He swam toward it, watching it grow larger again as he approached, until the whole cavern, the whole aquifer, the whole hidden universe was flushed with light. He kicked hard with his fins, driving downward, and entered it.

They could see now, but they were low on air and they could not find the way out. Sam looked at his pressure gauge. The needle was in the red. Libby was doing better, but they had no more than five or six minutes between them.

They were at the top of the room where it was not so deep and they could think a little. Libby held tightly to Sam's hand, guessing that they were going to die here. They swam slowly around the circumference of the room, looking for the line, but they could not find it, and Sam feared they had worked their way into an anteroom of the main chamber, or in their blind groping had entered another chamber altogether.

He avoided her eyes and tightened his grip on her hand. His next few breaths came hard, and then they stopped coming at all. He turned to Libby and signaled that he was out of air and she handed him her octopus. He looked at her gauge. It was in the red now too. He took the octopus from his mouth and handed it back, but she shook her head and signaled for him to replace it. She was right; there was no point in her watching him drown.

Libby held herself close to him, her fingers closed around his tank strap. They were still searching for a way out but they had more or less given up and they were looking at one another now with an unashamed frankness and fear.

Sam began to feel the crawling sensation in the tips of his fingers, the aftereffects of the snakebite in the Abuelos. It grew more intense, and he began to think it was a prelude to the

277

greater ghostliness that would soon engulf his whole being.

Then all at once the room seemed to explode with life, with thousands and thousands of black wriggling shapes surging upward. Libby looked at him, her eyes wide with terror. Sam studied the serpentine forms for a long moment before it registered on his depleted brain what they were. Eels. The room was filled with them, their narrow faces strained and concentrated.

Libby breathed wildly, profligately, horrified by the swarming nightmare before her. Yet something told Sam to pay attention. Where were these eels going, he asked himself, and the answer was so simple it stunned him. They were going out. They were going home to the Sargasso Sea to spawn.

He took her hand and they swam with the eels, following them down and under a shelf of rock that turned out to be the true ceiling of the room where they were lost. They could see the line, leading upward to the chute. Sam put one hand on it, taking the lead, and Libby followed with her hand on his weight belt. Just at the top of the chute they saw a light, with a hundred eels undulating in its beam. As they drew closer, Sam could make out Gary. He was swimming toward them, gazing in amazement at the congested passageway, and dragging the three safety tanks behind him.

Chapter 31

IT was the time of the hawk migrations. From the smooth summit of Enchanted Rock Sam could see them coming in waves, the gray sky knit tightly behind them.

The mountain was made of pink coarse-grained granite; when he looked through his hand lens or simply put his face close to the rock he could see it sparkling with crystals. Its broad dome was as bare as the moon, and it loomed above the countryside like an immense blister whose swelling had been arrested and transformed into stone.

All around him was evidence that the mountain was wearing down. There were potholes in the surface, which told him that certain minerals were being weathered out; there were graceful seams in the rock where he could trace the path of the eroding rainfall; and there were huge sheets of exfoliated granite, waiting for the time when they would drop off the rock's surface like flakes. It was all as temporary as a bubble in a pan of boiling water, but it was eternal enough for his purposes.

He saw her car on the road below, heading toward the base of the rock. When he had called her that afternoon from Fredericksburg she had agreed to come, but he had not allowed himself to believe that she truly would.

Her car entered the parking lot and disappeared beneath the brow of the mountain, and he did not see her again until she was climbing up its steep forward slope, following a path of arrows painted onto the rock. She was wearing a flannel shirt, which she stopped after a short distance to remove and tie to her waist by the sleeves. Beneath that was a green T-shirt. Her hair was longer, past her shoulders now. He watched her stride carefully as she climbed, grateful to see that she did not limp or show any other lingering effects of the bends.

The three of them had stopped at forty feet, Gary somehow making them understand that they had to decompress before they went any farther. He remembered how Libby kept looking back, caught between the desperate psychic need to reach the sunlight above them and the claim that still waited for her in the blackness below. As they hung there on the line he saw her eyes growing wide with terror and helplessness as her head cleared and she realized what had happened.

There was still a chance he would come out, that he had hoarded his breath so as to have enough left to reach them. But there was nothing they could do to help him, and for all the terror in Libby's eyes when she looked at Sam there was nothing accusatory there.

Gary waited until they were almost completely out of air and then motioned them upward, into the sunlit shaft. Sam could see the clouds above him, and feel the flow of the water urging him upward.

On the surface Libby tore off her mask and screamed Rick's name. She knelt in the shallow water at the edge of the Well, her face tearless and contorted, looking down, waiting for him to come.

Sam stared at her, not knowing what to do. His own shock was absorbed in her grief, so that he felt empty and dull.

"I've got to get you two to a recompression chamber," Gary told him. "There wasn't enough air in those tanks to keep you down long enough to decompress."

Sam nodded. He walked over to his wife.

"Libby," he said. "We have to go. We're going to get the bends."

She turned her head to him. "What about Rick?"

"We have to go," he said.

The recompression center was in a hospital at an air force base in San Antonio, seventy miles away. Sam felt the pain before Libby did; it hit him in all four limbs almost simultaneously, a terrible bone-deep hurt that rose in pitch as the frothing nitrogen gas squeezed off the oxygen to his joints.

While Gary drove, the two of them writhed in the backseat of the car, fruitlessly shifting for a position that was less painful. Gary did not have any symptoms; he had not been nearly as deep. He drove with clear-minded efficiency through the confusing streets of the city and picked up an escort at the base gate that led them to the hospital.

The recompression chamber was a claustrophobic space with no more room to move than in a restaurant booth. Sam and Libby sat on the benches, looking out the porthole at the operator who turned a dial to create an atmospheric pressure that would simulate the depth they had been exposed to. Sam knew when the operator hit the right depth because the pain started to filter away. And with that distraction gone Libby lay down on the bench and put her arm under her head as if she was going to sleep. But she shot upward almost immediately, like a dreamer shuddered awake by a nightmare.

"*No!*" she shouted. "*No!*" Her voice rose above the sound of the machinery and rushing air.

Gary led the recovery effort. A group of cave divers had flown in from Florida to help. It was a way of paying homage. But Rick's body could not be reached. He had gone too deep. The Florida divers spent an extra day replacing the barricade and then flew home.

Sam and Libby went into the Well together one last time and anchored a little plaque in the rock, where the first tunnel branched out from the opening shaft. They had picked a place where his name—that was all that was on the plaque—could be read without artificial lights, where the warm sunlight still fell on your shoulders.

Afterward, when they sat unbuckling their straps and laying their masks and fins and gauges on the bank beside them, it occurred to Sam that they would never use these things again.

So much was over. Libby sat there, her wetsuit still zipped to the collar. She was shivering a little from the cold water. She stared out at the Well with a composed look of pure sorrow. The water was so brilliant it seemed lit from within, as if there were some power source down there, deep in the rock, throwing light into the pale atmosphere.

"Maybe this is what I wanted," he said.

Libby turned her face, studying him.

"I don't believe that," she answered.

"I was willing for him to die," Sam said. "I tried to save him but I was willing."

"No," she said, "it was what he wanted."

Sam stood up and began to collect their gear and toss it indiscriminately into the trunk of his car. He drove her home. They were silent. When he dropped her off at the house they had once shared, he told her that he loved her and she nodded her understanding.

That had been two months ago. He had not seen her since, feeling it was his responsibility now to stay apart from her until they could identify what they needed from each other, what was left for them. But finally that afternoon he had given up on his tact and driven into Fredericksburg, where the closest phone was, and called her from a German bakery.

When she was halfway up the mountain she spotted him and waved. Sam began to walk down to meet her, calling Dumptruck away from a little depression of stagnant water where he had been wallowing for the past half hour. When Dumptruck saw Libby he bounded ahead with no more effort or caution than a puppy. Dumptruck was eleven or twelve years old now, Sam calculated, but it appeared that he would hover forever at his prime.

"It's steeper than I remember it," Libby said to him as they met. She touched her head lightly to his chest and then turned around to look at the hawks drifting along the edge of the front.

"What kind are they?" Libby asked him.

"Swainson's mostly, I think. We'd have to check the field guide."

"They're pretty."

They walked back up to just below the summit and sat down at the base of a long seam in the rock, a rent whose edges were smooth and rounded like a healing scar. Libby untied her shirt and put it back on. They could feel the norther now.

"How long have you been up here?" she asked him.

"Two days. I've got the tent pitched down in the campground."

"Are you working?"

"No."

"Then why are you here?"

Sam looked around him at the rock. "I just came to see how it's holding up."

Dumptruck breathed in Libby's face. She gently turned his muzzle away. She looked tired and worn to Sam. She had lost weight.

"How are things in your part of town?" he asked. "I hear Hudson's been putting the rush on you."

"Where'd you hear that?"

"From Bobby."

"It's not a rush. He called me up one day out of the blue and asked me to go steelhead fishing with him in Canada. I politely declined."

"And no sooner had you hung up the phone than I called."

"More or less."

"Thank you for coming."

"Everybody needs a vacation," she said.

Libby smoothed her hair back against her temples and turned to him, her face buried in his chest, her arms gripping him so tightly that after a while he had to loosen them and shift position so he could breathe.

She cried for a long time, with a violence that startled her. At the same time she was calmed by the feel of him, remembering how she had swum to him in the silted, white-blind waters of Jacob's Well, drawn to him finally by a force as powerful as the one that had guided Rick away from her into the endless dark rooms below.

He held her until her sobs subsided into hiccoughs. The cold wind swept over the summit of Enchanted Rock and they took

283

shelter behind a solitary boulder. They felt as ancient as the granite beneath them, formed in the same way, through heat and pressure and simple endurance, and ready like the rock to disappear into the timeless moment.

Chapter 32

LIBBY fixed on Sam's eyes as the pain bore through her. She could feel its rightful power; she was bewildered by its sheer strength. How could anything be so strong? At the peak of the contraction she thought the pain must be part of the overall cost, part of the hurt that she knew she was still owed. But she understood, as the awesome blunt pressure began to lessen, that this pain was linked to something new.

The next one made her scream. She forgot about the breathing, stunned by the insistent force inside her. She felt unequal to the terrible need of the baby to be born.

"Sam, help me!" she yelled. His face entered her field of vision. She knew there was nothing he could do. He said something, mouthing reassurances she could not bother herself to hear. But she fixed her eyes on his and he looked back without flinching, willing to go with her wherever she would take him. She drew him into the pain. They were together there, harbored away in some deep and distant place where they had never been before.

There had been snow, but it had melted quickly under a once-a-year sky so clear you could see all the way from the Olympic Peninsula to Mount Rainier. Sam drove home along Puget Sound, ragged from lack of sleep and witless over the still unprocessed fact of their baby daughter.

He drove to the house they had rented in Greenlake to feed

Dumptruck and pick up some notes on fluvial deposits that he meant to study in the hospital. He was working for the Washington Geological Survey, doing much the same work he was used to, though here in the Northwest the landforms still caught him off-guard after six months of getting used to them. The look of the place was so different from Texas. He did not like it as well, but he was satisfied. They had moved arbitrarily; they had all but thrown darts at a map. The point was to move, to stake something on the deeper shift they had recognized as occurring within themselves.

Dumptruck was seated on the floor next to the space heater, thumping his heavy tail with a look of such expectation that Sam felt obligated to tell him out loud what had happened. He filled Dumptruck's dish and changed his water, then grabbed his notes and hurried back to his car. Driving along the sound, he thought he saw the fins of killer whales.

The baby had been born in a birthing suite, a fake bedroom that was decorated like a cheap motel and dominated by a large, wooden rocking chair. When Sam came back to the room, Libby and the baby were still asleep. He sat down in the chair, meaning to read his notes, but he could not concentrate. Outside the window, swooping through the clear air, he saw a mockingbird, the state bird of Texas.

He stood up and went over to the bed, picked up the sleeping baby girl, and took her back to the rocking chair. Her eyes were closed tightly, as with an effort, and her fists opened and closed in her sleep. He looked down at her and felt the presence of the other baby, the boy. That was all right. The dead were welcome here.

Libby shifted position on the bed at the other end of the darkened room. He thought she would wake, missing the feel of the baby next to her, but she did not move again. Sam kept his eyes open for as long as he could, but after a while he too fell asleep in the rocking chair, the baby secure in his arms.